Rosie Goodwin

Crying Shame

headline

First published in Great Britain in 2008
by HEADLINE PUBLISHING GROUP

First published in paperback in 2008
by HEADLINE PUBLISHING GROUP

Apart ... this
public ..., in
any for ...g of
the p ... in
a

a

Catalogui ... Library

ISBN 978 0 7553 4224 2

Typeset in Bembo by Palimpsest Book Production Limited,
Grangemouth, Stirlingshire

Printed and bound in Great Britain by
CPI Group (UK) Ltd, Croydon, CR0 4YY

HEADLINE PUBLISHING GROUP
An Hachette Livre UK Company
338 Euston Road
London NW1 3BH

www.headline.co.uk
www.hachettelivre.co.uk

Dedication

I dedicate this book to my mum, who is fighting a
courageous battle. We are all behind you, Mum,
keep fighting. We love you.

Acknowledgements

Thanks to my editor, Flora, and all at Headline and my agent, Sonia Land, and the team at Sheil Land for unfailing support and encouragement. And special thanks to Joan Deitch, copy-editor extraordinaire!

Thanks also, to my many friends in Social Services, who were there to offer advice during the writing of his book.

Lastly, thanks to my husband, children and grandchild. Each of them so very special to me . . .

'The wind/spirit blows where it wills, but you do not know where it comes from or where it goes.'

John 3, 8

Prologue

It was as if some great, unseen hand had rolled back the years. She was a child again, back in the cold, sparsely furnished bedroom of the council house in Nuneaton where she had lived with her mother and younger sister. She could hear footsteps on the stairs and her heart was hammering as she cowered beneath the thin bedcovers, waiting for the door to open . . . And then suddenly she was a woman, living in a grand private house in Bispham, standing in the doorway of her stepdaughter Nikki's bedroom, watching in horror as her husband prepared to abuse the child. History was repeating itself. Now Christian, the love of her life, was there – imploring her to come with him. Offering her the sort of life she had only ever dreamed of. She was holding her hand out and walking towards him, but the more steps she took, the further away he appeared. She couldn't go to him yet, not while Nikki still needed her. She began to cry, great gulping sobs that shook her body, and then thankfully the hand released her and she was struggling through what appeared to be a fog to come back to the here and now . . .

Claire Nightingale started awake. She was lying in a damp tangle of bedclothes and she fought to get free of them. Through the bedroom wall that divided them she could hear Nikki's gentle snores and slowly her heart returned to a steadier rhythm. Glancing towards the curtains, she saw the first signs of light break through the chinks, and now she allowed her eyes to roam about the unfamiliar room. She was back in the Midlands, in Solihull, and had just spent her first night in her new home.

Settling further back onto her pillows, Claire tried to put her thoughts into some sort of order. Nikki, her adopted daughter, had not been too happy about moving so far away from her former home. However, she had grudgingly agreed to live nearer to Claire's home town when the latter had explained that she still had family and close friends living there whom she had not seen for many years. Now, already, Claire was wondering if the move had been such a good idea after all. It was many years since she had last set foot in Nuneaton. What if her sister Tracey and her former foster-carers Molly and Tom no longer wished to know her? So much had happened in the time since she had run away to make a new life for herself. Tracey would be all grown up now, possibly even married with a family of her own. And Molly and Tom – would they still be living in the smart semi-detached house in Howard Road?

The thoughts ran round and round in her mind, causing her to break out in a sweat again. But it was too late to run away now. She had tried that once before, and what had it got her but heartbreak? Claire knew that in order to move forward, she would have to confront the demons that constantly haunted her, and be true to herself. Outwardly, she was now the very wealthy widow of a much-respected Lancashire businessman, but just beneath the surface she was still the tormented teenager who had run away to London, expecting to find the streets paved with gold and thinking that she could put her past behind her. It was time to lay the past to rest. If there was to be any chance of finding happiness with Christian Murray, the tousle-haired young vet to whom she had lost her heart several years ago, then she must be strong and try.

Sighing deeply, she dragged herself to the edge of the bed. There would be no more sleep for her now, so she decided to go and unpack some of the many boxes that were piled high all over the house. She would leave Nikki to sleep in. The child was exhausted after the journey from Bispham and the stress of the move the day before. Grabbing her dressing-gown, which was draped across the back of a chair, Claire cursed softly as her knee connected with an unpacked box, then slipping out onto the landing she crept down the stairs.

Once in the kitchen, she clicked on the light and looked about her. The room was a little dated, but she intended to remedy that in time. In actual fact, the whole place was in need of a facelift, but Claire had looked beyond the faded wallpaper and fixtures and fittings when she had first viewed it and seen the potential there. It was a lovely kitchen in a lovely house, in Lovelace Lane in the better area of Solihull. Claire had fallen in love with it at first sight and did not regret her decision to buy it. The house boasted four good-sized bedrooms and a large family bathroom as well as an en-suite bathroom to the master bedroom, which she had allowed Nikki to have. Downstairs, there was an enormous lounge and beyond that a dining room that led to a fair-sized garden room. Two doors leading off the other side of the hall revealed a further sitting room and a study.

This was a house where she hoped she and Nikki could find peace. She had felt it the first time she had stepped through the door. But first, she must turn it into a home so, rolling up her sleeves, Claire Nightingale heaved the first box towards her and began to unpack it.

Chapter One

January, 1998

'Come on, Nikki, you'll be late for school at this rate.'

'Coming, Mum.'

Claire smiled as Nikki clattered down the stairs and snatched up her schoolbag before bending to stroke Gemma, her small gold and white shih-tzu.

'And make sure you put your warm coat on,' Claire ordered. 'It's enough to cut you in two out there.'

Nikki hurriedly tied her long fair hair into a ponytail before tugging a woollen hat on and grinning at Claire. They had been in Solihull for just over a week now and she appeared to be settling in well at Claremont, the select private school that was just up the road from them. It was her second day and already she had made new friends, which Claire took as a good sign. Standing on tiptoe, the girl planted a hasty kiss on Claire's cheek before charging towards the door, pulling her coat on as she went.

As yet, Nikki hadn't asked Claire when she was going to take her to meet the family she had told her all about. The pair of them had been too busy unpacking boxes and tidying the house to discuss it, but Claire knew that soon Nikki would start to probe. The thought made butterflies flutter to life in her stomach. She had come back to her roots feeling ready to face her past – but was she really strong enough to go through with it? She had explained to Nikki about how she had run away from home, and also confessed that she had once given birth to a child whom she had given up for adoption. Even now, after all these years, the thought of her baby daughter Yasmin could bring tears stinging to her eyes. But it wasn't the time to be thinking of that now, so she playfully nudged Nikki through the front door and onto the drive.

'Go on, be off with you and leave me to a bit of peace and quiet,' she teased. Nikki laughed before scampering off down the drive as if she hadn't a care in the world. It did Claire's heart good to see her smiling after all the girl had been through. Not that she was out of the woods yet, not by a long shot. Claire would still occasionally hear her crying out in the throes of a nightmare. Less frequently now though, thank goodness. The counselling Claire had arranged for her back in Bispham had gone some way towards helping Nikki come to terms with the abuse she had suffered at the hands of her adoptive father, and Claire made a mental note to seek similar help here in the Midlands once they were settled.

Claire shuddered as she thought of her late husband Greg, the wealthy accountant whom she had once thought could give her the lifestyle she craved. How wrong she had been – and how quickly her dreams had turned to ashes once he had put a ring on her finger. For all his so-called respectability, Gregory Nightingale had been no better than the men her mother had once allowed to abuse her and her younger sister Tracey.

Sighing, she filled the kettle then plugged it in to boil before going to stare out of the kitchen window across the fields that backed onto the house. Once again she found herself thinking of Yasmin, the baby daughter she had abandoned so long ago, and her eyes grew moist. Sometimes, when she looked at Nikki she would find herself wondering what Yasmin would look like now. The two girls were almost the same age. Would they be the same slim build? Would Yasmin still be fair like

Nikki? Were her adoptive parents being good to her? Claire hoped so, and although never a day went by when she didn't thank God for bringing Nikki into her life, still the yearning for her own child remained, as raw and as painful as it had been on the day she had signed the papers giving her up for adoption.

The sound of the kettle singing pulled her thoughts back to the present and after making herself a cup of instant coffee she sank down at the kitchen table and looked around. It was strange to think that Molly and Tom, her former foster-carers, and Tracey, the sister she hadn't set eyes on for years, were only forty minutes or so away down the road again. Should I write to them, she mused to herself, or just turn up out of the blue and take my chances on their reactions?

'I'll write to them!' she told the empty kitchen, and jumping up before she could change her mind, she took a pad and pen from the drawer. Once seated at the table again, she chewed the end of the pen thoughtfully before beginning.

Dear Molly and Tom,

I know this letter might come as somewhat of a surprise to you after all these years, but . . .

'No, *that* isn't right,' she scolded herself, and screwing the paper into a ball she flung it towards the bin before beginning again.

Dear Molly and Tom,

I know it's been a long time since I have been in touch, but . . .

No! That wasn't right either. The second sheet of paper followed the first. Half an hour later the bin was almost full and Claire was so frustrated that she could have cried. Instead, she began to question herself.

If Molly and Tom had moved house, which they might well have done by now, then a letter would be no good anyway. Perhaps it was a better idea to go for a ride into Nuneaton and just have a look? There was nothing to stop her while Nikki was at school, after all, was there? Taking a deep breath, she rose from the table and took the car keys from the worktop.

Striding purposefully towards the door, Claire paused to look back at Gemma, whose tail was wagging furiously. 'I won't be long,' she promised, then hurried outside to her car. Thirty-five minutes later, she was driving along Howard Road and she had the sensation of stepping back in time as she slowly cruised past Molly and Tom's tidy semi-detached house.

Everything was just as she remembered it. The small lawn was still neatly trimmed and the same wooden fence surrounded it. White net curtains still hung at all of the front windows and Claire found herself remembering how proud Molly had always been of them.

'You can always judge how clean a house is on the inside by the net curtains,' she would tell Claire on the first of each month when she would religiously take them down to wash them. Claire parked a few doors down the road and as she rested on the steering wheel she saw herself as a child again, arriving with the social workers who were taking her there to join Tracey. From that moment on, Molly and Tom had shown her nothing but kindness, but the kindness had come too late. By then, Claire had developed a deep mistrust of everyone and was determined not to let anyone close enough to hurt her ever again. Her sister, on the other hand, had lapped up the love and affection that Molly and Tom had lavished on her. And this, strangely, had made Claire feel even more alone. Until then, Tracey had needed her, but within months of moving in with her foster-parents she had become like a different child. The timid little girl who was afraid of her own shadow had been replaced by a confident child with a sunny smile and an extrovert personality. Until then, Tracey had relied on her alone and Claire had been like a little mother to her, but now it was Molly she would run to if she needed anything. Molly who would wash her hair. Molly who read her a bedtime story.

Lowering her head, Claire choked back a sob. The pain was still there even now. Tracey had also found a friend in Billy, Molly and Tom's young son, and soon the pair had become inseparable. Molly had used to joke that they could get into mischief in a padded cell while Claire looked on resentfully. Of course, she realised with a little shock, Billy would be grown up too now and she wondered if he still lived at home. It was while she was pondering that she noticed someone struggling up the road laden down with two heavy bags, and when she looked closer she saw with a jolt that it was Molly. Her foster-mother had lost a little weight and looked a little older. Her hair was streaked with grey and there were lines on her face that hadn't been there before, but even so, Claire would have recognised her anywhere. Her heart began to hammer in her chest. What if Molly noticed her? How could she explain her presence after all this time? Thankfully, the woman seemed too intent on getting home to notice anyone, and seconds later she placed a bag on the ground while she opened the little wooden gate and disappeared up the side path towards the back door.

Shaking uncontrollably, Claire fumbled in her bag on the seat at the side of her and lit a cigarette. Drawing on it deeply she willed her heart to settle down into a steadier rhythm. That had been a little too close for comfort, but then again, she would have to face them sometime. Perhaps it would be better to just get out of the car and go and get it over with right now.

Her mind rebelled at the thought. *No, not yet. I'm not ready . . . But will I ever be?* Having no answer to her question, she stubbed out her cigarette in the car ashtray and started the engine. She needed to get back home to think.

'Is everything all right, Mum? You seem very quiet.'

'What? . . . Oh, sorry, love, I was miles away.' Claire smiled at Nikki who was curled up on the settee with Gemma watching TV. Since getting back from Nuneaton earlier in the day she had been in a pensive mood that she couldn't seem to break free of. She supposed it was seeing Molly and her old home again that had caused it, although she hadn't told Nikki that.

'So what did you do today while I was at school?'

'Oh, I just pottered about here unpacking boxes,' Claire lied unconvincingly. 'I'm beginning to wonder if I'll ever get to the end of them.'

Nikki frowned as she helped herself to a handful of popcorn from the dish on the coffee-table. Her mum seemed to have been in a preoccupied mood ever since she had arrived home from school. But then she supposed she *had* been busy over the last few days.

'Never mind, I'll be able to help more at the weekend,' she told her and Claire felt a pang of guilt. Nikki was such a lovely child, she hated lying to her.

'Perhaps when we *do* finally finish all the unpacking, you could take me to meet your family? After all, that's why we moved back here, isn't it?'

The guilt kicked in again, sharp as a knife as Claire nodded. Of course, she was keen for the girl to meet them, but not just yet. First she would have to break the ice and do rather a lot of explaining into the bargain. Thankfully, the conversation stopped there when Nikki hopped off the settee and lifted Gemma's lead.

'Come on then.' Bending down to the little dog she fastened the lead to her collar before telling Claire brightly, 'I'll just take her out for her last walk, shall I? Then I reckon I'm going to get an early night. Do you want to come with us?'

'No, I won't tonight if you don't mind, love. I'm feeling a bit tired too so I'll make us a last drink while you're gone. Don't get going too far though. You don't know anyone around here yet. Make sure you keep to the main road and don't talk to anyone.'

'Oh, Mum,' Nikki chuckled as she headed towards the door with Gemma bounding along at the side of her. 'You are a worrier.'

Claire watched her go fondly. Nikki was such an innocent, despite what her father had done to her. She was growing up right in front of her very eyes and Claire was fiercely protective of her. As her face settled into a frown she wondered again what Nikki would think of her when she finally told her the whole truth about her past. How would she react to knowing that her mum was a former prostitute? A girl who had stood on the street corners of London selling her body? Claire had no way of knowing. All she *did* know was that eventually she would have to tell her – and Molly, Tom and Tracey too. The thought made her feel sick, but until she did so, she was still hiding behind a façade. Tears were stinging at the back of her eyes. The only people in the world she had ever confided in were Christian and Mrs M, and they had stood by her, telling her that they understood why she had done it. But would Nikki and her family be so understanding? Only time would tell. First she had to gather every ounce of courage she had, and go to see Molly.

The next afternoon, Claire glanced at the clock and inhaled deeply on her cigarette. Over the years, she had fought a constant battle to give up smoking, but she always slipped back into the habit when she was nervous, and now was one of those many times. She found herself thinking of one of Mrs Pope's many sayings: There's no time like the present! Mrs Pope had been her late husband's faithful house-keeper, and during the time they had been married and following his suicide, the gentle-hearted woman had been a tower of strength to her and Nikki. Perhaps she was right, Claire decided. After all, as Nikki had quite rightly pointed out, the whole reason for them moving back to the Midlands was for her to be close to her family again. Yesterday the opportunity to climb out of her car and face Molly had been offered to her on a plate, but as usual, she had chickened out. Well . . . she wasn't going to be a chicken any longer. It was time to face the music.

Stubbing the cigarette out in an ashtray, Claire strode towards the stairs. Half an hour later she came back down looking ready to go for a job interview in a smart navy two-piece suit and high-heeled shoes. She had swept her blond hair up into a sophisticated chignon and as she picked up her car keys and glanced in the hall mirror she knew that she was looking her best. 'Right then, it's time to get this show on the road,' she told Gemma, who was sitting at her feet with her tongue wagging furiously. Bending to stroke her, she then straightened her shoulders and walked towards the door with her head held high. It was time to build bridges – if at all possible.

Less than an hour later, she was once more sitting up the road from the Garretts' neat semi-detached house and her confidence had flown through the window again. Even so, she was determined to get it over with and so, taking a deep breath, she climbed from the car and locked the door before walking towards the house. It was Wednesday, the day when Molly had always done her baking. Even now, Claire could clearly remember the wonderful smells of fresh baked scones and cakes that would greet her when she got home from school. But of course, that had been many years ago. Molly's routine might have changed by now. She might not even be in, if it came to that. The cowardly part of Claire almost hoped that she wouldn't be, while the practical side of her prayed that she would, so that she could get the reunion over with.

Almost before she knew it, she was standing before the front door. The shiny brass knocker that she so vividly remembered looked exactly the same and she had the urge to turn and run. Resisting it, she plucked up every ounce of courage she had, then lifting her hand she rapped at the door. Almost instantly she heard footsteps coming towards her from the direction of the kitchen then the door was opening and there was Molly wrapped in a huge apron with flour smeared across her nose.

'Yes? Can I help you, love?'

Claire blinked. Molly didn't recognise her, but then, it had been many years since she had run away.

'I . . . er . . . Hello, Molly.' The words were sticking in her throat.

Molly narrowed her eyes and peered more closely at her before saying, 'I'm sorry, love, do I know you?'

Claire licked her lips. 'It's . . . it's me, Molly. It's Claire.'

The colour drained from the older woman's face as her hand flew to her mouth and she stared back at this elegant young woman in front of her. She was so white that she looked as if she had seen a ghost, but then in a way she had. It was many years since Claire had left her, and Molly Garrett had resigned herself to never seeing the girl again, but now here she was, as large as life, and Molly could hardly believe it.

'Claire.' A wealth of emotions were flitting across her face and Claire bowed her head in shame, unable to meet her eyes.

'I . . . er . . . I suppose you'd better come in,' Molly stuttered eventually, and as she held the door wide, Claire stepped past her and back in time. She saw at a glance that the carpets, curtains and three-piece suite had all been changed, but then she supposed that the ones she remembered would have worn out long ago. Even so, she had the sense of coming home and it was all she could do to stop herself from flinging herself into Molly's arms and begging her forgiveness.

'You'd . . . er . . . you'd better come through to the kitchen.' Molly looked hopelessly ill-at-ease. 'I was baking.'

'Oh, you still do it on a Wednesday then?'

'Yes, I do, though I'm surprised you remember.'

They were in the kitchen now and Molly nodded towards a chair as she went to fill the kettle at the sink. Claire noticed that the older woman was visibly shaking, and shamefaced, she sank down onto one of the chairs placed about the table. She had never felt so uncomfortable in her whole life, but then she knew that she didn't deserve to be welcomed back with open arms after the way she had treated Molly so long ago. An awkward silence settled between them. There was so much that Claire wanted to say. So many questions that she wanted to ask, but she knew that she must give Molly time to get over the shock of seeing her, so she kept tight-lipped as the older woman got out two mugs and warmed the teapot.

It was only when Molly placed a steaming mug in front of her and finally sat down opposite her that Claire dared to ask, 'So how are you, and Tom and Billy too, of course?'

'We're fine.' Molly stirred two spoonfuls of sugar into her tea and avoided her eyes, then suddenly blurted out, 'Though it seems as if we haven't done as well as you. You look like a million dollars.'

'Thank you.' Claire flushed. This was turning out to be even more difficult than she had expected it to be. 'And . . . Tracey?'

'She's fine too. She's married to an ambulanceman now and they're expecting twins in April. Done well for herself, she has. He's a lovely bloke and they've got a smashing home.'

'Oh.' Claire was struggling to hold back the tears again now. It was hard to believe that Tracey was all grown up with a family of her own.

'She took it really badly when you upped and ran off,' Molly told her, and now Claire could clearly hear the anger in her voice. 'The poor little mite. As if she hadn't gone through enough – and then for you to just disappear off the face of the earth like that. For years and years she expected you to just walk back through the door, but as they passed and you didn't, she grew bitter. I wouldn't expect her to roll out the red carpet for you. Do you have *any* idea at all what your running off like that did to us all? We were beside ourselves with worry. What were you *thinking* of, Claire? We loved you, and you turned your back on us. And now you waltz back in as if you've never been gone, and I don't mind telling you, I don't quite know what to say to you. You've fair taken the wind out of my sails.'

Claire stared down into her tea before saying, 'I'm *so* sorry, Molly.'

'Huh! And you think that one little word will make everything all right, do you? That it can make me forget all the nights I lay in bed worrying about you, wondering if you were lying dead in a ditch somewhere!'

'No, no, of course I don't. I just . . .' It was no good, the tears were burning now and they streamed from her eyes and splashed onto her clenched fists as she struggled to think of what she should say. Molly had every right to be angry and Claire knew that she deserved everything her foster-mother might throw at her.

After a few moments, Claire scraped back her chair and rose unsteadily. 'I shouldn't have come,' she choked. '*Please* try to forgive me, Molly. I know I can never make it right but I just wanted you to know that I was sorry.' She was almost at the door when the woman's voice stayed her.

'No – don't go. Not yet. It must have taken some guts for you to come here, and now that you have, I want to hear about what you've been doing all these years. But you can't stay too long. I'm expecting Tracey this afternoon and I think I ought to prepare her before you see each other. No doubt it will come as a right old shock to her. You do understand, don't you?'

Claire nodded blindly and then suddenly Molly covered the distance between them and wrapped her in her arms as Claire began to sob broken-heartedly.

'Come on, sit yourself back down,' Molly muttered as Claire clung to her. 'I think it's time we had a talk, don't you?'

Chapter Two

Claire and Nikki were curled up on the sofa together that evening, with Gemma snuggled between them when the first flakes of snow began to fall beyond the window. It was Nikki who noticed first. She pointed gleefully.

'Look, it's snowing,' she announced, and Claire nodded absently.

'I love the snow.' Nikki stroked Gemma, then leaning slightly away she asked, 'Is everything all right, Mum? You've been really quiet tonight. Right since I got home from school, in fact.'

'What? Oh yes, love, everything's fine. It's just that I . . . well, I went into Nuneaton today while you were at school and I saw Molly.'

'You *did*?' Nikki's face lit up brighter than a summer day. 'Why didn't you tell me earlier on? Was she glad to see you? Did you get to see your sister? Did—'

'Whoa!' Claire held up a hand to silence the excited child. 'One question at a time, if you please. You're making me dizzy.'

When the girl instantly lapsed into silence, Claire looked away and began falteringly, 'I'm not so sure she was actually *pleased* to see me, but she was certainly shocked, which I suppose is hardly surprising after all this time. And no, I didn't get to see Tracey. Molly thought it might be best if she prepared her first. She's going to have twins in a couple of months, you see, and shocks aren't good for her.'

'Wow!' Nikki grinned. 'So you'll be an aunty then, won't you? And they'll be my cousins. That's *so* cool. And when will I be able to meet them? Did you tell her about me?'

'Of course I did. But I can't say yet when you'll get to meet them. I left it with Molly to decide. It might be that Tracey won't even want to see me again after all this time, let alone meet you. We just have to wait now and see if Molly rings. I gave her our phone number but if she doesn't get in touch there's not a lot I can do about it. The last thing I want is to be a nuisance, so now we wait.'

'Oh.' Disappointment clouded Nikki's face. She had heard so much about Molly and Tom, her mum's foster-parents, not to mention Tracey, her sister. Still, even at her tender age she could understand what Claire was saying.

'I'm sure everything will turn out all right,' she told Claire encouragingly as she squeezed her hand. 'And even if they don't want us, we've still got each other, haven't we?'

'Of course we have, love.' Claire's heart filled with love as she pulled this precious girl into her arms and kissed her freshly washed hair. 'That's one thing you can always be certain of. You'll *always* have me. You're the most precious thing in my life and I love you.'

'I love you too, Mum,' Nikki replied contentedly as she rested her head on Claire's shoulder. 'For always.'

Claire blinked back the tears. Today's meeting might not have gone exactly as she had hoped it would, but at least she had taken the first step. Now it was all up to Molly and she could only hope that the woman could forgive her.

'I still can't understand why we didn't move back into Nuneaton though,' the girl went on.

Claire sighed. 'We've been through this before, love,' she told her patiently. 'I wanted to be close to them again but not on their doorstep. This way, there's just enough distance between us for them to get used to me being around again without me bumping into them all the time.'

'I miss Christian and Mrs M.'

The comment was so unexpected that for a while Claire was lost for words, but then she said softly, 'I do too, love.'

Nikki sat forward and looked Claire directly in the eye before saying, 'I think Christian loves you, and I think you love him too, so why can't you be together?'

'Because . . .' Claire licked her dry lips. 'Because I have a lot of demons to face before I can properly love anyone, Nikki. Things that I have to come to terms with before I can go on.'

'You mean things like giving your baby away when you were young and running away from your foster-home?'

'Yes . . . that, but there are other things too. Things I've done that I'm ashamed of.'

'What other things?'

'I can't tell you right now. But one day I will, I promise you, when the time is right. And when I do, I just pray that you'll still love me.'

'Nothing could make me stop loving you,' Nikki declared hotly. 'So why don't you just tell me now and get it over with?'

Claire chewed on her lip as colour flooded into her cheeks. 'I can't tell you yet because I'm a coward,' she whispered. 'Trust me, I'll tell you when the time is right.'

Nikki pulled a face as she dragged herself off the sofa and headed for the kitchen. 'Grown-ups can be very hard to understand at times,' she muttered, and as she disappeared through the door with Gemma at her heels, Claire bowed her head in shame. All the way home from Molly's that day she had asked herself why she hadn't just told Molly the truth and have done with it. She had tried to excuse herself because their first meeting had been limited in time. But deep down she knew that she hadn't really intended to tell Molly about her past today. She had simply said very briefly that she had worked in London after leaving home before moving to Blackpool and marrying Greg. She had then gone on to tell her that Greg had died, no explanation of how, and that she had now adopted Greg's adopted daughter as her own. Molly had been sympathetic and Claire had grasped at that. It was more than obvious from the woman's first reaction that she hadn't been altogether thrilled to see her, but after hearing Claire's story she had softened a little.

Perhaps it's best this way, Claire thought to herself. At least this way I might get to meet Tracey again. If I had told her everything straight out, she might have shut the door on me and that would have been an end to it. It was all too easy to convince herself that she had done the right thing and so now she swung her legs off the settee and followed Nikki into the kitchen, knowing deep down that she was still fooling herself and that the day of reckoning must surely come.

It was three days later before the call that Claire had been longing for finally came. Nikki was at school and Claire was hanging new curtains in the spacious lounge when the sudden shrill ringing of the phone almost made her topple off the chair she was standing on.

With her heart in her throat she hurried into the hall and snatched it up. 'Hello.'

'Hello, Claire. It's me, Molly.'

Claire gulped deeply. Now that the call had come she scarcely knew what to say, but she needn't have worried because Molly hurried on, 'I've had a chat with Tracey. I'm not going to lie to you and tell you that she was pleased to hear you're back on the scene because she wasn't. In fact, her first reaction was, "I've been without her for this long, so why would I want to see her now? She didn't care about me when she went swanning off without a word." Luckily, she calmed down a bit then and when she rang me earlier today she agreed to meet you. I thought here might be the best place, as she's comfortable here. But I can't say what she will be like with you, so there it is. I've done my best – now the rest is up to you. So what do you think?'

'I think you're absolutely wonderful,' Claire said truthfully. 'Thank you, Molly. I know I don't deserve your help after the way I treated you all. But I *will* make it up to you, I promise – if you'll all give me a chance.'

She heard Molly sniff at the other end of the phone and knew that she still had a long way to go before being welcomed back into the fold.

'Well, that remains to be seen. Now, when would you like me to arrange it for?'

'As soon as Tracey can manage it,' Claire told her hastily. 'I can come today, if you like, while Nikki's at school.'

'I'll phone Tracey and see what she thinks, then ring you back, but don't hold your breath. The mood she's in at the moment she might just change her mind.'

'I understand,' Claire told her quickly. 'And . . . thanks again, Molly.' The phone went dead in her hand and now all she could do was wait as she paced up and down the hallway. Ten minutes later she snatched the receiver up again on the first ring and said eagerly, 'Yes?'

'She says she'll be here in an hour. Is that too soon for you?'

'Oh, no,' Claire assured her. 'I'm on my way.' And this time it was she who slammed the phone down before hurrying away up the stairs. Once in her bedroom she grabbed the first suit she saw from its hanger, put it on then pushed her feet into high-heeled shoes. Hastily, she applied a little make-up and piled her hair on top of her head. Twenty minutes later, she collected her car keys from the table in the hall and ran out to her car, heedless of the snow that was creeping over the top of her shoes. Her heart was thumping painfully but the smile on her face stretched from ear to ear as she tried to picture what Tracey would look like now. She had been just a little girl the last time Claire had seen her, but she was a married woman now, and seven months' pregnant with twins. It was hard to believe.

Claire took the back way through the twisty lanes to Nuneaton and the weather conditions slowed her progress. At times she knew she was driving far too fast for the icy roads but she didn't care. She was finally going to see her sister again and she would have walked barefoot to do it, if need be.

It was exactly fifty-five minutes since Molly had phoned when she drew her car to a halt outside the house in Howard Road. A small Fiat was parked outside and Claire guessed that this must be Tracey's car. She quickly checked her hair in the car mirror then, picking up her bag, she took a deep breath and climbed from the car. Seconds later she was knocking at Molly's door. The snow had started to fall again but Claire was oblivious to it. She was oblivious to everything except the fact that she was seconds away from seeing the sister she had missed for too many long years.

'Hello, Claire. Come on in.' Unsmiling, Molly held the door wide and Claire stepped past her into the hallway.

'She's in the kitchen,' Molly told her without preamble. 'I'm going to make myself scarce for a while upstairs, but give me a shout if you need me.' With that she turned and left Claire staring at the kitchen door. It was all that divided her from her sister now, but suddenly she didn't know if she had the courage to go through it. Perhaps it would have been better if I'd never come, she thought to herself. Perhaps I should have just stayed in Blackpool and married Christian. He could live with what I've done in the past, but will Tracey – or Molly, for that matter – be able to?

As it happened, she didn't have time to turn tail and run because at that moment the door opened and Claire was confronted by an attractive young woman, heavily pregnant. Shock coursed through her. This couldn't be Tracey, surely? She was beautiful. Or at least, she would be if she smiled. As it was, her face was fixed in a deep frown.

They eyed each other warily until the woman suddenly snapped, 'So . . . you finally decided to come back then?'

Claire could only nod numbly and the silence seemed to stretch between them until Tracey said grudgingly, 'You'd better come through. You look frozen. There's a fresh pot of tea made. Would you like a cup?'

'Yes, I . . . I would. Thanks.'

There was a lump in Claire's throat and she was afraid to talk in case she burst into tears. She wanted to fling her arms around Tracey and tell her how much she had missed her, how often she had cried for her and thought of her over the years – but instead they were facing each other like two strangers.

When Tracey turned and strode into the kitchen, Claire followed her and stood at the side of the table as Tracey poured milk into two mugs.

'Still two sugars, is it?'

Claire felt ridiculously pleased that Tracey had remembered. She nodded solemnly. And then her sister was pushing the mug towards her and gesturing at a chair before sitting down herself. Claire studied her. Tracey still had the beautiful dark hair she remembered; it was fashionably cut in a feathered style that framed her face and curled slightly on her slim shoulders. She had grown tall; in fact, Claire was shocked to find that she was possibly even two or three inches taller than herself. But there any resemblance to the little girl she had carried in her heart all these years ended. Tracey was now a mature young woman. The years in between were gone, never to be relived.

It was Tracey who finally broke the uncomfortable silence when she asked tartly, 'So how are you then? Molly tells me that you've been married and have a daughter.'

'Yes, I do, her name is Nikki. She's twelve now. She was actually my late husband's daughter, and I adopted her when he died.'

'I see.' Tracey's eyes were moving over Claire's outfit. 'And just what made you decide to pop up out of the woodwork now, after all this time? I would have thought you would have forgotten all about us long ago.' There was no attempt to conceal the contempt in her voice and Claire cringed inwardly. But then, what could she expect?

'I could *never* forget you,' she replied. 'And I'll never forgive myself for leaving you the way I did. But I thought you were happy with Molly – that you didn't need me any more. And I was all screwed up.'

'Huh! *You* were screwed up! Don't you think that I was too? Oh, but then I forgot . . . you went and got yourself pregnant on top of everything else, didn't you? It's hardly surprising really when you were going with every Tom, Dick or Harry you could get your hands on. And then, to cap it all, you go and give the poor little mite away as soon as it was born, even though Molly told you she'd stand by you.

And now you have the nerve to sit there and tell me that *you* were screwed up! Still, I suppose that's as good an excuse as any,' Tracey spat scathingly. 'You *must* have known that you were my whole life. Granted, I loved Molly, but that didn't make me love *you* any the less. You should have known that. When you left, I . . . I . . .'

Tracey's voice trailed away for a moment but then her chin came up, and her eyes were bright with angry tears as she glared at Claire and told her, 'I kept thinking you'd come back, Claire. Can you even *begin* to imagine what that was like? I couldn't eat or sleep for weeks. And then slowly, as time passed, it dawned on me that you *weren't* coming back and I had to try and forget about you or I would have gone mad. And now you breeze in and want to play Happy Families. Well, I don't really think that's going to happen overnight, do you?'

'No, I don't,' Claire told her truthfully. 'Not a day has gone by when I haven't regretted what I did, and I'll never forget the child I gave up. It's too late for me to do anything about her now, but if it takes me the rest of my life I'll make it up to you . . . I promise.'

'Words are cheap.' Tracey stared at her over the rim of her mug. She then gave a long, shuddering sigh before asking in a slightly calmer voice, 'So what did you do when you left? Where did you go?'

This was the moment that Claire had been dreading, and after the greeting she had received she was wise enough to know that she mustn't divulge too much too quickly or she could be at risk of losing Tracey for ever.

'I hitched a lift to London,' she told her sister, and that much at least was true, 'hoping that all the misery you and I had endured would just vanish in a puff of smoke and I could leave my past behind.' She lowered her head before going on. 'Of course, I soon found myself disillusioned. I couldn't get a job and then I got mugged by a gang of youths who took every penny I had. Luckily, a girl who lived in London befriended me and took me in off the streets.'

'And what did you do for a living?'

'Oh, this and that.' Claire was on very thin ice now and she knew it. 'Mainly book-keeping and management.'

Even this was not strictly untrue, she told herself. She had done courses in both, but she had omitted to tell her sister that her main income had been earned on street corners – until she had worked her way up to being a high-class call girl, that was.

'And your husband, where did you meet him?'

Claire gulped deeply. 'I went to live in Blackpool when I had saved enough money and bought myself a small hotel. Greg was my accountant. He was a widower.'

'Lucky you,' Tracey drawled sarcastically. 'It sounds like you really landed on your feet.'

Claire chose not to answer that remark and eventually Tracey rose from the table to carry her mug to the sink. 'And Nikki, your adopted daughter. Do you love her?'

'I adore her.' This, at least, Claire could answer truthfully. 'She's a wonderful child. I'm sure that you'll like her when you meet her. If you want to meet her, that is,' she finished hastily. 'And by the way, congratulations about your marriage and about the babies.'

Tracey's hands dropped protectively to her stomach. 'Callum, my husband, is the best thing that's ever happened to me,' she told Claire. 'And this,' she stroked her abdomen, 'this is just the icing on the cake. So you see, Claire, eventually life did go on without you. It had to. I couldn't spend my whole life waiting for you to come back.'

'But we could go on from here, couldn't we?'

Tracey looked at her solemnly. 'I don't know,' she answered. 'Let's just take one day at a time, eh?'

Claire nodded eagerly. At least it was a start. Tracey could have told her that she never wanted to see her again, but she hadn't. For now, this was the best that she could hope for.

Chapter Three

April, 2000

Through the bedroom wall, Claire could hear Nikki pacing up and down, up and down. It was now one o'clock in the morning and the girl had gone to her room just after nine following yet another row.

Claire sighed. Nikki was now fourteen years old. When Claire had adopted her, she had been a pretty child, but now she was fast developing into a beautiful young woman – a fact of which she had suddenly become very aware. As Claire lay there staring into the darkness, she tried to put her finger on exactly when things had started to go wrong between them.

Following their move to Solihull from Bispham, Nikki had appeared to be happy for a time; particularly so after she started at Claremont School, not far from their new home. She had quickly made friends and Claire hoped she was coming to terms with the abuse she had suffered at the hands of her adoptive father. Nikki had had no counselling since coming to live here, as she had promised Claire that she did not want – or need – it. But then she had reached her teens and Claire had begun to notice a subtle difference in her. It was just minor things at first – staying out a little later than she should, answering back, refusing to do something when asked. At first, Claire had put it down to teenage mood swings, but over the past two years things had gotten progressively worse until now, she knew that soon she would have no choice but to call in some professional help. Nikki was fast becoming beyond parental control.

Her thoughts turned to Christian, and tears pricked at the back of her eyes. She had hoped that eventually, when she had helped Nikki and faced her own abusive childhood, she would be able to return to Seagull's Flight, the small vet's practice he ran in Fleetwood on the edge of Blackpool, as his wife. Christian had been so patient over the past two years. They still spoke regularly on the phone and she had even visited him and his grandmother on a few occasions, but never once had he tried to rush her into returning to Fleetwood. He was too much of a gentleman for that.

Up to a point Claire *had* faced some of her demons, although it had been hard. Since coming back to the Midlands her relationship with her former foster-mum had improved immensely, but the same could not be said for her relationship with Tracey. The latter was now the proud mother of beautiful twin baby girls. Claire absolutely adored her nieces but even after two years, Tracey still held her sister at arm's length. She was a long way from forgiving Claire for abandoning her, and Claire knew that it would be a considerable time before Tracey fully trusted her again. Of course, it was no more than she should expect, but the fact still cut like a knife each time they met.

A loud bang from the room next door jolted her thoughts firmly back to the present. The latest row had started when Nikki had asked to be allowed to go to an all-night party at a friend's house. Claire had pointed out that as she was not yet fifteen years old she felt it would be inappropriate, and then the balloon had gone up big time. Even when Claire had offered to fetch her back at bedtime, Nikki had continued to rant and rave until eventually she had stormed off to her room, and there she had stayed ever since, pacing up and down like a caged animal.

As the sounds continued, Claire swung her legs out of the warm bed and padded to her dressing-gown, which was slung across the back of a chair. She put on her slippers and after leaving her room, tentatively tapped at Nikki's bedroom door.

'Nikki, I can't sleep and I can hear you're still awake. Why don't you come down and I'll make us both a nice hot cup of cocoa, eh?' she asked.

The noises stopped abruptly although there was no reply to her question. Tightening the belt of her dressing-gown she tried again. 'Won't you *please* come and talk to me, love? If you go on at this rate you'll be worn out in the morning.'

Again only silence answered her, so pursing her lips she slowly descended the stairs to the spacious hallway and made her way into the kitchen where Gemma bounded towards her, her tail wagging furiously. Gemma had been one of the strays that Christian had taken into his animal sanctuary at Seagull's Flight and was much loved by both Claire and Nikki, which was funny now that Claire came to think of it, for while Nikki seemed to be rebelling against her at every turn, her love for the little dog remained unchanging. After turning the kettle on to boil she sat at the table and looked about her with Gemma on her lap.

Nikki's schoolbooks were spread haphazardly across the table. There was a perfectly good study where Nikki could do her homework – when Claire could get her to do it, that was – but lately she had started to leave it all over the house as if she was deliberately trying to start a row. As the kettle began to sing, Claire hurried to the hob and was just in the process of spooning some cocoa into a mug when Nikki appeared in the doorway. Her hair was tousled and standing there in her pyjamas she looked incredibly young and vulnerable. Ignoring her sulky expression, Claire motioned her to a seat.

'Sit down. This will be ready in a jiffy and then we'll have a little talk, eh?'

Nikki's lips curled back from her teeth as she ground out, 'Why should I want to talk to you? All you ever do is nag at me . . . *do this, do that*! I'm sick of it, do you hear me? You're not my mum – not my *real* mum anyway!'

With that she turned and stamped away back up the stairs as tears spurted from Claire's eyes and coursed down her pale cheeks. Sadly, she clicked off the kitchen light and made her way to bed. There would be no use in trying to talk to Nikki any more tonight. It would just end in a row; better to wait until the morning and try again then.

'Nikki, can you hear me? Your breakfast is on the table and if you don't get a move on, you'll be late for school.'

Claire paused outside Nikki's bedroom door waiting for a sign that the girl had heard her, and when no reply was forthcoming she gently began to inch it open. 'Nikki, come on, love. It's gone eight o'clock.'

The room was in darkness, so striding to the curtains, Claire pulled them back, allowing the early-morning sunshine to stream into the room. She turned towards the bed with a smile on her face but it died instantly when she saw that it was empty. Moving quickly to the door of the en-suite bathroom she saw at a glance that this was empty too and her heart turned over.

Hurrying back to the window she looked down the long drive that led to their smart detached house. It was deserted just as she had thought it would be. Nikki could have been gone for hours, for all she knew.

Sinking onto a chair at the side of Nikki's bed she dropped her head into her hands and fought to hold back the tears that were threatening. This was the second day this week that Nikki had pulled this trick and no doubt Claire would have another call from Claremont telling her that Nikki had not turned in for school again. Her schoolwork was suffering as a result of her truanting but Claire was at a loss as to what she could do about it.

She rose and after slowly making her way back down to the kitchen she scraped Nikki's breakfast into Gemma's bowl and stood and watched as the little creature wolfed it down. Before she and Nikki had adopted her, the poor little creature had been starved and Claire was sure that if she'd allowed it, Gemma would still have eaten until she burst, almost as if she was trying to make up for all the years she had gone without. It was as she was standing there that the phone rang and when Claire answered it, Molly's voice came to her.

28

'Hello, love. How are things?'

'Hello, Molly. They're . . . er . . . all right, thanks.' Remembering how badly she had treated Molly when she herself had been in her teens, Claire was always somewhat reluctant to confide the way Nikki was behaving. After all, the way she saw it, Molly would probably say it served her right.

'Good. In that case I was wondering if you'd fancy doing a bit of shopping while Nikki's at school?'

Claire chewed on her lip. There was nothing she would have liked more than to head off to Nuneaton to spend a day with Molly and pop in and see Tracey and her adorable twins. But until she knew where Nikki was, she just couldn't.

'Thanks, Molly. I would have loved to, but unfortunately I'm booked up for today. I promised my boss I would pop in and catch up with a few letters that he needs to get out.' This was not strictly a lie, as Claire had taken a part-time job at a solicitor's in the town.

Molly sighed. 'Oh well, perhaps another time then. Though why you need to work is beyond me.'

Molly was right. Financially, Claire had no need to work, but it gave her an interest and something to occupy her while Nikki was at school.

'Tracey was wondering if you and Nikki would like to come to the twins' birthday party on Saturday?' Molly went on. Claire was delighted. This was definitely a step in the right direction – as long as she could persuade Nikki away from her friends for long enough for them to go, that was.

'I'd love to,' she assured Molly, and they chattered on about nothing of great importance for another few minutes. When Claire eventually put the phone down she felt slightly better. It was nice to be on good terms with Molly again, even if Tracey hadn't completely accepted her back into the fold yet. She began to think of what she could buy the twins for their presents and decided to stick to clothes. That way, she would have less chance of buying them something they had already got, if that was possible. Tracey and her husband obviously doted on the little ones,

Jessica and Isabelle, and each time Claire had visited their comfortable detached house on the Nicholas Park Estate in Nuneaton it had seemed to be bulging at the seams with every toy imaginable. But before she thought of shopping she would have to find Nikki – and that could prove to be easier said than done if her recent jaunts were anything to go by.

She walked to the phone in the hall and lifted the address book. Once again she would have to ring round all Nikki's friends in the hope of finding her, and if that failed it would mean climbing into the car and cruising the streets hoping for a sight of her. Sighing with resignation, she dialled the first number.

'So . . . what shall we do today then?' Nikki asked.

Her friend Erin took a packet of cigarettes from her smart blazer pocket and lit one. Offering the packet to Nikki, she shrugged nonchalantly. 'Whatever you like. We may as well make the most of it though, 'cos we know we're going to get a roasting when we both go home.'

'Huh! As if I care,' Nikki sneered as she inhaled a lungful of smoke. 'Why are grown-ups always so smug? They seem to think they know *everything*. I mean, look at this . . .' She poked the lapels of her royal-blue blazer with disgust. 'Nearly fifteen and still having to wear baby things like this! They don't have to wear uniforms, do they, so why should we?'

Erin grunted. 'Beats me.' She stared into the swirling waters of the canal that ran along the back of the church. This was one of their favourite places because from here they couldn't be seen from the road. Nikki looked at her admiringly. Of all the girls that attended Claremont, Erin Morgan was her favourite. She wasn't afraid of stepping out of line like the other girls in their class and had the reputation of being something of a rebel. Erin and Nikki made an unlikely pair. Nikki was tall and slim, to the point of being skinny, whilst Erin was short for her age and inclined to be dumpy. Her mousey-coloured shoulder-length hair was as straight as a poker and did nothing to flatter her round face, which had already erupted into teenage acne. On top of that, her slightly buck teeth were now encased in thick braces both top and bottom. Erin lived in Lady Byron Road, a stone's throw from Nikki, and over the last couple of months they had become inseparable, both in and out of school.

'So, will you be seeing your dad this week?' Nikki now asked and Erin's face set into an angry mask.

'Yes, I dare say he'll be round to take me out on Saturday,' she said sulkily.

'That'll be another new outfit then,' Nikki commented.

'You're probably right, but it doesn't cut any ice with me. It's just conscience money 'cos he's left me and Mum,' Erin retorted. Her father had left them several months ago and since then she had extorted every penny she could out of him. The way she saw it, he had betrayed them by running off with his blonde bimbo of a secretary, so why shouldn't she bleed him for all she could? He deserved no better.

'How is your mum now?' Nikki dared to ask, and Erin's lips set in a firm straight line.

'Still hitting the bottle like it's going out of fashion,' she hissed. 'I don't know why she doesn't just go out and start to enjoy herself again. I mean, my dad isn't the only man in the world, is he? I know she's old . . . well, thirty-five is old, isn't it? But even so she isn't bad looking when she makes an effort. Instead of that though she just sits there drinking herself silly and crying all the time. When we bunked off school the other day she was so drunk by the time I got in that she didn't even bother to give me a rollicking. The sad old sop!'

Despite the brave face Erin was putting on, Nikki knew that her parents' break-up had affected her badly, and the way she was fleecing her father was her way of getting back at him. She could understand how she felt. From where she was standing, fathers were wicked, bad people who didn't deserve respect. For just a second she felt a flicker of shame as she thought of Claire. Claire had stood by her when her father had abused her, but then Nikki had begun to suspect it was because of the guilt she felt for once having given her own baby away

– as if she, Nikki, could somehow take the place of that child, just as Claire thought she could take the place of her mother. Well, she couldn't. Her mother, her birth mother, was out there somewhere and Nikki was going to find her. The need to do just that was like a festering boil inside her. Exactly *how* she would do it she had no idea as yet, but she knew there would be no peace until she did.

The girls finished their cigarettes in silence and when they had tossed the nub ends into the dark water, Erin asked, 'Do you fancy going into town?'

'Won't we be a little conspicuous dressed in these?' Nikki looked down at her hated uniform uncertainly.

'Nah. If anyone asks us why we aren't at school we'll just tell them we have a free lesson. Look, we can spend some of this.' As she spoke, Erin pulled a small wad of notes from her blazer pocket.

Nikki's eyes popped out of her head as if they were on stalks. 'Crikey,' she gasped. 'Where on earth did you get all that?'

'Out of Mum's purse while she was lying sozzled on the sofa last night.' Erin displayed not so much as a trace of remorse. 'And the best of it is she hasn't even *missed* it. She's so drunk for most of the time now that she doesn't even know if she's on her arse or her elbow, so from where I'm standing she doesn't deserve any better.'

Nikki put her hand across her mouth to stifle a giggle. Erin was so brave. Nothing seemed to worry her, not even Fatty Harbin. Mr Harbin, their headmaster – or Fatty Harbin, as he had been nicknamed – could strike terror into Nikki's heart with one stern glance, yet Erin seemed to have no fear of him at all. She didn't fear anyone, from what Nikki could see of it, which only made her admire the other girl all the more.

Erin stood up, and after taking off her school tie, she stuffed it into her pocket. She then undid her blouse right down to her small cleavage and began to roll the waistband of her navy and white striped skirt over until it reached way above her knees.

'That's better. Let's go and buy a bottle of vodka and then we'll bring it back here where no one will disturb us.' She proceeded to swipe the loose grass from her skirt as Nikki followed suit and then they turned and headed for the town.

It was now three o'clock in the afternoon and despite phoning everyone she could think of, and driving round in her car for hours looking for Nikki, Claire hadn't caught so much as a glimpse of her. As she entered the house, the phone rang.

Snatching it up, she barked, '*Yes?*'

'Oh dear, someone is not in a very good humour.'

At the sound of the familiar voice, Claire's face softened. 'Christian, I'm sorry, I didn't mean to snap. It's just that Nikki has played hookey from school again and I've spent the entire day trying to find her.'

'I see.' His voice became serious. 'Have you reported her missing?'

'No, not yet. She usually rolls in before bedtime when she pulls this stunt so I don't want to get the police out unnecessarily.'

Hearing the tremor in her voice he asked, 'Do you want me to come over? I could be there in less than three hours.'

'Thank you, but no. It might just make things worse. She'd think we were ganging up on her if she came home to find you here too.'

'Damn!'

She could hear the frustration and irritation in his voice. He felt as if there was a great gulf between them again. And he knew that the gulf would always be there while Nikki was playing up because Claire would always put Nikki before herself. 'Look,' he suggested as a thought occurred to him, 'why don't you bring her here for the weekend? Gran would love to have you both and once you manage to get her here, Nikki usually seems to enjoy it.'

'I would have loved to but it's the twins' birthday on Saturday and I've promised Molly that I would go to their party,' Claire told him regretfully.

Christian's sigh came to her down the line. 'Fair enough, it was just a thought. But of course I understand that you need to attend the party. You and Tracey have a lot to catch up on. I hope you'll be able to come soon though, 'cos . . . I miss you, Claire. *So* very much.'

Claire choked back tears, but her voice when she answered was calm. 'We've been through this before, Christian, a hundred times. I have to put Nikki first for now, but our time will come, you'll see.' Yet deep inside she was thinking . . . would it?

Chapter Four

'Just where the hell do you think you've been, young lady? I've been almost frantic, worrying about you. Another half an hour and I would have phoned the police – and then where would you have been?'

Nikki smirked and shrugged her slight shoulders as Claire stepped out of the lounge to confront her in the hall. It was almost 10 p.m. and Claire had been beside herself with worry as she watched the hands of the clock ticking away the hours. Now the fear was replaced by anger that surged through her veins as she stared into Nikki's defiant face. The girl suddenly wobbled slightly to one side and Claire realised that she had been drinking.

'My God – you're drunk!' Claire would have said much more, but at that moment Nikki suddenly turned a sickly shade of green and clamped her hand across her mouth.

'I . . . I'm going to be sick,' she murmured, and rushing into the downstairs toilet, she promptly emptied the contents of her stomach, which was pitifully little except for liquid, into the pan.

Despair washed over Claire as she thought of the pain she must have caused Molly when she had done exactly the same to her all those years ago. But now was not the time for whipping herself. Nikki needed her, so grabbing her by the elbow, she yanked her into the kitchen and sat her down at the table.

'Now you just sit there, my girl, while I make you some good strong coffee,' she ordered. 'And something to eat wouldn't go amiss either, judging by the state you're in. I bet you haven't eaten a thing all day, have you?'

Nikki stuck out her chin, obstinately quiet as Claire put the kettle on and turned on the heat beneath the soup that was ready on the stove.

In no time at all she had a meal in front of the girl and a steaming mug of coffee, but Nikki just crossed her arms and stared at it as if it was poison before telling her, 'I'm not hungry.'

'Whether you're hungry or not I want you to eat something,' Claire informed her shortly. 'No wonder you feel ill, drinking on an empty stomach.'

Nikki remained still and now Claire's voice took on a wheedling tone as she lifted the spoon and tried to put it in Nikki's hand. 'Look, just eat a little bit for me, eh? I promise you'll start to feel better if you do.'

Nikki suddenly bounced up from the table and slapped at the spoon, sending it clattering across the ceramic tiles on the kitchen floor. 'Are you deaf?' she shouted, red in the face as Gemma scooted away into her basket with her tail tucked between her legs. 'I told you I'm not hungry! What part of that sentence don't you understand? You're doing it again, aren't you – trying to rule me. God, *and* you're trying to spoonfeed me! Just leave me alone and go and find someone else to pick on, can't you?' With that and a toss of her head she stormed from the room, leaving Claire to stare after her open-mouthed.

Eventually she retrieved the spoon from the floor and sank onto a chair as she listened to Nikki thumping about upstairs in her bedroom. I handled that all wrong, she thought to herself, and not for the first time she wished that teenagers could come complete with books on how best to deal with them.

Gemma now crawled across the floor on her belly to her and after stroking her, Claire headed resolutely towards the staircase. She would never give up on Nikki, never. She loved her far too much for that.

Once on the landing she tapped at the door and not waiting for a reply she pushed it open and quietly entered the room. Nikki was curled into a tight little ball beneath the bedcovers and Claire sat down at the side of her. Stroking the fair hair that was fanned across the pillow she whispered, 'I'm sorry, love. I didn't mean to go at you like that. I was just worried about you, that's all.'

Nikki sniffed loudly, resisting the urge to throw herself into Claire's arms as she had done so many times before.

'I'm sorry too,' came a little voice from beneath the bedclothes.

Claire smiled as she switched off the bedside lamp and straightened the covers. 'It's okay,' she whispered. 'Things will come right in the end, you just see if they don't.' She moved towards the door where she paused to look back at the young girl who was bathed in the moonlight that was flooding through the window. 'Good night, sleep tight.' Closing the door carefully, she moved on to her own room.

'So, how are you feeling this morning then?' Claire pushed a bowl of cereal across the table to Nikki as she sat down.

'Not so good, to tell the truth,' the girl muttered.

'Well, get something inside you and a couple of good strong cups of tea and no doubt you'll start to feel better.'

Nikki lifted her spoon and began to push the cornflakes around her bowl as Claire poured tea into two mugs and placed one in front of her. After the trauma of the day before, Claire had slept like a log from the second her head hit the pillow, and she was feeling a lot more optimistic about things again today. After all, she asked herself, don't all young girls go off the rails from time to time when they reach adolescence?

'I had a phone call from Christian yesterday,' she said brightly. 'He wants us to go to Seagull's Flight as soon as we can for a weekend. That will be something to look forward to, won't it? Oh, and I had a call from Molly too. Jessica and Isabelle are having a birthday on Saturday and we've been invited to their party. I thought perhaps we could go shopping and buy them some presents on Saturday morning?'

Claire kept up her cheerful chatter until half past eight when she rose from the table and fetched Nikki's schoolbag for her. 'Here you go, then. Don't forget that or they'll be sending you home again to fetch it if your homework is in there. Have a good day.'

Nikki took the bag without a word and after collecting her blazer she nodded at Claire and left the room. Claire flashed her a dazzling smile but once she had gone she blinked back tears as she crossed to the hall window to watch Nikki walking away down the drive. There was a stoop to her shoulders as if she was carrying the weight of the world on them and it hit Claire like a blow how thin the girl looked from behind. Her legs were like matchsticks, and now Claire hurried back into the kitchen. Just as she had thought, she found Nikki's breakfast bowl under the table with Gemma lying contentedly at the side of it. She must have given it to her when I was pouring the tea, she thought to herself. Frowning, she lifted the bowl and carried it to the dishwasher. She was due in to work today and was suddenly glad of the fact. At least while she was working she didn't have time to worry about anything else.

Nikki had almost reached the end of the road when she heard someone coming up behind her. Turning, she saw Erin running to catch up with her, so she stopped and waited.

'I've been yelling my head off,' Erin scolded. 'I reckon you must have been off with the fairies not to hear me.'

'Sorry.' Nikki gave her a weak smile. 'I was just thinking.'

'Oh yes, what about?'

'Oh, nothing in particular really.' Nikki kicked at a stone and dropped her eyes as Erin fell into step beside her.

The sun was already shining and it looked set to be a lovely day, which prompted Erin to suggest, 'What about if we wag off school again? I could take you to meet my friend Poppy. She lives over on the Chelmsey Park Estate. She's really good fun – she don't give a damn about anything and I think you'd like her.'

The thought was tempting and just for a second Nikki hesitated, but then she shook her head. She was feeling guilty enough about the way she had treated Claire over the last few days and had promised herself that she would try harder to be good in future.

'Thanks, but I think I'd better go in today. My mum was really upset when I got in last night and I feel a bit rotten about it.'

'Huh!' Erin looked at her scathingly. 'I thought you were tougher than that? Mums are always upset about something or another.'

'You're probably right, but all the same I think I'll go in.'

'Have it your own way. It's your loss if you want to turn into a goody-goody.' Erin turned round and strode off down the road as Nikki watched her regretfully. Already her good intentions were wavering and she was sorely tempted to run after her friend, but then she thought of Claire's red-rimmed eyes again and resolutely set off for school.

She had barely settled at her desk when the teacher entered the room and she wished she hadn't bothered.

'Nikki Nightingale, Mr Harbin wants to see you in his office right now!' Miss Baker snapped.

'Yes, miss.' Nikki slunk from behind her desk and headed for the door, very aware of the sniggers from the other girls in the room as she passed. She wasn't very keen on Miss Baker at the best of times. The woman was middle-aged, old-fashioned and always looked as if she had been sucking on a lemon, but today, Nikki hated her with an intensity that was frightening.

When she arrived at the headmaster's door she tapped on it tentatively and his voice boomed, 'Enter.'

Nikki gulped deeply before doing as she was told. Mr Harbin was sitting at his desk and he peered over the top of his glasses at her before asking sharply, 'And where were you yesterday and on Monday, Miss Nightingale? Do you have a note from your mother excusing you from school?'

'N . . . no, sir.'

'Hmm . . .' He shook his bald head, setting his many chins wobbling as colour flamed into Nikki's cheeks. 'Then you are in very deep water, my girl, and you leave me no choice but to ring your mother again. I can only imagine that you must be proving to be a great disappointment to her.'

Could he have known it, the words cut deep but still Nikki said nothing as she continued to stare at the carpet.

'Very well, you will report to the detention room every day after school next week and do an hour's detention,' he now informed her.

Nikki's head shot up and she stared at him incredulously. 'Every day?' she repeated, before she could stop herself.

'Yes, young lady. *Every* day – and any more of your insolence and I will make it two weeks. Now go, and don't let me hear of you truanting again. Your mother pays a lot of money for you to attend this school and it would do you good to remember that. When you don't bother to attend, you are not only letting yourself down but her as well.'

Nikki turned on her heel and strode from the room, resentment coursing through her. Just who the hell did Fatty Harbin think he was anyway, talking to her like that?

Pausing in the corridor, she looked towards the entrance. There was no way she was going to stay here now. She just wished she had gone off with Erin in the first place. After marching through the entrance doors she left them swinging open behind her and stamped off down the tree-lined drive. However, she had barely taken a dozen steps when Mr Harbin's voice carried to her. '*Nikki Nightingale, just what do you think you are doing?* Get back inside the school *this minute* or I shall ring your mother immediately.'

Nikki had forgotten that his office overlooked the drive. 'So ring her and see if I care,' she shouted insolently, and swinging her bag higher onto her shoulder, she turned her back on him and walked on.

It wasn't until she had gone some way along the road that the anger left her and her shoulders sagged. She'd really done it now. Her mum would go berserk when she went home; she had no doubt about that. It was too late to do anything about it now though, so what should she do? As her eyes settled on the church she hurried towards it and after walking through the churchyard she came to the canal bank where she and Erin had passed some time away the day before.

Throwing her bag on the ground, she slouched down onto the grass and looked around at the tombstones. Back in Blackpool, her father was lying beneath one just like them; cold and rotting as he deserved to be. She shuddered as she remembered the feel of his hands on her bare flesh and tried to push the memories away. Even now, nightmares of what he had done to her would cause her to thrash and turn in the bed until she woke in a cold sweat. For a while after he had taken his life when Claire had discovered him abusing her, Nikki had seen Claire as her saviour. But lately her feelings had changed and she was asking herself, Why hadn't Claire realised what was going on earlier? If she had, she could have stopped it all the sooner.

It didn't occur to Nikki that she herself could have stopped it, if only she had confided in her. There was this great well of anger inside that seemed to be eating away at her. *Why* had it happened to her? What would Erin think of her, if she knew what her father had done to her? And then there was the other concern that seemed to have suddenly sprung up from nowhere: where was her *real* mother – her birth mother – and why had she given her away? She knew that she had been over a year old when she had been adopted by her first mother and father, so surely if her real mother had kept her for a year, she must have loved her? What could have happened to make her give her up? Perhaps she had been ill – perhaps she had died! Or perhaps, right now at this very minute, she was looking for her? Nikki sniffed as a tear splashed onto her joined hands. She wished she could feel differently but all her feelings were jumbled up at the minute, even her feelings for Claire.

A sound disturbed her thoughts, and glancing over her shoulder she saw an old lady bend to place a bunch of brightly coloured tulips in front of a gravestone. Nikki guessed it was probably her husband's grave and once again her thoughts turned to her late father. There would be no one to place flowers on his grave and she was glad. She hoped he was burning in hell, where he belonged.

'Good morning, Claire. And how are you today, my dear?'

Claire smiled into the friendly face of Mr Dickinson, the elderly solicitor she worked for as she hung her jacket on the small coat-rack behind the office door. Mr Dickinson had run this office in the centre of Solihull for over thirty years and was close to retiring. He was a small, stooped, grey-haired old man. Despite this, his reputation was second to none, and his client list was more than he could comfortably manage, which was why he had recently taken on not only Claire to do the typing and the reception work, but also a young man fresh from university, called Bradley King. King, his new partner, was proving to be invaluable to him. What's more, to Mr Dickinson's amusement, he had taken a shine to Claire, which he did nothing to hide.

Bradley was just a year younger than Claire and unmarried, and Mr Dickinson lived in hope that eventually, Claire would accept one of his many invitations out to dinner. Up to now, she had politely declined every one. Mr Dickinson supposed that this was because she was still mourning her husband. He knew that she was a widow with a young daughter and that they had recently moved to the Midlands, but little more than that. He had found Claire to be a very private person but exceptionally professional and good at her job. Mrs Dickinson, his wife, had also taken to Claire and had invited both her and her daughter to tea at their home in the nearby village of Catherine De Barnes on a number of occasions, but again Claire had politely refused.

Now, as Claire slid into the chair behind her desk, she smiled primly and told him, 'I'm very well, Mr Dickinson, thank you.'

'Are you sure, my dear?' He peered more closely at her over the top of his gold-framed glasses. 'You're looking terribly pale.'

'I'm quite all right,' she assured him, and turning to her computer she booted it up and began to study the list of letters waiting to be written.

Mr Dickinson frowned and went about his business. He knew when to keep his mouth shut. Soon they had both become absorbed in what they were doing and Claire was shocked when she next glanced at the clock to see that it was almost time to go.

Tidying the papers on her desk, she shut her computer down and looking towards the elderly man she asked, 'Would you like me to make you a drink before I go, Mr Dickinson?'

'Oh, is that the time already? How it flies! Yes, yes, that would be very nice, my dear. A cup of tea, I think. Won't you join me?'

Claire opened her mouth to refuse but then seeing that he was watching her hopefully she nodded. 'Very well then. I'll just put the kettle on. Is Bradley not in today?'

'No, he's in court all day. It's taken a great burden off me since I've been able to pass the less serious cases over to him. He's doing very well too. In fact, I wonder now how I ever managed without him. Such a nice chap too, don't you think? Good husband material for some fortunate girl, if I'm not very much mistaken.'

Claire grinned from ear to ear. As a matchmaker, Mr Dickinson was about as clumsy as an elephant in a china shop, not that he offended her. She knew that he meant well.

Once the tea was made he joined her at the window and they gazed down into the street below.

'And how is that lovely daughter of yours?' he asked conversationally.

When Claire's brow creased into a frown he guessed the reason for her quietness.

'How old is she now?'

'She'll be fifteen in November,' Claire replied quietly.

He chuckled. 'Oh dear – the terrible teens. They can be very trying at that age, can't they? Especially nowadays. Most of them are fourteen going on forty in the head. I remember my daughters had poor Mrs Dickinson almost pulling her hair out at that age. I was glad to come to work to get out of the way, I don't mind telling you. All those hormones causing havoc . . . and the mood swings. Oh yes, I remember it well.'

Claire peeped at him out of the corner of her eye. She could never imagine Mr Dickinson's children causing him or his wife so much as a moment's grief. They had always appeared to be such a close, loving family.

He glanced at her and as if reading her thoughts, he laughed again. 'Don't think a good education and a stable home-life qualifies you for being exempt from teenage tantrums. We had our share of troubles with ours, I admit. Still, they came through it in the end. Most of them do, given time. Half the cases I have on at the minute are teenagers due up in court for one thing or another. Drugs, shoplifting . . . you name it. Some of them are earmarked for a life of crime, but thankfully most of them go on to become respectable citizens.'

Claire was very tempted to tell him of the troubles she was having with Nikki. She opened her mouth to do just that, but then clamped it shut again. She had never found it easy to confide in anyone, and that was something that hadn't changed with the years. At that moment the phone rang and she hurried to her desk to answer it. It was a call for Mr Dickinson so after transferring the call to him she waved, took her coat and slipped out of the office. Strangely, she felt slightly better after their conversation. After all, as he had quite rightly pointed out, all teenagers went through a rebellious period, so was Nikki really so very different? And she did have a lot more than most to come to terms with. A smile lifted the corner of her lips as she suddenly wondered what Mr Dickinson would think of her if he ever got to learn about her own past. To him she was an efficient little secretary; a respectable widow with a young daughter. But what if she were to tell him that she had given birth to a child at fourteen, run away to London and become a prostitute?

As she emerged onto the street she paused to glance up and down. She looked no different from the many women who were gazing into shop windows or hurrying home with their shopping bags full of food for their families. And yet she *was* different. Her childhood had seen to that. And now she must be strong and stop the same thing happening to Nikki. Stop her going off the rails; stop her building a barrier that no one could ever penetrate. Only then could she think of joining Christian and beginning a new life with the man she loved where she could put the past behind her once and for all. Before that could happen she would have to tell Molly and Tracey the truth about her past. They were still blissfully unaware of how she had really earned her living in London, and Claire was happy for now for them to remain so. After all, until her relationship with Tracey improved it could only be detrimental for them to know. That was what she told herself, but deep down she knew that it was only an excuse. She wasn't strong enough just yet to face that particular confession. As she moved on, the thought of how she might ever do it was daunting, to say the very least. One thing was for sure: until she did, she could never be with Christian and find the peace she had always craved.

Chapter Five

Claire had only been home for half an hour when the phone rang.

'Mrs Nightingale?' It was Mr Harbin – she would have recognised his voice anywhere. And if he was ringing her yet again it could only mean one thing; Nikki must have been up to more mischief.

'Yes, Mr Harbin, this is Claire Nightingale. May I help you?'

'I wondered if it would be convenient for you to call into the school and see me, Mrs Nightingale? This afternoon, if it's at all possible.'

'Yes, I could manage that. But is there a problem?'

'I'm rather afraid there is. Nikki stormed off the school premises some time ago after I had cause to speak to her. I hate to say this, Mrs Nightingale, but her behaviour is having a somewhat disruptive influence on some of the other girls now. This is a very exclusive private school, as you are of course fully aware, and you must appreciate that we find this sort of behaviour intolerable, especially with the exams looming so close.'

'I shall be with you within half an hour,' Claire told him quietly, and after replacing the receiver she leaned heavily against the wall. What could Nikki have done to warrant being called into Harbin's office? And worse still, why had she then stamped off? Where was she now?

Wearily she headed back out to her BMW, which was parked on the drive. The way she saw it, she might as well go and face the music and get it over with.

When she left the school almost an hour later, Claire was in a deep depression. Mr Harbin had been most indignant about the way Nikki had stood up to him, and although Claire knew that her daughter had been in the wrong to do so, by the time she left his office she felt like strangling him herself. Harbin was such an arrogant, bombastic man that she could only wonder how he had ever managed to become the headmaster of Claremont in the first place. From where she was standing, he would have been better placed back in Victorian times. Claire had tried to treat Nikki as the young adult she was fast becoming but Mr Harbin seemed incapable of compromise on any issue regarding the young women in his care. Not for the first time she wondered if she shouldn't remove Nikki from the school. The fees were extortionate and if Nikki was unhappy there, which she obviously was, then there seemed very little point in making her continue. Claire decided that she would talk to Nikki about it, but first she had to find her, so once again she began to cruise the streets of Solihull as a dull headache throbbed behind her eyes.

She eventually turned the car in the direction of home after a fruitless search, and when she got there, was shocked to see Nikki sitting despondently on the front doorstep.

The girl looked so unhappy that Claire's annoyance fled immediately. She parked the car and walked up to her without a word as Nikki stared at her nervously.

'I suppose you've been to see Fatty Harbin then?' she asked as Claire calmly unlocked the door.

'I've been to see Mr Harbin, yes. But this is hardly the place to talk about it, Nikki. Let's go inside and get a drink, eh?'

Once in the kitchen, the girl dropped to her knees and began to stroke Gemma, who had come hurtling towards them.

'Why don't you take her out into the garden?' Claire suggested. 'I'll bring the drinks out there.'

Nikki threw open the French windows that led out onto the lawn and much as a small child would have done she ran the considerable length of the garden as Claire watched her with a lump in her throat.

Nikki was so very special to her; had been since the very first day she had set eyes on her. Claire didn't know how she would cope if ever anything came between them. Nikki was her life – and Christian too, of course. Thoughts of him and the little sanctuary at Seagull's Flight made the lump in her throat swell even more. Would she and Nikki ever be ready to join him there? Hastily placing the two glasses of lemonade on a tray she hurried out into the late-afternoon sunshine.

She sat down at the patio table and after a few moments Nikki came and joined her. She had expected Claire to shout at her and wasn't sure what to say so remained silent until Claire asked, 'Are you unhappy at Claremont, Nikki?'

Nikki stared thoughtfully off down the garden for a time before replying, 'Not really. I just – well, I get these funny moods that I can't seem to handle.' After glancing at Claire from the corner of her eyes she went on, 'I think it's because I . . . well, I wonder where I came from. Who my *real* mum was. It's not that I want to hurt you or anything,' she hastened to assure Claire. 'I *do* love you. I know I don't always show it, but . . .' Suddenly she burst into tears and rushing round the table, Claire wrapped her in her arms.

'Shush,' she soothed. 'If you really feel so strongly about finding out where you came from, then it's time we did something about it.'

'B . . . but how will we do that?' Nikki asked, gulping down her sobs.

Claire wiped the tears from her cheeks tenderly. 'I'll get in touch with Social Services; they'll tell us how we can go about it. But I'm not making any promises, mind.'

Nikki flashed her a look of such pure joy that Claire's heart began to thump wildly. She had the strangest feeling that they were about to embark on a journey that they might live to regret. But it was too late to go back on her word now. Tomorrow she would ring as she had promised and then what would be, would be.

* * *

On Saturday morning, Claire, Nikki and Gemma set off for Nuneaton. They had decided that they would shop for the twins' birthday presents there before going on to the party in the afternoon, and Nikki seemed much more relaxed and at ease, which Claire was grateful for. There had been no further incidents over the last couple of days and Claire was beginning to feel a little more optimistic about things.

Nuneaton town centre was teeming with shoppers when they got there and Claire struggled to find a parking place, but eventually they found one behind the Co-op and walked into the marketplace. Today was a typical April day and they had gone no more than a few yards when the heavens opened and they were caught in a heavy shower.

'Great,' Nikki grumbled as she tried to cover her fair hair with the hood on her jacket. 'My hair will go all fuzzy now with the damp.'

Claire smiled at her indulgently. Nikki had beautiful hair, thick with a tendency to curl, but she hated it and was forever trying to straighten it.

They passed through the market stalls, stopping here and there to admire the goods on display. Nikki persuaded Claire to treat her to a new pair of jeans that she insisted she *must* have, and then of course she needed a new top to go with it. She already had a wardrobe bulging with clothes back at home, but Claire found it hard to refuse her anything. The way she saw it, Nikki should have everything that she herself had never had as a child. The thought made her sad as she recalled the time when she and Tracey had lived with their mother in the council house in Gatley Common. Her mother had always put her own needs before those of her children, even more so after Claire's father had left them. She remembered the endless stream of boyfriends her mother would bring to the house, believing that each one would turn out to be the special one who would stand by her and make her life better. Of course, none of them had, as Claire and Tracey had found to their cost. She was shocked to discover that although she was now almost thirty years old, the memories could still strike terror into her heart. And then she had ended up marrying a man who was abusing Nikki as men had once abused her and her sister.

'Mum? *Mum* – what's the matter? I was talking to you. You were miles away.'

'Oh . . . sorry, love. I was just thinking. What were you saying?' Claire pulled her thoughts back to the present with an effort, to find Nikki holding up a little pair of denim jeans, heavily embroidered with flowers and butterflies.

'I was saying these would be nice for the twins. What do you think?'

'They're lovely,' Claire agreed. 'And they'd be just right for them to play out in the garden in. We could perhaps get them a little top each to go with them.' She bought two identical pairs and they moved on. By the time they arrived back at the car they were loaded down with bags.

'I reckon you've bought enough clothes here to last them right through to their next birthday,' Nikki commented as they piled the bags into the boot. Claire laughed; Nikki was right. There were pyjamas, coats, socks, vests and knickers as well as the jeans and tops they had bought first.

'I suppose I did get a bit carried away,' she admitted, but it was so nice to shop for little girls' clothes. Again she grew silent as she thought of the little daughter, Yasmin, she had given away at birth. She had never had the privilege of shopping for clothes for her. She would be fourteen now, almost the same age as Nikki.

Adopting Nikki had gone a long way to easing the heartache of losing Yasmin, and yet she still thought about her all the time; wondered where she was, what she would be doing. Were the people who had adopted her good to her? Was Yasmin happy?

'Mum, you're doing it again. What's wrong with you today?'

'Sorry.' Claire looked shamefaced. 'I think it must be being back on home ground that's making me broody. Come on. We'll go into Topper's and have a nice fish and chip dinner before we pick Molly up, shall we?'

Nikki didn't look too thrilled with the idea. Claire always seemed to be trying to get her to eat just lately, but she followed her back through the marketplace anyway, and soon she had the largest plate of fish and chips in front of her that she had ever seen.

'I'll never get through all this,' she complained as she stared at the loaded plate in horror.

Claire laughed. 'Well, you won't if you sit there looking at it. Go on, dig in. It won't bite you, you know.'

By the time Claire had finished her meal, Nikki had barely touched hers.

'I'm just popping to the loo,' Claire informed her, and Nikki watched her working her way through the tables to the back of the shop. The second she disappeared through the door, Nikki scraped almost all of the food on her plate onto an empty one on the next table that someone had just vacated. She then lifted her knife and fork and when Claire came back she smiled with pleasure.

'There you are, you see?' There was a note of approval in her voice. 'You were hungry after all, weren't you?'

'I must have been,' Nikki agreed as she laid her knife and fork down. 'I'm full up now though.'

'Right, I'll just go and pay and we'll get off for Molly then.' Claire glanced at her wristwatch. 'We should be just about right by the time we get there.'

When they drew up in Howard Road, Molly was looking out of the window for them. Tom, her husband, was mowing the front lawn and he smiled at them as he hurried to open the gate.

'Hello, loves. All ready for the party, are you?'

'Yes, we are, but aren't you coming, Tom?'

'Not on your Nelly!' He laughed aloud. 'I'm not daft. I reckon it will be less hard work staying here and seeing to the gardens.'

A flood of affection for this kind man swept through Claire. It had been many years since he and his wife had taken her and Tracey in after their mother had abandoned them, but now she realised how important they both were to her, although she hadn't realised it back then, of course. Just as Nikki was now, she had been young and headstrong and had thought she knew better than them. And so she had run away to London without a word, thinking that she would find the streets paved with gold. Huh! She had soon discovered how wrong she was, but by then she had been too proud to swallow her pride and come home. If only I had she thought to herself now, I could have saved myself all those years of heartache; of standing on street corners selling my body for a pittance.

At that moment, Molly erupted out of the front door and toddled down the path to meet them. She was still the nearest thing to a mother that Claire had ever known and as she was caught in a tight embrace she silently vowed to make it up to the Garretts for all the heartache and worry she had caused them.

'Eeh, I bet it's bedlam at our Tracey's,' Molly sighed. 'She's been baking cakes for the last two days. If truth be told I bet she'll be glad when the party is over. I offered to go early to help get everything ready, but you know what an independent little madam she is. Still, we can always help her to clean up afterwards, can't we?' She turned her attention to Nikki and smiled broadly. 'And how are you, love? You're looking as pretty as ever. Eeh, you look so grown-up you make me feel old. But that's enough of my chattering. Come on – let's hit the road, eh? Bye, Tom. Your tea is in the fridge with a plate over it. Expect us when you see us. And don't get touching that joint of beef I just took out of the oven. Our Billy and his family are coming for dinner tomorrow so I don't want half the meat missing, do you hear me?'

'I should think half the street heard you,' Tom answered with a wink at Nikki. 'Now get yourself away and give a bloke a bit o' peace.'

Nikki grinned back at him. She liked Tom – and Molly, of course. She wasn't so sure about Tracey though, Claire's sister. She was always polite and even made them welcome, but Nikki always got the feeling that she was holding Claire at arm's length for some reason. She supposed it was because she hadn't completely forgiven Claire for leaving her when she had been a little girl to go and work in London. It suddenly occurred to Nikki that Claire had never told her exactly what her job in London had been, and she determined to ask her when the opportunity arose –

not that there was much chance of that happening today. When Molly and Claire got together they never seemed to stop talking and she doubted if she could have got a word in even if she had wanted to. Settling herself into the back seat of the car, she waved through the window at Tom and sat back to listen to the gossip coming from the front.

When they pulled up outside Tracey's house in Windermere Avenue, Nikki grinned. There were children running all over Tracey's flowerbeds in the front garden and balloons were tied to the front door. Thankfully, the April shower had disappeared as if by magic and now the grass was gently steaming in the heat of the sun. The noise when they opened the car door was almost deafening and she suddenly wished she had stayed at home and gone out with Erin. Still, she was here now, so she might as well make the best of it.

Molly and Claire went into the house first while Nikki got the presents and cards from the boot, then wandered through the screaming tots to join them.

'Hello, Claire. It's good to see you. How are you?' Despite the fact that she was surrounded by hordes of screaming kids, Tracey still managed to look cool and collected, and not for the first time it struck Claire afresh how much she had changed. Gone was the frightened little girl who had clung to her skirts and insisted on sleeping in her bed as a child. In her place was a poised young woman, who was happy with her lot.

Callum, her husband, was rampaging around the back garden with the twins and yet more children in hot pursuit, and as Tracey glanced towards the window and smiled at his antics, Claire felt a pang of envy. She and Callum were obviously very much in love. Tracey had done well for herself. Before marrying Callum she had gone to university and then gone on to become a nurse in the George Eliot Hospital in Nuneaton. It was there that she had met him. Callum Brady was an ambulanceman and had arrived in the Accident & Emergency Department one night with a drunk in tow. The unenviable task of cleaning and sobering him up had fallen to Tracey. Callum had helped her get the man into a cubicle and from that night on they had been inseparable. And now they had two beautiful baby girls, and looking at Tracey no one would ever have known that she had once suffered from nightmares caused by the horrific childhood she had been forced to endure.

Claire dragged her eyes away from her sister to admire the two identical birthday cakes that took pride of place in the middle of the laden table. They were covered in pink icing, each with two little candles on and she asked, 'Did you buy those, Tracey?'

'No, actually, I made them myself.'

'Really?' Claire was greatly impressed. 'I didn't know you were such a good cook.'

'Well, you wouldn't, would you?' There was a trace of sarcasm in Tracey's voice. 'You haven't been about for most of my life. But you'd be surprised what you can do when you put your mind to it.'

She turned her back on Claire as she continued to beat some cream in a bowl, and feeling in the way, Claire drifted out into the garden. She supposed she had deserved that cutting comment. The second the twins set eyes on her they hurtled towards her, their chubby little legs going like pistons.

As Claire wrapped them in her arms and buried her face in their sweet-smelling hair, her heart ached. They were so like Tracey had been at their age that it almost felt as if she had slipped back in time. If only I could, she thought to herself. I would have done things so very differently. But the time for *if only* was long past and Claire knew that now she would have to work very hard indeed to re-establish the closeness that had once existed between her sister and herself.

The afternoon passed pleasantly. Nikki actually seemed to be enjoying herself and Molly was in her element as she handed out cakes and ice creams as if they were going out of fashion. A large Bouncy Castle had been erected in the spacious back garden and by the time the mothers began to arrive to collect their offspring, they were tired and sweaty but happy.

Molly put the kettle on as Tracey saw the children off and handed out goody bags. 'I dare say the grown-ups will be glad of a cuppa before we start the cleaning up,' she commented.

Claire meanwhile took a bin liner and began to collect all the discarded paper cups and plates from the lawn, while Nikki collapsed in a heap on the swinging hammock.

'Crikey, if this is what having children means, then I'm definitely never having any. It's too much like hard work,' she declared.

'Well, I'm pleased to hear it – for now at least,' Claire said immediately. 'You've got plenty of time to think about having children when you have a career and you're older.'

Nikki rolled her eyes and folded her arms and although she said not a word, Claire could read her thoughts. *Here we go again.* Still, all in all, she felt the afternoon had gone well and was glad that she had made the effort to come. There were still a lot of bridges to mend as far as Tracey went and this might go a way towards it.

It was dark by the time she and Nikki arrived home and after fussing over Gemma, Nikki yawned. 'I reckon I might go up and get an early night.'

'Good idea. As soon as I've fed Gemma and locked up I think I might do the same. Good night, love.'

'Night, Mum.'

Claire listened to Nikki climbing the stairs and then a silence settled and loneliness came with it. Her thoughts turned to Christian and she had the urge to ring him, but she resisted it. If she heard his voice it would only make the loneliness even more unbearable. She walked through the French doors and into the garden, letting the serenity of the place wash over her like a soothing balm. It was a beautiful evening with the stars riding high in a cloudless, black velvet sky. The moon was shining brightly like a queen on her throne and only the sound of the night creatures broke the silence. Somewhere, Christian might be looking up at the same moon, missing her as she was missing him. But as yet there was nothing they could do about it. Before she could go to him, Claire must find peace and at that moment it still seemed a long way away.

Chapter Six

Exactly one week later, Claire straightened the cushions on the settee for at least the tenth time then looked about the room. It was a lovely lounge, tastefully decorated in cream and gold, although the paper was beginning to look a little tired now. Claire had been meaning to get round to redecorating it, but up to now hadn't found the time. The old lady she had bought the house from had had impeccable taste, but ill-health had forced her to move in with her daughter. Claire had negotiated with her for most of the furniture, which the old woman had been more than happy to leave behind, so apart from the few bits and pieces of hers and Nikki's that were scattered about the place and the cream leather settees that she had purchased, it was still very much as the woman had left it.

On one wall, French windows framed by heavy swags and tails opened out onto the garden. On the opposite wall was another large window with matching curtains that overlooked the front drive. The wall-to-wall carpet was in a soft shade of gold and the walls were decorated with cream wallpaper that lent an airy feel to the room. Claire's settees stood facing each other at either side of a marble Adam-style fireplace, and on the fourth wall was a large mahogany display cabinet that Claire had filled with china collected from antique fairs and flea-markets. The house was nowhere near as large or as imposing as Nightingale Lodge, where she and Nikki had lived with Greg in

Bispham, yet somehow they had felt at home since the second they had set foot in it.

Over the last week, Claire had spent hours talking to the Social Services Department about the possibility of tracing Nikki's real mother, and she had been passed from one social worker to another. But now, at last, one of them had agreed to come and see her, and Claire's nerves were on edge. She realised that she would have to be totally honest with the woman about the circumstances that had led to her and Nikki being here. But then if it gave Nikki a measure of peace it would be worth it. As she glanced towards the clock on the mantelpiece, the front doorbell rang and although Claire was expecting it, she still almost jumped out of her skin.

'Pull yourself together, woman,' she muttered to herself and straightening her back she walked into the hall and opened the front door with a smile on her face.

'Mrs Nightingale?'

'Yes.' Claire held out her hand. 'And you must be Miss Blake? Do come in.'

For some reason, Claire had expected someone older, but the woman stepping past her looked to be even younger than herself. Claire ushered her into the lounge then hurried away to make a pot of tea. When she came back with a tray she found the woman looking at the pictures of Claire and Nikki that were spread across the mantelpiece.

'This is Nikki then, I assume?' Miss Blake was holding a photo of Nikki and Claire that had been taken in front of the sand dunes at Seagull's Flight. They were both happy and laughing.

'Yes, it is,' Claire replied politely. 'Of course, she's grown since then. That was taken over two years ago. Do you take sugar and milk?'

'Yes, please.' Miss Blake sat down on the settee opposite Claire, who was busily pouring tea into two china cups and saucers. 'So, from what you were telling me, Nikki is your adopted daughter but she now wishes to trace her birth mother?' she asked.

'That's about it, Miss Blake.'

'Oh please, Miss Blake sounds awfully formal. Call me Zoe. Everyone else does, and I'll call you Claire, if you don't mind?'

Claire relaxed a little as she nodded. Zoe actually seemed very nice and was easy to talk to. She was a pretty young woman with laughing blue eyes and fiery red hair that seemed to have a mind of its own, for it stood out around her head like a halo of curls. She was dressed in jeans and a bright yellow top that clashed with the colour of her hair. She wore trainers on her feet and Claire thought that she looked more like a student than a social worker; she liked her all the same though.

'Perhaps it would help if we started at the beginning?' Zoe suggested as she sipped at her tea, so hesitantly Claire began to tell her how she had met Greg and took it from there. Twenty minutes later, when she had finished, Zoe frowned.

'Poor little thing. Fancy being adopted only to be abused by the man you thought was your father.' Zoe realised that it couldn't have been easy for Claire to tell her all this and sympathised with her. 'The problem we are up against is the fact that Nikki isn't eighteen yet,' she went on. 'And even if she were, there's no guarantee that her birth mother would want to see her if we tracked her down. What usually happens in cases like these is that the child who is searching begins to build fantasies about what their birth family were like – and then when they find them, nine times out of ten they're sadly disappointed. What we could do for now though is to create a life story book.'

When Claire raised a quizzical eyebrow she went on, 'We start with the birth. I would try to find out where Nikki was born, which hospital, what she weighed, what length she was, et cetera. And then we would gradually build up a picture of her life from there. If, as you told me, she was a year old before she was adopted, that should make it slightly easier, but I have to tell you, this will take time and a lot of work on my part. She isn't going to discover who she really is overnight. Do you think Nikki would be prepared to do it?'

Claire chewed thoughtfully on her lip before slowly nodding. 'She might,' she replied, 'though I think she'll be disappointed that you can't just wave a magic wand and find her mother just like that.'

'If only it were that easy,' Zoe said ruefully. 'But let's take one step at a time. I think the behaviour that Nikki is currently displaying is down to the fact that she was abused as much as the fact that she was adopted. It's an awful lot to come to terms with at her age.'

Claire had to bite down on her lip to stop a hasty retort; she could have told Zoe that she knew *exactly* what it was like to feel as Nikki did, but this meeting was about Nikki's needs, not hers, and it must stay that way.

'I'll leave you to talk to Nikki about what I've suggested then, and if she agrees to the life story book I'll make another appointment and come back out to see her,' Zoe promised, and placing her cup on the tray she stood and held her hand out. Claire shook it before showing her to the door.

'Thank you. I'll do that as soon as she gets in from school and then I'll give you a call.'

Claire watched Zoe cross to a small car that looked as if it was only the rust that was holding it together. When she started it up there was a great bang and a cloud of black smoke issued from the exhaust pipe. And then she was reversing erratically down the drive and Claire closed her eyes, expecting to hear one of her trees come crashing down at any second. Thankfully, it didn't, and when she opened her eyes again she saw with amusement that Zoe was gone although the old car could still be heard clearly as it rattled off down the street.

Smiling to herself, she went back in and closed the door. At least she had made a start. Now all she could do was relay what the social worker had told her and see how Nikki reacted to it.

The opportunity arose later that afternoon over dinner. The pair of them were sitting at the kitchen table when Claire broached the subject and Nikki glared at her suspiciously as she pushed her food about the plate.

'So what did she have to say then?' Colour had risen in her cheeks and Claire chose her words carefully.

'She said that it might be difficult to actually trace your mother until you are eighteen.' She had never lied to Nikki before and saw no need to start now, although she knew that Nikki would not be happy with the answer. 'What she did say though was that there's no reason why she shouldn't do a life story book with you so that you know more about your past.'

'I already know about my past,' Nikki stated sullenly.

'You only know what happened since you went to live with your adoptive mother and father,' Claire pointed out. 'What Zoe is offering to do is fill in the time from your birth until then; don't forget, you were a year old when you were adopted. She will find out where you were born, what you weighed and so on. Even what area you lived in. She might even be able to discover why your mother gave you up and who your birth father was, and then when you're eighteen if you're still in the same mind you'll have a lot better chance of tracing them.'

'And just how would she be able to do all that?'

'Well, there must be records somewhere and she'll be able to get access to them whereas we couldn't. But, of course, it's up to you. You don't have to do anything you don't want to do, and if you decide to drop the whole idea I can phone her and tell her you're not interested.'

'But why can't they let me get in touch with my real mum *now*?'

'I've already told you, Nikki. It's the law and for some reason you have to be eighteen. I'm sorry if you're disappointed, but I am trying.'

Nikki pushed her almost untouched meal away and scraped her chair back from the table.

'Then the law *sucks*,' she declared petulantly. 'I'm not even fifteen yet so that means it will be over three whole years until I even get the chance to find her.'

'I know it's hard, love. But I don't see what else we can do.'

Nikki was now striding towards the door with a deep scowl on her face and Claire stared at her plate in dismay.

'Can't you just come back to the table and eat your dinner?' she implored. 'It's one of your favourites. Up until a few months ago you would have eaten sausage and mash every day if I'd let you.'

'That was a few months ago, I've gone off it now.' And the door banged shut resoundingly behind the teenager, making Gemma scuttle away beneath the table with her tail between her legs.

'I think we can safely say that went down like a lead balloon, don't you?' Claire muttered to the small dog and lifting Nikki's plate, she emptied it disconsolately in the bin.

Chapter Seven

Upstairs, Nikki threw herself onto her bed. A whirlwind of emotions were sweeping through her and she didn't know how to handle them. She knew that Claire was doing her best for her and yet sometimes she felt like running away. But, she asked herself, what am I trying to run away from?

The answer came back loud and clear: *It's no good running away because you can't run away from yourself!*

She bit down so hard on her lip that she tasted blood, as a vision of her father's face floated in front of her eyes. Gregory Nightingale had abused her, and she knew that for as long as she lived, she would feel dirty. Sometimes, even now when she was in the bath, she would scrub at herself until her skin felt raw, but it did nothing to make her feel any cleaner. Lately, some of the girls at school had giggled and whispered about boyfriends and what they had been up to. Nikki could never understand how they could bear to let any male touch and fondle them. As far as she was concerned, sex was a dirty thing; something that was forced on you. So how could the girls let the boys do it to them willingly?

She shuddered and once again thought of Claire downstairs. She knew that she was being unfair but couldn't seem to stop herself. She also knew that Claire was worried about the fact that she wasn't eating properly. Nikki could have told her it was because she was worried about

63

her fast-developing figure. Other girls at school were proud of their breasts but Nikki was terrified that if hers developed she would become desirable to boys and they would try to abuse her again as her father had. Until recently she had had a very healthy appetite and sometimes now her stomach would rumble with hunger. But she would rather suffer hunger pains than the feel of a man's hands on her again, although she couldn't tell Claire that, of course. She doubted that Claire would understand. After all, what did she know of how it felt to be abused? Sometimes if Claire really nagged, Nikki would force herself to eat the meal her mother had put in front of her. But then as soon as she left the table she would hurry away to the bathroom and force her fingers down her throat till she brought the undigested meal back up. She had got it off to a fine art now and could empty her stomach in seconds.

Her thoughts were interrupted by the sound of something tapping on her window. Hurrying across to it she peered down into the drive below, where she could just make out the shape of Erin. She was throwing pebbles up in the light of the street lamp that shone through the trees on the drive.

Nikki quietly opened the window and leaned out precariously. 'What are you doing here?' she hissed to the dark shape below.

'I'm going over to see my mate in Chelmsey Park and wondered if you fancied coming along?' Erin whispered back.

'But it's nearly nine o'clock. Does your mum know you're planning on going out this late?'

'Huh! She wouldn't know if a tornado swept through the house,' Erin snorted in disgust. 'She's as drunk as a skunk and flat out on the settee. She's in no state to worry about herself, let alone me, so are you up for it or what?'

Nikki hovered indecisively for a moment before saying, 'Wait down the bottom of the drive for me. I'll be with you in a jiffy.'

Closing the window, she snatched up a denim jacket and crossed to her bedroom door. Along the landing she could hear the sound of the shower running in the bathroom, so she scooted down the stairs and let herself out of the front door, closing it softly behind her. At the end of the drive she found Erin waiting for her in the shadows of the trees and she grinned.

'Right then, lead the way.'

Erin tucked her arm into Nikki's and they set off along Lovelace Lane feeling very grown up. Neither of them was allowed out after dark, which only added to the sense of adventure.

'Will you get it in the neck when you come back?' Erin asked.

Nikki shook her head. 'No. My mum thinks I'd gone up for an early night so she won't even know I've gone.'

'But how will you get back in?'

Nikki felt in her pocket then dangled a key in front of her. 'I pinched the spare.'

Both girls giggled and quickened their steps until eventually they came to the town centre where they hopped on the bus that would take them to the outskirts of Chelmsey Park council estate. It was so different to the area they lived in that Nikki stared about her in amazement. Gangs of youths with cans and cigarettes in their hands stood on street corners, and as the girls passed they wolf-whistled at them and made lewd suggestions.

Gates hung drunkenly from the fences dividing the houses and mangy-looking dogs were roaming up and down. Most of the gardens they passed were overgrown and they had to step over rubbish that had been thrown into the streets. Nikki began to feel nervous but Erin was obviously enjoying herself.

'It's great round here,' she declared. 'People here aren't stuck up like they are where we live.'

Eventually she stopped in front of a gate and pointed up the path. 'This is where my friend lives,' she informed Nikki, as if she was about to introduce her to royalty. 'You'll like her. Nothing bothers Poppy, she's as tough as old boots.'

Feeling decidedly uncomfortable, Nikki followed her up a path past a rusting car that was parked on the overgrown grass on the front garden. One door was hanging off it; Nikki saw that its wheels were missing and it was propped up on house bricks.

Following her eyes, Erin laughed. 'They've probably been nicked,' she informed her. 'Anything that stands still round here for long gets nicked.' She then strolled up to the front door and pushed it open without knocking, causing colour to flood into Nikki's cheeks. Loud music was blasting from a doorway leading off the small entrance hall and as Erin opened it, a cloud of cigarette smoke drifted out to them and the sound of a Phil Collins song was deafening. The room they stepped into seemed at first glance to be full of people lounging about on mismatched chairs and settees that were pushed back against the walls. The smell was indescribable; a mixture of unwashed bodies, cigarettes and a sickly smell that Nikki could not identify. A man was lying on the settee nearest to them puffing on what appeared to be a roll-up. Next to him was a woman who was wearing so much make-up that she looked as if it had been plastered on with a trowel. She too was smoking and as Erin entered she smiled at her.

'Hello, love. An' how are you? Our Poppy is upstairs puttin' her slappy on. Give her a shout, eh?'

Erin smiled and leaving Nikki momentarily, she walked back into the hallway and yelled, '*Poppy!*' It was just as well she did shout, for Nikki had no doubt that she would never have been heard above the volume of the music that was throbbing out if she hadn't. She then rejoined Nikki who was staring around trying to take in the sights. A huge television took up one corner of the room and a bare nicotine-stained light bulb dangled from the centre of the ceiling. All the walls appeared to be a dull brown colour, as did the paintwork. She could feel the carpet beneath her feet sticking to the soles of her shoes and the cushions that were scattered about on the furniture here and there were so dirty that their colour was indistinguishable.

Two youths were lying on the floor, apparently off in a world of their own, and yet another youth was slouched in a chair next to the television. Empty lager cans were scattered across the floor and everywhere she looked were dirty overflowing ashtrays. Nikki was speechless until the woman said, 'So, you're a mate of Erin's then, are you, love?'

Now, as Nikki nodded and looked at her more closely, she saw that the woman was not as old as she had first taken her for. At a glance she had appeared to be middle-aged but now Nikki guessed that she was probably only a little older than Claire. But years of heavy drinking and chainsmoking had taken their toll, and even the heavy make-up she was wearing could not disguise the deep wrinkles on her face.

'Yes. I . . . er . . . I'm Nikki,' she told her falteringly.

'Right, an' I dare say you're from over the posh side o' town an' all, ain't you?'

'I . . . I live in Lovelace Lane.'

The woman laughed; a deep throaty sound. 'Thought as much. Go to the private school with Erin, do you?'

Nikki nodded but was saved from having to say any more when a young girl who appeared to be about sixteen walked into the room. She too had a cigarette dangling from her fingers and after glancing curiously at Nikki she then looked towards Erin.

'Hiya, mate. An' what have you got for me tonight?' she asked.

Erin fumbled in her jacket pocket and produced a glittering gold chain from which was suspended a crucifix that looked to be encrusted with diamonds.

'Phew!' The girl took it from Erin and examined it. 'Real diamonds, are they, or cubes?'

'Real, I should imagine,' Erin told her indignantly. 'My mother is very fussy about her jewellery. She wouldn't wear anything that wasn't the real McCoy.'

'An' you're sure she won't miss it?'

'Not a chance, Poppy,' Erin assured her. 'You could take the settee from underneath her at the minute. She's that drunk she wouldn't even know it was gone.'

'In that case, ta very much.' The girl pocketed the jewellery and looking towards Nikki she now asked, 'An' who's this?'

'This is Nikki.' As Erin introduced them, Poppy nodded solemnly. It was at that moment that the large man who had been lounging next to the woman pulled himself to the edge of the sofa and looked admiringly at Nikki, causing her cheeks to grow even redder than they already were.

'Well, Nikki,' he slurred. 'You can come round here any time you like.'

'Oh give over, Dad, you old perve,' Poppy snapped at him, then turning her attention back to the two girls she asked, 'Do yer fancy a drink? There's some cans left in the kitchen – that's if these greedy bastards ain't necked 'em all.'

'Fuck off, you little bitch,' her father snapped back at her and now Nikki's eyes were almost out on stalks and she was glad of an excuse to get out of the room as she followed Erin and Poppy back into the hallway.

If Nikki had been shocked at the state of the lounge, she was even more shocked at the sight of the kitchen; there didn't seem to be an inch of work surface that wasn't covered in a clutter of dirty pots. A great Rottweiler lurched towards her growling deep in its throat as she walked in, causing her heart to leap into her throat, but at a stern word from Poppy it slunk back into its basket.

Poppy swept a pile of old newspapers and magazines from a chair and beckoning towards it she told Nikki, 'Sit yourself down, gel. You don't have to stand on ceremony here. You take us as you find us, else yer keep away. Ain't that so, Erin?'

Erin nodded eagerly as Poppy fumbled about in a dirty fridge that was standing next to the sink. She produced two cans of lager with a flourish and as Nikki looked on, proceeded to pour some into three glasses that she hooked from amongst the pile of unwashed pots in the sink. Nikki eyed the glass dubiously as Poppy handed it to her. She then looked at Poppy more closely. Just like her mother she was heavily made-up, and her long fair hair was tied high on top of her head in a ponytail. She was slim and Nikki thought that under all the layers of make-up she would be quite pretty. As it was, in her tight-fitting mini-skirt and skimpy halter-neck top she looked what Nikki knew Claire would have termed as 'common'. But she was certainly friendly enough, and as she perched on the edge of the kitchen table she asked Nikki, 'So how old are you then?'

'Sixteen,' Nikki lied without thinking then flushed as she saw Erin raise her eyebrows. She didn't contradict her though and the moment passed as they all sipped at their drinks. Nikki found that she quite liked the lager after the first few tastes and had soon drained her glass. By then for some reason the kitchen didn't appear quite so grubby and she found herself warming to Poppy who, she had to admit, was quite a character.

They spent a pleasant hour discussing clothes and boys and make-up. At least, Erin and Poppy did, but eventually Erin glanced at the clock and stood up.

'I reckon we ought to be going,' she told Nikki regretfully. 'No sense in pushing our luck, is there? If we don't get off now we'll miss the last bus back into town.'

Nikki hastily stood up and joined her at the kitchen door where Poppy was waiting to wave them off.

'Nice to meet you, Nikki.' When she smiled, Nikki knew that she had been right in her assumption that Poppy was pretty. Her teeth were straight and white and she saw now that her eyes were a deep blue colour, very much like her own.

'Thank you for your hospitality,' she said politely and Poppy almost fell about laughing.

'Christ, Erin, where did you pick *her* up?'

Erin grinned back at her. 'Nikki's had what you might call a very sheltered upbringing.'

'Has she now? Then it's about time she saw a bit o' life, ain't it? An' she'll certainly see plenty o' that round here.'

As they passed the door to the lounge the woman that Nikki had met when she first arrived lurched towards them. She was obviously very drunk but she smiled cheerily at them all the same.

'Shee yer both again shoon, loves,' she slurred, and crossing to the stairs she began to climb them unsteadily.

Poppy rolled her eyes to the heavens. 'That's me mam for you,' she declared. 'Always pissed up, she is, but she's got a heart as big as a bucket, believe it or not. She needs to have, to put up wi' him.' She thumbed towards the lounge door with a look of contempt on her face. 'Knocks her from pillar to post, he does,' she muttered beneath her breath. 'An' the silly old cow still goes back for more. If I were married to the lousy old bastard I'd have stuck a knife in his ribs long before now.'

Nikki gulped deep in her throat but had no time to comment because Erin was now ushering her down the path as Poppy shouted after them, 'Watch how yer go now an' I'll see yer both again soon, eh?'

Neither of the girls had time to answer as Poppy slammed the door shut on them as they stepped over the broken gate and onto the pavement. Nikki was shocked to see that young children were still kicking tin cans up and down the street.

'Shouldn't they be in bed at this time of night?' she whispered as they passed them.

Erin looked at her scornfully. 'This is the *real* world, Nikki, not the one where you and I live, and where our parents try to wrap us in cottonwool. And I'll tell you something: I prefer this world any day of the week. At least the people round here don't pretend to be something they're not. Take my mum for instance – she's no better than

Roxy back there. The only difference is, Roxy doesn't try to put on airs and graces.'

Nikki chewed on her lip as they moved on until eventually she asked, 'Why did you give Poppy that cross and chain?'

Erin shrugged. ''Cos she's a bit strapped for cash and it will buy her a few spliffs. My mother will never miss it as she's got so much jewellery lying about. And if she does, she'll just think she's mislaid it.'

'You mean it was your *mother's* necklace?' Nikki asked incredulously.

'Yes.' Erin seemed completely unperturbed by the fact.

'And what exactly is a spliff?' Nikki asked. 'I know it's drugs, but what sort?'

Erin shook her head. Nikki could be very naïve at times. 'A spliff is cannabis. I thought everybody knew that.'

Nikki's eyes widened as she asked, 'Have you ever tried any?' It all sounded very exciting and a million miles away from the humdrum life she lived with Claire.

'A couple of times,' Erin admitted.

'And what was it like?'

Erin frowned as she tried to think how best to explain. 'Well, you smoke it and it makes you feel sort of . . . relaxed, I suppose you could say. Nothing seems to bother you for a while and you feel all kind of happy inside.'

'Do you think I might get the chance to try some?' Nikki asked excitedly.

Erin nodded. 'I don't see why not. But it doesn't come cheap.'

'That's all right, I have some savings. Quite a lot of savings, in fact,' Nikki informed her.

'In that case then, the next time we go round you can slip Eddie a couple of quid and he'll give you some to try.'

'Will he sell it to me, knowing how old I am?' Nikki asked innocently and Erin grinned.

'I asked Poppy the same thing once and she said he'd sell his own

71

mother for cash. I'll tell you something else as well. Every copper in the town knows Eddie Miller. According to Poppy, he's up to all sorts of mischief. When I was round there the other day some youths turned up with a telly and a video recorder, and I saw him pay them some money.'

'Where did they get them from?' Nikki wanted to know.

Erin laughed softly. 'Oh Nikki, you're such a baby. They were nicked, of course! Eddie's well-known for handling stolen goods. Poppy reckons he's got away with murder over the years, 'cos although the police know he's a villain they've never managed to pin anything on him and get him sent down yet.'

The girls walked on towards the bus stop in silence. Nikki's head was reeling and she knew she would never forget this night; she had had a brief glimpse of a completely different way of life, and more unsettling still was the fact that she had found it all very exciting.

When they finally arrived at the bottom of the drive leading to Nikki's home they said their goodnights and Nikki began to walk up the drive through the overhanging trees that led to the front door.

Up above her she could see Claire's bedroom light on. The rest of the house appeared to be in darkness, so after fumbling in her pocket for the key she inserted it into the lock and quietly began to inch the door open. It was then that everything seemed to happen at once. Gemma came hurtling towards her with her tail wagging, barking furiously, and before Nikki had had time to quieten her, the hall light clicked on and Claire appeared in her dressing-gown with a face as dark as thunder.

'Just where the *hell* do you think you've been this time, young lady?'

Claire so rarely raised her voice to her that Nikki was temporarily nonplussed and could only stare back at her guiltily. She had been caught out good and proper, and knew that it wouldn't be easy to talk herself out of this one.

'I went out with Erin for a while,' she said shortly.

'Oh yes, and just where exactly is *out*?'

'*Just out!*' Nikki shouted back, and now they were facing each other like two opponents in a boxing ring instead of mother and daughter.

'Do you have any idea at all just how worried I've been?' Claire was far too relieved to see her safe and sound to worry about how she was sounding at present. 'I was just minutes away from phoning the police.'

'*So?*' Nikki squared up to her insolently.

Claire glared back at her but then her anger dispersed and despair washed over her. 'Nikki, what's happening to us?' she asked brokenly. 'I love you more than anything in the world, yet all we seem to do is argue just lately.'

'And whose fault is that?' Nikki shot back. 'You're always nagging me and treating me like a baby. Well, I'm not a baby any more, do you hear me? And I'm *sick* of being treated like a prisoner.'

With that she pushed past Claire and stamped away upstairs. As Claire watched her go, tears trickled down her cheeks. She knew that she had handled the situation badly but it was too late to do anything about it now. If she tried to speak to Nikki any more tonight she had an awful feeling that they would simply end up arguing again.

Lifting Gemma, who was shaking like a leaf, into her arms, she turned off the lights and slowly climbed the stairs. As she passed Nikki's bedroom door she could hear her clattering about inside but she strode straight past. Once in the privacy of her own room she looked at the telephone on her bedside table. She was longing to ring Christian; to hear his voice, but she resisted the urge once again. This was her problem and only she could sort it out.

Chapter Eight

'So that's about the long and the short of it, Nikki, and unfortunately the best I can offer you for now. So how do you feel about doing a life story book?'

Nikki stared at Zoe Blake resentfully. It was all right for her to sit there and tell her that she wouldn't be allowed to trace her birth mother until she was eighteen. But she wondered how the social worker would have felt if the shoe was on the other foot, if it had been *her* trying to trace *her* mother. And what use would a life story book be? It all seemed like a complete waste of her time to her. Of course, she was too polite to say so out loud, so she simply sat staring sullenly at the floor.

Eventually, Claire rose from the settee and said, 'I need to go and empty the washing-machine.' She was hoping to give them a few minutes alone to get to know each other a little better and to break the ice.

Tactfully, she left the room and now that they were alone, Nikki waited for the interrogation to begin. But instead, Zoe rose and went over to the French windows where she stood with her arms crossed, gazing out across the lawns.

'You have a lovely garden here,' she commented, and when Nikki didn't answer her she went on, 'It's been quite a while since your new mum adopted you now, hasn't it?'

'You mean Claire, my *third* mum?' Nikki quipped sarcastically. 'I bet you haven't got many kids on your books that have had *three* mums, have you?'

Ignoring the sarcastic tone, Zoe replied, 'No, I must admit I haven't. But at least you've always been loved and wanted.'

'Oh yes, a little *too* loved if what my dad did to me is anything to go by,' Nikki ground out.

Zoe turned and looked at her sympathetically. 'I know it must be a very hard thing to have experienced.' Her voice was soft. 'And as soon as you feel ready for it I can get you some counselling to help.'

'I don't *need* any more counselling,' Nikki shot back as hot colour crept into her cheeks. 'A counsellor can't make me forget what he did, can they?'

'No, of course they can't, but they *can* help you come to terms with it and show you how to carry on.'

Nikki suddenly leaped from the chair. 'Oh, this is all just a waste of time,' she snapped, and without another word she turned on her heel and walked from the room, leaving Zoe to stare after her with a deep frown on her face.

When Claire re-entered the room some minutes later she looked around in bewilderment. 'Where's Nikki?' she asked.

Zoe nodded towards the stairs. 'I'm afraid my suggestion of a life story book and counselling didn't go down very well,' she said.

Claire ran a hand through her hair distractedly. 'I didn't think it would. So what do we do now?'

Seeing that Claire was deeply upset, Zoe said, 'How about we sit down and have a chat between ourselves? Nikki might have a change of heart and decide to join us.'

'I doubt there's any chance of that,' Claire said solemnly. 'Nikki is as stubborn as a mule just lately.' She sat down heavily, and for a moment the two women were silent.

'You know, a lot of what you are experiencing is just teenage mood swings,' Zoe told Claire eventually. 'All teenage girls tend to get shirty at this age. And nine times out of ten, with girls it's their mothers they take it out on.'

Shame made Claire flush as she thought back to how she had treated Molly at that age, but she kept her thoughts to herself. She shuddered to think of what Zoe would do if she were ever to discover how she had once earned her living on the streets of London. Strangely, the urge came on her to tell Zoe the whole sorry story, but as always, when she tried to talk about her past the words stuck in her throat. She realised with a little start that she had not as yet completely faced her own demons. She owed it to Nikki to tell her everything, and yet up to now she had been unable to do so. Deep down she knew that she should; it might make what Nikki had gone through easier to bear if she knew that she herself had been abused as a child too. She had confessed that she had once had a baby and given it up for adoption, but Nikki had used that against her lately.

'So surely you can understand why I need to find *my* mum then?' she had screamed at her the last time they'd had a row. 'Have you ever stopped to think that your own child might be looking for you right now? Wondering why you gave her away and what you're like?' The words had cut like a knife. Claire had never considered that possibility.

Zoe rose from her chair. 'Right, I suppose I'd better get on,' she said. 'Let's give Nikki a little time to think about what I've suggested and then I'll call round to see her again.'

Claire smiled at her gratefully. 'Thank you. I'm sure she'll calm down soon.'

She saw the young social worker to the door and once Zoe had left, she climbed the stairs and tapped tentatively at Nikki's door. 'Do you fancy a bit of shopping?' she called. 'I've got to go into town and thought you might like to come with me?'

'I'll stay here,' Nikki answered, without bothering to open the door.

'Are you sure?'

'Yes, I said so, didn't I? I'm not a baby, you know. I *can* be trusted to stay on my own for a while.'

'All right then. I shouldn't be gone long.' Only silence answered her, so sighing sadly, Claire went on her way.

Once she heard her mother's car pull off the drive, Nikki put on her jacket and decided she'd go round to see what Erin was doing. She didn't fancy just sitting about the house for the rest of the day.

Erin's mother answered the door after the first knock, looking bleary-eyed and ill.

'Erin is out,' she told Nikki. 'She didn't say where she was going though.'

Nikki had a pretty good idea. 'Thank you, Mrs Morgan,' she said politely and turned in the direction of the bus station in the town centre. Erin would probably be round at Poppy's and she just hoped she could remember the way there once she got off the bus.

In no time at all she found herself standing outside Poppy's house and she hesitated. What if Erin wasn't there after all? Would Poppy mind her just dropping in? There was only one way to find out, so climbing over the rubbish that littered the path she made for the front door and tapped on it. If anything, the house looked even worse in the daylight. The windows were grimy and dull and the curtains looked as if they had never been washed. It was as she was standing there that she heard raised voices and she wondered whether she ought to leave. She might have done just that, but at that moment Poppy opened the door and gave her a bright smile. 'Hello there, Nikki,' she greeted her cheerily. 'Erin's inside. Come on in. We were just debatin' whether or not to go into town.'

Feeling somewhat cheered at the greeting she had received, Nikki followed her through the drab hallway to the kitchen where Erin was sitting at the littered table. Again the curious smell was hanging on the air and the sound of a furious row was coming from the lounge.

'It's me mam an' dad at it again,' Poppy said as she saw Nikki looking towards the sound. 'They go at it hammer an' tongs when they get goin'. He's just had a call from one of his runners to say that one o' his vans has been pulled up by the customs, so he's in a rip-roarin' rage. That's why he's takin' it out on me mam. Poor bugger always gets the backlash if owt goes wrong.'

When Nikki looked slightly confused, Poppy went on to explain, 'Me dad has blokes who take old vans over to France for him to bring back fags and wine. Then me dad sells 'em on cheap to the people on the estate an' makes a nice tidy profit. He won't be makin' none today though. The customs have confiscated the whole bloody lot, includin' the van.' She chuckled. 'Serves 'im right. He's as tight as a duck's arse! I only asked him for a tenner this mornin' for a top I've seen in town an' he told me to piss off, the miserable old sod.'

Nikki was still struggling to accept the way Poppy swore. Every sentence she uttered seemed to contain at least one swearword, which Nikki thought was very grown-up and impressive. Had she used the sort of language Poppy did in front of Claire she would have raised the roof, but then Claire was old, or at least she appeared so to Nikki.

It was then that the row that was raging in the front room erupted out into the hallway, and Nikki turned startled eyes towards Poppy's mother and father who were shouting loud enough to waken the dead. The fact that Poppy had friends there didn't seem to faze them in the least and now Nikki heard the man shout, 'I tell you it'll be all right! I'll pay Jed to take the rap. He's got the London mob after him anyway so he'll probably be glad of a stretch inside to keep him out o' their way for a time.'

As Nikki stared at them she was shocked to see that Roxy looked totally different without her make-up on. She was still dressed in a washed-out old dressing-gown, although it was now mid-afternoon, and with her bleached hair falling onto her shoulders and her eyes red-rimmed from crying, Nikki suddenly felt sorry for her.

'I can't go on like this,' Roxy Miller screamed. 'It's all your bloody fault, Eddie!'

'That's enough now, woman, else you'll feel the back o' me bleedin' hand.' Eddie advanced on her threateningly.

Roxy stood tall and glared back at him. 'I'm tellin' you, Eddie,' she warned, 'if you so much as lay one hand on me again today, I'll do for you – I swear I will.'

He moved closer with his fist clenched and Nikki held her breath, but then to her relief he suddenly swung about and snatched up a coat that was flung across the bottom of the banisters.

'I've had enough o' this,' he declared in disgust. 'I'm off to the pub. Expect me when yer see me.' With that he slammed out of the house and Roxy seemed to shrink before Nikki's very eyes. As the woman walked into the kitchen, Nikki saw that one eye was darkening and there was a split on her lip. She was going to have a right old shiner on her by the next day.

'Why do you put up with it, Mam?' Poppy tossed her head in the direction her father had taken. 'Yer should never have come back after the last goin'-over he gave yer. You, me an' Katie were all right in that women's refuge they put us in.'

'We might have been all right, but it weren't home, were it?' Roxy replied wearily. 'An' don't forget I have the lads to think about an' all, not just you an' Katie.'

Nikki briefly wondered who Katie was but before she could ask, Poppy snorted, 'Huh! Jake an' Luke are more than capable o' takin' care o' themselves. It ain't as if they were babies, is it? They're turnin' into as big a pair of villains as me dad is. A hard day's work would kill the pair of 'em.'

'Don't talk about your dad like that,' Roxy scolded. 'He ain't that bad – not really. He don't mean to lose his temper.'

She looked apologetically towards Erin and Nikki. It never ceased to amaze her how Erin and Poppy had become friends in the first place. Her daughter and Erin were as different as chalk from cheese. Erin had been born with a silver spoon in her mouth, from what she could make out, and now here was yet another little girl come to join her. It was Nikki she was concentrating on now. For no reason that she could explain she felt sorry for the girl, little realising that Nikki felt the same towards her. It was something to do with the haunted look in her eyes, she supposed, as if she were carrying some deep dark secret inside that was weighing her down.

'Don't take no notice of us,' she told her. 'We're always at it like cat an' dog but I love the old bastard really. I must do, to have put up with him for as long as I have. I were just thirteen when I met him an' I knew from that day on that he were the only lad for me.'

Nikki saw Poppy raise a scornful eyebrow at her mother's comment. Roxy must have seen it too because she rounded on her and snapped, 'An' don't come the holier than thou wi' me, my girl. The others are just . . . Well, they're a means to an end. You don't complain about the money I earn when you're off out spendin' it, do yer?'

Poppy sniffed as she walked towards the door, ignoring her mother as if she wasn't even there now. 'So, are you two comin' or what then?' she said to her friends.

Erin and Nikki almost collided in the doorway as they hurried to follow her. Nikki paused to look back and say, 'Goodbye, Mrs Miller.'

'Ta-ra, love. Come an' see us again, won't yer?' As Roxy watched the girls leave, she touched her split lip reflectively. There was definitely something about Nikki that she had taken to. She then put her hands on her hips and looked around the dirty kitchen. The row that had just taken place had started when Eddie had discovered that he didn't have a clean shirt to put on. When he had begun to rant and rave about it she had retorted that he was big enough and ugly enough to iron his own. But now as she looked about, shame washed over her. She had let the house go badly just lately – and herself, if it came to that. Whatever must that young girl think of her, coming into a pigsty like this? No doubt the house she lived in with her parents would be like a little palace. She'd go and get dressed right this minute and give the whole place a bit of a blitz. Lord knew, it was long overdue for one. And then she'd pop up the shop and get something nice in for dinner. That would shock Eddie when he decided to come back in. On a mission now, she hurried away upstairs.

It was nearly four o'clock by the time the girls strolled into the town centre. Erin glanced at her watch but Poppy told her, 'Don't worry. We've still got plenty o' time. Come on, I want to go into the boutique in High Street. I saw a top in there the other day that I've got me eye on.'

'But I thought you said you hadn't got any money off your dad?' Erin reminded her.

'So what? I didn't say I was goin' to buy it, did I?'

The girls followed her until they came to the boutique and once inside Poppy told them, 'You two have a look around. I'm just goin' to try a few bits on.'

Minutes later, Nikki looked up to see Poppy disappearing into a changing room with a selection of clothes slung across her arm. Knowing that she had no money, Nikki wondered why she was bothering, but deciding that it wasn't her place to comment, she and Erin continued to browse, holding up one thing after another for inspection when they found something they liked.

The shop assistant had been busy serving a customer when they first entered the shop but now she was free, she came over to them to ask, 'Is there anything I can help you two girls with?'

'No, thank you,' Erin replied. 'Our friend is just trying some things on in there; she should be out in a minute.'

The woman nodded and went back to the counter thinking what wonderfully polite girls they were. Not like some she got in here from the nearby council estate. You needed eyes in the back of your head when they stepped through the door, because some of them would steal anything that wasn't screwed down.

Minutes later Poppy reappeared from the changing rooms with the clothes slung over her arm.

She dumped them on the counter as she told the woman, 'Thanks, but there's nothin' that took me eye today.' She then nodded at Erin and Nikki who smiled at the woman as they followed her out of the shop. They had gone some way down the road when Poppy whipped a top out from beneath her jumper with the tags still attached to it and waved it in front of their faces.

'There yer go. *That's* how to do it if you're strapped for cash.'

Nikki stared at the top in horrified disbelief. 'You mean you *stole* it?' she gasped incredulously.

'Too bleedin' right I did.' Poppy grinned. 'With the mark-up they put on new clothes they can afford for the odd thing to go missin'. Don't tell me you ain't never nicked owt?'

Nikki shook her head, feeling suddenly very young and foolish.

Poppy sighed with exasperation. 'An' how old did you say you were?'

Shamefaced, Nikki replied, 'Well, I told you I was sixteen but actually I'm fourteen. But I'll be fifteen in November.'

Poppy playfully punched her in the ribs. 'You didn't really think I believed you were sixteen, did yer? I guessed straight off that you weren't. Mind you, if you'd let me make you up I can guarantee I could make yer *look* sixteen at least. It's surprising what a bit o' slappy can do. An' you're a looker as well. So – are you up for it?'

Nikki nodded eagerly. To her, Poppy appeared very grown-up and streetwise, and if she could make her look like her she would be over the moon.

'Right then, let's get back to my place an' we'll see what we can do, eh? You don't have to get home yet awhile, do yer?'

Nikki glanced at her wristwatch. It was already past tea-time and Claire would probably be pulling her hair out by now. But what the heck? She was enjoying herself far too much at the minute to worry about the row that would inevitably erupt when she finally arrived home.

'I'd like that,' she told Poppy shyly, and tucking the ill-gotten top into her pocket, Poppy linked her arm through Nikki's and they went on their way, with Erin feeling more than a little put out as she shuffled along sullenly behind them.

When they re-entered Poppy's home some time later, Nikki looked about her in amazement. The hall had been cleared of clutter and in the kitchen there was not a dirty pot in sight. Of course, Roxy had been unable to do anything about the smoke-stained walls and paintwork, but even so the whole room looked a million times better.

'Bloody Nora,' Poppy uttered, astonished at the transformation. 'Have we come to the right house? Me mam must have had a brainstorm.'

Roxy chose that moment to walk out of the lounge and it was all the girls could do to stop themselves from laughing aloud.

'Bloody 'ell, Mam. Yer look like a charlady,' Poppy quipped.

Roxy smiled ruefully. 'I feel like one an' all. I don't think I've worked so hard for years. An' now I have, you bleedin' lot had better make an effort to keep it tidy.'

Poppy sniffed at the air as her stomach rumbled with anticipation. 'What's that I can smell cookin'?'

'I've got some roasties an' lamb chops in the oven,' Roxy informed her as if she had performed some miraculous feat.

'Well, I don't know what's brought all this on, but long may it last,' Poppy declared, and then she ducked and slid back into the hall as Roxy playfully swiped at her with the duster she was holding.

Poppy beckoned Erin and Nikki to follow her up to her bedroom. There didn't seem to be a square inch of furniture or floorspace that wasn't covered in clothes, but Poppy seemed oblivious to the chaos and pushed Nikki onto a stool that stood in front of a cluttered dressing-table. The dust on it was so thick that Nikki was sure she could have written her name in it, but she tactfully didn't say anything. She was too intent on wondering how Poppy was going to make her look.

As her newfound friend took up a tube of foundation cream, the door suddenly swung open and a little girl of about six or seven appeared. Nikki blinked in surprise as Poppy told her, 'This is Katie, me youngest sister.'

Nikki smiled at the little girl as Poppy set to work on her face. 'Katie's me mam's pride an' joy,' Poppy rambled on. 'There's six of us altogether, but only four of us at home now. We all ended up in care a long time ago an' only three of us came back, then Katie here came along, didn't yer, pet?'

Nikki saw that the little girl was remarkably pretty; she had long fair hair like Poppy's but there was something about her that didn't seem quite right somehow. Her big blue eyes had a slightly blank expression about them and her head kept wagging from side to side.

'Katie is autistic,' Poppy explained as she saw Nikki watching her in the mirror. 'There's only me mam can control her for most o' the time. I tell you, when she has a tantrum it's enough to bring the roof down.'

The child was watching Nikki avidly and when Nikki smiled at her again it earned her a poke in the arm as Poppy told her, 'Keep still, can't yer? Else you'll end up lookin' like a bleedin' clown.'

Nikki did as she was told as Poppy leaned over her. When she had finished applying the make-up she released Nikki's long blond hair from its ponytail and brushed it till it shone and then she stood back to ask, 'So, what do yer think?'

When Nikki looked in the mirror she was shocked to see a young woman staring back at her. She could easily have been taken for sixteen and suddenly felt very grown-up and confident.

'Why, it's a-amazing,' she stuttered. 'What do you think, Erin?'

Erin shrugged. She was feeling very left out. In all the time she had known Poppy, the older girl had never offered to make her up, and she was beginning to wish she had never introduced her to Nikki. They were getting on just a little too well for her liking and her nose was badly out of joint.

'It's all right if you like heavy make-up, I suppose,' she muttered sullenly. 'But don't you think it's about time we were going?'

Nikki really didn't want to go. She was beginning to enjoy herself now. There was no one here to nag her, to tell her, *do this, do that.* Poppy and her family were like no one else she had ever met. They seemed to be a law unto themselves, which she found strangely exciting. However, one glance at Erin persuaded her that it was time to head for home.

As she rose, she wondered what Claire was going to say when she saw her. Her mother did allow her to wear a little make-up for special occasions, but nothing like this.

'Thanks, Poppy,' she told her as she followed Erin to the door. Katie was still standing silently watching her and she stroked the child's hair as she passed.

Poppy saw them out. At the front door she said, 'Be sure an' come again very soon now. See you both.' And then she was gone and Nikki walked through the estate in a daze. It had been quite an afternoon, one way or another.

'So how old is Poppy?' she asked Erin as they walked along.

'Fifteen, nearly sixteen,' Erin answered curtly.

Nikki was surprised. She had thought the other girl was already sixteen at least, but then she had seen at firsthand how different you could look with make-up. No doubt Poppy would look much younger without hers on too.

She noticed that Erin was very quiet and peeped at her out of the corner of her eye. Until today, Erin had been her best friend and Nikki had been slightly in awe of her, but now she appeared almost dull in comparison to Poppy. The latter didn't seem to give a jot for anything or anybody. What she wanted she got, even if it meant stealing it, without so much as a qualm.

They passed a gang of youths who whistled at them appreciatively. Nikki's small chest swelled as a feeling of power swept through her. The makeover had made her feel like a different person and she hoped the feeling would last. She was sick of being scared of her own shadow, of nightmares and the way she felt when she looked at herself in the mirror. From now on, she silently promised herself, things are going to be different. From now on, it will be me calling the shots!

Chapter Nine

It was early June and Nikki had left for school almost an hour ago. Or at least, Claire hoped she had gone to school. The way Nikki was behaving recently, it was difficult to tell what she might do. Claire had tidied around and now she was getting ready for work when she heard the sound of the mail plopping through the letterbox. There were five envelopes in all today. At a glance she saw that at least two of them were junk mail. The third was from the dentist, which reminded her that she and Nikki were due for a check-up. The fourth looked suspiciously like the electric bill, but the fifth was handwritten. She frowned; she certainly didn't recognise the handwriting. A glance at the clock told her that if she didn't leave right now she would be late, so she stuffed the letter into her bag and picked up the car keys. Reading it would have to wait until later, during her tea-break at work. She had just set foot out of the door when the phone rang and she hesitated. Another glance at her watch and she slammed the door shut behind her. If it was something important then whoever it was would just have to ring back later.

Bradley was sitting at his desk when she walked into the office and as always, his handsome face lit up at the sight of her. Claire had guessed some time ago that he had a soft spot for her and wished that she could reciprocate his feelings, but the only man she had ever truly loved was Christian, and she knew that if she couldn't have him she would never have anyone.

'Morning, Claire. Do you fancy a coffee before you start?' He was already striding towards the kettle.

She nodded absently, her mind on the letter in her bag. Who could it be from? She was sorely tempted to read it there and then, but instead she forced herself to sit in front of her computer and sift through the work that Mr Dickinson had placed on her desk for her. It all looked fairly straightforward today. Mainly court reports to type up. Glancing back up at Bradley she asked, 'Where's Mr Dickinson today?'

'Oh, he phoned in earlier to say that he'll be in court all day.' As he spoke, Bradley spooned some sugar into two mugs. 'He's defending that Eddie Miller again from the council estate. I offered to do it but he insisted on going himself. I sometimes wonder how that chap gets away with it. He's the biggest villain on two legs, fingers into all sorts of pies. From what I can gather he practically runs the estate he lives on. I think Mr Dickinson must spend more time in court with him than any of his other clients, and yet he always manages to get him off. He must have the luck of the Irish.'

'Eddie Miller?' There was something about the name that was vaguely familiar, but try as she would, Claire couldn't think why. 'What's he up for today?' she asked, more out of politeness than for a real need to know.

'A bloke got caught by customs at the docks coming back from France with a van full of cigarettes, beer and wine and they confiscated the lot. Trouble was, it was one of Miller's vans he was in, so Miller will have to explain that away. He will, of course – he'll probably just say that the chap who was driving it had borrowed it and he didn't know what he wanted it for. He'll get away scot-free, but I reckon the other chap will go down because it's about the third time he's been caught. Everyone knows that he's doing the runs for Miller. He sells fags and beer all over the estate he lives on. But whenever one of his runners gets caught, Miller denies knowing anything about it. Between you and me, I've had a tip-off that he sells more than just wine and fags too, but proving it is a different thing.'

'You mean drugs?'

He nodded as he poured milk into the mugs. 'Yes, and if what I'm hearing is right it's the hard stuff. I can't understand why he hasn't been raided before now. The police must have an idea what he's doing. That man must have made thousands with his wheeling and dealing over the years. With the money that's passed through his hands he could have bought a mini-mansion by now, and yet they reckon his house is barely fit for a dog to live in. He spends most of it over the bookies' counter apparently. And then there's his wife June, or Roxy as she's known. She's a right one as well. Mr Dickinson has had to go to court for her too. When things are a bit tight, Eddie sends her out on the game.'

Claire felt colour rise into her cheeks and eager to change the subject, she asked quickly, 'Do they have any children?'

He nodded. 'Oh yes, two girls and two boys. The older ones are already following in their father's footsteps, and the girl, she's about fourteen or fifteen I think, has been in court for shoplifting twice already to my knowledge.'

The shrill ringing of the phone stopped the conversation from going any further, and from then on the morning passed in a blur. Claire was so busy that she forgot about everything as she answered one call after another and struggled to get through the pile of work on her desk.

It was Bradley who eventually told her, 'Claire, it's time you were gone. You've done twenty minutes more than you should have already.'

Claire was shocked to see that it was already twenty past one. Flashing him a smile, she finished the letter she was typing and after turning her computer off, took her jacket from the coat-rack that stood next to the door.

'Shouldn't you be thinking off knocking off too for some lunch?' she asked him.

His grin spread from ear to ear. 'Now that sounds like a very good idea. Particularly if you would agree to join me. What do you say – my treat?'

She shook her head regretfully. 'Thanks, Bradley. That's really kind of you. But I have a million things I should be doing, so I'd better get straight home. But thanks again for asking.'

Masking his disappointment with a smile he told her affably, 'Aw well, you can't blame me for trying.' He found Claire quite intriguing. She had worked at the office for almost a year now and yet apart from knowing that she was a widow with a teenage daughter, she was a mystery and tended to be a very private person. Mr Dickinson was forever singing her praises and Bradley could understand why. Claire was very efficient at her job and the soul of discretion.

She was at the door now where she paused to say, 'I'll see you tomorrow then.'

'Yes, have a good afternoon, Claire.' As the door closed softly behind her he sighed before burying himself in his work again.

It was a beautiful afternoon and as Claire drove home she decided that she would work on the garden after she'd had some lunch. It seemed a shame to be shut away indoors with the weather being so nice. Besides, after Bradley's comment about Eddie Miller's wife being on the game she felt strangely unsettled. He had spoken of the woman with disdain, little knowing that she herself had once chosen the same path, and she wondered what he would say if he ever found out. She parked the car on the drive, intending to garage it later, and had just put the key in the lock when she heard the phone ringing. Hurrying now, she stepped into the hallway and picked it up. 'Hello?'

'Oh Claire, love. I'm so glad I've caught you. I've been trying to get hold of you all day.'

Recognising Molly's voice, Claire asked, 'Is there anything wrong? You sound a little upset.'

'Well, not wrong exactly. But I need to talk to you, love. Have you had a letter, by any chance?'

Suddenly remembering the letter stuffed down in her bag, Claire told her, 'Yes, I have, as a matter of fact. It came just as I was leaving for work this morning but I haven't had time to read it yet. Why do you ask? Do you know who it's from?'

'Yes, I do, as it happens.' Molly sounded very distraught now and Claire began to feel anxious as she went on, 'Will you pop over and see me, love, before you open it? I need to explain what's been going on.'

Claire frowned. If she were to shoot off to Nuneaton now she would be cutting it very fine to be back in time for Nikki coming in from school. She explained this to Molly and asked, 'Couldn't you just tell me what it's about over the phone?'

'I'd rather see you face to face,' Molly replied. 'I think what you're going to hear will come as a bit of a shock to you. But I tell you what – I'll get Tom to bring me over to you. How would that be? And then you won't have to panic about getting back in time for Nikki.'

'Of course you're welcome to come,' Claire assured her. 'You don't have to ask.'

'Right, I'll be there in forty minutes or so. And Claire . . . don't open the letter until I get there, please.'

The phone went dead in her hands. Deeply bemused, Claire headed for the kitchen to get a nice long cold drink.

Forty-five minutes later, Molly and Tom's old car pulled onto the drive. Claire was watching for them from the lounge window and hurried to open the door. She kissed them both soundly and ushered them through to the kitchen.

While Claire put the kettle on, Tom, who seemed strangely ill at ease, asked, 'You wouldn't mind if I were to go and sit out in the garden, would you? It will give you women a chance to have a bit of a gossip.'

'Of course I don't mind. Go and sit on the bench in the shade under the apple tree, Tom. There's a newspaper there you can take with you to read and I'll bring you a cup of tea a bit later on.'

Tom flashed Claire a relieved smile, and taking up the paper, he set off down the garden at a fair old trot with Gemma following closely behind. Claire turned her attention back to Molly.

'Right. Now we have less than an hour until Nikki gets home, so perhaps you'd like to tell me what exactly is going on? I can see that something is troubling you.'

Molly was wringing her hands together and chewing nervously on her lip as if she didn't quite know where to start.

Eventually she stuttered, 'I . . . I hope you're not going to be mad at me, Claire. But the thing is, I had a letter about a month back. It was from – from your dad.'

Claire felt the floor rush up to meet her and she clutched at the sink. And then her mind slipped back in time and she was a little girl again, holding tight to her daddy's hand as they stood on the top of the hill side-by-side overlooking Gatley Common, the small village where they had lived.

'Is this the top o' the world, Dad?' she had asked him, her small face glowing as she gazed in awe at the panoramic view, and he had laughed and tousled her hair, replying tenderly, 'No, lass. It just feels like it is.'

And then her mind moved on in time and he was leaving them. She was at the door of their council house, hanging on to his coat and pleading with him. 'Please don't leave us, Daddy.'

He too had been crying as he gently pressed her aside. But he *had* left her, despite her heartbroken pleas, and it was after that that the bad things had started to happen . . . bad things that had shaped the rest of her life.

She suddenly became aware of the fact that Molly had her arm around her waist and, pulling herself together with a great effort, she told her, 'I'm sorry, Molly. It just came as a bit of a shock . . .'

'Of course it did. But now sit down and let me make that tea. And then I'll tell you everything.' Molly bustled away as Claire stared off into space trying to absorb what Molly had just told her.

Some time later, when she had taken Tom's tea down the garden to him, Molly pressed a mug into Claire's hand and told her with authority, 'Now have a sip of that and I'll tell you what's gone on.'

Now that the initial shock had worn off, Claire felt like crying as

92

she remembered how devastated she had been when her father had left her and Tracey. For years afterwards, she had clung like a lifeline to the hope that he would come back, but as time passed her hopes had faded until eventually she had pushed him from her mind. And now here was Molly telling her that she had heard from him just like that.

'So,' she said dully. 'You'd better explain.'

Molly gulped at her tea before saying, 'Well, I had this letter come out of the blue about a month back from someone calling himself Robbie McMullen. He said in the letter that he was your father. As you can imagine, it fair knocked the wind out of my sails. It seems that your mother had got in touch with him and so he'd come back from Scotland where he'd been living, to meet her. You see, love,' Molly paused, then went on, 'it appears that your mam is ill – very ill, in fact – and she wanted to make her peace with him.'

The look on Claire's face was breaking Molly's heart but she forced herself to go on. 'It put me in a rare old quandary, because in his letter he said he wanted to see you and Tracey. I didn't know what to do but when Tracey called in at the weekend I showed her the letter and she decided that she wanted to see him. I intended to ask you this week how you felt about it. I'd given him your address but asked him not to get in touch until I'd spoken to you, and then this morning I had another letter from him saying that he'd written to you. I was worried sick how you would react so I've been ringing you all day, off and on.'

'I see.' Claire stared out into the garden. 'And what exactly is wrong with my mother?'

'She's got lung cancer – and according to your dad, she hasn't got much longer left.'

For long years, Claire had felt nothing but hate when she thought of her mother, remembering how she had allowed Tracey and herself to be abused. But now her emotions were in so much turmoil that she didn't know how she felt.

'What do you think you'll do?' Molly asked softly.

Claire could only shrug. 'I honestly don't know yet,' she replied truthfully. 'I'll have to think long and hard about it. Has Tracey seen him yet?'

'No, I think they're meeting up tomorrow. But you know, you don't have to do anything you don't want to. If you decide you'd rather not see him, after all that's gone on, no one would think any the less of you.'

'I really loved my dad,' Claire now told her brokenly, and Molly put her arms around her, wishing that she could take away her pain.

'I know you did,' she whispered into her hair. 'But the other thing you're going to have to think about is whether you want to see your mother. She's very ill.'

'But she *abandoned* me and Tracey!' Claire was crying now. 'When we were first taken into care and brought to live with you and Tom, it was supposed to be just a temporary thing. But what did she do? As soon as she saw that we were all right, she cleared off with one of her boyfriends and never gave us a second thought.'

'Well, I've no doubt she regrets what she did now,' Molly told her. 'None of us are perfect and we all do things we live to regret.'

Could she have known it, her words had sliced through Claire like a knife, for hadn't she herself lived a lie for years? Her head wagged from side to side as she tried to put her thoughts into some sort of order. There were so many rolling around in her head that she felt as if it might burst.

Seeing how distraught she was, Molly crossed to the French windows and called Tom before telling her, 'I think we ought to get off now, love, and give you a bit of thinking time. Read your dad's letter and see how you feel then. And just remember, I'm right at the end of the phone if you need me. I'm sure whatever decision you make will be the right one.'

'Oh Molly, I really don't deserve you after the way I've treated you.' Claire threw herself into the older woman's arms and began to sob.

'Like I said, we all make mistakes and we all deserve a second chance from where I'm standing. You did what you did through circumstance, but it's all in the past now. Just think on that when you get round to reading your dad's letter, eh?' Molly soothingly stroked her hair.

Claire wiped a hankie across her tear-drenched cheeks as she nodded. Molly could be very wise, which was just one of the many reasons why Claire loved her. She saw the Garretts off, and once they had gone she crossed to her bag and took out the letter. She then went through the kitchen and out into the garden, and once she was seated on the bench that Tom had just vacated she slit the letter open and began to read.

There was no address on it but she saw there was a mobile phone number in the top right-hand corner.

My dear Claire,

I have no doubt that my writing to you like this will come as something of a shock after all the years we have been apart, and for that I am sorry, as I am for so very many other things. Molly tells me that you now have a daughter of your own. It's funny, but I always still thought of you and Tracey as children, so I was amazed when Molly told me that you and Tracey had made me into a grandad.

I was surprised when your mother got in touch with me and have to admit that I wasn't sure whether I should come back to the Midlands again. But then I thought about it and decided that life is too short to bear grudges. I fear your mother's life is coming to an end and I know it is her dearest wish to make her peace with you and Tracey before she dies. She knows now that the way she treated you both was wrong, but then I am not blameless either. I should never have left you all as I did and have regretted it every single day in the years since. I shall be staying in Nuneaton for the foreseeable future and hope you will agree to meet with me. I will of course understand if you decide not to. Even so, I will live in hope that you reply to this letter.

With love,
Dad xx

Claire sat staring at the paper in her hand. She could hardly believe that her father wanted to come back into her life after all this time. And suddenly she was a little girl again, lying in bed with Tracey telling her stories of how wonderful it would be when their dad came home to them. But he never had come home – and deep down, Claire had never forgiven him for leaving them as he had.

Then there was her mother. The last she had heard of her, Karen McMullen had disappeared off the face of the earth with one of her numerous boyfriends and without so much as a thought for her kids, fostered with the Garretts. And now she was dying of lung cancer. Molly had told her that she didn't think she had much longer and wanted to see her and Tracey before she died. Claire's face set in a grim mask. That was typical of her mother, always putting her own feelings before those of anyone else. Resentment rose like bitter bile in her throat. Why should she bother to go and see her now, or her father for that matter? They had both let her down in different ways, and because of them she had spent most of her life hating herself, wishing that she could be someone else – even wishing that she were dead at times. Even now she was constantly looking over her shoulder, terrified of seeing a face from her past.

Screwing the letter up, she tossed it beneath the bench. Her decision was made. As far as she was concerned, her parents could both rot in hell. They deserved no better. One way or another, she had gotten by without them for this long, so why bother with them now, simply so that they could ease their consciences? Let them stew and suffer as she and Tracey had done.

Standing up abruptly, and with Gemma scampering close to her heels, Claire made her way back up the sunlit lawn to wait for Nikki to come home. Nikki was all she needed now. The past was done with.

Chapter Ten

It was the evening after Molly and Tom's visit. Nikki had gone off to meet up with her new friend from the council estate again, and the evening stretched endlessly in front of Claire. She had tried to read the new Martina Cole book she had just bought, but gave up after the first three pages when she realised that she hadn't taken in a word. She had then tried listening to music, but it just seemed to interrupt her thoughts, so that too was switched off, and now she sat staring vacantly off into space with Gemma curled up on her lap.

The sound of the doorbell ringing made her start. Claire kept herself very much to herself. She had no friends in the neighbourhood and wondered who it might be. Lifting Gemma down, she straightened her skirt and hurried into the hallway to open the door. Her mouth dropped open with shock and delight when she saw Tracey standing there. Tracey had never taken the trouble to visit her before, despite numerous invitations, and Claire saw this as another step in the right direction. Perhaps now she was ready to accept her back into the fold again?

'Come in. It's lovely to see you and you're looking so well.' It was all Claire could do to stop herself from dragging her sister across the threshold, she was so pleased to see her.

Tracey stepped past her into the hallway as Claire looked out at her car parked on the drive. 'Are you on your own?' she asked.

'Yes. Callum is looking after the twins.'

'Oh well, come on through to the kitchen then. I'll make us a cup of tea, or perhaps you'd prefer a glass of wine?'

'Tea will be fine, thank you. I'm driving,' Tracey replied shortly.

Claire felt her cheeks burn as she led Tracey into the kitchen and filled the kettle at the sink. Tracey looked about her at the sparkling glass in the French doors, the uncluttered worktops and the ceramic tiles on the floor that were so clean she felt she could have eaten her dinner off them, before commenting, 'You have a beautiful home, Claire. It's far tidier than mine. I'm afraid I fight a losing battle trying to keep on top of housework with the twins rampaging about.'

'It's worth the mess for those two.' Claire smiled at her. 'You're very lucky to have them. They're beautiful little girls.'

'You surprise me,' Tracey said caustically. 'If you're so fond of little girls, I wonder why you once gave yours away?'

Claire felt as if she had had the air knocked out of her lungs as Tracey stared at her coldly.

'I was just fourteen years old when I had Yasmin. How could I have kept her? What did I have to offer her?' she managed to say eventually.

Tracey was glaring at her now and it was obvious from the torrent of words that poured out of her in a stream that she hadn't forgiven, or forgotten, anything. 'You had me and Molly and Tom behind you,' she said bitterly. 'We would all have done everything we could to help you. But you were too intent on getting away and bettering yourself, weren't you? Even *I* wasn't enough to keep you there – let alone your own daughter. Still, that's all water under the bridge. I've known where I stood with you since the day you left me. It isn't that I'm here for. I'm here to talk to you about our mum and dad. Or at least, *your* mum and dad. If what Mum told us some years ago is true, then there's a big question-mark over whether Robbie is *my* dad, isn't there? Which, if I remember rightly, is why he left us in the first place.'

Claire was shaking. This wasn't turning out to be the sort of visit she had hoped for at all.

'I don't have a mum or a dad,' she muttered, and now Tracey raised her eyebrows.

'Oh, Claire. That's just so typical of you. All you ever thought about was yourself, and time obviously hasn't changed you.'

'That's unfair,' Claire denied hotly. 'When you were little I was like a mother to you. Have you forgotten that?'

'No, I haven't forgotten. But it still didn't stop you leaving me, did it?'

'I left because you didn't need me any more. You had Molly and Tom – and Billy,' Claire defended herself.

Tracey curled her lip. 'Oh yes, I had Molly and Tom, and it's a good job I did because from the day you left I didn't know if you were dead or alive, until you suddenly deigned to put in an appearance all these years later. I bet you never even gave me a thought while you were in London playing the great I am and making your millions. We weren't good enough for you to bother keeping in touch with, were we? Not even a phone call to let us know that you were all right. Do you have any idea *at all* what that did to Molly? She was almost beside herself with worry. She blamed herself for your going and ended up suffering with depression and on tablets. Of course, that wouldn't worry you. You were too busy off enjoying yourself!'

'*Enjoying myself?* Why, if only you knew . . .' Claire suddenly clamped her mouth shut. It was clear that Tracey had little time for her, and if she were to tell her of how she had worked the streets at King's Cross, she would probably disown her altogether.

She was feeling utterly devastated. If only Tracey could have known how many times she had thought of her, fretted about her and longed to ring her during their time apart. But of course, Tracey could have no way of knowing that, so Claire supposed she deserved all that her little sister was dishing out. It was as if a dam had broken free inside her and all the hurt she had kept bottled up over Claire's leaving was gushing out of her.

Claire's shoulders suddenly sagged; the great weight was still there on them, just as surely as it had been when she had run away all those years ago. When she had left Bispham, she had promised Christian that she would sort herself out and return to him. But apart from moving back to the Midlands and mending bridges with Molly and Tom, she had got no further on. The secrets she had been forced to keep were all still trapped inside her, like great festering boils waiting to burst. They all knew that she had made her money in London before moving to Blackpool and marrying Greg, but they still had no idea of how *exactly* she had made it. And until she could be honest with other people, how could she ever be honest with herself?

Seeing the look of utter despair on her sister's face, Tracey's tone softened slightly as she said, 'I came here to talk about Mum and Dad. Perhaps we should just stick to that for now, eh?'

Claire shrugged helplessly and Tracey went on, 'I met Dad today. It was quite . . .' she struggled for a way to explain how she had felt before ending, 'emotional.'

'And?'

'He . . . he's changed. But then of course he would have, wouldn't he? I was just a tiny girl when he left us. I went ready to do battle with him, I admit, but somehow I couldn't. He's so sorry for leaving us, Claire. If he hadn't, things might have been so very different, and he knows that now. The biggest shock though was how he still feels about our mum. He *still* loves her, even after all this time and all that's happened. It's quite incredible, isn't it? Apparently he's lived near Glasgow ever since he left, but he never formed another serious relationship and lives alone in a little rented flat. When Mum got in touch with him through a cousin of his that she remembered, he decided it was time to let bygones be bygones, and when he told me that, well, it got me thinking and I ended up visiting her in the hospital this afternoon with him. She's in Dorothea Ward in the George Eliot, if you decide to go.'

'And . . . how is she?'

'Not good, by all accounts. The nurse I spoke to reckons she could have another couple of weeks at most. She certainly won't be coming out of hospital again, except in a box that is, so Dad has decided to stay here for a while until . . . Well, he said he wanted to make sure she had a decent funeral, which I suppose is good of him, all things considered.'

Claire nodded solemnly. She had been trying to convince herself that she never wanted to set eyes on either of her parents ever again; the way she saw it, they had both contributed to the terrible life she had once been forced to lead. But now she had to ask herself if this was really true. For no reason that she could explain, the thought of her mother dying all alone in hospital was painful. Did *anyone* deserve to die like that? And if Tracey was ready to forgive her and their father, then shouldn't she? She just wished deep down that Tracey could show the same compassion to her.

Seeing that Claire was still indecisive, Tracey slowly rose from the table and lifted her shoulder bag.

'Right then, you have a lot to think about so I'm going to leave you to it.'

'Do you have to go so soon? You've only just got here.' Claire was dismayed and it showed, but Tracey shook her head.

'Yes, I'm afraid I do. Callum has had the twins for most of the day and as you know they're a bit of a handful so he'll probably be pulling his hair out by now.'

Claire followed her to the door. She wanted to say so very much and the words were all there waiting to pour out, but somehow they stayed lodged in her throat.

Tracey held her hand out as if she were saying goodbye to a stranger and Claire's heart broke just a little bit more as she shook it.

'Thanks for coming. I'll think about what you've told me.'

Tracey nodded curtly and then her car was pulling off the drive and Claire once more felt an overwhelming sense of loneliness. The opportunity to be honest with Tracey about her past life had been handed to her on a plate, but fool that she was, she had stayed silent and let the chance slip away. Cursing softly, she walked back into the empty house.

★ ★ ★

It was well after ten o'clock when Nikki returned home that night and by then, following her visit from Tracey, Claire's nerves were stretched to the limit. More so when she saw at a glance that Nikki had been drinking.

'Just what the *hell* are you playing at?' she snapped.

Nikki giggled and hiccuped. 'I'm playing at having a good time. You should try it, instead of being so prim and proper all the while.'

Prim and proper! The words bounced around inside Claire's head. Could former prostitutes be prim and proper? And yet, this was obviously how Nikki perceived her.

Another glance at Nikki told her it would be pointless trying to talk any sense to her tonight. They would just end up in the middle of another blazing row.

'Come on, young lady. I think you could do with a good strong cup of coffee inside you.' So saying, she took the girl firmly by the elbow and led her into the kitchen where she plonked her unceremoniously down onto a chair.

Half an hour later, after helping her undress, Claire tucked the duvet around her daughter and kissed her on the cheek. Inside, she was crying; it was the first time she had seen Nikki without her clothes on for some time and she was so thin that it was frightening.

I'll get her to the doctor's next week, Claire promised herself as she crept towards the door. There she paused to look back at the girl who was already fast asleep and snoring softly. All the anger she had felt seeped away. Nikki had her arm curled around Gemma and she looked so young and innocent. Claire loved her so very much. Nothing would ever change that, she knew it, but she loved Christian too and felt as if she was being pulled in half.

After having a hot bath she went to bed where once more she tried to become absorbed in a book. But it was useless, so eventually she snapped the light off and burrowed down under the duvet where she tossed and turned. Half an hour later, she put the light back on again. It was no good; she knew that she would never sleep feeling as she did. Slipping into her dressing-gown, she walked along the landing, hoping that a glass of hot milk would perhaps do the trick. At Nikki's bedroom door she paused to listen and when the sound of her gentle snores reached her she moved on.

Two glasses of milk and two hours later she was still wide awake, so now she opened the French doors and stepped out into the garden. A hedgehog who was shuffling across the patio stopped to look at her curiously as she moved past him onto the lawn. She had no idea at all why she had felt the need to come outside until she got to the bench under the apple tree, and then it came to her. This was where she had discarded her father's letter. Before she was even aware that she was going to do it she found herself on her hands and knees scrabbling beneath the time-worn seat in the damp grass. And then the letter was in her hand and she was heading towards the house again, suddenly feeling very nervous of the night sounds all around her. The moon unexpectedly slid from behind the scudding black clouds and she started as two white eyes stared at her from the shrubbery. Realising that it was only a stone statue she shot up the rest of the garden like a bullet from a gun.

Once back in the safety of her kitchen, she smoothed out her father's letter and read it again. Yet still she was no nearer to reaching a decision as to what she should do. Sighing, she clicked off the kitchen light and went back to bed.

Claire overslept the next morning and when she glanced at the bedside clock she was shocked to see that it was gone ten o'clock. Thankfully it was a Saturday, so she yawned and stretched before climbing out of bed. Apart from a little food shopping, she had nothing planned and intended to ask Nikki if she would like to go to the cinema. As she descended the stairs she heard Nikki pottering about in the kitchen and wondered how she would be feeling today. No doubt she would have a terrible hangover, which would also mean that she would be in a bad mood. Not that she was in any other kind of mood just lately, Claire thought to herself.

The second she entered the room, Nikki rounded on her. 'And what's *this* then?' she shouted accusingly as she waved a sheet of crumpled paper in Claire's face.

Claire cursed silently as she realised she must have left it on the kitchen table. Nikki had obviously read it, so she told her resignedly, 'It's a letter from my father – though why you're bothering to ask I really don't know, since it's obvious you've read it.'

'And what are you going to do? He says here that he wants to see you. That your mum is *dying*!'

'I don't know what I'm going to do yet,' Claire admitted. 'I haven't decided.'

'You haven't decided!' Nikki was staring at her incredulously. 'Your mum is *dying* and you have to *decide* if you are going to go and see her?'

'Look, Nikki. I know how it sounds but things have happened that you don't know about. My mum left me and my sister in care when we were very young and I've never set eyes on her from that day to this.'

'You heartless cow!'

'*Nikki!*'

Tears filled the girl's eyes. 'Well, you are!' she shouted insolently. 'No matter what she's done, she's still your mum. And he's still your dad. He didn't *have* to come back, you know? What do you want him to do – beg? How could you *not* go and see your mum when she's going to die? I would give anything to know who my real mum is, and yours is waiting for you and you can't even be bothered!'

With that she turned and stormed out of the room. Claire's first instinct was to hurry after her and to drag the girl back into the room; to make her apologise for the terrible things she had said. But then commonsense took over and she stood as if she were rooted to the spot. She could see why she must appear heartless to Nikki. She had told her very little about her young life, so it was natural that the girl should feel sorry for Karen, her mother.

Crossing to her bag she rummaged inside it until her fingers closed around an almost full packet of cigarettes. She was desperately trying to quit but right at this minute in time she felt a desperate need for tobacco. She lit one with shaking fingers and drew on it deeply, feeling slightly dizzy as the smoke entered her lungs, and it was then that she reached a decision. She would ring her father. What harm could it do? Grinding the cigarette out in a saucer that happened to be nearby, she then strode away to her room to get showered and dressed.

It was now almost three o'clock in the afternoon and once again, Nikki had left to go to her friend's. She had flatly refused Claire's offer of taking her to the pictures, and Claire knew that she probably wouldn't see her again now until at least ten o'clock that night.

After straightening the crumpled sheet of paper in front of her she dialled the number at the top of the page and waited.

'Hello?'

Claire's stomach did a somersault at the sound of the voice she still remembered so well, even after all these years. She opened her mouth to answer but no sound came out and now the voice again said, 'Hello? Is anyone there?'

'Yes. It's me, Claire.'

The silence stretched down the line until he whispered, 'Ah, sweetheart. I've been prayin' you'd phone.'

'You wanted to see me?' She knew her voice was sharp but could do nothing about it.

'Oh yes – yes, please. When . . . and where?'

'I could be in Nuneaton in an hour. I'll meet you outside the library.'

'I'll be waiting for you, lass.'

She replaced the receiver, and calm again now, she lifted her bag and her car keys and went outside to her car.

When she got into Nuneaton she parked at the back of Woolworth's, then took the short-cut through Mill Walk and across the bridge over the River Anker.

It was market day and people were milling about everywhere, but she spotted him straight away. Robbie McMullen was standing on the steps leading to the library looking anxiously up and down the street, glancing at his watch every few seconds. He looked older than she remembered him, but then it had been well over twenty years since she had last set eyes on him. Even so, time had been kind to him. He was still tall and upright, with the same shock of wavy black hair that she had loved to run her fingers through when he was telling her a bedtime story. There were streaks of grey in it now above the ears that gave him a distinguished look, and more wrinkles on his face than she remembered, but even so she would have recognised him anywhere. He was her dad. Her heart began to thump as she waited for a gap in the traffic, and then she was walking towards him and at sight of her she saw his eyes well with tears.

And then she was standing in front of him, her chin held high. 'Hello, Dad.'

He stared in amazement at the beautiful, sophisticated woman in front of him.

'C-Claire . . . is it *really* you?' He wanted to hug her but something about the way she was holding herself and the cold glint in her eyes stopped him. Instead he held his hand out awkwardly and after a moment's hesitation she took it and shook it very briefly.

'So . . .' He was at a loss as to what to say. 'Shall we go for a coffee or something?'

She nodded and they fell into step as they headed into the market-place. When they came to a café he held the door open for her and she stepped past him into the warm aromatic atmosphere.

'Tea or coffee?' he asked once he had her settled her at a table by the window.

'Tea, please. Two—'

'I know. Two sugars and plenty of milk.'

He had remembered and she felt the familiar stirrings of love she had always felt for him spring back to life. But she knew that she would have to suppress them; he had hurt her once and he could hurt her again if she allowed him back into her heart. She watched as he walked to the counter and by the time he returned she was cold and composed again. He sat down opposite her and she felt her cheeks grow warm as he stared at her.

'I didn't think you'd come,' he said softly. 'And who could have blamed you if you'd ripped my letter up and ignored it? I know I did a terrible thing when I walked out on you, Claire, and all I can say is I'm sorry from the bottom of my heart.'

'You're sorry,' she repeated scornfully. 'And that one little word will put everything right, will it?' It didn't seem so very long ago since Molly had said the very same words to her, but she wouldn't allow herself to think of that now.

'No, no, of course it won't. Nothing will ever put it right. I know now that I was to blame for your mam doing what she did. I knew she liked a good time when I married her. She was always the life and soul of the party. Trouble was, I was a pipe and slipper man and she couldn't stand it, which is why—'

'Which is why she went off with any man who made eyes at her – is that what you were about to say?'

'No, I wasn't actually. I think she only had the one serious fling while we were together. When I found out about it and she told me that Tracey might not be mine, I just lost it and cleared off. And don't think I haven't regretted it every single day since. You see, I couldn't forget her – or you two girls, for that matter. But I was too proud to come crawling back with my tail between my legs, and so I stayed away and ruined all our lives. Again I say, I'm so sorry, Claire. If there were anything I could do to make it up to you, I'd move heaven and earth to do it, and that's the God's honest truth.'

Claire stared through the window. Half of her wanted to throw herself into his arms and sob out all the hurt she had endured. The other half still hated him.

'Couldn't we start again?' he pleaded softly. 'I've nothing to rush back to Glasgow for yet awhile. We could get to know each other again and I could perhaps try to make up for what I put you through.'

'You could never make up for what you put me through,' Claire told him, and the way she said it made him drop his eyes with shame.

'I could try?' He was not going to give up without a fight. 'And Molly tells me I have a granddaughter. Nikki, isn't it?'

'You have two, actually. I gave the first one up for adoption when I gave birth to her at fourteen. Did Molly tell you that too?' The shocked look on his face answered her question and she felt a small thrill of satisfaction at seeing his distress. 'It was shortly after that, that I ran away to London. I didn't feel I had anyone of my own any more, you see?' she told him, twisting the knife in his heart. 'I imagined that I would be happy there, but I must have been mad.'

'But it worked out all right for you in the end, didn't it? Look at you. You're a fine young woman, and wealthy too, from what I'm hearing though I was heartsore for you when Molly told me that you'd lost your husband.'

'Did she tell you *how* he died?'

Robbie shook his head and now, her face distorted with hatred, Claire leaned across the table and told him, 'He took his own life after I found him abusing his daughter, who I have since adopted. He couldn't face the shame when I told him that I was going to expose him for the pervert that he was. *So*, do you *still* feel sorry for his loss now?'

His own face seemed to crumple but now it was Claire who was shocked when he looked up at her and muttered brokenly, 'I know, Claire. What you went through when I left and why you ended up in care. Your mum has told me everything and I'm so very, very sorry. No child should ever be subjected to what you and Tracey went through. When I first found out, I was physically sick.'

The room was swimming about her. Her mother had told him. But why? As if reading her thoughts, he tried to take her hand but she snatched it away.

'She didn't want to die without trying to make her peace with you,' he told her. 'You wouldn't recognise her now, Claire. Believe me, she is nothing like the woman you remember, and she too is sorry.'

'I . . . I have to go now.' The walls seemed to be closing in on her and she felt the need to get outside – to feel fresh air on her face. She rose and stumbled to the door, aware that he was right behind her, and once outside she leaned heavily against the wall.

'Are you all right, lass?'

Gulping deeply, she nodded, feeling foolish. She shouldn't have come; she knew that now. It was too late to turn the clock back and play at Happy Families. Eventually she pulled herself from the wall and began to head back to her car.

'May I walk with you, lass?'

She nodded as she felt his hand gently take her elbow, but didn't pull away and once again in her mind's eye she could see them walking hand-in-hand above the village, with not a care in the world. He was her father. He would *always* be her father – and she knew that deep down, there was a tiny part of her that still loved and needed him.

They reached the car and as she unlocked it, he asked, 'Will you think on what I've said – consider going to see your mum?'

She nodded numbly, afraid that if she answered him she would burst into tears.

He smiled at her, a sad smile that touched her heart despite all the promises she had made to herself that she wouldn't allow him to hurt her again.

'I'll hope to hear from you then, lass. And Claire . . . I do love you. I never stopped.'

She dropped into the driver's seat, knowing that she had to get away before she broke down completely. He closed the door and she watched him walking away, his shoulders stooped, and then she started the car and turned it in the direction of home.

Chapter Eleven

'Sorry, love, if it's our Poppy you've come for, I'm afraid she's out.'

'Oh.'

Hearing the disappointment in Nikki's voice, Roxy Miller held the door wide. 'Why don't you come in anyway an' keep me company fer a bit? Yer look as if you're on a bit of a downer.'

'I just had a blazing row with my mum. Or what I should say is, I just had *another* blazing row with my mum.'

Roxy's face broke into a sympathetic smile as Nikki stepped past her.

'She's always on at me,' Nikki complained. 'No matter what I do, it's never right.'

'Well, I don't want it to seem as if I'm siding with your mum, love, but it sounds to me like you're suffering from teenage mood syndrome. I've been through it enough times wi' my lot to recognise the signs. Was the row over anything important or something and nothing?'

'It all depends what you'd class as something or nothing,' Nikki retorted as she dropped down onto the settee. Katie was sitting on the hearthrug with a dolly in her lap rocking to and fro as she stared sightlessly off into space, and as Nikki looked at her, she felt sorry for her. One thing she had noticed in the time that she had been coming here was that no matter how dirty or untidy the house was, Katie always looked clean and well kept. Roxy obviously doted on her, as did her brothers and sister.

The woman sat down opposite her and after lighting a cigarette she drew on it before asking quietly, 'Is it anything you need to talk about?'

Nikki chewed on her lip then suddenly it all came spilling out. 'My mum's dad left her when she was small and she ended up in care because her mum couldn't look after her properly. Then she got pregnant when she was just fourteen and gave her baby away. Not long after that she ran away to London. She worked there till she was a bit older when she moved to Blackpool where she met my dad and married him. I thought things would be good once Claire came to live with us, but they weren't. My dad still . . .' Her voice trailed away as terrible memories came rushing back, but then she went on, 'Well, to go back to the row – my mum has had this letter off her dad. It's been years and years since she saw him. He wants to see her and in the letter he told her that her mum is in hospital. She's dying and she wants to see my mum. But Mum's being stubborn and says she won't go. Don't you think that's awful? That she won't go and see her own dying mother, I mean?'

'Hmm.' Roxy studied Nikki's pale, indignant face. She was shocked to the core. If what Nikki was telling her was true, then Nikki wasn't her mum's child by birth. Claire must have adopted Nikki after her husband's death. And here she'd been thinking what a perfect family they were. Even Nikki's mum had been through the mill by the sounds of it. In care, pregnant at fourteen? At this moment in time she was feeling sorrier for Claire than Nikki. But she didn't say that, of course.

Choosing her words carefully she said, 'Perhaps your mum just needs a little time to think about things? I mean, it must have come as a shock when her dad's letter arrived out o' the blue after all these years.'

Nikki tossed her head. 'That's no excuse to ignore him, is it?'

'It all depends on why he left her,' Roxy replied sensibly. 'It must have hurt her deeply when he went, an' then fer her mum to let her end up in care . . . it hardly bears thinkin' about. And another thing, if your dad already had you when he married her, then she must have adopted you when he died. Think on it, she wouldn't have done that if she didn't love yer, would she?'

'I don't suppose so,' Nikki admitted somewhat reluctantly. 'But Claire is my *third* mum. You see, I found out after my dad died that he and my other mum had adopted me when I was one year old. I didn't even know. Until then, I'd thought they were my real mum and dad.'

Roxy's heart was racing; she could hardly believe what the girl was telling her. It was like something you could read in a book. 'So, what happened to your dad's wife?' she now asked. 'Did they divorce?'

Nikki shook her head, setting her long fair hair dancing on her shoulders. 'No, my mother died in a road accident one night after she and my dad had had a row. She'd taken me in the car with her, but I didn't get hurt.'

Roxy whistled through her teeth before asking, 'Just for curiosity's sake, how old are you, Nikki? An' don't tell me fifteen or sixteen. Me head ain't up me arse an' I weren't born yesterday.'

'I'll be fifteen in November,' Nikki told her, flushing guiltily.

Roxy looked away and nodded. It just went to prove that what you saw wasn't always what you got, as her own mother had been fond of saying. Katie began to whimper and now Roxy was down on the floor beside her with her arms tight about the little girl. She would have died for this child, as her husband would testify. Many a time he had clouted one of the others and very often Roxy herself. But even he knew better than to raise his hand to Katie, for as Roxy would often warn him, if ever he did then he had better not dare go to sleep 'cos the moment he did she would stick a knife in his ribs.

The sound of the door opening made both Roxy and Nikki look towards it and seconds later, Eddie walked into the room, looking very smart in a dark suit and tie.

'How did it go?' Roxy asked him and her husband shrugged as he slid his long arms out of his jacket.

'All right. The boss has given me a little more time,' he said.

'Then you'd better get off your arse an' get back what you owe him,' Roxy told him darkly. She had never had any idea who this invisible 'boss' of Eddie's was, but she did know that her husband lived in fear of him. Which was quite surprising, considering Eddie practically ran this estate. If anyone wanted drugs, they came to him. If they had stolen goods to get rid of, they always ended up here. The boss sent money that Eddie lent out, charging the poor sods that were reduced to borrowing it extortionate rates of interest. She was also aware that he had a few girls tom-ing for him – herself included if they hit a lean time – and she put up with it all because, God help her, she loved the bastard. Always had done, even though he had put her in hospital more times than she cared to count.

Now as Eddie's eyes settled on Nikki he put on his most charming smile. She was a nice little piece and ripe for it, if he wasn't very much mistaken. He liked 'em young and slim.

As if she could read his mind, Roxy told Nikki apologetically, 'Perhaps you ought to come back an' see if Poppy is in later, love, eh? There's no tellin' how long she might be when she walks out that door.'

Realising that Roxy wanted to get rid of her, Nikki nodded, and rising from the settee she left the house despondently, wondering why grown-ups always had to be so complicated.

She had barely got through the gate when Roxy rounded on her husband furiously. 'Don't you *dare* go makin' cow eyes at that child,' she spat. 'She's barely out o' nappies.'

'I can think of a few punters who like 'em just like that,' he quipped.

'I'm warnin' you, don't even *think* about it. She comes from a good family.'

He was shocked to see that she meant it, and glaring at her with contempt now he ripped off his tie and walked out of the room. After the day he had just had he didn't want to get into an argument with her because he knew if he started on her he was likely to kill her or put her back in hospital again at the very least.

'So you decided to go and meet him after all then?'

'Yes, I did,' Claire replied flatly as she pushed a plate full of hot buttered cheese on toast across the table to Nikki.

Nikki stared at it as if it was poison. It was obvious that Claire didn't want to talk about the meeting, but she was curious.

'Had he changed much? I know it's been a long time since you've seen him.'

'Actually, he hadn't changed that much at all. I recognised him straight away.'

Claire was usually a bright chirpy person, but at the moment Nikki noted that she was very subdued.

'Did you . . . er . . . get on OK?'

'Look, Nikki, if you don't mind I don't really want to talk about it just yet. I feel a bit drained.'

Nikki crossed her arms as she slipped into a fully-fledged sulk. Normally she had the whole of Claire's attention, to the point that sometimes she felt as if she was being suffocated. But right at this moment, she had the feeling that Claire was only tolerating her presence and would rather have been on her own, which if truth were known she would have.

'Just one more question then,' she persisted. 'Have you agreed to go and see your mum now?'

'No, I haven't. I still don't know what I'm going to do yet.' The words were uttered more sharply than she had intended and the instant they were out she was contrite. 'Sorry, love. I didn't mean to snap at you. It's just as I said, I'm a bit emotionally drained at the moment.'

Claire might as well have saved her breath; Nikki was already walking away from the table, and as the door banged behind her, Claire's chin drooped to her chest and she asked herself, *When will I ever find peace?*

★ ★ ★

An hour later, Nikki was once again on Poppy's doorstep and this time it was Poppy who answered the door.

'Hello, mate,' she greeted her affably, then glancing over her shoulder she asked, 'No Erin again?'

Nikki shook her head. 'No, she doesn't seem too happy with me at the minute.'

Poppy giggled. 'Jealous cow. Probably 'cos you an' me have started to knock around together. Leave her to stew in her own juice, eh? She'll come out of it. But me mam said you'd called round earlier an' you weren't too happy. So, what's up?'

Nikki was following Poppy up the stairs and once they'd reached her room, Poppy crossed to her music centre and the next minute, a Britney Spears record was bouncing off the walls.

Almost shouting to make herself heard above the din, Nikki began to tell her and when she was done, Poppy sighed.

'Fuckin' hell. You couldn't make sommat like that up, could you? What's your mam goin' to do now?'

Nikki shrugged. 'I haven't got the foggiest, and the way I'm feeling at the minute I really don't care.'

'Here, have one o' these an' chill out a bit.'

Nikki's eyes almost popped out of her head as Poppy took a tobacco tin from beneath her bed and proceeded to roll a couple of spliffs.

She lit one and handed it to Nikki who looked at it uncertainly.

'Go on then.' Poppy was laughing. 'It ain't goin' to bite you, an' I guarantee when you've smoked that, *nothin'* will trouble you.'

Nikki took a drag and was pleasantly surprised by the very mild effect.

'See, I told yer. It won't hurt yer,' Poppy chortled. 'Go on. Finish it off.'

Nikki swung her legs up onto Poppy's unmade bed and did just that.

* * *

Claire started awake, and after rubbing the sleep from her eyes, she looked at the clock. She had settled down on the sofa earlier on with a *Take A Break* magazine to wait for Nikki to come in, and realised that she must have dozed off. It was way after midnight, and she felt a flush of annoyance. Nikki could have taken the trouble to wake her when she came in. Yawning, she stretched painfully before making her way into the kitchen to turn off the lights. Gemma was still in there, curled up in her basket, which was strange to say the least, as she always went to bed with Nikki.

'Come on, girl.' Claire bent to stroke her. 'Let's take you up to your pal, eh?'

Gemma's tail wagged as she followed Claire out of the kitchen and once on the landing she waited expectantly as Claire opened Nikki's bedroom to let her in.

'In you go,' Claire told her, glancing towards the bed, and then her heart seemed to stop as she saw that it was empty. Snapping on the light she looked around the room as panic began to get a grip of her. The window was still open and the curtains were blowing gently in the cold night breeze. Hurrying over to it, Claire closed it before turning about. Lately, she had gotten used to Nikki rolling in at all hours. But she had never, ever stayed out this late before. Where could she be? As an idea occurred to her, she opened Nikki's bedside drawer. Her phone book was in there. Perhaps she was at Erin's? With shaking fingers she turned the pages until she came to Erin's number and then glanced worriedly at the clock again. It was now going on for one o'clock in the morning and if Nikki wasn't there, Erin's mother was going to be none too pleased at being woken at this time of the morning. But what choice did she have?

Taking a deep breath she dialled the number, strumming her fingers impatiently on the bedside cabinet as she waited for someone to answer.

Ten rings later, when Claire had been just about to give up, a sleepy female voice said, 'Hello?'

Claire gulped, feeling very guilty. 'I'm so sorry to trouble you so late, Mrs Morgan. It's Claire Nightingale, Nikki's mother, and I was wondering if she was there, by any chance?'

'No, she's not here. Erin has been in bed for hours,' the woman told her.

'Oh, I see. Then in that case I'm very sorry to have troubled you. Goodnight.'

The phone went dead in her hand and now Claire began to frantically go through the other numbers in the book. There was no one else she could think of that Nikki might be with, apart from the girl on the council estate who had lately befriended her. Claire tried to think what her name was and suddenly it came to her. *Poppy* – that was it. She should have remembered straight away, since all she had heard off Nikki for weeks was, Poppy this and Poppy that! But there was no Poppy or even a number in the book for her.

Hugging herself, she tried to stay calm. It was no use falling apart or she would be no good to Nikki at all. What should she do? What should she do?

I'll go and have a drive round and see if I can see her, she thought to herself, and hurried back to her own room where she threw on the first clothes that came to hand and charged back down the stairs.

She knew that Poppy lived somewhere on the Chelmsey Park Estate, but she had no idea which street, so she found herself cruising around aimlessly. The streets were deserted apart from a few boisterous youths on their way home from a night club. As she slowed down to pass them they began to shout and whistle. She tried another road but after an hour she realised that it was pointless and turned in the direction of home. Perhaps Nikki would be back by the time she got there? But the second she set foot through the door, she knew that she wasn't. Gemma was still waiting patiently by the door where she had left her and the house felt strangely empty.

Despair washed over her as she realised that she now had no option but to phone the police.

As she waited for them to arrive, Claire's mind was working over-time. Perhaps Nikki had been kidnapped by a pervert and was lying dead in a ditch somewhere? Or perhaps she had run away? They hadn't been getting on all that well lately, and she herself had run away, hadn't she? Only now did she realise the full extent of the distress she must have caused Molly and Tom when she left for London all those years ago. How would she feel if Nikki now disappeared without trace for years as she had? Perhaps this was God's way of paying her back for the hurt she had caused them? Claire had often questioned if there was a God in the dark days, but now she prayed as she had never prayed before. *Oh dear Lord, please keep her safe. She's all I have. Please. Please . . .*

The police arrived at three o'clock. There was a man and a woman and they both looked very young to Claire as she led them into the lounge.

'So when did you last see your daughter then?' was the first ques-tion and then they went on and on as they filled in the Missing Persons form.

'What was she wearing?'

Claire tried to think back to when Nikki had stormed out of the kitchen. 'I think she had jeans and a denim jacket on.'

'Had you had a row?'

Claire flushed. 'Well, not a *row* exactly.' She went on to tell them what had happened as they continued to scribble furiously.

'Have you tried all her friends?'

'I've tried the one where I thought she might be, but she wasn't there. The only other one she has been mixing with quite a lot lately lives on the Chelmsey Park Estate but I don't have her address.'

'Do you know her name?'

Claire flushed again. She should have asked things like this herself. Why hadn't she? What sort of a mother was she anyway?

'I only know her first name is Poppy.'

'I see. Could you give us a description of her?'

'No, I'm afraid I couldn't. Nikki has never brought her to the house to my knowledge. She tends to go to Poppy's.'

'Then could you give us a description of Nikki and a recent photo?'

As Claire began to describe Nikki the tears rose up in her throat and threatened to choke her. Hurrying to the sideboard she brought back a photo of her and Nikki that had been taken at the twins' birthday party. They had their arms about each other and looked happy and carefree, and now the tears spilled over and coursed down her cheeks.

'Do you think something has happened to her?' she asked fearfully.

'Truthfully, no, I don't,' the young policeman assured her kindly. 'I wouldn't mind betting she's at this mate's house. You'd be shocked how often this happens with teenagers, particularly the girls. I've no doubt she'll breeze in, in the morning, as cool as a cucumber. But in the meantime we'll be looking out for her, of course. And we'll also radio a description of her to the other cars in the area. Try not to worry too much, Mrs Nightingale.'

She managed a tearful smile as the officer and his female colleague walked towards the door.

'If she should arrive home, could you let us know she's back? We'll come and have a word with her then. And as I said, try not to worry. If I were you I'd go to bed and try to get some sleep.'

Claire nodded, but inside she was thinking, Has he totally lost his marbles? How could she *possibly* think of resting while Nikki was out there missing?

She thanked them politely and after closing the door behind them she walked back into the lounge. Crossing to the sideboard, she rummaged about in one of the cupboards until she found an unopened bottle of vodka. After opening it she poured herself a stiff measure and as she lifted it to her lips she suddenly thought of all the times she had drunk it before going to stand on a street corner in London with

Cindy. She had had to, or she would never have been able to bear what she was about to do. Cindy was the young prostitute who had taken pity on her when she had first arrived in London and allowed her to stay in her flat with her in King's Cross while Claire looked for a job. Of course, Claire had never managed to find one. Not a legitimate one, at least. And so eventually she had resorted to prostitution under Cindy's guidance.

During the time they had lived together, she and Cindy had become firm friends. When Cindy had eventually returned to the little town where she had been brought up, after a severe beating from one of her clients, Claire had stayed on in the flat alone. And slowly she had made herself into the person she wanted to be. Or she thought she had, until she met Christian Murray, a struggling young vet who had saved the life of Cassidy, a little stray dog she had taken in. She had soon realised that, despite all the promises she had made herself to never trust anyone again, she loved Christian with all her heart. But how could she go to him? He believed that she was the wealthy orphan of upper-class parents. How could she ever bear to tell him that she was a former prostitute? And so she had married Greg, her accountant, and look how that had turned out. He had been no better than the men who had paid for the use of her body. In fact, he had been even worse, for he had abused his own adopted child.

Lighting a cigarette, Claire took another gulp of her drink, coughing as it burned its way down her throat, but already it was taking the edge off the pain she was feeling. After finishing the drink she quickly poured a second one, then lit another cigarette with shaking fingers. And then she sank onto the sofa and prepared for the long wait ahead.

Chapter Twelve

Roxy was spoonfeeding Katie some porridge when Poppy and Nikki put in an appearance in the kitchen late the next morning.

'You're an early bird,' she told Nikki, for this was early for them to get up on a weekend.

Poppy stared at Roxy's black eye as she put the kettle on before telling her, 'She ain't an early bird. She stopped the night.'

'Oh.' Roxy frowned. 'You did tell yer mam you were stayin', I hope?'

When Nikki flushed, Roxy sighed. 'I think the best thing you could do is to get your arse back home as fast as your legs will take yer then, young lady. Your poor mam is probably pullin' her hair out by now.'

'Huh! Why would she be?' Poppy took the milk from the fridge and took a long swig straight from the bottle. 'I stay out all the time an' I ain't never heard you ask where *I've* been.'

'Yes, well, that's 'cos I'm used to it wi' you, an' I know yer can take care o' yourself. From what I can see of it, Nikki here has been brought up a bit different.'

Poppy now focused on her mother's eye again before saying, 'Been at it again, has he? The bastard. I never heard it this time.'

'I'm not surprised,' Roxy shot back. 'From the smell that were comin' from your bedroom last night, you were probably so high yer wouldn't have heard a bleedin' bomb drop. You'll set the house alight wi' your bloody wacky baccy one o' these nights, you just mark my words.'

121

'Oh, give over naggin', Mam.' Poppy now turned her attention to Nikki. 'I hate to say it but she might have a point, mate. Perhaps it'd be as well if you did get back an' let your old girl know you're OK. If you don't get home soon she might do sommat daft like ringin' the Old Bill.'

Nikki nodded as she walked towards the door. Her mouth felt like the bottom of a birdcage and there was a dull headache behind her eyes. Not that it would put her off trying the stuff Poppy had given her again. It had made her feel like a different person for a while. Nothing had mattered and she had felt relaxed and happy.

'I'll see you later then.' She smiled at Poppy and Roxy, then started for home, ready to face the music. Claire would probably go mad at her but Nikki wasn't overly concerned. She could wrap Claire round her little finger when she wanted to, and the night before was worth a telling-off. She would just hang her head and say she was sorry and then Claire would forgive her and it would all be forgotten.

Eddie was in the Pig and Whistle with the pub phone pressed tight to his ear as he tried to hear what his boss was telling him. He made all his phone calls to the boss from here. That way, no one could trace them back to his house. The pub was full of men all smoking, drinking and playing cards and darts.

'Yes, boss. By Tuesday I swear it, as God's me witness,' he shouted into the mouthpiece. His voice was confident but when he put the phone down he found that he was shaking. Why the hell had he had to go and blow the boss's last payment on the dogs? Sure Thing, the dog had been called, and it had been favourite to win. Huh, that was a joke, the bloody dumb mutt had come in second to last. And now the boss wanted the payment that was already overdue, so what could he do? His mind began to work overtime as he took a long swallow from his glass. Well, he could get Roxy out to do a couple of turns for a start, and some of the toms owed him a fair bit and all. Then there were the drugs that were stacked under the stairs in neat little plastic bags. If he brought some of that down here tonight he'd no doubt shift a bit when the blokes had got a few pints down their necks. Slightly heartened, he downed his pint and ordered another.

The sight of the police car on the drive made Nikki break out in a sweat. So Poppy had been right then – her mum had called the police. She briefly thought about turning around and walking away, but then common sense took over. If she was to go in all apologetic and tell them that she had fallen asleep at a friend's, it would be all over and done with and out of the way.

Taking a deep breath, she walked through the front door – and just as she had thought, Claire was there in a second. Different emotions seemed to be playing across her face. Anger, fear, pain . . . but overriding them all was relief.

'Nikki. Oh, thank God you're safe.' She had covered the short distance between them and now she was hugging Nikki as if she might never let her go. Then she was holding her at arm's length and barking at her, 'Just where the *hell* do you think you've been? I've been out of my mind with worry and I've had the police out looking for you.'

A young policeman and policewoman had now joined them in the hallway and for their benefit, Nikki dropped her head and muttered apologetically, 'I'm so sorry, Mum. I was at my friend's. We were lying on her bed watching a video and the next thing I knew it was morning. We must both have dropped off. I didn't do it on purpose. Honest, I didn't.'

'And where does this friend of yours live?' This was from the policewoman.

Nikki felt like telling her to mind her own business but instead she told her, 'She lives on the Chelmsey Park Estate, but I'm afraid I don't know the address.'

From the look on her face, the policewoman clearly did not believe her and now she asked, 'And what is this friend's name?'

'Poppy.'

'And I don't suppose you happen to know her last name either?' The question was loaded with sarcasm but ignoring it, Nikki looked back at her innocently, her big blue eyes wide.

'No, I'm sorry, but I don't.'

'Then I suggest you get to know a little more about the people you stay out with next time. The police have better things to do than spend whole nights searching for girls who can't be bothered to let their mothers know where they are.'

The officers now walked towards the front door and Claire followed. 'Thank you so much,' she told them. 'And I'm so sorry I had to bother you.'

Nikki had already disappeared off into the kitchen and now the young policewoman leaned towards her and told her in a hushed voice, 'If I was you, Mrs Nightingale, I'd try to find out who this mysterious Poppy is. She might be a perfectly nice girl, but even so, if Nikki is going to start pulling stunts like this you need to know where she might be.'

'I'll do that,' Claire assured her, and once she had closed the door behind them she leaned heavily against it. She had just gone through one of the worst nights of her life and her nerves were as taut as wires. Even so, she was determined to try and be reasonable with Nikki. After taking a deep breath she joined her in the kitchen. Nikki was kneeling down fussing Gemma, waiting for the fireworks, so she was surprised when Claire said calmly, 'Right, perhaps you'd like to tell me the truth now?'

'I've already told you the truth,' Nikki stated indignantly.

Claire raised her eyebrows. 'Oh yes, and since when have you just fallen asleep on a whim? You've never been a good sleeper. You know it and so do I.'

'Look, I have no intention of letting this turn into a row, so I'm going to my room now.' With that, Nikki turned on her heel and walked sedately out of the room, leaving Claire to wonder just who the adult was, and who the child was here?

Once upstairs, Nikki pulled a small packet from her pocket. Inside it were two more roll-ups that Poppy had given her. She had assured her that they weren't addictive. In fact, as she had pointed out, some people smoked them for medicinal purposes, so where could the harm be? Of course, Nikki knew that if Claire were to find them she wouldn't look at it that way and the shit would hit the fan big time. Nikki chuckled softly; she was already picking up some of Poppy's sayings and she liked the way it made her feel. All grown-up and devil-may-care. The way she saw it, she was growing up fast and Claire had two choices: she could either like it or lump it!

Crossing to her chest of drawers she opened it and pushed the joints between her knickers; as far as she was concerned, what Claire didn't know wouldn't hurt her.

As Robbie McMullen stared down at the wreck of a woman in the hospital bed his heart ached. It was hard to believe that this was the girl he had married; the girl who had been able to turn heads wherever she went. She was fast asleep, which was just as well. Robbie needed a little time to compose himself before he faced her. He glanced around the ward. All the other lockers were loaded with flowers and bowls of fruit and magazines. Karen's was empty except for a water jug and a glass. He made a mental note to bring something in, the next time he came. That was the least he could do. He sat down in the chair next to the bed, his eyes never leaving her pain-ravaged face. She seemed to have shrunk to half the size he remembered her being, and she looked very, very old although she was only in her early fifties. Once upon a time this woman had been able to make his heart dance at the sight of her; now it felt like a lead weight in his chest.

His thoughts turned to Claire and he had to blink away the tears. She had been nothing like he had expected her to be. She was poised and sophisticated and beautiful. It was hard to believe that he had had a part in her being. She was a daughter any man could be proud of, but he had let her down, and judging by the way she had reacted to him at their meeting, he doubted if she would give him a chance to make it up to her. He supposed that he couldn't blame her. Why should she forgive him? Because of him her childhood – her whole life, in fact – had been ruined. And then there was Tracey. It was strange; he had left Karen because there was a question about whether Tracey was his child. And yet she had received him back far more welcomingly than Claire. She had invited him to her home to meet her twins tomorrow and he was looking forward to it. Jessica and Isabelle they were called, she had told him, and he could hardly wait to see them.

He had become so lost in thought that it was a shock when he realised that Karen had woken up and was staring at him.

'Hello, Karen. How are you feeling today, lass?' The question sounded ridiculous even to his own ears.

'How would you expect me to feel?' Surprisingly, the words were said without malice. 'Have you seen the girls?' she went on.

'Yes, I have. Both of them. You'll be proud when you see how they've turned out.'

'They're coming to see me?'

He looked away from the hope shining in her eyes. 'Well, Tracey certainly is. I think Claire might need a little more time.'

'Ah, then we have a problem. You see, time is sommat I'm fast runnin' out of, Robbie.' Her eyes were tight on him and she knew in that moment that she still loved him. She had always loved him. Why had she once thought him boring? What had prompted her to go off and have a fling? But it was too late to think about it now. What was done was done. She had blown the chance of having a happy family years ago.

Robbie sat quietly, trying not to look at the tube in the back of her hand that dripped morphine into her at regular intervals. Even on

126

the highest dose they dared give her, her face still looked drawn and haggard.

'So, tell me about the girls,' she requested in a weak voice.

He thought for a minute before saying: 'Well, Tracey is married and lives in a very nice house in Windermere Avenue. You know, on the Saint Nicholas Park Estate? She's married to a nice chap called Callum Brady. They have twin girls, Jessica and Isabelle, who are two years old. And she seems to be happy.'

'Saint Nicholas Park, eh? She's done well for herself then. That's the posh side of town. And Claire . . .'

He cleared his throat and looked away. 'She's done very well for herself too. She adopted her stepdaughter after her husband died and she's living in Solihull now.'

'I can't believe she's a widow so young.' Karen slowly shook her head. She had lost her hair during the chemotherapy she had received, and it was beginning to grow back in grey wispy curls. 'Does she still hate me, Robbie?'

The question took him by surprise and he wondered how he should answer it. He had no wish to hurt her when she was already as low as she could get, so he told her, 'I've only seen her once, but I think she's very mixed up. She's been through a lot and I have the feeling she doesn't know what she feels.'

Karen nodded in dull acceptance. 'I'm not surprised. When they first went into care she used to look at me as if I was something that was stuck to the bottom of her shoe when I visited her and Tracey. That was what finally decided me to not have them back. I was lonely, Robbie. So lonely that I went from one man to another; always thinking that this would be the one to take your place. But do you know something? None of them ever did and I sacrificed my children for that. Huh! If only I could have my time over again, things would be so different. Do you know I even got hooked on drugs at one stage? How shameful is that, eh?'

'Karen, you don't have to put yourself through this.' His eyes were brimming with tears and now as he gently stroked the hand that was lying limply on the starched white sheet she took his and gripped it with surprising strength.

'I *do* have to,' she muttered with an urgency that frightened him. 'I want you to know that I've been a real bad 'un. But I also want you to know that there was never another for me who meant the same after you left. I've done unforgivable things to the girls. Allowed terrible things to happen to 'em. If there really is a hell then I must have a first-class ticket booked straight there. But I *am* sorry. An' . . . well, the thing is, I still love you, Robbie. I never stopped.'

He continued to stroke her hand as the tears spilled over and trembled on his thick dark lashes.

'I still love you too, Karen.'

He suddenly saw a trace of the woman she had once been as she flashed him a smile that lit up her eyes.

'Then will you do something for me?'

'Of course – anything.'

'Will you try to persuade Claire to come an' see me? Even if it's only just the once so I can tell her how sorry I am. I don't expect her to forgive me. But I just need to see her one more time.'

'I'll do my very best,' he promised, and then as they both sat thinking of all the wasted years, a silence settled between them.

It was late afternoon when Nikki next put in an appearance. Claire was standing at the cooker stirring a large pan of bolognese sauce. It had always been one of Nikki's favourites and she hoped that it would tempt her to eat.

All day she had been wondering how best to handle the situation about Nikki staying out. After a lot of thought she had decided to ground her for a couple of days, then let the matter drop and hope that it had been a one-off. Now she smiled at her.

'Ah, there you are. I was hoping you'd come down when you smelled this.' She noticed that Nikki was dressed up and had her make-up on and prayed that this wasn't a sign that she was going to try and go out again.

'Come on, get yourself to the table,' she went on. 'I hope you're hungry. I've cooked enough here to feed an army.' For an awful moment she thought Nikki was going to refuse, but then she bent to stroke Gemma and did as she was told as Claire carried the steaming meal to the table.

'Help yourself,' she told her as she placed the bowl in front of her. Nikki obediently spooned some onto her plate as Claire took a seat opposite her.

Once Claire had helped herself too she peeped at Nikki out of the corner of her eye. 'This . . . er . . . Poppy that you stayed with. I think I ought to have her address, don't you? You seem to be spending an awful lot of time round there and I really need a contact number.'

'Why?' Nikki asked resentfully.

Claire tried to keep her voice light. 'Just in case I ever needed to get in touch with you if you are round there,' she told her casually.

'I've already told you, I don't *know* her address.'

Claire saw Nikki's face set in resentment and knew that this conversation was in danger of developing into yet another row. Even so, she was determined to find out where this girl lived. Ever since she had come on the scene, Erin seemed to have disappeared off Nikki's horizon, yet until then they had been as thick as thieves. Claire was ashamed to admit to herself that she had never been very enamoured of Erin, yet now she appeared like a positive angel compared to this Poppy that Nikki had got involved with. Deciding that it might be wise to change the subject for now, she announced, 'I thought we might go to Blackpool within the next couple of weeks to see Mrs M and Christian.'

Nikki pulled a face. 'Do we have to? It's boring there. There's nothing to do. And anyway, in case you've forgotten, your mum is dying in hospital at the minute. Don't you think you ought to stick around and go and see her?'

Claire tried to keep the shock from showing on her face. Nikki had always loved it at Seagull's Flight until now. In fact, usually once they had arrived there on the very few occasions they had visited since living in Solihull, she had barely seen the girl. She was either walking the stray dogs down on the beach or paying home visits with Christian. Furthermore, Claire had no intention of getting into a further discussion about her mother until she had decided what she was going to do.

The lure of this Poppy must be very strong, she thought if she doesn't even want to go to Seagull's Flight any more. Mrs M and Christian had always spoiled Nikki shamelessly, but it seemed that even they could not compete with her newfound friend.

'Perhaps we'll leave it till you break up from school for the summer holidays then,' Claire said tactfully, still trying desperately to avoid a row. She felt as if she was walking on egg shells and couldn't say the right thing.

Nikki shrugged as Claire watched her pushing her food around the plate. 'I thought we might pop into the doctor's sometime in the week,' Claire added casually. 'I notice you've lost a lot of weight and thought he might perhaps be able to prescribe you a tonic or something.'

'Oh, for God's sake.' Nikki shoved her plate away. 'Can't you just stay off my case for one minute? You're trying to run my life. I'm not a baby any more, you know.' Throwing herself away from the table she headed for the front door as Claire hurried after her. Her own temper was rising now in spite of all her good intentions.

'Hold on one minute, young lady!' she snapped. 'Just *where* do you think you're going?'

'Out!' Nikki snapped back.

'Oh no, you are not.' Claire was standing in front of the door now. 'You don't really think I'm just going to let you back out after your little escapade last night, do you? You keep telling me that you're not a baby, so why don't you stop acting like one? You are grounded until further notice, young lady, do you hear me?'

'Oh, I hear you loud and clear,' Nikki told her insolently. 'But you're not going to keep me in. If you stand there I'll just go out of the back door, and you can't stand in front of them both all night, can you?'

Claire felt the anger seep out of her and her shoulders sagged in defeat as Nikki stepped past her. She was trying very hard to keep the girl on the straight and narrow, but right at this moment in time she felt as if she was fighting a losing battle. And worse still was the fact that she had no idea what she could do about it.

She had tried so hard since Greg had died to make Nikki feel loved and cared for. But what she had not allowed for was how Nikki would feel when she reached her teens and how she would deal with the abuse she had suffered. Just as she herself had done many years before, Nikki was building a barrier that no one could penetrate. More than anyone, Claire knew what Nikki must be going through and now, just as she had taken her feelings out on Molly, Nikki was taking hers out on her.

'Oh Christian, I miss you so much,' she whispered to the empty house as the door slammed behind Nikki, but only silence answered her.

Chapter Thirteen

'I've made a decision,' Claire told Nikki over breakfast the next morning. 'On Friday afternoon when you get in from school we're going to stay at Seagull's Flight for the weekend.'

'But I don't want—'

Claire held a warning hand up and stopped the girl mid-sentence. 'Just for once I don't care what you want, Nikki. I'm putting myself first this time. I think a short break away will do us both the world of good, so don't even bother arguing. When you get in from school I shall have the car packed and ready to go, so that's an end to it.'

'And what about your mum? She's running out of time – doesn't that matter to you? Are you really happy for us to go swanning off when she is lying in a hospital bed dying?'

'We are going, and that is that.'

As Nikki pouted, Claire was reminded that beneath the grown-up attitude she was trying to display to the world she was still little more than a child. It might be that a short break would put them back on good terms. And of course, it was also an excuse to see Christian. Thinking about him brought the familiar tears stinging at the back of her eyes. During the time they had been apart he had been so patient, never pressuring her to join him. The trouble was, he was only human and how much longer would he wait?

She pushed the thought away. The prospect of life without him waiting for her in the background was unthinkable. Somehow she had to get Nikki through this difficult stage so that she could be with him.

She also had to make a decision about whether or not she wished to see her mother again. Nikki had been right about Karen's time running out, if what her dad had told her was anything to go by. But first they would have a break. It could be that this was all it would take to get Nikki's mind off this new friend she was suddenly so obsessed with.

Claire had a bad feeling about the girl, even though she had never met her. Only the day before while she had been cleaning Nikki's room, she had noticed a strange smell. She had opened the window and emptied the bin but the smell had persisted. Standing at the bottom of the bed with her hands on her hips, she had tried to think why the smell was so familiar and then it had hit her like a slap in the face. It was cannabis; she had known enough girls who had smoked it when she had shared a flat in London with Cindy. But surely Nikki would not be foolish enough to try drugs? Many people were of the impression that joints were non-addictive but Claire could have told them otherwise. She had seen far too many of the toms she had worked the streets with hooked on far stronger stuff after starting off on spliffs.

She had almost tipped Nikki's room upside down then but found nothing and she had started to think that she had imagined it. She had to think that or she would go mad with worry. Nikki was getting to be a handful but she was a sensible girl and Claire could not envisage her doing anything so foolish. And so she had said nothing, but from now on she would be on a mission to keep Nikki away from this Poppy as much as she could, even if it meant taking her away for weekends or coming up with something that they could do together.

Now as Nikki walked down the stairs in her school uniform with her schoolbag slung across her shoulder, Claire forced a smile to her face.

'Have you got your dinner money off the kitchen table?' She had a sneaky suspicion that the dinner money went on cigarettes more often than not, but refrained from saying so.

'Yes, I have.' Nikki's expression was sullen, and without the heavy make-up she had taken to wearing she looked exactly what she was, a fourteen-year-old girl. And a very thin one at that. Claire looked at the stick-like legs poking from beneath her school skirt and silently promised herself that she would try and get an appointment with the doctor for after school that very afternoon. Nikki would probably kick off big time about it, but if Claire met her at the school gates and took her straight there, there wouldn't be a lot she could do about it.

'Well, have a good day then. And Nikki . . . I love you.'

Nikki rolled her eyes as she let herself out of the door, and before she could change her mind, Claire lifted the phone and dialled Christian's grandmother in Blackpool to let her know that she and Nikki would be arriving on Friday evening.

Mr Dickinson was on the phone to a client when Claire entered the office shortly before ten o'clock and he smiled at her. Bradley was sitting in front of his computer and he immediately stood up to put the kettle on. He always made Claire a cup of tea when she arrived, which was one of the things she liked about him. Someday he would make someone a wonderful husband, but it wouldn't be her. Her affections lay elsewhere, if he could only have known it.

She worked steadily through the pile of paperwork on her desk until twelve o'clock when she asked the men, 'Is anyone ready for another coffee-break yet?'

'I could kill for one,' Bradley told her with a smile. At that moment the phone rang and Mr Dickinson answered it. He then placed the phone back down and walked towards the small office where he spoke to the clients when he needed to be private.

'Claire,' he said, 'I wonder if you could put this call through to me in here, please?'

134

She nodded affably. 'Of course, Mr Dickinson.' She transferred the call and then went on to make their drinks.

She was just about to take Mr Dickinson's through to him when he reappeared, telling her apologetically, 'I'm so sorry, my dear, but something urgent has come up and I have to go out. I had an appointment at one o'clock. The number is on my desk in my diary. Do you think you could ring them and reschedule it for me?'

'Certainly.'

When he had gone, Bradley leaned back in his chair and scratched his head as Claire lifted the diary and looked for the number of the client.

She rang them and booked them another appointment and as she put the phone down, Bradley commented, 'How strange. It isn't like the old man to shoot off and let a client down like that, is it? It must have been something important, yet he didn't even take his briefcase.'

'Well, I just hope it isn't a personal problem.'

They then both lifted their mugs and continued with their work.

The car was packed with everything they could possibly need for the weekend and now all Claire had to do was collect Nikki from school. The girl had been in an awful mood ever since Claire had taken her to the doctor's a couple of days before; particularly since the doctor had insisted on weighing and measuring her, before agreeing with Claire that she was a little underweight. Claire had felt like telling him that from where she was standing, Nikki was very underweight, but had managed to hold her tongue. He had then prescribed a tonic and some foul-tasting sachets that she had to mix with milk and which he had promised would, to use his terms, *put a little meat back on her bones.*

Since then Claire had stood over her daughter every morning and night like a sergeant-major until the whole gruesome concoctions were finished to the last drop. Thankfully, she could have no way of knowing that Nikki was then going to the toilet and vomiting the whole lot back up.

And so now she lifted Gemma onto the back seat and set off. She knew that Nikki would not be happy at having to arrive at Seagull's Flight in her uniform, but she was afraid that if she had allowed her to come home first to get changed, she might slip out and head straight off for Poppy's instead.

Claire arrived at the school a few minutes before home time and after parking the car, she stared at a young girl who was standing at the gates smoking a cigarette. She looked to be about sixteen. She was heavily made-up and was wearing one of the shortest skirts that Claire had ever seen and a low-cut top that left little to the imagination. Claire was reminded of the toms she had worked with, and thought she would not have looked out of place standing on a street corner, and yet for all that she could see that beneath the paint and powder was a very pretty young girl. She looked towards Claire now, as if she could feel her scrutiny, and before Claire looked swiftly away she noticed that the girl's eyes were a striking shade of blue.

At that moment the school bell sounded and within minutes girls of all shapes and sizes, all dressed in the same uniform, began to stream out through the elaborate wrought-iron gates. Claire watched closely and sure enough, seconds later, Nikki emerged. But instead of turning towards Claire, she made straight for the girl and after greeting her they began to walk away in the opposite direction. She quickly started the car engine and when she was abreast of them, she drew the car into the kerb and wound down the window.

'*Mum!*'

Hearing the shock in Nikki's voice, Claire knew that she had been right in her assumption. Nikki had had no intentions of coming straight home, which meant that this then was probably the infamous Poppy.

Knowing that she had been caught out, Nikki had the grace to blush. 'I was . . . er . . . just walking with Poppy to the corner and then I was coming home.'

'Well, I've saved you a walk then, haven't I?' Claire deliberately kept her voice light. 'Hop in and we can get off. I've packed you every-thing you'll need.'

Nikki reluctantly walked around the car and got into the passenger seat with a dull flush on her face as Claire smiled charmingly at Poppy. 'Goodbye then, Poppy. It was nice to meet you.'

Poppy inclined her head as Claire steered the car back out into the traffic and now Nikki snapped, 'There was no need to show me up like that. Poppy will think I'm a right cissy, having my mum meet me from school.'

'I had no intentions of showing you up,' Claire answered reason-ably. 'I just thought it would be nice if we could get off early enough to miss the worst of the traffic. You know what it's like on the M6. If we meet the rush-hour traffic it could take us hours to get there and Mrs M is cooking us a meal.'

Nikki slouched down in her seat with a frown on her face and her arms tightly crossed.

'Put your seat belt on,' Claire told her, and with a long exagger-ated sigh Nikki did as she was told before settling into a sulky silence.

It was almost three hours later when they finally pulled onto the track leading to Seagull's Flight. Nikki had had the radio blaring out all the way there and there was the beginning of a dull headache behind Claire's eyes. Even so she experienced a sense of coming home and her heart started to beat a little bit faster at the thought of seeing Christian again. The sandy track slowed the car down but then they turned a bend and some way ahead of them was Seagull's Flight nestling in the sand dunes with the sea sparkling in the late-afternoon sunshine beyond them.

From the long outhouse that housed the stray dogs they could hear barking and as they drew closer to the house they saw that the kitchen door was open. Mrs M suddenly appeared in it, wiping her hands on her apron, and when she saw the car cruising towards her,

her wrinkled old face lit in a smile and she hurried out into the yard to meet them.

'Claire, Nikki! Oh, loves, it's so good to see you. Come here an' let me look at you.' She had them both wrapped in her arms as Gemma scampered about her feet and now she stood back, and staring at Nikki she declared, 'Why, you seem to shoot up another foot every time I see you. At this rate you're going to be a nuisance to the aeroplanes. You could do with a bit more meat on you though. You're not on one of those silly diets, are you?'

Nikki frowned and looked away from her, but thankfully, Mrs M was bending to stroke Gemma now. 'Well, I can see I don't have to worry about you.' She chuckled. 'Look at you. No one would ever believe that when you were first brought here you were at death's door. You could be entered for Crufts now.'

She straightened back up with difficulty before telling them, 'Your dinner is all ready. Christian is just seeing to the last patient in the surgery but he should be done any time now. How was your journey?'

'A bit slow coming through Birmingham on the M6,' Claire told her. 'And then we hit some roadworks, but it wasn't too bad.'

They walked into the little house and as Claire looked around, a feeling of peace settled over her. She always felt safe here. It was like a sanctuary to her as well as the strays that ended up there.

'Shall I fetch the bags in?' Nikki asked.

Claire nodded gratefully. 'If you wouldn't mind, love.'

As the girl went back out to the car, Mrs M raised an eyebrow. 'Causing you a few problems, is she?'

Claire's face became solemn. 'Just a bit. But it's probably her age. Anyway, let's not talk about that now. How are you?'

'Oh, I suppose I shouldn't complain. I ain't no spring chicken, so I dare say I do well for me age, though Christian has had to get a kennel maid in to help out about the place. I'm afraid I'm not up to cleaning all the dog pens out any more. It's the bending that does me. She's a nice enough girl though. She's at university, so she works here part-time and we couldn't have found anyone better because she's training to be a vet.'

'Oh, she sounds ideal then.'

Nikki reappeared carrying two overnight bags and Mrs M nodded towards the stairs. 'Take 'em straight up, love. Your rooms are waitin' for you.'

As Nikki went to do as she was told for a change, Claire headed towards the door.

'I'll just pop into the surgery and let Christian know we're here and then I'll be back,' she promised. But once outside she turned first towards the tiny pet cemetery that nestled in the sand dunes where Cassidy, her old dog, was buried. She opened the gate that led through the little picket fence and soon came to his grave, which was marked with a small wooden cross with his name engraved on it, that Christian had carved.

She let the peace of the place wash over her as she pictured him in her mind. She had taken Cassidy in after he had been involved in a road accident when she had owned her hotel in Blackpool. His leg had been badly broken and by pure chance she had looked through the numbers of the vets and phoned Christian. Their relationship had gone from there. Until Claire met him she had never loved a man, apart from her father, who had let her down. And by the time she did meet him, she knew it was too late. Christian had fallen in love with the image she had created, of the wealthy orphan of well-to-do parents who had her own hotel, but deep down she knew that she was still Claire McMullen, the girl from a council house, a former prostitute, and she loved him too much to be less than honest with him, so instead she had married Greg Nightingale, a rich handsome man whom she imagined could give her the respectability she had always craved. And what a farce that had turned out to be! She was nothing more than a trophy to Greg; a younger woman to hang on his arm and show off to his colleagues. The only thing that had been worthwhile in their marriage was Nikki, who had inadvertently brought about the end of it when Claire had found Greg abusing her one night. Following his suicide, Claire had again contacted Christian when Cassidy became ill, and as soon as she set eyes on him again, she knew that she still loved him. It was then that she had given him her diaries to read so that he would understand who she really was. But the biggest shock had been when he came back after reading them and told her that he still loved her – that she had only been forced into the life she had led because of circumstance. Claire had known that she was being offered the only chance at happiness she might ever have, but she had also known that in the time ahead, Nikki would need her – and now she was being proven to be right. Nikki *did* need her now, although she didn't know it.

'Oh, Cassidy,' she whispered to the sand-swept grave, 'will I ever find peace?'

The sound of laughter made her turn and look towards the small surgery that was tacked on to the side of the house. Her heart skipped a beat as Christian appeared with a young woman following close behind him. She appeared to be in her early twenties and was tall and slim with long dark hair tied up in a ponytail.

Christian had a small dog in his arms and Claire watched as he carried it to the dog enclosure with the young woman at his side. Once they had disappeared inside the building she glanced once more at Cassidy's grave before walking to the edge of the little cemetery where she quietly closed the gate behind her.

She had almost reached the dog house, as Christian had nicknamed it, when he and the girl reappeared, and his face lit up more brightly than the sun in the sky above when he saw her.

'Claire!' Hurrying towards her, he took both her hands in his as she smiled up at him. He was so handsome that he made her feel weak at the knees. 'How are you?'

'I'm fine,' she told him.

They looked at each other for a long moment and then suddenly remembering his manners, Christian turned to the woman standing behind him and told Claire, 'This is Amanda Duncan. She's been helping out here for the last few months and she's been a godsend. Mandy, this is Claire.'

'How do you do, Amanda.' Claire politely shook the young woman's hand. Close up, she realised that she had somehow just missed being pretty. Her mouth was just a little too wide, and her face was covered in freckles, yet when she smiled, she was very attractive.

'Call me Mandy, please,' she told Claire. 'Amanda is too formal. It's so nice to meet you. Christian often talks about you.'

Claire felt herself warming to the girl. It would have been hard not to as she was so nice-natured and friendly.

'Well, I hope what he's been saying about me has been good,' she joked.

Mandy nodded, setting her long dark ponytail swishing around her shoulders as she patted the side of her nose.

'That would be telling,' she came back, but her eyes were twinkling and Claire knew that here was a young woman she could become friendly with if . . . if she hadn't been having so much to do with Christian.

Claire felt a little pang of jealousy and silently scolded herself. How could she feel jealous of someone she didn't even know? And yet she undeniably did. But then she knew that she would feel jealous of anyone who got to have regular contact with Christian, particularly someone like Mandy, who was undeniably a lovely person.

While these thoughts were racing through Claire's head, Mandy glanced at her watch and after rubbing her grubby hands down the side of her jeans she told Christian, 'I'm afraid I'm going to have to love you and leave you unless you need me for anything else? I have an assignment to finish that needs handing in at Uni by Monday, and if I don't get stuck into it soon I'm going to be up till the early hours.'

Love you and leave you. There it was again, that awful flood of jealousy. Claire was well aware that it was just an expression, so why, she wondered, did the words stab at her heart? Could it be that Christian and Mandy were becoming close? She found herself thinking back to Lianne, who Christian had been engaged to when she had first met him. Lianne had been stunningly pretty and always immaculately turned out. She had also been very career-minded and Claire had thought from the offset what an ill-matched pair they were. But Mandy was a different kettle of fish altogether. She obviously didn't mind getting her hands dirty and Claire could imagine her as the wife of a vet. The wife of *her* vet.

They were all walking towards Mandy's little car now. Christian had loosed Claire's hand and they were walking slightly apart, almost as if they were polite strangers.

'Right then, I'll see you tomorrow,' Mandy told them cheerily as she clambered into the car and with that and a final wave, she roared off up the drive, sending showers of sand in all directions.

'She seems very nice,' Claire commented innocently as she and Christian turned towards the house.

'Oh she is,' he answered without hesitation. 'I don't know how I would have managed without her these last few months. The practice is starting to get really busy now.'

His praise had come just a little too quickly for Claire's liking, and again she wondered if she had left it too late. Had Christian grown tired of waiting for her and transferred his affections to Mandy? She knew deep down that if he had, she had only herself to blame, but the knowing brought her no comfort whatsoever and she felt her spirits sink.

Chapter Fourteen

It was that curious time between day and night when the sky could not seem to decide which colour it should be. As Christian and Claire strolled along the beach with Gemma and some of the strays scampering ahead of them, the sun was sinking towards the sea. The sky was streaked with mauves and purples as if some unseen artist had used it as a great canvas, and the sea was calm. The beach was deserted and as Claire took deep breaths of the clean salty air, the stress she had felt for weeks slowly began to ebb away.

She sighed deeply, wishing this moment could go on for ever. Nothing seemed to matter here. There was nothing to fret or worry about. She supposed it was because Christian and Mrs M were the only two people in the whole world who knew who she really was. Since she had allowed them to read her diaries there had been no need to pretend in front of them. They had accepted her, had even swallowed the way she had earned her living on the streets of London, pointing out that as far as they were concerned, it had been through no fault of her own. Yet strangely, Claire still felt that in some way it was. That she was somehow to blame for it all. She shuddered now as the words the men had whispered in her ear when she was a child came back to her. *You made me do it, didn't you?* And after hearing this so often, she had come to believe it. After all, it hadn't happened to the other girls she had known, had it? So there must have been something she was doing that had caused it to happen.

She better than anyone knew that Greg would have probably whispered those exact same words to Nikki, which was why the girl was now putting up barriers as she struggled with her childhood having been snatched away from her, just as she herself had all those years ago.

Until she had met Christian, Claire's own barrier had been impenetrable, but he had managed to unlock the door to her heart and, could he have known it, he was still in sole possession of the key. Yet they seemed fated to be apart, for just as Claire was coming to terms with her own past, she now had Nikki's to contend with.

She had become so lost in thought that she started when his voice brought her sharply back to the present.

'So, how is Nikki behaving now then?'

'Oh, you know – up and down.' She flashed him a sad smile. 'She's changed so much over the last few months that sometimes I hardly recognise her. She's taken up with this girl from a nearby council estate and I have to say that since then, things have definitely taken a turn for the worse.'

'In what way?'

Claire looked at the waves lapping on the shore. 'Bunking off school, not coming in until all hours, drinking, smoking . . . Should I go on?'

'Sounds like you've got your hands full,' he said.

'You could say that.' She smiled ruefully at him again. 'Trouble is, I can hardly blame her, can I? If I were to be honest I'd have to admit that I was even worse at her age. But it isn't just that I'm struggling with at the moment. You see, my mum and dad have come back on the scene.'

His face mirrored his shock. 'But I thought your dad had hot-footed it back to Scotland when you were just a little girl?'

'He did, but apparently my mum is very ill in hospital and she sent for him. The biggest shock was the fact that he came, and believe it or not, he *still* cares for her. Don't you think that's incredible, after all the years they've been apart? I do, and I have to say I'm finding it hard to accept the fact that he can forgive her.'

Christian stared thoughtfully off across the dancing waves before saying, 'Bitterness is a terrible thing, Claire. If you allow it to, it will eat you away. You say your mum is very ill, but exactly *how* ill is that?'

'She's dying,' Claire told him flatly. 'She's got lung cancer and according to my dad, her days are numbered.'

'Then I can understand why he would want to make his peace with her. He has to live with himself after she's gone, and no matter how they feel about each other now, or what went on in the past, once they must have loved each other. Have you been to see her?'

'No, but I did meet my dad briefly. It was . . . well, very strange and a little fraught, as you can imagine. He says he's sorry for leaving us now, but saying sorry can't change things, can it? If he hadn't gone, then things might have been so very different.'

'You're quite right – I've no doubt at all they would have been. But you know, Gran is a great believer that everything happens for a reason. If you hadn't suffered, you would probably never have met Greg and Nikki. You would have had no idea what she is going through now, you wouldn't have been able to help her, and you probably wouldn't have met me either.'

Claire pondered on his words. She had certainly never thought of it like that before, but now she could see the sense in what he said.

'So, are you saying that you think I ought to go and see her then?'

Christian shrugged. 'I'm not telling you what to do one way or another. You must do what you feel is right. But I know what *I* would do. If she's as ill as you say she is, then time is running out – and if you don't go, you'll have to live with that fact for the rest of your life.'

Claire came to a standstill as a picture of her mother's face flashed in front of her eyes. She certainly had a lot of thinking to do, and what better place to do it than here where she felt released from the pressure Nikki was putting her under? She moved on, resisting the urge to take

Christian's hand. She knew that she still had a long way to go before she could commit to him. If she hadn't already left it too late, that was.

'Ah, there you are,' Mrs M greeted them when they returned to the house an hour later. They had just settled the dogs down for the night and were feeling tired and pleasantly relaxed. Mrs M and Nikki were playing cards at the table and without the heavy make-up she had taken to wearing, Nikki looked her true age and happier than she had for some time.

'I'm winning hands down,' Nikki boasted as she dealt the cards for another game of crib.

'You're probably cheating,' Claire teased her and Nikki laughed.

'No, I am not, am I, Gran?'

'Not at all,' Mrs M replied good-naturedly. 'You're winnin' fair an' square from what I can see of it.'

Christian settled in the chair and stretched his legs out with a sigh of pleasure. It had been a long day and now he was tired, though he didn't want to go to bed and miss being with Claire and Nikki. They saw each other so infrequently that he was determined to make the most of their time together. Ten minutes later, as Claire carried a tray of cocoa and biscuits to the table, Mrs M gathered the cards together and placed them to the side with a huge yawn.

'Lordy, I'm so tired I could fall asleep on a clothes-horse,' she declared as she lifted a mug from the tray.

When Nikki yawned too, Mrs M playfully poked her in the ribs. 'There you are, you see. You're yawning too now. They say as it's catching.'

'I'd rather say it's something to do with the air here,' Claire quipped. 'I often wish we could bottle it. We'd all end up millionaires if we could.'

'Well, whatever. I'm going to watch *The Bill* and then I'm off to me bed.'

She turned the television on and they all settled down to watch it. Claire was feeling more contented than she could remember feeling for a long time. As she looked around the room it occurred to her that anyone looking in from the outside would take them for a family. But then she thought of Mandy and a frown flitted across her face. She wanted to hate her for the simple fact that the young woman got to see far more of Christian than she did, but she found that she couldn't. Mandy was too likeable and looked completely at home at Seagull's Flight. She obviously knew her way around the place like the back of her hand and she was studying to be a vet into the bargain. What a wonderful match she would be for Christian. In Mandy he would find someone who would share his love of animals. Someone who would not be afraid to work alongside him at ungodly hours and who wasn't afraid of getting her hands dirty.

Claire pushed the worrying thoughts away. She was here for such a short time that she didn't want to spoil a second of it.

Nikki retired to bed an hour after Mrs M, and Christian and Claire finally found themselves alone. Christian was pretending to read the newspaper as Claire sat at the side of the open back door and stared out into the balmy starlit night. Eventually he put the newspaper down and asked, 'Would you like to go out for a while? We could perhaps go and have a drink or something?'

'Thanks, but no. I'm quite happy here. I can't tell you how nice it is not to be sitting in alone worrying what time Nikki is going to roll in.'

'Things as bad as that, are they?'

She nodded glumly. 'Sometimes I think she really hates me,' she told him, and when he went to answer she stopped him by saying, 'It's true. She's totally obsessed with this new friend she's made. I have an awful feeling that she's having a bad influence on her. The other day I thought . . . well, I thought I smelled cannabis in her bedroom. I didn't find any, thank goodness, but I'd stake my life I'm right.'

'Good grief!' Christian looked suitably horrified now. 'You mentioned on the phone the last time we spoke that you were going to bring in Social Services to help. Did you?'

'Yes, I did. But it wasn't entirely successful. Nikki has to be eighteen before she can start to trace her real mum, so the social worker offered to do a life story book with her. Nikki refused, of course.'

When he raised a quizzical eyebrow, Claire explained what it was and he fell silent for a time as he thought about it before suggesting tentatively, 'Have you thought about moving house? Somewhere far enough away to keep Nikki unable to see this new friend of hers?'

'Yes, I have,' she admitted, 'but the problem with that is her schooling. I don't really want to move her from Claremont. Another change right now before GCSEs might just make things worse.'

'Mm, I see what you mean.' He cleared his throat before asking tentatively, 'And what about you, Claire? You went away to put your own feelings into some sort of order. How are things with Tracey, and Molly and Tom?'

He saw the sadness in her eyes before she lowered them. 'Well, Molly and Tom have been wonderful. They've eventually welcomed me back into the fold as if I've never been away. But I think it's going to take Tracey a little longer to forgive me. She's very civil when we see each other, but . . . cold.'

'I see. And have you told her everything? All that you went through in the years you were apart?'

'I . . . no, I haven't.'

'So . . . you are still living a lie then?'

The disappointment in his voice cut through her like a knife. And it was true – she was still maintaining the image she presented to the world. And now, here she was trying to keep Nikki away from Poppy because the girl came from a council estate when she herself had been brought up on one!

'I will do it,' she assured him. 'It's just choosing the right time. With Nikki feeling as she is, it doesn't seem right.'

'It will never seem right, Claire. Not while you keep using Nikki as an excuse.'

'And just what is that supposed to mean?'

'I don't think you need me to tell you that. Time is rushing by.' His eyes held hers and she was shocked to see the hurt there. 'While you are supposedly helping Nikki to face her problems, you can pretend that you haven't time to deal with your own. Isn't that true?'

Colour had stained Claire's cheeks and her voice rose. 'How could you say such a thing to me?'

He shrugged as he rose from his chair and headed towards the stairs door. 'I can say it because I thought you cared for me – that we would be together by now. Obviously I was wrong though. And now if you'll excuse me, I'm suddenly feeling rather tired so I'm off to bed. Goodnight, Claire.'

'*Christian.*' She watched his broad back as he walked away from her without looking back; heard his footsteps on the stairs, and then she sank heavily down at the table. Was Christian trying to tell her that it was over between them? That he was tired of waiting? It was no more than she had expected, but the pain was overwhelming. She had blown it big time. A picture of Mandy's smiling face flashed in front of her eyes and the pain inside deepened. Perhaps Mandy was the reason he wanted to end it – not that she could blame him.

The ringing of her mobile phone made her wipe her hands across her wet cheeks and sniff as she hurried across to her handbag.

'Hello.' Her hand was shaking but her voice when she answered it was calm. Over the years, Claire had become a master at hiding her true feelings.

'Oh Claire, I'm so glad I've got through to you, love.'

'*Molly!* What's wrong?'

'It's your mother.' Molly was almost gabbling in her panic. 'She's right bad. Tracey went to see her tonight in hospital and she was asking for you again. They reckon it could be anytime now. I thought I ought to let you know.'

'I see.' The pain seeped away and Claire felt empty. She knew that she should be feeling something, but it was as if someone had turned a tap on and drained all the emotions out of her.

'So will you be coming or what then? Your father asked me to ask you. He's at the hospital with her now.'

'I ... er ... the thing is, Nikki is already in bed,' Claire babbled. 'Let me think about it, Molly. If I do decide to come I'll be there sometime in the morning.'

She could almost feel the disapproval travelling along the phone line and now Molly's voice was quiet as she said, 'Don't think about it for too long, will you? And just remember, you only ever get one real mother. No matter what she's done, she's still your mother, and she wants to make her peace with you before she goes to meet her Maker. It's my belief that everyone deserves a second chance. Just think on that while you're making your decision.' With that the phone went dead in Claire's hand and she stared at it in stunned disbelief.

Molly had been her backbone since she and Nikki had arrived back in the Midlands, yet during the conversation they had just had, Claire had got the feeling that her former foster-mother was disgusted with her. But why should she be? Molly had seen first-hand what Karen had done to her and Tracey. Had seen how callous Karen could be – how she had abandoned her two young daughters without so much as a second thought.

Dropping the phone back into her bag, Claire crossed to the open back door where she stood staring sightlessly out across the sand dunes with her arms hugging her chest. Why did life always have to be so complicated? Each time she thought she had got it back on track, something seemed to happen to send it awry again.

Her eyes were drawn to the little pet cemetery and just for an instant she could have sworn she saw a little dog rolling in the sand; a little dog with three legs and huge soulful brown eyes. She blinked and the vision was gone as she scolded herself. One of these days her imagination would be the death of her.

Turning about, she took a notepad and a pen from her bag. She had reached her decision. She would go and wake Nikki; they were going home. The weekend had not got off to a good start anyway, so Christian would probably be relieved when he got up in the morning to find them gone. She scribbled hastily and propped the note against the sugar bowl that was standing in the middle of the table. Her eyes then dropped to the hearthrug in front of the empty grate and now the pain she felt was indescribable. It was there, on that very rug, that she had once given herself to Christian, and even now, all these years on, she could remember every detail of their coming together as if it were yesterday. That had been the one and only time in the whole of her life that she had given herself to a man willingly. The only time that she had ever allowed a man to kiss her on the lips. There had been a fire licking up the chimney and snow clinging to the window-panes. And just for that short time, she had felt clean and good – a feeling she had never felt before or since. Tears slid down her cheeks as she looked about the familiar room. She had the strangest feeling that once she left it tonight, she would never see it again – or Christian for that matter.

Chapter Fifteen

'How much longer now till we get home?' Nikki grumbled. She had scarcely stopped moaning since the second they drove away from Seagull's Flight and now Claire's nerves were almost at breaking-point. Thankfully, the M6 was quiet so they were making the return journey in record time.

'We should be home within an hour,' Claire told the irate teenager, struggling to keep her voice calm. 'So why don't you curl up and go to sleep? We'll be back before you know it.'

Nikki snorted with disgust. She could see no reason at all why they had had to leave so suddenly, particularly as she hadn't wanted to come in the first place. Surely they could have set off in the morning? But Claire had practically dragged her out of bed despite her loud protests.

'What are Christian and Mrs M going to think when they get up to find we've done a disappearing trick?' she had complained.

'Don't worry about that, I've left them a note,' Claire had told her.

'Well, why can't we go in the morning? Why do we have to go now?'

Claire had begun to lose her patience at that stage as she snapped, 'We have to go now because I say so. Now get a move on. At the rate you're going it will be morning before we get off anyway!'

And so they had driven away and Nikki had whined constantly ever since. Now she sighed dramatically as she tried to get comfortable in the seat, but thankfully within minutes she had dropped off and Claire could finally try to put her thoughts into some sort of order.

Already she was beginning to wonder if she had done the right thing, shooting off like that. But it was too late to worry about it now. They were over halfway home and she was not going to turn around now.

As her thoughts moved back to the phone call she had received from Molly, she bit down on her lip. If what Molly had told her was true, her mother was very close to death. She knew deep down that she had only gone to Seagull's Flight to delay a decision on whether or not she should go to see her, but now the time for delaying was over. Time was running out. What was it Christian had said? *If you don't go, you'll have to live with that fact for the rest of your life.*

And Molly: *It's my belief that everyone deserves a second chance.*

A second chance. The words bounced round and round in Claire's head. Perhaps she should go to the hospital, if only to put her own conscience at rest.

They were back at home and as Claire carried Gemma into the house, Nikki followed, bleary-eyed and moody.

'I'm going to bed,' she declared petulantly as she swept past Claire and made for the staircase. 'Some weekend this has turned out to be!'

Claire watched her disappear into her bedroom and after carrying the bags in she tapped softly at Nikki's door and told her, 'I'm going into Nuneaton. I'll be back by the time you get up in the morning.'

Nothing except a grunt as Nikki burrowed under the duvet. Claire glanced at her watch. It was gone one o'clock in the morning. Would the hospital let her in at such an ungodly hour? She supposed there was only one way to find out, so she made her way back out to the car wondering if this long night was ever going to end.

The car park of the George Eliot Hospital was almost deserted when she pulled up and now her courage was beginning to fail her. Perhaps she should have waited until the morning, after all. But then, she was here now and it seemed silly to drive all the way back to Solihull without at least trying to see her mother. If the worst came to the worst, and the staff on the ward turned her away, at least she could say in truth that she had been.

She followed the arrows pointing to Dorothea Ward and with each step she took, a feeling of resentment grew inside her. What the hell was she doing here anyway? Her mother didn't deserve to have people running around after her, after the way she had treated Tracey and herself. The entrance to the ward was in sight now and she began to waver as her footsteps slowed. Perhaps she should just turn around and go home . . .

'Claire.'

The sound of the voice seemed to echo in the empty corridor and when Claire swung round she was surprised to see Tracey walking towards her.

'I didn't think you'd come. Molly told me you'd taken Nikki away for the weekend.'

'I had.' Claire could see that her sister had been crying. 'But when Molly told me that Mam was really bad, I drove straight back.'

The two sisters surveyed each other solemnly, and then to Claire's surprise and delight, Tracey suddenly launched herself at her and wrapped her arms around her. It was the first physical contact that they had had since Claire had returned to the Midlands and she was deeply touched.

'Just how bad is she?' she asked as Tracey sniffled on her shoulder.

'It could be any time now. Dad's been in with her all night and I'd just popped out to use the loo . . . I'm glad you came, Claire. It will mean a lot to her.'

Claire nodded. 'Shall we go in then?'

After disentangling herself from Claire's arms, Tracey pushed the double swing doors open and led the way.

They crept through a ward full of sleeping patients, some of whom were snoring softly in the dim glow of the night lights. Everywhere was uncannily quiet and Claire found that she was almost afraid to breathe. At the other end of the ward were two private rooms and it was in front of one of these that Tracey eventually stopped. She smiled at Claire reassuringly before gently pushing the door open, and Claire followed her in with her heart in her mouth. The first thing she saw was her father. He was sitting at the side of a bed, and when he turned to look at her she was sure that she had never seen so much raw pain in anyone's eyes before. Now as they settled on Claire they filled with tears and he rose hastily to greet her.

'Ah, lass. I knew deep down you'd come.'

She gulped, deliberately keeping her eyes averted from the figure on the bed. But now he was stepping away and she had no choice but to look. What she saw caused her hand to fly to her mouth to stop the cry of disbelief that had risen in her throat.

'*Aw, Mam!*' This poor pathetic wreck of a woman was nothing at all like the woman she had remembered and hated for so many years. Her mother seemed to have shrunk to half her size, and the thick hair that Claire remembered had been replaced by thin tufts of grey that now surrounded the once-pretty face.

At the sound of her voice, the woman's eyes fluttered open and as they settled on Claire a look of wonder crossed her face.

'Claire? Is it really you?' Even the once vibrant voice came out as little more than a whisper.

Claire felt as if she had been rooted to the spot, but her father's gentle hand in the small of her back sent her stumbling forward.

'Yes, it's me . . . Mam.'

Tears began to roll down the woman's cheeks and find their way past the oxygen tubes that were inserted into her nostrils. She lifted her hand and Claire haltingly took it.

'I . . . I didn't think you'd come. Wouldn't have blamed you if you hadn't.' A coughing fit seized her and Claire could only look on in distress until it had passed. A nurse who was standing discreetly in the corner of the room stepped forward and tenderly wiped the sweat from Karen's face, before stepping back into the shadows again.

Claire had hated this woman for many years; blamed her for every single bad thing that had ever happened to her. But now as she looked down on her suffering, the hatred finally slipped away, to be replaced by pity. Karen's mouth was working but for a while no sounds were forthcoming until she squeezed Claire's hand and with a superhuman effort told her, 'You . . . you've grown into a beauty. I always knew you would.'

Claire could think of no reply so she remained silent. Karen's eyelids were fluttering and Claire thought that she was going to go back to sleep, but then they suddenly blinked open again and the grip on her hand became urgent as Karen pleaded, 'Say you forgive me, Claire. I know I don't deserve it. I've been a selfish cow all me life. I should have kept you safe . . . but I were lonely, you see?'

Claire bit down hard on her lip as a dam opened up inside her and then suddenly the tears were spurting from her eyes. Karen was staring up at her, and as they looked deep into each other's eyes, Claire told her, 'I forgive you, Mum.'

Karen seemed to sink into her pillows as a look of pure pleasure passed across her face.

'Thank you.' The eyes fluttered shut again for what was to be the very last time, and now Claire cried as she had not cried for many long years. Robbie stepped forward and put his arms about her as she sobbed on his shoulder. And then they all sat down at Karen's bedside.

Karen McMullen died peacefully at four o'clock in the morning without regaining consciousness and with her family gathered about her, which had been her final wish and more than she had dared to hope for.

Chapter Sixteen

Eddie Miller ground his cigarette out in the ashtray and cleared his throat nervously as he stared from the window of his council house.

'What's wrong with you?' Roxy demanded. 'You're like a cat on hot bricks.'

'The boss is sending some stuff over. It should be here any minute.'

Roxy frowned. *Stuff* usually meant drugs, which would mean she would live on tenterhooks until Eddie had got rid of it all again. She had no objection to cannabis, in fact she was partial to the odd spliff herself, but she knew that lately Eddie had been handling the stronger stuff, and it worried her. Not least because she was aware that he had been sampling the goods and was already in the boss's bad books. Only the night before, she had walked into the kitchen to find him snorting a line and she had gone mad at him.

'What if our Katie had walked in and caught you at it?' she had cried indignantly. 'And how are yer ever supposed to pay back what you owe him if yer keep snortin' it yourself?'

'Shut your fuckin' mouth, woman, an' keep your nose out o' what don't concern you. I pays the rent an' keeps food on the table, don't I?'

Roxy had looked around their small council house and sighed heavily. Yes, he did pay the rent, when he had got it. But over the years he must have earned a small fortune with his wheeling and dealing and yet here they still were, living in a council house. Had he looked after his money, instead of spending most of it on the dogs and gambling, she had no doubt that they could have been living over in Lovelace Lane where Nikki lived by now. As she thought of the girl, her eyes grew sad. She hated to say it but she felt that the lass was too good to be hanging around with the likes of their Poppy. Much as she loved her, Poppy was her father's daughter through and through. Money slipped through her fingers like water, and her only ambition in life was to make sure where the next spliff and the next night out were coming from. The boys were no better. They were already following in their father's footsteps and had their fingers into all sorts of pies. Neither of them had done an honest day's work since they had left school, and she doubted now that they ever would. She supposed this was why she was so protective of Katie. Because she was severely autistic, she would be an eternal baby. She would never be able to go off the rails and would always need Roxy to look out for her. Instead of finding this prospect daunting, Roxy found it kept her going, gave her a purpose in life.

As Eddie's wife, she was respected on the estate, which was one of the reasons she stayed with him. No one crossed Eddie Miller without living to regret it. At one time she had thrived on the fact, but lately she was looking at her husband differently. Seeing him as he really was: a villain who made a living out of other people's misfortunes. Not so long back, a family in Greaves Road had hit hard times and had come to borrow money from him. The father had fallen from scaffolding at work and was unable to pay their rent. Eddie had lent him several hundred pounds, courtesy of this invisible boss of his, but the man's injuries had turned out to be worse than what they had thought and he was unable to pay it back plus the exorbitant interest rates at the agreed time. Roxy had asked Eddie to go easy on him. But the next thing, she heard the man's teenage son had met with a little 'accident'. Both his legs had been broken in a mugging in a dark alley. Roxy had known without doubt who had instigated this and the knowledge had sickened her. Eddie only had to say the word and there were heavies who were only too happy to dance to his tune. Since then she had regarded him, and her life, with dismay. She was no longer a young woman and now she felt that she had nothing to look forward to. She had always known that Eddie was a womaniser. She had lost count of the times he had come home smelling of the scent of another woman. At one time she had swallowed it, grateful for the fact that he always came home to *her*. But lately, she didn't care if he stayed out all night – if he didn't come home at all, in fact.

She looked at him now, lighting one cigarette after another as he nervously stared from the window. In all the years she had been with him, he had never confided to her who this mysterious boss of his was. She had a pretty good idea the boss was a bent copper. It stood to reason, otherwise how would they have avoided being raided as many of their neighbours constantly were?

She saw him start and hurry from the room without a word and she now crossed to the window and peeped past the grimy net curtain. A shining Mercedes was parked at the kerb but she couldn't see who was inside it due to a combination of the darkness outside and the tinted windows.

Shrugging her shoulders, she switched the telly on and soon she was so intent on watching *Holby City* that Eddie was all but forgotten about.

'Cheers.' Eddie took the small bag from the man and pushed it deep into his coat pocket before asking, 'Anything else?'

The well-built man nodded as he leaned over the steering wheel, his eyes straight ahead. 'The boss wanted me to pass on a message.'

'Oh yes?'

'Seems he's got his eye on one of your daughter's little mates. You know what the boss is like. He wants 'em young an' pretty – in fact, the younger the better. He saw her goin' into the house one evenin' by all accounts, an' now he wants you to arrange for her to meet him at the usual hotel.'

Eddie scratched his head in bewilderment. His daughter's mate?

Poppy had got loads of mates, so how was he supposed to know which one the boss had his eye on?

'Can't you be a bit more specific? Poppy's always got mates in and out.'

'Tall, slim, about fourteen – blond hair and blue eyes.'

Eddie's heart skipped a beat. He must be on about Nikki, the posh kid that Poppy had taken up with from the swanky side of town.

'An' what would be in it for me?'

The man laughed into the darkness, an ugly sound that made the hairs on the back of Eddie's neck stand to attention.

'You're hardly in a fuckin' position to ask that, Eddie. The boss is gettin' a bit tired of waitin' for what you owe him, so if I were you I'd just try an' keep in his good books. Know what I mean?'

Eddie gulped and nodded quickly. 'Point taken, mate. Tell him to leave it wi' me an' I'll see what I can do.'

He slid across the seat, the smell of the new leather upholstery sharp in his nostrils. Once on the pavement he ran his fingers distractedly through his hair as the car purred away from the kerb. From where he was standing he was really in Shit Street now. For some reason, Roxy had taken to this kid big time, and if she were to find out what he had in mind, she'd lynch him. He could see why the boss was attracted to the girl though. She was a pretty little thing – a bit skinny for his taste, but then each to his own. He glanced towards the house then quickly began to stride away down the road. First things first. There were people waiting for the coke he had tucked in his pocket, so he would get that delivered and then worry about how he was going to manipulate the kid the boss had his eye on. He might even keep a bit of the coke back for himself. He imagined the rush he would get as he snorted it, the bitter taste as it hit the back of his throat before the feel-good factor set in.

Robbie, Tracey and Claire stood shoulder to shoulder as Karen's coffin was carried into the crematorium in Eastboro Way in Nuneaton. Robbie had seen to all the arrangements and as Claire looked towards the heavy, brass-trimmed casket, she saw that he had spared no expense.

He had even chosen the hymns and now as the pallbearers laid the coffin down they lifted their hymn books and began to sing.

There were pathetically few mourners. Apart from themselves, only Molly and Tom had taken the trouble to attend. Claire supposed it wasn't surprising really. Her mother had never gone out of her way to make friends, apart from men friends that was, and this was reflected today.

As the vicar intoned the words of the funeral service, Tracey began to cry quietly and Claire placed her arm protectively about her younger sister's shoulders. That was one good thing that had come out of their mam's death. At least Tracey was being a little kinder towards her now. She peeped out of the corner of her eye and saw that her dad was crying too.

Strangely, she found that she herself was dry-eyed. She had cried all her tears on the night her mother had died. She was only here today for Tracey's sake and to pay her last respects. The service droned on and on and then suddenly the curtains were closing, and she gazed at the box containing her mother's remains for one last time. For long years she had wished her dead, wished that she would rot in hell. But now she hoped that if there was a heaven, her mother would find her way there. She had made her peace with her at last and no good could come of wishing her bad things now. Another chapter of her life was about to close.

The small posse of mourners trooped from the church and as black smoke began to belch from the cemetery chimney, Claire averted her eyes. It was done.

'Why don't you all come back to our place for a cup of tea?' Molly suggested kindly.

Claire shook her head, 'Thanks, Molly. I'd love to but Nikki will be in from school soon. I had a real job to get her there today. She wanted to come to the funeral but I didn't think it was appropriate so I ought to be back for when she gets home.'

'What about you, Tracey?'

She too shook her head as she wiped the tears from her cheeks. 'I have to get home as well,' she said apologetically. 'Callum is looking after the twins but he has to go into work later this afternoon and I don't want to make him late.'

Claire turned to her father now and was shocked when she heard herself saying, 'Why don't you follow me back home, Dad? You could stay for a bit of dinner and it would give you a chance to meet Nikki.'

Robbie's cheeks started to glow and he smiled. This was the first time Claire had invited him to her house and he saw it as a major step forward.

Molly beamed her approval as she steered Tom in the direction of their car. 'Right. We'd better be making a move too then. We've got our Billy's little one this afternoon after school.'

They all said their goodbyes and now Claire asked her father self-consciously, 'Would you like to follow me in your car then?' Already she was beginning to wonder why she had asked him, but it was too late to do anything about it now.

Swallowing the lump in his throat, he nodded vigorously as Claire climbed into her car and waited for him to pull up behind her before setting off.

She was standing outside the door of her home as he got out of his car and walked towards her. He stared in awe at the leaded windows, glinting in the sunshine and told her, 'You've done well for yourself, lass. I'm glad.'

She led him into the hall and through to the kitchen where she put the kettle on as he stared around.

'Your husband must have left you very well provided for.'

Claire flushed. 'He did, but I was actually very comfortably off before I met him. I owned my own hotel in Blackpool.'

'Oh.' Robbie looked suitably impressed. This was the first chance he and Claire had had to talk properly since their first meeting, and he felt ashamed. She had gone through so much and he hadn't been there to help her. There were so many questions he wanted to ask, but Robbie was a very astute man and didn't want to push his luck. Claire seemed to be a very independent young woman and now that he had found her again he didn't want anything to spoil it, so he held his tongue. There would hopefully be time for personal questions when their relationship was on a more even keel.

It was actually Claire who now asked him, 'So what will you do now? Go back to Scotland?'

'I'm not sure yet,' he answered, avoiding her eyes. 'I'd quite like to stay around for a while, if you and Tracey felt all right about it.'

With an imperceptible shrug of her shoulders she looked back at him. 'It isn't really up to me or Tracey, is it?'

He could feel her keeping him at a distance and knew that he would have to work very hard to win back her trust. He had deserted them both, after all.

It was then that they heard the slamming of the front door and seconds later, Nikki breezed into the room. She stared at Robbie curiously as she slung her schoolbag onto a chair before looking towards Claire and asking, 'So how did the funeral go?'

'Oh, about as well as you could expect,' Claire told her, then looking somewhat embarrassed she went on, 'I've someone here I'd like you to meet, Nikki. This is my father. Dad, this is Nikki.'

They approached each other and solemnly shook hands. Nikki was surprised to see that Claire didn't look anything at all like Robbie, and supposed she must have taken after her mum.

'Hello.'

'Hello, Nikki.'

Nikki decided that she liked him. He had kind eyes, though they looked sad at the minute. Nikki thought this quite strange. Admittedly he had just come back from his wife's funeral, but from what Claire had told her, they had been apart for years. The way she saw it, if he had loved her that much he wouldn't have left her in the first place.

Turning her attention back to Claire she now asked, 'How long is dinner going to be?'

'About an hour. But why the rush?' Claire answered.

'I'm going out,' Nikki informed her. 'And before you start to nag, don't worry, I'll do my homework first.' With that she flounced out of the room with Gemma close on her heels as Robbie grinned.

'Teenagers, eh? They seem to have an answer for everything.'

Claire swallowed the hasty retort that sprang to her lips. Seeing as how he had left her and Tracey when they were still very small, she wondered what had made him such an expert on teenagers. He certainly hadn't practised his parenting skills on them. She realised then that she still felt very bitter towards him. But it was early days and she could only hope that her feelings towards him would soften with time. Sighing softly, she turned her attention to peeling the vegetables for dinner.

A silence settled between them until he suddenly said, 'Nikki is a lovely young girl, Claire, and so like you. No one would believe that she was your adopted daughter. You must be very proud of her.'

Claire nodded as she dropped another carrot into the saucepan. 'Yes, I am proud of her and you're not the first to remark on how alike we are.'

He cleared his throat before asking tentatively, 'Were you and your husband planning to have any more children before he . . .' His voice trailed away as he realised how tactless the question had been.

Claire swallowed the painful lump that rose to her throat before telling him, 'Actually I had a little boy, William. He died shortly after his birth.'

Feeling her pain, Robbie wished that he could bite his tongue out. Trust him to go and put his big foot in it. There were so many things that he wanted to ask, so many things that he wanted to say, but it was too soon yet.

'I . . . I'm so sorry.' The words sounded inadequate even to his own ears but they were all he could think of to say.

Sensing his embarrassment she smiled sadly. 'It's all right. You weren't to know.' This was the perfect time to tell him of all that had happened.

Of the circumstances that had led up to William's death, but as always they stayed trapped in her throat. She silently cursed herself, knowing that until she could talk of it she would never start to heal. And so the silence settled between them again as Claire relived the few precious moments she had shared with her lovely baby boy, and her heart broke all over again.

'So how do you think it went then?' Molly asked on the journey back to Howard Road in Nuneaton.

'As well as these things can do,' her husband answered wisely.

'Mm.' Molly stared thoughtfully off into space. 'Do you think Robbie will be able to win the girls back?'

'I certainly think he stands a chance with Tracey, but I think Claire will take a little longer to accept him.'

She nodded in agreement then went on, 'You know, whenever I see Claire I always get the feeling that she isn't quite what she appears to be.'

Tom laughed. 'Oh yes, and what makes you think that?'

'The look in her eyes,' Molly answered promptly. 'That look was there when she was a girl. A sort of haunted look that never goes away. As if she's got something deep down that is troubling her.'

'Oh Molly, you and that imagination of yours.' Tom squeezed her hand briefly. 'Aren't you forgetting that she lost her husband? You don't get over something like that overnight, you know.'

'Yes, I do know, but I think it goes deeper than that,' Molly insisted. 'Haven't you noticed that she rarely talks about him? Nor does Nikki, for that matter.'

'Perhaps that's because they find it too painful?' Tom suggested.

Molly shook her head. 'No. There's something else that neither of them are telling us. I could read Claire like a book when she came to live with us and I still can. You just mark my words; everything isn't quite as it appears in that house!'

'Well, we'll see. Best let sleeping dogs lie for now, eh?' Tom was desperate to change the subject before Molly got on her high horse.

If she did, she would no doubt rattle his ear off all the way home and he was hoping for a bit of peace and quiet.

'Have it your own way then.' She hitched her breasts up, a sure sign that she was annoyed. 'But one of these days you'll tell me I was right – just you wait and see.'

Chapter Seventeen

'Why don't you just pick the phone up and ring her and be done wi' it? I don't know how much longer I can stand you mopin' round the place.'

Christian glared at Mrs M. 'And why would I want to do that?'

'Much as I hate to say it, it's as obvious as the nose on your face, lad. Claire left so suddenly because she wanted to go and make her peace wi' her mum before she passed away. That is, unless there's something else as you're not telling me? You didn't have a row, did you?'

Christian had the grace to flush as he stared out of the window at Mandy who was just emerging from the dog enclosure.

'Well, not a row exactly,' he muttered, shamefaced. 'I suppose things did get a bit heated though. I told her she was using Nikki as an excuse for not facing up to her own past.'

'You told her *what!*' Mrs M was horrified and it showed. And now she began to carry the pots from the table and slam them into the bowl of hot soapy water in the sink as she shook her head in disbelief. 'Whatever possessed you to say that to her? Claire's been through a lot and she should be allowed to recover from it in her own time.'

'I realise that now,' he admitted. 'But I can't take it back, can I?'

'No, you can't. But you *can* ring her and tell her you're sorry. What with Nikki playing up, her dad turning up out of the blue like that, and then her mam dying, the poor love mustn't know if she's on her arse or her elbow. I can't think what came over you.'

'I suppose I'm fed up of waiting,' he said soberly and now her heart went out to him. She had hoped to see her grandson and Claire married and settled by now, but it still seemed to be a long way from happening – if it ever did; and lately she was beginning to question that.

Deep down she knew that Christian had a point. Claire doted on Nikki and would never do a thing to harm a single hair on her head, even if it meant putting her own life on hold. She followed his eyes to where Mandy was now bending down, stroking one of the dogs in the yard. Mandy was a lovely girl. Since she had come to work at Seagull's Flight she had gone a long way to cheering Christian up. No one could stay miserable around Mandy for long. Her bright smile and sunny personality saw to that. There were no airs and graces about the lass – she had been raised on a farm in Yorkshire by a Scottish father and an English mother who doted on her and her siblings, and it showed. She now shared a small two-bed flat in Blackpool with another girl who was attending university with her.

'Don't look so glum, lad,' Mrs M said, patting his arm lovingly. 'Things have a way of working out in the end.'

He nodded glumly – but she knew he didn't believe a word of it.

'Hiya, Nikki. Come in.'

Poppy held the door wide and Nikki stepped past her into the hallway. Once again it was clutter-free and as Poppy saw her looking around, she chuckled. 'I reckon me mam's gone looney,' she confided as she cocked her head towards the lounge door. 'She's gone off on this cleanin' binge. It's drivin' me bleedin' mad, between you an' me. You get yer head snapped off if you so much as leave a thing lyin' about nowadays.'

She started to blow on her nails, which she had just painted a deep shade of purple as Nikki followed her into the kitchen.

'So, how's things at home then?'

Nikki raised an eyebrow. 'Well, you're not going to believe this but my mum went to her mother's funeral and came back with her dad in tow. He was still there when I left just now.'

'Bloody 'ell. How's that for a turn-up for the book then, eh? An' yer say he left her when she were nowt but a kid. I wonder what he wants now then?'

'Actually, he seems really nice.' Nikki pulled a chair out and joined her at the table. The air was heavy with the distinct smell of cannabis and Poppy gestured towards a spliff that was resting in an ashtray.

'You can finish that off, if yer like,' she said, and needing no second telling, Nikki lifted it and toked on it deeply, smiling at the warm feeling it created as she sucked it into her lungs.

Poppy leaned towards her and whispered, 'Me dad's got some stronger gear in at the minute an' I know where it is. Do yer fancy tryin' a bit?'

Nikki looked back at her indecisively before asking, 'What stuff is it?'

'Coke. Yer sniff it an' if you think that spliff is good, just wait till you've tried this. It blows you away. So what do yer say?'

Nikki would have died rather than look like a chicken in front of Poppy, so she smiled tremulously. 'I suppose trying it couldn't hurt.'

Poppy disappeared, only to return minutes later with a tiny plastic bag full of white powder. She then smoothed out a small sheet of kitchen foil and tipped some of the powder onto it before dividing it into three neat lines.

'Right, shall I go first?'

When Nikki nodded, she told her, 'Now watch me, OK?' Pressing one nostril flat with her finger, she leaned down close to the powder and sniffed it straight up the other nostril in one clean sweep. She then stood up and swiped the loose powder from her top lip before telling Nikki, 'Now you try.'

Nikki leaned towards the powder and did as she was told, then gagged as the powder hit the back of her throat. But by the time she had straightened up, the bitter taste had all but gone and she felt a strange kind of warmth creeping through her. Poppy had been right, this stuff was even better than the spliffs she was getting so fond of.

169

Within minutes she felt as if she could have flown, and nothing and no one seemed to matter any more.

When Roxy entered the room some minutes later her eyes went straight to the neat white line of coke that remained on the kitchen foil.

'Poppy, for fuck's sake tell me you ain't let Nikki have none o' that!' she said in horror.

When her daughter answered her with a silly grin, Roxy slapped her forehead with the flat of her hand.

'You *stupid* little mare. Are you tryin' to get us all bleedin' locked up?'

Roxy's mind was racing ahead. Nikki was staring off into space with a vacant smile fixed on her face. There was no way she could let the girl go home tonight in this state. Unless her mother was a complete fool she would know at a glance what had gone on and she could have the coppers down on them like a ton of bricks.

'Come on, you gormless little bugger.' Yanking Poppy to her feet she pushed her none too gently towards the door. 'We'd better get this kid to bed. Whatever were you thinkin' of, lettin' her try this? A spliff is one thing, but this is another entirely. Your dad is goin' to knock your block off when he comes in, if I ain't very much mistaken.'

She hoisted Nikki to her feet, which she soon found out was no hardship, for the child was as light as a feather.

'Come on, lovie.' Her voice was kind. 'Let's get you upstairs, eh? You'll be right as rain in the mornin'.'

Unresisting, Nikki allowed herself to be led away. Once they were in Poppy's room, Roxy threw the quilt back and after removing Nikki's shoes she helped her on to the bed next to Poppy, who was already slipping into a deep drug-induced sleep. She then stood with her hands on her hips looking down on the pair of them. The balloon would go up big time tonight when Eddie got in and learned what they had been up to.

Sighing heavily she left the room, closing the door behind her.

Nikki as usual had hot-footed it to Poppy's straight after their meal and Robbie had left over an hour ago. Now as Claire strolled down the garden with Gemma under the light of a full moon she glanced up at the sky. If there really was a heaven, her mum would be up there now. Or at least, Claire hoped she was. It was funny; she had spent so many years hating Karen, even wishing her dead at times, yet now that she was gone, she could forgive her.

As she thought back to Karen lying in the cold hospital bed she shuddered. If she hadn't known it was her mother lying there she would never have recognised her; she had been nothing like the picture Claire had carried around in her head for all those long years. And then there was her dad. Strangely, apart from being a little older and a little plumper he had barely changed at all. Not in looks anyway. His personality seemed to have changed though. The sparkle she remembered in his eyes had dimmed and there was a stoop to his shoulders now that Claire could not remember seeing before. She wanted to go on hating him, blaming him for leaving them, yet somehow she found that she couldn't. There was a part of her that still loved him, still wanted him to be proud of her, which he obviously was. She thought of him now when he had first seen the house and her eyes filled with tears. He had been so full of praise. But what would he say if he knew how the house had been earned? Sinking down onto the bench under the tree, she lifted Gemma onto her lap as her mind drifted back in time.

She could remember the day she had run away from Molly and Tom as if it were yesterday. Her head had been full of dreams and she had thought the world was at her feet. Huh! She had soon been disillusioned on that score. And then the endless quest to better herself had begun: the night courses, the elocution classes, the painful rise from street girl to a high-class escort.

It suddenly struck her for the first time how Tracey must have felt when she had abandoned her, and again Claire thought of her father. Had he really done any worse than she had? He had run away from his wife when she had an affair with another man. He too must have been hurting and he too was regretting his action now, just as she was. But at least he had been strong enough to admit to his mistake. Honest enough to tell the truth. She wondered if she would ever be able to confess to the people she cared about what her past had really been like.

'Ah Gemma, it's a hard life, isn't it?' she whispered into the darkness and the wagging of Gemma's tail as she licked her mistress was her answer. It was then that she heard the faint ringing of the phone back in the house and dropping Gemma gently onto the grass she ran back up the lawn. By the time she lifted the receiver in the hallway she was breathless. 'Hello?' she gasped.

Only silence greeted her, so again – more loudly this time – she said, 'Hello?'

She could hear music playing but no one answered, so after waiting for another second or two she dropped the phone back down, shuddering as she wondered if she had just received what Molly would have termed as 'a funny phone call'.

'So, just what the bloody hell is goin' on here then?'

Roxy was just scraping the remains of the drugs the girls had sampled earlier into the sink when the sound of her husband's voice made her swing about.

'I'll tell you what's goin' on, yer careless bastard,' she squawked. 'You left this stuff lyin' about where Poppy could get her hands on it, an' now her an' young Nikki are lyin' upstairs stoned out o' their bleedin' heads. What were you thinkin' of, eh? If I'd sent the kid home like that, her mam would have probably had the coppers down on us.'

Eddie looked momentarily shocked, then shrugging his arms out of his jacket he flung it carelessly across a chair. Roxy could see that he had been drinking, which was a sign to keep her distance, but tonight she was so angry with him that she was past caring.

'Shut your mouth, woman,' he told her threateningly. 'Or do I have to shut it for yer?'

'That's right. You've done sommat wrong so let's sweep it under the carpet, eh? I've told yer before, Eddie. I can stand the nicked stuff yer stash here, I can stand you bein' at the beck an' call o' your invisible bleedin' boss, but I draw the line at heavy drugs. What if our Katie had found it? She could have killed herself.'

'Well, she didn't fuckin' find it, did she, so what yer harpin' on about? A couple o' lines won't kill 'em. In fact, they'll probably enjoy it. What you gettin' all holier than thou for, anyway? You can stand the nicked stuff. In fact, if I remember rightly, it were *you* as sent the shoplifters out only last week to lift a new pair o' shoes an' a new coat for Katie.'

'Yes, well, perhaps if you'd give me regular money I wouldn't have to!'

Eddie was losing his temper now but instead of backing off and making herself scarce as she usually did, Roxy stood her ground and thumbed towards the stairs.

'That girl up there comes from a good family, yer know? She ain't been *dragged* up like our lot.'

'An' just whose fuckin' fault is that? I ain't askin' her to come round here, am I? She's practically bleedin' livin' here, though I've no idea why. She an' our Poppy have hardly got a lot in common, have they? An' anyway, if it worries you so much, why don't yer put your foot up her arse an' tell her to piss off an' keep away.'

'Oh, that's just typical o' you, ain't it?' Roxy blazed at him. 'The first chance our Poppy has o' mixin' wi' someone half-decent an' you want to go an' spoil it for her.'

When his clenched fist shot out and connected firmly with her cheek her head snapped back on her shoulders. But then she was glaring at him and for the first time he saw hatred shining in her eyes. Roxy had always danced to his tune. Taken anything he cared to throw at her, but now he came to think about it, she had changed lately. It was ever since that Nikki had started to come around. She wasn't so keen to go out and stand on the street corner when he was strapped for cash any more, and she had taken to cleaning everything in sight. As his eyes travelled around the kitchen he snorted in disgust. Admittedly, she hadn't managed to do anything about the tobacco-stained walls and cupboards. If truth be known she was as much responsible for the state of them as he was. Roxy had chainsmoked for as long as he had known her. But the rest of the kitchen was gleaming. The sinks were bleached, the worktops were clear and there wasn't a dirty pot in sight when not so very long ago he had had to wash a cup if he wanted a drink.

'You ain't goin' to start goin' all religious on me, are yer?' he suddenly asked.

Roxy's eyes narrowed to slits. His fingerprints were showing on her cheek now, but instead of backing off as she normally did, she was standing up to him.

'It would take more than Him Upstairs to save you or me now, Eddie, from where I'm standin'. But I ain't gettin' any younger an' I'm startin' to think I ain't really done all that much to be proud of in me life. One thing I can do though is see that you don't get your filthy mitts on that child upstairs. You're to keep away from her, do you hear me?'

'You must be mad, woman,' he spat, but she noticed his furtive expression and knew that her suspicions had been right. His so called 'boss' was partial to a little bit o' young stuff and she had heard via the grapevine that Eddie usually supplied him with it. Well, he wouldn't be supplying young Nikki – not if she had her way. Over her dead body.

A sick feeling started up in the pit of her stomach. The only sensible thing to do would be to ask Nikki to keep away from here in future. She would do it in the morning before she packed her off home to face the music with her mum. She would miss her though. Nikki had been like a breath of fresh air with her lovely smile and her pleasant voice. She spoke nicely, making her lot sound like a load of country peasants. And she always said please and thank you too, words that had always seemed to be missing from her brood's vocabulary. Sighing sadly, she rubbed at her cheek; it was stinging now and the tooth that had been troubling her for the past two weeks was hanging on by a thread. She put two fingers into her mouth and after a sharp twist it came out easily. Oh well, Eddie had done her a favour if he did but know it. At least he had saved her a trip to the dentist's. Lifting her head high she walked past him and his mouth gaped.

"'Ere, woman, what about me bacon butty? Me stomach thinks me throat's cut!'

'So cook it yerself then,' she flung at him over her shoulder and then after going into the lounge and scooping Katie into her arms she walked away up the stairs as he stared after her in shocked disbelief.

A gentle hand on Nikki's arm brought her eyes blinking open. She gulped and stared up into Roxy's smiling face. One side of the woman's face was swollen and her eye had a deep purple bruise spreading across it, but her voice was kind as she said, 'Come on, love. Let's get some breakfast inside yer an' get you pointed in the direction o' home, eh?'

Nikki gulped again. Her mouth felt dry and her tongue was cleaving to the roof of her mouth; she had a headache too and felt very off-colour. Turning slightly, she saw that Poppy was still curled up at the side of her, fast asleep and snoring softly.

'Come on now. I don't want your mam hammerin' on the door and raisin' the roof.' Roxy turned and made towards the door and Nikki felt sorry for her as she saw how weary she looked.

She moaned quietly as she sat up. She really did feel very ill, but even so as she thought back to the night before she had no regrets. Once the effects of the drug she had snorted had taken hold she had felt like a different person. Free, and able to do anything she chose. She only wished that she could feel like that all the time.

As she padded along the landing she was just in time to see Poppy's older brother walking out of the bathroom in his boxer shorts. He laughed when he saw her blush but passed her without comment. Nikki was too young for him, he liked his women with a bit of experience under their belts and didn't mind if he had to pay for the pleasure half the time.

Nikki quickly walked into the room he had just vacated, bolting the door behind her, then hurrying to the cracked sink she splashed her face with cold water and tried to comb the tangles out of her hair with her fingers. Feeling slightly better now, she went back out onto the landing and as she did so, the smell of bacon frying wafted up the stairs towards her, making her stomach revolt. It was at that moment that Eddie walked out of the bedroom he shared with his wife. Nikki lowered her head; he too was dressed only in boxer shorts and she wondered if this family had ever heard of such things as dressing-gowns. She would have walked straight past him as she headed towards the stairs but his hand suddenly snaked out and stayed her.

'Here, wait there a minute. I've got something for yer.' The words had barely left his mouth when he shot back into his room to return seconds later with a small plastic bag in his hand. 'Take this,' he urged. 'But don't get sayin' nothin' to her downstairs about it. If you enjoyed it last night yer might like to try a bit more later on.' He tapped the side of his nose and leaning towards her he winked. 'It's our little secret, an' if you want any more, just come an' see me. But remember, not a word.'

Nikki felt uncomfortable. Eddie was so close that she could feel his stale breath fanning her cheek and she had the urge to pass the bag back to him. But before she had the chance he playfully slapped her bottom and after belching loudly, continued on along the landing and disappeared into the bathroom. She glanced at the small package in her hand then pushed it deep down into the pocket of her jeans and went on her way.

Roxy was standing at the cooker when she entered the kitchen, flipping the bacon in the pan with a cigarette dangling from the corner of her mouth.

'Ah, there you are, love,' she greeted her. 'Sit yourself down at the table. This should be ready in a second.'

Nikki wanted to tell her that she didn't want any breakfast but she sat down anyway and helped herself to a cup of tea from the pot simply to get rid of the bitter taste in her mouth. The tea was lukewarm and stewed but it helped to rid her of the horrible tang so she swallowed it gratefully.

Seconds later, Roxy carried the frying pan to the table and slid some bacon onto a plate before pushing it towards Nikki.

'There, get some o' that down you,' she urged.

Nikki stared down at the plate in dismay as Roxy stubbed her cigarette out in a chipped saucer and headed towards the door.

'I'll just pop upstairs to fetch our Katie, and then I'll make us a nice fresh pot o' tea,' she promised as she swept from the room. Nikki quickly snatched the bacon from the plate and threw it to the dog under the table who wolfed it down as if he hadn't been fed for a month. Smiling with relief, Nikki wiped her hands on the tea towel that Roxy had flung on the table then crossing to the kettle she quickly filled it at the sink and turned it on to boil as she waited for Roxy to come back.

Twenty minutes later, with a second cup of tea inside her, she was ready to leave. As Roxy had pointed out, she might as well go and face the music. When she stood up, Roxy followed her to the front door where she glanced nervously across her shoulder before saying in a whisper, 'Nikki, what you an' Poppy got up to last night . . . yer won't get mentionin' it to your mam, will you?'

'Of course I wouldn't,' Nikki told her indignantly.

Roxy sighed with relief then mustering her courage she went on, 'Yer know, love, I know you an' your mam ain't seein' eye to eye at the minute but I've no doubt she only has your best interests at heart, an' the thing is . . . Well, the thing is, you an' Poppy have been brought up differently. What I'm tryin' to say is, it might be better if you were to mix wi' girls from your own school.'

When she saw the hurt register in Nikki's eyes she swiftly looked away. This was proving to be more difficult than she had thought it would be.

'Are you saying that you don't want me to come round here again?'

The hurt was sounding in the girl's voice and Roxy felt worse than ever. 'It ain't that I don't *want* yer here, love. It's just that I think it would be for your own good if yer didn't come any more. I ain't blind, an' much as I love her, I know our Poppy ain't no angel. I . . . I wouldn't want her leadin' you astray, yer see? She could be a bad influence on yer. Poppy is streetwise but you ain't been brought up that way an' I wouldn't want yer gettin' into no trouble.'

Nikki breathed in deeply, feeling completely desolate. Since getting to know Poppy she had felt as if she had someone she could talk to. Someone who understood how she felt. Now, Roxy was telling her that she didn't want her here any more.

Roxy held her hand out to her but, mustering what dignity she had left, Nikki put her nose in the air and sauntered away down the path. Fine, she knew when she wasn't wanted. Straight-backed she walked off down the street but when she finally heard the door close her shoulders slumped and tears started to her eyes. She might have had a good time last night but today certainly hadn't got off to a very good start, and worse was still to come when she got home and faced her mum. No doubt Claire would be pulling her hair out by now and would rant and rave at her. Nikki knew that Claire did her best for her, so why was it that she felt so resentful towards her? Was it because she saw Claire as the last link to her father? Strangely, there were still times when she wanted to throw herself into Claire's arms and be held tight. To pour out all her troubles and fears, and tell her of the terrible nightmares that still plagued her. But of course, she was far too old for that sort of thing now. So instead, she kept the feelings bottled up inside where they festered and grew.

Pausing at the end of the road, she looked back at Poppy's house. She had been happy there, but once again her happiness had been short-lived, just as it always was. She turned the corner and went on her way. There was no point in staying where she clearly wasn't wanted. Patting the small packet resting against her thigh, the girl thought that at least if she had to stay in tonight, she would have something to take her mind off her problems.

Chapter Eighteen

'Nikki, I've been thinking.' Claire placed her daughter's Sunday dinner in front of her. Today she had done roast beef with all the trimmings, which had always been one of Nikki's favourites, though no one would have guessed it from the way she was looking at it now. In fact, from the look on her face, they might have thought that Claire had put a plate full of poison in front of her.

'Thinking what?' Nikki asked without interest.

Ignoring her tone, Claire sat down opposite her and took up her knife and fork. 'Well, that we don't get to do enough together, so I've come up with an idea. Now that you're at school all day and I have the house and garden how I want them I tend to get a bit bored. I know I have my little job at the solicitor's but that doesn't really fill all my time in, so I've been trying to think of something we could do together and I've come up with just the solution.' She waited for Nikki to show some interest and when she didn't, she went doggedly on.

'I've seen this little shop in the High Street that's up for rent and I wondered how you'd feel about us opening a boutique? You could come and help me in there after school and on Saturdays, and we could fill it with clothes that would appeal to your age group. You could even come with me to choose the stock. What do you think?'

When Nikki shrugged, Claire sighed. Since the night she had stayed out the week before, the girl had been moping about the place with a face like a wet weekend. She had made no attempt to go out at all and Claire could only assume that she and Poppy, her new friend, must have had a row and parted company. Secretly, she was relieved. Ever since the day she had seen Poppy standing at the school gates she had worried about the influence she might have on Nikki. She had looked years older than Nikki for a start-off, and the way she was dressed had reminded Claire of the way she and the girls she had used to work with in London dressed. Now as she loaded her fork with a crispy roast potato she suggested, 'Why don't we take Gemma for a walk after lunch and you can have a look at the shop and tell me what you think?'

Nikki shrugged again, but made no reply. Aw well, at least she hasn't completely dismissed the idea, Claire thought to herself and then a silence settled between them as they ate their lunch.

Two hours later, Claire stopped outside a small shop in town and told Nikki, 'This is the one. It could be really nice if we spent a little time doing it up. We could call it Nikki's Boutique if you like?'

Nikki peered through the window but there was very little to see. The shop was empty apart from a counter that ran along the back wall. 'I've already been to the estate agents and got the particulars on it,' Claire told her with an edge of excitement in her voice. 'Apparently there's a decent-sized room out the back, which we could use as a stockroom, and there's a toilet in the yard that we'd share with the shop next door. I know there are already quite a few dress shops in town, but I don't think there's one that caters specifically for teenagers. So, do you think we could make a go of it? I thought we could stock some costume jewellery too – and perhaps bags and shoes.'

Nikki nodded slowly. She supposed it would be quite nice to have a shop named after her. It would certainly sound good at school when she told the other girls that she had her own shop.

'I suppose it could work,' she admitted, trying not to sound too enthusiastic, 'but the inside of the shop would need a lot of work. The wallpaper in there is gross, all flowery, and we'd need some fitting rooms where people could try the clothes on.'

'I've already thought of that.' Claire was delighted that Nikki was finally talking to her again. 'I spoke to my dad on the phone yesterday and told him what I was thinking of doing, and he informed me that he's a dab hand at DIY and said that if we decide to go ahead he'd be more than happy to lend a hand. It would be a good chance for you to get to know him a little too.'

'I don't know about *me* getting to know him. You hardly know him yourself, do you?' Nikki remarked cuttingly.

Seeing the hurt look in Claire's eyes she felt a slight pang of guilt. But then she had only been telling the truth, after all. Claire had mentioned him often during the previous week, and yet since the day of her mother's funeral she hadn't invited him over again, which only went to show that she still hadn't forgiven him for leaving her and her Aunt Tracey all those years ago. The girl could understand that. After all, she still struggled every single day to come to terms with what her own dad had done to her – not that she would ever tell Claire that.

'So, is that a yes then?' Claire was looking at her expectantly and Nikki sniffed.

'I suppose it would give us something to do on a Saturday,' she admitted grudgingly and then she moved on, dragging Gemma behind her on her lead.

Claire was bubbling with excitement. Since the night she had stayed out the week before, Nikki had remained indoors every single night. It was obvious that she and Poppy had parted company but Claire was too afraid of having her head snapped off to ask why. It broke her heart to see Nikki looking so miserable all the time, which was what had prompted her to put her thinking cap on and try to come up with something they could do together. The shop seemed the ideal solution, and now that Nikki had agreed to it, Claire decided she would ring the estate agent who was letting it first thing in the morning.

Nikki had slouched off to her room shortly after tea and ever since then, the only thing to be heard was the throb of the loud Madonna CD floating down the stairs from her bedroom.

Claire was in the kitchen washing up when the phone rang and she hurried into the hall to answer it.

'Hello, Claire.'

'Oh . . . er . . . hello.' It suddenly occurred to her that every time she heard her father's voice, something inside her seemed to switch to polite mode, as if she were talking to a stranger.

'I was wondering if you'd gotten round to mentioning the shop to Nikki yet?'

'Yes, I took her to see it this afternoon, as a matter of fact.'

'Oh aye, and what was her reaction?'

It was obvious that Robbie was trying really hard to make his peace with Claire, but it was as if she had put up shutters that he couldn't get past.

'She seemed to think it was a good idea, but you never know with Nikki just lately. I think I'm going to go ahead with it though. Even if she loses interest it will give me something to occupy my time.'

'That's marvellous, lass. And as I told you, I'll be more than willing to help with anything that needs doing inside the shop. You could perhaps take me to see it so that I can give it the once-over?'

He sounded so hopeful that Claire didn't have the heart to refuse, although she had grave misgivings about how they might get on if they spent too much time together. She could easily have afforded to pay tradesmen to come in and do any alterations, but her father wouldn't hear of it and now she felt backed into a corner.

'Well, I was planning on picking the keys up tomorrow morning and going to have a good look at it,' she told him quietly. 'I suppose you could come along if you hadn't got anything else planned.'

'I'd love to,' he replied. 'What time are you going?'

'As soon as I've got Nikki off to school.'

'In that case I'll come over to the house for nine o'clock then.'

Claire groaned inwardly, feeling that she really didn't have much choice in the matter, before telling him, 'Very well, I'll see you in the morning. Goodbye.' She stared at the receiver as she placed it down with a frown on her face, but then she tried to look on the bright side of things. After all, he was only coming to look at a shop with her, he wasn't moving in. And anyway, he would no doubt be returning to Scotland before too much longer, and then she could forget all about him again.

'My goodness me, you're looking smart today, lass.'

As Claire held the front door open for her father she smiled at him coolly. She had taken a lot of trouble over her appearance today and was wearing one of the expensive, timeless designer suits from her days in London. It was a lovely shade of blue that set off her blue eyes to perfection, and she had swept her long fair hair up into an elegant pleat on the back of her head. The whole look was completed by high-heeled shoes that gave her a sophisticated air, and anyone seeing her could easily have taken her for a businesswoman, which of course, she had been once upon a time.

'I've just made a cup of tea,' she informed him. 'Would you like one before we go?'

'It'll be a cold day in hell before you hear me refuse a cup o' tea,' he told her with a cheerful wink.

Once he was seated, she began to pour the tea, choosing her words carefully as she told him, 'I don't want you to feel obliged to do any work in this shop, you know. I mean, it was very kind of you to offer, but I promise you I can afford to have it done professionally, and I wouldn't want you to delay going back to Scotland on my behalf.'

He looked like a puppy that had been kicked as he told her, 'I dare say you could afford to, Claire – but I'd like to do it, and I'm in no rush to go anywhere for now.'

She shrugged. 'Very well. But I will insist on paying you the going rate.'

'You'll do no such thing,' he spluttered indignantly. 'Can't a father do a favour for his own flesh and blood now?' Suddenly keen to change the subject, he sipped at his tea then said quietly, 'Actually there's something I have to ask you, Claire.'

'Oh yes, and what's that then?'

She watched as he tugged uncomfortably at his tie before telling her, 'I collected your mam's ashes from the crematorium yesterday.'

Claire felt sick as she suddenly realised for the very first time that her mother was really dead. Since the night of her death and the day of the funeral she had not allowed herself to think about it too much, but now she could deny it no longer.

'I thought perhaps . . . Well, I thought perhaps it would be nice if you and Tracey came with me to scatter them.'

She gulped deep in her throat before asking, 'Where did you have in mind?'

'The hill that overlooks Gatley Common. Do you remember it? I used to take you for walks up there when you and Tracey were little. Your mum used to come too sometimes, before I . . . Well, I just thought that was somewhere that would have happy memories for all of us.'

Happy memories. In her mind's eye, Claire was suddenly a child again; she could see herself holding his hand and looking up at him trustingly as he pointed out places of interest. And then she and Tracey, after he had left them, staring down at the village below as Tracey clung to her hand and asked innocently, 'Is this the top o' the world, Claire?'

They would often go there after school before moving on to the Blue Lagoon, where they would skim stones across the surface of the water in the winter, or splodge in the edge of it in the summertime.

It was one of the few places she knew that held happy memories, and she too felt it would be a good resting-place for her mother.

'What does Tracey think of the idea?' she asked.

'She thinks it's a fine idea, but we wanted to consult you before we agreed on anything.'

'All right,' Claire nodded, and her composed tone belied the deep emotions that were spinning out of control inside her. 'Just let me know when you plan to do it and I'll try to get there. But now if you've finished your tea, shall we get on?'

'Yes, yes, of course.'

He followed her out to the drive, where he gestured at his car. 'Why don't you come in mine? It seems silly to take two.'

He held the passenger door open and then they fell silent as he drove her into the town centre and parked the car before heading off to the estate agent.

An hour later, she opened the door of the shop and they stepped inside. Claire was dismayed to see that, on closer inspection, there appeared to be much more that needed doing than she had thought, but her father was smiling broadly.

'It's a bonny little shop,' he declared.

Claire kicked at a piece of loose skirting board which immediately dropped off the wall. 'The whole place needs gutting,' she remarked despondently. 'It didn't look this bad from the outside. It would take weeks and weeks to get this dump up to scratch. No wonder it's stood empty for so long.'

'Rubbish!' Robbie loved a challenge and was in his element. 'There's nothing here as a little elbow grease won't put right, and you'd have to go a long way to find another shop in such a prime location. That's probably why the rent is so cheap, because it needs a little work done.'

'A *little* work! I think that's rather an understatement.' Claire looked around. The dated flowery wallpaper was peeling off the walls and the skirting boards looked as if they were full of woodworm. The air smelled damp and musty, and she pulled a face as she spread her hands, feeling totally over-faced with it all.

'Look.' Robbie drew her towards the corner of the room. 'The first thing we'll do is get rid of this paper. You'll be shocked at how different it will look with that gone. Then we'll rip these skirting boards off and put nice new ones on. Now I think the fitting rooms should be just here.' He strode to a corner of the room and spread his hands. 'Once we've got those up we'll repaper using something bright and trendy that will appeal to the younger customers. And I think perhaps we'll need a little platform running along the front of the window where you can do a nice display. Over there we could have some shelves where you can put your bags and knick-knacks, and down there some open-fronted cupboards for the shoes.' He crossed to the counter and after closely inspecting it he declared, 'All this needs is a good rub down and a coat of varnish and it will look as good as new. Now surely you can see it all in your mind's eye?'

Despite her initial feelings of doubt, as Claire listened to him she did begin to picture it all clean and spruced up, and a slight smile played across her lips.

Seeing that she was coming around to his way of thinking he hurried on, 'You could perhaps use some of that nice voile in a colour that would match the paper and the curtains on the fitting rooms in the window. You know, just sort of drape it so that it doesn't block the display but looks pretty? Of course, I'm dreadful with colour schemes so I'd have to leave that part of it to you and Nikki. You two could be the brains and I'd be the brawn of the outfit.'

Claire chewed thoughtfully on her lip before asking, 'How long do you think all this would take? I'd have to start paying the rent on the place straight away so I couldn't afford to have it standing empty for too long. Then even when it's done I'd have to buy all the stock in.'

Staring around him for a few minutes he mentally calculated how long each job would take.

'How long would it take you to stock it?'

'Oh, about a week, I should think.'

'Then I reckon you could open the doors within a month,' he said optimistically. 'That's without doing the room out the back, of course. But that could be done once you were open, if you didn't mind keeping some of the stock at home while I tackled it. Come on, let's go through and have a look at it.'

They were both pleasantly surprised when they entered the back room. The walls in there were bare plaster, which would only need painting to spruce them up, and there was even a little sink where they could get water for their tea and wash their hands.

'This will be a doddle,' he told her with a smile. 'I can have this looking all shipshape and Bristol fashion in a couple of days or so. Possibly even within the month, and in time for you to open.'

'In that case, I think I might give it a try,' Claire told him tentatively. 'I realise that I may be making a horrible mistake and may fall flat on my face with hundreds of pounds' worth of stock on my hands, but I suppose I ought to give it a go.'

'I don't see how you can fail,' her father assured her. 'You've got Nikki who will be more than happy to tell you what the teenage girls are after. Though looking at you, I don't really think you need any lessons in dress sense. I reckon you could have a little gold mine here in no time and I am sure that Nikki will love it.'

Claire was suddenly decided and as she flashed him the first real smile he had seen off her since his return, it warmed his heart.

'Right then. If we're going to do it, there's no time like the present,' she told him. 'Let's get back to the estate agent before I change my mind and give him the first month's rent in advance, and then I can get stuck in.'

'Then *we* can get stuck in,' Robbie reminded her, and side by side they left the shop with matching grins on their faces.

The Claire who arrived back at the shop bright and early the next morning after getting Nikki off to school, looked nothing like the sophisticated young woman who had visited the day before. Today she was dressed in faded jeans and a loose shirt, and her hair was tied up in a ponytail. She had given Robbie one of the two keys that the estate agent had passed to her and was shocked to see that he was already there and had begun stripping the walls.

Hearing her enter, Robbie turned and stared at her. Scrubbed clean of make-up, she reminded him of the little girl he had left behind all those years ago, and tears of regret sprang to his eyes. He had a lot of making up to her to do, and if it took him until his dying breath he was determined to do it. There had been so much heartache but now they would put it all behind them.

'This is practically falling off the walls,' he told her gleefully. 'I reckon I'll have the lot stripped for this evening and all rubbed down ready for some nice new stuff to be hung.'

Claire scratched her head as she looked around. Everywhere was such a mess that she didn't quite know where to begin.

'What would you like me to do?' she asked.

'Well, for a start-off we're going to need paint and paper. You'll have to choose that, so perhaps you could go and have a look round while I get this done. I've already ordered the new skirting boards and wood for the platform and the fitting rooms. That will be delivered later today. Then once it's all stripped out we can give the whole place a scrub before we start redecorating. What are you like with a paintbrush?'

Claire chuckled as she thought back to when she had bought her hotel in Blackpool. During the first winter season before her guests had arrived she had done most of the painting and papering herself because she had used all her money to buy the place and had none spare to bring in decorators. Most nights she had dropped into bed exhausted with almost as much paint on her as she had managed to get on the walls. Thoughts of the hotel were followed by memories of Christian, and the smile slipped away. Whenever she thought of him, a great empty hole seemed to open up inside her, but now wasn't the time for dwelling on that, so she simply told her father, 'I get by.'

'Good, then you get off and see if there's anything that catches your eye. But before you go – did you think to bring a kettle and some tea bags?'

'Everything is in the car,' she told him with an amused twinkle in her eye. 'I've parked round the back so I'll make you a brew before I shoot off, shall I?'

'Not half!'

She hurried away to unpack their supplies, and soon after she set off again in search of wallpaper and paint. She herself would have liked to choose something classy and elegant, but seeing as how she was hoping to make the shop appeal to teenagers she knew that she would have to be on the look-out for something a little more trendy. She found just the thing in the third shop she visited. It was a cream paper scattered with gold stars and moons, and as soon as she saw it she knew that it would be just right. She then went and bought ten metres of gold voile and some plain gold fabric that would serve as curtains on the front of the fitting rooms. It was almost lunchtime by the time she arrived back at the shop. When she went in, her mouth gaped in surprise. Two of the walls were completely stripped, the old skirting boards had been ripped off the walls and already the place was beginning to look better.

'Someone's been busy,' she commented as she placed a large tin of paint and a bag full of wallpaper in the corner of the room.

'Looks like I'm not the only one. Did you find what you wanted?'

Claire took a roll of paper from the bag and held it up for his inspection. 'I found this and thought Nikki might like it. What do you think?'

'I think she'll be over the moon.' He chuckled. 'Excuse the pun!'

Claire shook her head, then, serious again she told him, 'I think we ought to go and have something to eat now. There's a McDonald's just down the road. Would that suit you?'

'Well, seeing as how I'm hardly dressed for the Ritz I think that would suit me just fine.' After clambering down off the ladder he hurried out to the back room where he quickly rinsed his hands before telling her, 'I'm fit then. Come on, every minute we're out of here is wasted work time so I don't want to be long.'

Claire rolled her eyes as she followed him from the shop locking the door securely behind her. The atmosphere between them had been relaxed during the morning but now as they sat down to lunch together, Claire could once again think of nothing to say to him. He seemed equally as ill-at-ease as she was and so the meal was a silent affair and they were both secretly glad when they could return to the shop and resume work. The wood that Robbie had ordered arrived early in the afternoon and he then replaced the old skirting boards he had torn off that morning with new ones while Claire set about undercoating them. The time passed quickly and they were both surprised when Nikki suddenly appeared in her school uniform with her bag slung carelessly across her shoulder.

She looked surly, although when she saw Claire she did manage a smile. 'Crikey, Mum, you've got more paint on you than on the skirting boards,' she told her, and when Claire glanced down and saw the state she was in, she couldn't deny it.

'Well, I never said I was the best in the world at painting,' she admitted. 'But you, miss, can put the kettle on. I bet you wouldn't say no to a cuppa, would you, Dad?'

Dad. The word sounded strangely alien on her tongue after all their years apart but she forced herself to say it for Nikki's sake. Nikki walked into the back room without giving Robbie so much as a second glance and he grinned at Claire ruefully.

'I don't think Nikki is too keen on me,' he whispered.

'Oh, don't think that. Nikki is like that with everyone just lately,' Claire assured him.

He nodded and carried on with what he was doing until Nikki reappeared with a small tray loaded with cups of steaming tea and a plate of gingernut biscuits.

By half-past four Nikki was getting bored and she asked Claire, 'What time are we going home?'

Claire glanced towards Robbie, who said immediately, 'You get off, pet, and sort the lass something to eat. I'll be fine here.'

'Are you quite sure?'

'Positive. I just want to get the rest of these walls stripped and then I'll call it a day. Don't worry, I won't forget to lock up after me.'

Claire went into the back room to wash her hands feeling very guilty. Robbie had hardly stopped all day and looked tired. Before she could stop herself she asked him, 'Why don't you come round to the house when you've done? I could get you a bit of dinner ready before you go home.'

There was nothing he would have liked more yet he was afraid of rushing things, so he told her, 'Thanks, I appreciate the offer but me landlady will have somethin' ready for me an' I don't want to go upsettin' her. You get yourself away and I'll see you in the mornin', eh?'

'Actually I won't be in till the afternoon,' Claire told him, feeling guiltier than ever. 'I have to go into work, you see. I need to hand my notice in and explain what I'm going to do. I can't say I'm looking forward to it though because Mr Dickinson is a dear old soul and he's been very good to me since I came to live in Solihull.'

'I'm sure he'll understand,' Robbie told her kindly.

She nodded. 'I'll see you tomorrow sometime then?'

It was his turn to nod now as she led Nikki out to the car.

'So did you have good day then?' Claire asked, hoping to start a conversation as they drove along.

Nikki shrugged. 'How good can going to school be?'

Taking the hint, Claire clamped her mouth shut as they continued on their way. The silence continued until they turned into the drive when Nikki suddenly leaned forward in her seat and said animatedly, 'There's Poppy. At the door – look.' With that she threw the door open before Claire had had time to draw the car to a halt and went haring off up the drive towards her friend.

Claire sighed. Aw well, she thought to herself, I should have known it was too good to last.

'Nikki, will you please come and eat this dinner?' Claire had to practically scream up the stairs to make herself heard above the noise coming from Nikki's bedroom. She and Poppy had been closeted up there for over an hour now and Claire's nerves felt as taut as piano wires.

The sound of a door opening and banging shut again told her that Nikki had heard her and now the girl leaned over the banisters, and staring down at her mother she snapped, '*What!*'

'I said your dinner is ready. Could you please at least take the trouble to come and eat it? There's plenty for Poppy too if she's hungry.' Claire was trying very hard to be reasonable but it was getting harder by the minute.

'She's not, and we're going out,' Nikki informed her shortly. 'Leave mine on the side and I'll warm it up and have it when I come in later.'

'And just where are you thinking of going?'

'I told you, didn't I? *Out.* Now if you don't mind, I'm trying to get ready.' And the girl turned and pounded back to her room.

Claire felt depressed. The day had got off to such a good start but now it seemed to have taken a nosedive again, and she wasn't quite sure what she could do about it.

Nikki appeared in the kitchen doorway some time later with Poppy, who was made up to the eyeballs, close behind her.

'I'll see you later then.'

'All right, love. Don't be too late in, will you? Remember, you've got school tomorrow.'

Nikki stared at her scornfully before following Poppy to the front door. Claire listened to them giggling as they strolled off down the drive and then a silence settled on the house that only minutes before had been echoing with loud music.

Claire chewed on her lip. Now that Nikki was back under Poppy's influence again, the chances were that she wouldn't come home at all. Even worse, Claire still had no idea where Poppy lived so she couldn't even go to fetch Nikki home. As an idea suddenly occurred to her, she snatched up the lead and fastened it to Gemma's collar.

'Come on,' she told her. 'You and me are going for a little walk. There's no harm in that, now is there?'

Gemma wagged her tail as if she was in full agreement as she waddled along at Claire's side.

Chapter Nineteen

As Poppy walked along with Nikki she felt a surge of resentment sweep through her. Since Nikki had suddenly stopped coming to the house her dad had been constantly on her back with questions like, *Where's your little mate then?* Or, *So when is your pal gonna put in another appearance?*

She had soon noticed that the questions were always asked when her mam was out of earshot, which she found rather strange. Her dad had never shown any interest in any of her mates before, so she wondered why Nikki should be so special.

Eventually she had turned on him and demanded, 'What's it to you if she's stopped comin'?'

He had scratched his head for a time as if he was unsure of his answer before saying, 'Oh, I just wondered what had gone wrong, that's all. She were practically livin' here for a time an' then suddenly it's as if she's dropped off the face o' the earth. Did you have a row or sommat?'

'No, we didn't!' Poppy had wondered herself why Nikki had suddenly stopped coming, but being as she wasn't that much bothered, she had hardly given it any thought. In truth, Nikki had got on her nerves at times with her la-di-da voice and her prim and proper manners. The only reason Poppy had put up with her was because Nikki was good for touching up for a few quid when she was short, which seemed to be all too often. Much to her surprise, her dad had then started to slip her a bit here and there. He had never bothered to do so before, so Poppy had found it odd to say the very least – until the night before, when he had slid into her bedroom and told her, 'I've got a favour to ask of yer, love.'

'Oh yeah, an' what's that then?'

By now, Roxy had lapsed into a drunken sleep. She had hit the bottle again big time over the last couple of weeks and the house had now returned to the sorry state it had been in when Nikki had started visiting.

'Well, the thing is, me boss saw Nikki an' he's took a bit of a shine to her.'

When Poppy raised an eyebrow he hurried on, 'He likes the company o' young girls, but don't worry. He ain't goin' to harm her in any way or nowt like that. An' I were thinking . . . well, if you could persuade her to start comin' round again, I might be able to introduce 'em. It would be up to Nikki then, wouldn't it? What I mean is, she wouldn't be forced into doin' nothin' she didn't want to do.'

Poppy's eyes had narrowed to slits as she asked quietly, 'An' what would be in it fer me?'

'Same as would be in it for her,' he'd answered abruptly. 'You know you like the odd snort, an' from what I could see of it, so did she. She might have been brought up posh but she's only flesh an' blood at the end o' the day, an' even at that age you can have a leanin' towards a little bit o' what you fancy. So, what do yer say? Will you call round an' see her an' get the lay o' the land? Find out what's upset her, like?'

When Poppy had hesitated he had delved deep into his trouser pocket and produced a note. 'Here,' he told her shortly, pushing a fiver into her hand. 'That's a bit to be goin' on wi'. *Now* will you go an' see her?'

Poppy had snatched the money before he had the chance to change his mind. And so here she was, but now that they were away from

Nikki's luxurious home she found that she didn't quite know what to say to her.

Nikki too had fallen silent until she asked, 'So how are things then? I thought you'd forgotten all about me.'

'I could say the same about you. After all, it weren't me as stopped you comin' round, were it? Why did yer stop, by the way?'

Nikki stared straight ahead as she thought how best to answer Poppy's question. She had no wish to tell Poppy that Roxy had asked her in a roundabout way to stop coming to the house in case it caused trouble between them, so instead she lied. 'Oh, I didn't stop intentionally,' she muttered. 'I've just been rather busy with homework and the new shop and one thing and another.'

She had mentioned the shop earlier to Poppy and the girl was all ears as she asked, 'When did yer say it will be ready to open?'

Nikki shrugged. 'According to my mum's dad it should be all ready within a month or so.'

'Your mum's dad? Why don't yer call him "Grandad" then?'

'Because he isn't my grandad, is he? I was adopted, if you remember, so he's not really any relation to me at all. Neither is Claire, my mum, if it comes to that. But my *real* mum is out there somewhere, and as soon as I'm eighteen I'm going to find her if it's the last thing I do.'

There was such determination in Nikki's voice that Poppy was momentarily stuck for words. But then she thought of the shop again and asked, 'An' you say this shop is goin' to be named after you?'

'Yes, and it's going to sell clothes that will appeal to our age group.'

Poppy was impressed and it showed in her voice as she said, 'Yer lucky little cow. You'll probably get to have first pick of anythin' that takes your fancy.'

'I dare say I will,' Nikki said nonchalantly, and Poppy felt like slapping her. Today was the first day she had ever actually been inside Nikki's home, and the place had nearly taken her breath away. Compared to the shit-hole she lived in, it was like a palace and she had been green with envy. Nikki's bedroom was like something she had only ever seen on the pages of a magazine and yet she seemed to take it all for granted. The ungrateful little cow.

By now they were nearing the bus stop that would take them to Chelmsey Park and Poppy became silent as she slid onto a seat, leaving Nikki to pay her fare for her. When they eventually turned into the estate, Nikki realised with a little start that she had missed coming here more than she had realised. Everything seemed so easygoing here. Nothing at all like where she lived, where the neighbours appeared to be governed by routine. Every Sunday morning, come rain or shine, the men were out on their drives washing and polishing their cars until you could see your face in them. Meantime the women were in their gleaming houses cooking the traditional Sunday roast. It all seemed very mundane and boring to Nikki, who would much have preferred to go to McDonald's as Poppy often did.

They walked by a group of snotty-nosed children who were busily painting graffiti on the side of someone's fence, and as they passed, one little chap shouted, 'Wotcher, Poppy. Got any spliffs on yer?'

'No I ain't, yer cheeky little bleeder,' Poppy shot back, and chuckling, the boy went back to what he was doing without batting so much as an eyelid.

Nikki grinned as she stared at her idol, and to her that's what Poppy was – someone to look up to and admire.

Soon afterwards, they turned into Grove Road where Poppy lived and the house came into sight. For the first time, Nikki began to feel a little apprehensive. Roxy had asked her to keep away. How would she feel now when she just waltzed in again? But it was too late to back out now. They were approaching the gate, which she saw was still hanging drunkenly off its hinges and then they were walking up the path and Poppy was pushing the front door open.

Poppy's mam and dad had cashed their dole cheque today, as the empty lager tins lying about the place testified. Now they were both sprawled in front of the television set with cigarettes dangling from their mouths and empty chocolate wrappers thrown on the floor at their feet.

Poppy stuck her head round the lounge door before snorting with disgust and heading for the kitchen. Nikki quickly followed her, but as she passed the door Katie saw her and to everyone's amazement let out a whoop of delight before flying across to her and wrapping her arms tightly about Nikki's waist as little grunts of pleasure issued from her lips.

A fleeting look of surprise crossed Roxy's face but then she forced a smile, saying, 'Hello there, stranger. I thought you'd forgotten where we lived.'

Nikki was at a loss as to what to answer, considering it was Roxy who had asked her to keep away in the first place, so instead she concentrated on cuddling Katie. During the short time she had been visiting them she had shown the little girl a lot of attention, but this was the first time the child had ever reacted to her and she found it strangely touching.

'Looks like somebody missed yer.' Eddie had pulled himself up in the chair and as he too smiled at Nikki, Poppy felt a rush of jealousy. What was it about this kid that could elicit so much attention from her family anyway? Half the time she felt as if she herself was invisible; sometimes she wondered if they would even notice if she were to vanish off the face of the earth altogether.

She moved on, her face set in resentment, and Nikki followed with Katie still clinging to her skirt as if she was afraid that Nikki might disappear again if she let her go.

Poppy had hardly had time to rummage in the fridge when Eddie appeared in the kitchen doorway, all sweetness and light.

'So how have yer been then, love?' he addressed Nikki.

'Fine, thank you.'

Poppy snatched a chunk of cheese from the fridge and flung it onto the table as she glared at him. 'I don't suppose anybody bothered to cook owt?' It was more of an accusation than a question and Eddie didn't even bother to answer her as she crossed to the bread bin, which she had no doubt would more than likely be empty except for stale crumbs.

She rolled her eyes at Nikki as she said, 'It's the same every pay day. The first place they head to is the off-licence an' us lot can whistle. All except Katie, o' course. I sometimes wonder if these pair even know the rest of us exist.'

'Now that's unfair, Poppy, an' yer know it,' Eddie snarled. 'You lot are bleedin' big enough to take care o' yourselves. Katie could hardly do that, now could she?'

Poppy sneered and Nikki saw that the exchange was fast turning into a row as she held fast to Katie and looked from one to the other of them with frightened eyes.

'Huh! Perhaps I should have been born thick like her an' then happen you'd have taken notice o' me an' all!' she retorted.

Her father raised his fist and lunged towards her, but at that moment Roxy appeared in the doorway and screamed, '*Eddie, that's enough! Do you hear me?*' Then, turning her attention to Poppy, she told her, 'An' that's quite enough from you an' all, young lady. If I *ever* hear yer call our Katie thick again you'll feel the back o' me hand quicker than yer can say Bob's yer uncle! Katie can't help bein' the way she is.'

Poppy hung her head. 'Sorry, Mam', she muttered. 'I didn't mean it. He just rubbed me up the wrong way, that's all.'

'Right, well, that's enough said.' Roxy leaned heavily on the corner of the table as Eddie turned on his heel and stormed out of the room. Lowering her voice she told Poppy, 'You'll push him too far one o' these days, me girl, an' I might not be here to stick up for yer, an' then you'll be sorry. You let your gob run away wi' yer, that's your trouble, an' in front of a guest an' all.'

'Nikki ain't a guest, she's just me mate,' Poppy shot back sullenly.

'That's one an' the same thing. Now come on, Katie. Say good-night. It's time I was gettin' you ready for bed.'

Katie left Nikki's side and obediently crossed to her mother who now led her from the room without another word. It was then that Nikki heard yet another ruckus coming from next door and the sound of something smashing.

Poppy grinned at her. 'Sounds like the neighbours have had their dole cheque an' all,' she joked, and then she proceeded to chew on the piece of cheese in her hand as if nothing had happened in the last few minutes at all.

Some time later they again heard raised voices coming from upstairs and shortly after that, Roxy appeared in the kitchen doorway. This time she was dressed up to the nines and her make-up looked as if it had been applied with a trowel.

'I'm off out for a bit,' she informed Poppy, keeping her eyes averted from Nikki.

'Oh yeah? Bingo, is it?' Poppy smiled knowingly and Nikki was surprised to see Roxy flush.

Ignoring Poppy's question, she snapped, 'Keep your ear out for our Katie till I get back, would yer?'

Poppy nodded as Roxy turned and tottered off down the hallway, her high heels clicking on the worn linoleum floor covering.

The girl looked back at Nikki and shrugged. 'She's off out on the game again, by the looks of it,' she said calmly.

Nikki almost choked on the mouthful of lager she had just drunk. 'On the game! You mean she's a . . .'

'A pro? Yeah, half the women round here are, though in fairness me mam only goes out when she has to. No doubt me dad is in debt again an' she's got to try an' get him out o' the shit. Most o' the women round here go out to feed their drug habit. The best of it is though, it's usually me dad that supplies 'em. Trouble is, he can't stop himself from taking his share, an' then when it comes to payin' his supplier, or his "Boss" as he calls him, he never has enough to cough up what he owes so out me mam has to go again to make the cash up.'

Nikki was appalled. She knew the neighbourhood had a bad reputation but she had never dreamed that Roxy would sink so low. Without quite knowing why, she once more found herself feeling sorry for the woman. Her eyes moved around the grubby little kitchen. There was not a single thing in there worth having, so it was no wonder that Roxy took no pride in the place.

Poppy now rummaged behind the bread bin and held up two fat spliffs. 'Here, I dare say yer wouldn't say no to one o' these, would yer?'

Nikki took it gratefully. She had missed this. After smoking one of these her troubles seemed to just drift away. And the coke Poppy had given her was even better. She had soon discovered that after a bit of that, the nightmares disappeared and nothing seemed to matter. With a contented sigh she lit up and inhaled deeply.

It was almost ten o'clock when she finally set off for home feeling relaxed and at peace with herself. There had been no sign of Roxy since she had left earlier in the evening, closely followed by her husband who had told Poppy that he was going out too as he had business that needed attending to.

Nikki had reached the end of Grove Road and had just turned in the direction of the bus stop when a car cruised to a stop alongside her. She began to walk faster until the car door opened and she heard a familiar voice say, 'Nikki? Hold up, it's me.'

Pausing to look over her shoulder, she was surprised to see Poppy's father half in and half out of the car with a broad smile on his face.

'I spotted yer from up the road as I were comin' back an' thought yer might be glad of a lift,' he told her obligingly. When he saw her hesitate he rushed on, 'Come on, love, hop in. It ain't safe fer little 'uns like you to be walkin' the streets all on their own so late at night. Especially ones as pretty as you.'

Nikki was vaguely surprised. Eddie had never seemed to mind her getting home on her own before. Even so, she knew it would look impolite to refuse so she crossed to the car and climbed into the passenger seat.

'Thank you, Mr Miller.'

As he drew away from the kerb he laughed aloud and taking his hand momentarily from the steering wheel, he squeezed her knee.

'Mr Miller? Christ, that's a bit formal ain't it, love? Call me Eddie, everybody else does. Now where are we goin'? Lovelace Lane, ain't it?'

'Please.' Nikki kept her eyes directed ahead. The place where his hand had rested on her leg felt as if it was on fire and she didn't know what to say. They drove on in silence for some minutes until he suddenly said, 'It's nice to see you again, love. I was beginnin' to think you'd washed yer hands of us.'

'Oh no, no, I wouldn't do that, it's just that I've been . . . busy,' Nikki finished lamely.

'Well, that's all right then.'

When they eventually turned into Lovelace Lane, Nikki told him, 'Anywhere here will be fine, thank you.'

He steered the car into the kerb and Nikki began to fumble in the darkness for the door handle. She was just about to get out when he suddenly reached across and pressed something into her hand.

'Here. Don't let yer mam find it, mind. Poppy said as how you enjoyed it an' no doubt you'll pay me for it when you're able to.'

Nikki stared down at the packet of white powder in her hand before staring back at him questioningly.

He laughed. 'Look, I know what you young 'uns are like. Always bein' treated like kids. Well, I reckon you're old enough to decide what yer like, so as I said, pay me when yer can, an' when that's gone happen I'll be able to find yer a bit more o' the same, eh?'

Nikki flushed with pleasure. Why couldn't her mum treat her like a grown-up as Eddie was doing?

'Th . . . thank you,' she stuttered, hardly daring to believe her luck. 'I'll bring you some money around tomorrow.'

'As yer will,' he answered. 'But be warned, coke don't come cheap. Thirty quid should see you right for that little lot.'

Nikki swallowed. *Thirty pounds?* That would mean she would somehow have to get into town and take some money out of her savings account unless Claire left her purse lying about.

She managed a smile as she slammed the door then stood and watched as he drove away. Her heart was hammering loudly in her chest and she found that she couldn't stop smiling. Apart from her father, who had violated her, and Christian who treated her as if she was still a child, she had had very little to do with men but Eddie had made her feel . . . she sought in her mind for the right word and then it came to her: special, that's how he'd made her feel. She watched the car until it turned a bend in the road and disappeared from sight, then humming merrily to herself she hurried on her way.

Eddie meanwhile was also feeling well pleased with himself. He had just taken the first step towards getting Nikki right where he wanted her. If things ran true to form she would soon owe him so much that she would be only too glad to pay the debt off any way he suggested, rather than let her mum find out what she had been up to. Chuckling to himself, he turned the car in the direction of the pub.

Chapter Twenty

On a beautiful day in July 2000, when the sun was riding high in a cloudless blue sky, Robbie stood with his daughters on either side of him high on the hill overlooking Gatley Common, their old home.

In his hands was the urn containing his late wife's ashes, and as Claire peeped at him from the corner of her eye she saw that he was struggling to contain his emotions.

Tracey was openly crying and Claire had a lump in her throat that was threatening to choke her, although she had managed to remain dry-eyed.

'A lot o' water has passed under the bridge since we last stood here, ain't it?' Robbie muttered regretfully.

'Oh, Dad.' Tracey reached out to squeeze his hand and he returned the pressure on her fingers.

'I suppose one of us ought to say somethin'?' he suggested and when neither of the girls answered he looked down into the valley pensively. From here he could see the roof of the council house that had once been their home. They had been a family then – a real family – but he had ended all that on the day he had walked out on them and he would never forgive himself for it.

In his mind's eye he could see Karen as she had been then; pretty, vivacious and full of life. Nothing like the wreck of a woman she had become before her death. But it was too late to ponder on that now.

What was done was done and he wanted to make it up to his girls. Karen was gone but they were still here and life was for the living.

Slowly taking the top off the urn he cleared his throat before saying softly, 'Goodbye, Karen. May you find peace at last, me bonny lass.'

He then tipped the urn and as the ashes fluttered out of it, the gentle breeze snatched at them and they swirled away into the air.

'Oh, *Mam* . . .' Tracey began to sob, and then suddenly they were all in each other's arms and their tears were mingling as they silently said their goodbyes to the woman who had once meant so much to each of them. It was done. Karen was finally at peace.

'I shall miss you, Claire.' Bradley's face was sad as Claire pushed the last of her things from her desk into a bag. It was her final day at the solicitor's office and both Bradley and Mr Dickinson were obviously more than a little sorry to see her go.

'I shall miss you too,' Claire told him truthfully. 'And you too, Mr Dickinson. You've both been very good to me.'

'Nonsense.' Mr Dickinson sniffed loudly. 'You've practically kept this office running single-handed at times. I doubt the new girl will be able to hold a candle to you.'

'Rubbish.' Claire smiled. 'I'm sure she'll have the place running like clockwork in no time at all.'

'Well, that remains to be seen, but here . . . we've got you a little something. I hope you like it.'

Mr Dickinson produced a small package from his desk drawer and after opening it, Claire gasped with delight. It was a small gold locket set with diamonds and she saw at a glance that it must have been very expensive.

'But I . . . I can't accept this,' she stammered. 'It's too much!'

'Oh my dear,' Mr Dickinson told her. 'You deserve it. You've been a godsend and you'll be sorely missed, as Bradley said. Nevertheless, I think I can speak for both of us when I say we wish you well in your new business.'

Claire blinked tearfully. 'Thank you.' She suddenly wanted to be gone. There had been so many goodbyes in her life and here was yet another one to add to her list.

'Now you be sure to come and see us. Don't be a stranger,' Mr Dickinson warned her, and then before she could stop him, Bradley had lifted her bag and was striding towards the door.

'I'll pop this in your car for you while you say goodbye,' he told her obligingly.

Claire crossed to Mr Dickinson and planted an affectionate kiss on his wrinkled old cheek.

'You take care now, and don't get overdoing it,' she told him. 'And don't worry. You haven't seen the last of me yet. I shall turn up like a bad penny to check on you when you least expect it.'

He nodded and after a final glance around she turned and left the office. She found Bradley standing at the side of her car with a face like a wet weekend and she grinned.

'Oh Bradley, don't look like that.' She opened the car and he placed her bag on the back seat. 'I'm not about to leave the country. I'm sure we'll still see each other from time to time.'

'Yes, I'm sure we will,' he said seriously. 'But that's the trouble, Claire. I don't want to just see you from time to time – I want to see you *all* the time. You must have guessed how I feel about you?'

She looked up into his handsome face. Bradley was a lovely, kind man, and not for the first time she wished that she could return his affections. But while Christian was in the background she knew that there could never be anyone else for her and she owed it to Bradley to tell him so.

'I think you would be a good catch for any woman, Bradley,' she said gently. 'I mean that from the bottom of my heart. But the thing is, my affections lie elsewhere. I have a vet friend back in Blackpool – well, no, he's more than a friend if I'm being honest. I've been in love with him for years and one day . . . well, one day I hope that we'll be able to come together.'

Shock registered on his face. He had assumed that Claire was a grieving widow, and yet here she was, telling him that she was in love with someone else – and had been for some time, if what she was saying was true.

'I'm only telling you this because I think you should have someone who will love you as you deserve to be loved,' she went on. 'And I don't think it's fair to have you wasting your affections on me. Somewhere out there is a woman who will be worthy of you, and I know you will find her. But I hope we can remain friends? I am very fond of you.'

'I see. Well, thank you for being honest with me, Claire. And yes, of course we can still be friends.'

He held out his hand and she shook it warmly, knowing that she had just blown yet another chance at happiness. Bradley would defin-itely be a wonderful catch for someone – although that was what she had once thought about Greg, she reminded herself. He had been handsome and charming too, or so she had believed. One thing she was sure of, Bradley King wasn't for her. Her heart belonged solely to Christian and she knew that it always would.

The young solicitor watched as she climbed into the car and drove away before turning slowly and making his way back into the office.

'My goodness! You've done wonders,' Claire declared as she walked into the shop later that day. Robbie was perched on a stepladder, pasting a sheet of wallpaper to the final wall and he grinned at her across his shoulder.

'It is takin' shape, ain't it?' He looked around. 'I aim to get this wall finished today and then I can start on the platform for the window displays and the fitting rooms.'

Claire stood, hands on hips, surveying his handiwork. The room looked completely different. The paper gave it a light and airy feel, and just as she had planned, it looked trendy and modern. But she also saw that her father looked tired and she felt a stab of guilt. He had been working tirelessly for three weeks now, weekends included, and she wondered how much longer he could keep it up. An idea had been forming in her mind over the last couple of days and now she tentatively broached it to him, hoping that she wasn't about to make a big mistake.

'Dad? I . . . er . . . I've been thinking.'

'Oh aye? What about, lass?' Clambering down from the ladder, Robbie wiped his hands on an old towel and gave her his full attention.

'Well, the thing is, it seems a long way for you to travel here every day, so I was wondering if you might like to move in with me and Nikki? Just until the shop is finished, of course. It would save you a lot of to-ing and fro-ing, and we have plenty of room for you. But only if you wanted to,' she finished hastily.

Robbie cleared his throat, feeling emotional. Over the last couple of weeks they had become easier in each other's company and he saw this as a major step forward to rebuilding their relationship.

'Well, I suppose it does make sense,' he replied cautiously. 'As long as you're quite sure you can put up wi' me for a time, that is. O' course, I'd be happy to pay you me board an' lodgin'—'

'There will be no need for that,' Claire told him immediately. 'I think you are more than earning your keep working in here all the hours God sends.'

'In that case then, I think it's a grand idea, and I thank you kindly,' he told her. 'I'd have to go back an' settle up with me landlady and get me stuff though.'

'Of course, but that shouldn't take long, so how about you do that when you've finished here today?'

'I dare say there's no time like the present, so you're on.' There was a twinkle in his eye and a wide smile on his face now, and suddenly embarrassed, Claire turned abruptly and walked towards the back room.

'Fine, that's settled then. You go and pack your things and by the time you get back I'll have your bedroom and a meal ready for you. Meantime, I dare say you wouldn't say no to a cuppa.'

He nodded solemnly.

★　★　★

'What? You've asked him to move in here? But why?'

'Oh Nikki, don't be such a drama queen,' Claire sighed. 'I would have thought it's more than obvious why. He's working his socks off getting the shop done for us. And it is only a temporary thing. The shop should be ready for opening in a couple of weeks and then no doubt he'll be heading back to Scotland.'

'Hmph!' Nikki folded her arms across her chest; a sure sign that she was sulking. She had only met Claire's father on a few occasions and she could see no reason at all why they should suddenly be lumbered with him actually living under the same roof. Still, if it was only going to be a temporary thing, she supposed she would have to grin and bear it. She didn't have much choice, did she, if Claire had already asked him. As her hand dropped to the money in the pocket of her school skirt, her thoughts were temporarily diverted. She had gone into town again at lunchtime and withdrawn yet another fifty pounds out of her savings for Eddie, but God knew what Claire would say if she found out. Her savings were dwindling fast and she wondered what she would do when they were gone. She shrugged; she would worry about that when the time came. For now, what Claire didn't know wouldn't hurt her. Meantime, she supposed she had better try to be civil at least to Robbie, else Claire would be on her case again.

It was almost eight o'clock that night when Claire heard Robbie's car pull onto the drive and she hurried out to meet him. He was just lifting a small case from the boot of the car and she saw that he had washed and changed.

'Ah, you're here then?' she said, for want of something to say. 'Come on in. I've got your dinner ready but first I'll show you to your room, shall I? I've put you at the back so the traffic doesn't disturb you – not that it's that noisy here.'

'I really don't mind where I go,' he answered self-consciously. 'I'm sure it will be lovely.'

He followed her into the house and up the stairs, and when they reached the end of the long landing she threw a door open and told him, 'I've put you in here. I hope you'll be comfortable.'

His mouth fell open as he looked around. 'Comfortable? Why, lass, compared to where I've been stayin', this is like a palace,' he told her truthfully. 'Not that me lodgin's weren't perfectly adequate,' he hastened to add.

'Well, it is a nice big room,' Claire admitted as her eyes followed his. 'I've been meaning to get around to decorating it, to be honest. The wallpaper is a bit dated, to say the least, but seeing as Nikki and I have never used it, I've never found the time.'

He looked admiringly at the king-sized bed and the tall mahogany wardrobes and matching drawers. There was a wall-to-wall carpet on the floor and bright flowered curtains hanging at the windows.

'I'm afraid there isn't an en-suite with this room,' she went on apologetically. 'So you will have to share the bathroom with me. Nikki has her own.'

He chuckled. 'That won't exactly be a hardship, seeing as where I've been living I had to share with five other blokes.'

'Right then, I'll leave you to unpack. Shall we say dinner in ten minutes? I've done us a chicken casserole. I hope you like it?'

He nodded eagerly and turning about, Claire left him to it. Once alone, he crossed to the window where he stood gazing out across the huge garden and there he said a silent prayer, *Dear Lord, let this be the start of better times.*

He then turned back to his case and began to put his clothes away.

Claire was just lifting a steaming dish from the oven when he joined her a short while later and she nodded towards the table, which he saw was set for two.

Glancing towards the door he asked, 'Isn't Nikki joining us?'

Claire shook her head. 'No, I'm afraid not. She went out about an hour ago. Even when she is in she's started taking a tray up to her room – but that's teenagers for you. They go through these little fads. Anyway, help yourself. I hope it isn't overcooked.'

'It looks wonderful,' he assured her, and began to load his plate as he realised how hungry he was.

The meal was a silent affair, with each of them feeling a little awkward but once they had eaten and retired to the lounge with a glass of wine, Robbie began to relax a little.

'That was a lovely meal, Claire,' he told her sincerely. 'I didn't realise you were such a good cook, lass.'

'I had to learn young, didn't I? Mum wasn't in all that often to see to us when we were little so I had to look after Tracey.' Seeing him flush she silently scolded herself. She hadn't meant for that to come out as it had and he had obviously taken it as a slight.

'And then, of course, when I got my hotel I had to learn slightly fancier dishes for my guests,' she hurried on, hoping to soften her last statement. 'I don't mind admitting there were some real culinary disasters in the early days. If I hadn't had Betty, a lady who worked there, to help me, I think I would have gone bankrupt.'

'Oh, I'm sure that isn't true, lass,' Robbie said kindly. 'You seem like the kind of young woman who could do anything she set her mind to. Look at this place for a start. There aren't many your age who own a beautiful house like this.'

Claire looked around, trying to see it as he would. 'It is a nice house,' she admitted eventually. 'Though I have to say I haven't done much to it since Nikki and I moved in. The old lady who owned it had very good taste, though I know it could do with updating a bit.'

'Well, just say the word and I'd be happy to help,' Robbie told her.

Claire blushed. 'Oh, I wasn't hinting that you should—'

'I know you weren't,' he cut in with a grin. 'But as I said, I'd be more than happy to decorate anywhere you want doing once we've finished at the shop.'

Claire looked at him curiously. 'You're not in any hurry to get back to Scotland then?'

'No, I'm not.' He stared into the empty fire-grate as colour rose in his cheeks. 'I have more to keep me here than there is for me there, but we'll see, eh? At the minute I'm happy to take one day at a time, and I'm more than grateful that you've asked me to stay.'

'It was the least I could do,' Claire told him, suddenly feeling embarrassed again. 'Now, how about we have a top-up? We may as well finish the bottle off. It will only go flat and get poured away if we don't.' Without waiting for an answer she hurried away to fetch the wine bottle from the kitchen.

It was almost an hour later when Claire saw Robbie stifle a yawn and so she asked, 'Would you like to go up to bed? You must be worn out. It's been a long day, hasn't it?'

'I wouldn't mind, lass,' he replied. 'Shall I help you with the pots before I go up?'

'No, there's no need for that. I'll stick them in the dishwasher.'

He saw her glance at the clock and asked, 'What time will Nikki be in?'

It was almost ten o'clock and Claire frowned. 'She should have been in an hour ago. But you go up. I've got plenty to do while I wait for her.'

Robbie bit down on his lip. He wanted to say that Claire should put her foot down with the girl. From what he had seen she was far too soft with Nikki, but then he didn't want to be seen as interfering, so instead he said, 'Goodnight then, lass. Sleep tight.'

'Hope the bedbugs don't bite . . .' Claire pursed her lips as she finished the sentence he had always said to her while tucking her in when she was just a little girl. Just what did I have to go and say that for? she cursed herself, but Robbie merely smiled and left the room without so much as another word, though his heart felt as if it was breaking. So she had remembered, then. All these years on and she still remembered.

Claire meantime was staring off into space. Soon, very soon, she would tell her father the truth about her past. She had fully intended to do it this very evening, but somehow, as always, the words had stuck in her throat. Still, she consoled herself, there will be lots of other days now that he's living with us, and then when I've told him, I'll tell Nikki then Molly and Tracey. She tried to imagine the relief she would feel when the truth was finally out in the open, and the thought of it consoled her as she settled down to wait for Nikki.

Chapter Twenty-One

Nikki was standing at the end of Grove Road; Eddie had promised to meet her there at ten. It was now almost twenty past and she had no doubt that her mum would be going mental by now, which would mean yet another shouting match when she got in.

She sighed, wondering if she should set off for home, but then decided against it. If she didn't get her bag of coke it would mean a sleepless night so she would hang on and hope that he would soon put in an appearance. At that moment, Eddie's car turned the corner and drew to a halt at the side of her. She scooted round to the passenger side and slid into the seat beside him.

''Ello, sweetheart,' he greeted her. 'Sorry if I'm a bit late, I got held up. Not to worry though, eh? I've got your stuff for you.' So saying, he slipped a small bag into her hand as she fumbled in the pocket of her jeans for the money. She passed it to him without a word and he grinned into the darkness.

'I think you're gettin' fond o' this, ain't yer?' he said.

She nodded. There was no point in denying it. It was getting now that she felt shaky and ill when she didn't have a regular supply, which was a little worrying with the way her savings were dwindling.

'I . . . er . . . the thing is, I don't think I dare take any more money out of my savings for a while,' she muttered. 'If my mum got to see my bank book she'd have a fit.'

'No one ever said this stuff came cheap,' he retorted. 'But never mind, I'm sure we'll think o' some other way you can pay for it, if cash is gettin' tight.'

Nikki peered at him questioningly in the light from the street lamp.

'Don't worry about it for now,' he told her with a grin. 'Just you let me know when that's gone an' you need some more, an' then we'll see what we can come up wi', eh? You should know by now that I'd never deny you anythin'. Now off you go. We don't want yer mam round here raisin' hell, do we?'

Nikki smiled and tucked the bag into her pocket before clambering out of the car to watch as Eddie pulled away and continued up the road. What could he have meant? *Some other way o' payin' for it.* Shrugging, she turned about and headed for the bus stop, praying that she hadn't missed the last bus home.

When she turned into Lovelace Lane and saw that the lights were still on in her home, her heart sank. Claire was obviously waiting up for her, which meant she was in for another telling-off. Oh well, she thought, best go and get it over with. She was becoming used to it by now.

The second she set foot through the door, Gemma pottered towards her and Claire stepped out of the lounge. She looked pale and tired and worried sick, and just for an instant Nikki felt guilty, but then she stuck out her chin and demanded, 'What are you looking like that for? It isn't *that* late!'

'From where I'm standing I would say it *is*,' Claire shot back. She was trying hard to keep her voice down, desperately aware that her father upstairs must be able to hear every word she said.

Nikki sniffed as she elbowed past her. 'Look, we'll talk about this in the morning, shall we?' she grunted rudely, and she then climbed the stairs, leaving Claire standing there clenching her fists with frustration. Until Nikki had started going round to Poppy's again things had seemed to settle down for a while, but now they were as bad as ever. Even the novelty of having a shop named after her had worn off and it wasn't even open yet.

Sighing, Claire began to switch the lights off. At least Nikki had come home, so she supposed she should be grateful for small mercies. It was then that the harsh ringing of the phone interrupted the silence and she snatched it up, fearful of waking her dad, just in case he was still fast asleep.

'Hello?' There was no reply. 'Hello, is anyone there?' Again there was only silence so she put down the receiver and headed for the stairs. These wrong numbers were becoming a damn nuisance.

'Good morning.' Robbie flashed Nikki a friendly smile as she entered the kitchen the next morning. He was sitting at the table tucking into a plateful of bacon and eggs that Claire had cooked for him and was in a good mood.

'Morning,' she answered sullenly, barely looking towards him as she made for the fridge to pour herself a glass of orange juice. Deciding that now wasn't the best time to discuss the incident of the night before, Claire glanced at her daughter with concern. Nikki seemed to have lost even more weight and her cheeks looked sunken and pale. On top of that, there were dark circles under her eyes.

'You look a bit peaky,' she commented. 'Are you feeling poorly? If you are, we could get you down to the doctor's.'

'I'm fine,' Nikki retorted as she headed back towards the kitchen door.

'Well, what about some breakfast then?'

It was on the tip of Nikki's tongue to say she didn't want any, but seeing the determined look on Claire's face, she mumbled, 'I'll just have a slice of toast.'

Claire instantly began to butter one for her as she asked, 'Would you like any marmalade on it?'

'No, thanks.'

Claire placed the plate on the table but Nikki instantly lifted it and carried it towards the door.

'I'll eat it upstairs while I'm getting ready for school,' she informed her, and with that she was gone.

'Kids, eh – who'd have 'em?' Robbie commented, seeing the look on Claire's face. Smiling ruefully she joined him at the table and the rest of the meal was eaten in silence.

It was mid-morning and Claire had stopped to put the kettle on when there was a tap on the shop door. Hurrying through the back room and past Robbie, who was working on the new fitting room, Claire was surprised to see Bradley King smiling at her through the glass.

'Why, Bradley, what a lovely surprise,' she told him after unlocking the door and ushering him into the shop. 'What brings you here at this time of day? I thought you'd be at work.'

'I have been actually,' he told her with a grin. 'I've been in court with a client, but seeing as I don't have another appointment till after lunch I thought I'd stop by and see how things were going . . . Oh, and to give you these, of course.' When he held out an enormous bunch of red roses, Claire felt herself blush to the roots of her hair.

'Why, thank you. They're lovely,' she said shyly, then suddenly remembering her manners, she announced, 'Dad, this is Bradley King. He's Mr Dickinson's partner – the solicitor I used to work for. Bradley, this is my father, Robbie McMullen.'

Robbie stopped what he was doing and strode across to them. The two men shook hands as Robbie told him, 'Nice to meet you, Bradley. Are you missing her at work then?'

'Very much so,' Bradley replied with a wide smile. 'The new girl we have is dizzy compared to Claire. She had everything well under control.'

'I can quite believe it.' Robbie returned the smile, thinking what a nice young man Bradley seemed to be. Just the sort he would like to see Claire with, in fact, and it was obvious the poor chap was smitten with her. Claire, on the other hand, looked desperately embarrassed, so hoping to divert things, Robbie asked him, 'So what do you think of the place now then? It's taking shape, isn't it?'

'It certainly is,' Bradley answered, looking round admiringly. 'The wallpaper looks grand, just the sort of thing to appeal to the customers you're aiming at.'

Robbie then led him round the shop telling him of their plans for the place and showing him what he had done as Claire carried her flowers into the back room, found a vase and got another mug out of the cupboard.

'We were just about to have a tea-break,' she shouted through the open door. 'Would you like a cup, Bradley?'

'I'd love one,' he called back. 'Milk, two sugars, but then you should know that by now.'

'I've certainly made you enough,' she retorted laughing, and minutes later she carried a tray in to them. 'There you go. I managed to rustle up some custard creams too. Help yourselves.'

The next fifteen minutes passed pleasantly as they spoke of this and that, and Claire was amused to see that her father and Bradley were getting on famously. Eventually, the young man glanced at his watch and placing his empty mug on the tray, he told them regretfully, 'I dare say I ought to be going now, else the boss will be after my blood. But it was lovely to meet you, sir.'

'You too, Bradley, you too. Call in and see us again, won't you?' Robbie rejoined. 'I aim to have the place ready for opening by next weekend.'

'Wonderful, but if you get stuck, give me a shout. I could always come in and give you a hand after work. I'm not afraid of getting my hands dirty, I assure you.'

'In that case then, how about you come in and help me with getting this fitting room up on Saturday morning? It's difficult to do it on your own and it's a bit heavy for Claire.'

'You're on,' Bradley told him good-naturedly. 'I'll be here for nine o'clock sharp. How does that sound?'

'Perfect,' Robbie beamed.

Once again the men shook hands warmly, then after placing an affectionate kiss on Claire's cheek, Bradley lifted his briefcase and headed towards the door.

'Goodbye, and thanks for the flowers,' she smiled.

'It was my pleasure,' he told her, and with a final friendly grin he let himself out.

'What a nice chap,' Robbie remarked. 'Looks like he's smitten with you, my love.'

'Oh Dad, don't get reading anything into it,' Claire said, more irritably than she had intended. 'Bradley and I are friends, nothing more, and that's how it's going to stay.'

'Don't you like him then?'

'Of course I like him. There is nothing about Bradley *not* to like, but . . . Well, let's just say my affections lie elsewhere.'

'I see.' Robbie scratched his head. 'From where I'm standing, he's going to be a great husband for some lucky girl.'

'You're quite right,' Claire said, and she couldn't help smiling. 'But you can stop your match-making because that girl won't be me.'

'Aw well,' Robbie told her with a twinkle in his eye, and turning about, he went back to work, whistling merrily.

It was Friday evening and upstairs in her room, Nikki was getting ready to go out as Claire prepared the evening meal. Robbie had stayed on at the shop for a while, insisting that he had a job to finish, and Claire could not fail but be impressed with him. He had worked tirelessly and was proving to be remarkably easy to get on with. She had also found that she quite liked having him staying at the house; it was nice to have a man about the place, it made her feel safe. Not that she would have dreamed of telling him so.

Glancing towards the ceiling, she frowned. Upstairs, she could hear Nikki crossing the landing on her way back to her room from the family bathroom. It was strange, now she came to think about it; Nikki had been using it for the last couple of days, although she had her own en-suite bathroom adjoining her room. Crossing the kitchen she climbed the stairs and tapped at Nikki's door. It inched open and Nikki peered out at her.

'Hello, love. I heard you using the main bathroom again and wondered if there was a problem with yours?'

'There is, as a matter of fact,' Nikki said with a scowl. 'The toilet seems to be blocked up and I can't flush it.'

'Then you should have said. I'll get Dad to have a look at it later this evening, shall I?'

Nikki shrugged, not much caring one way or another, and Claire smiled before hurrying back down to the kitchen. But inside she was crying. She felt as if a wall was building up between herself and the child she loved as her own, yet had no idea at all how to break it down. Nikki barely had a civil word for her these days and at times she had been downright rude to Robbie, who had taken it all in his usual cheerful way.

Slumping down at the table, Claire rested her chin on her hand and stared out of the window. Perhaps things would improve when the shop was open? She and Nikki would be spending a lot more time together then and she could only pray that they would get back to being close as they had once been. Her thoughts moved on to Christian; he would be feeding the dogs in the sanctuary now, no doubt with Mandy helping him. As jealousy surged through her she mentally shook herself and hurried back to the stove to check on the joint.

Leaning over the banister, Nikki listened to Claire clattering about the kitchen before tip-toeing across the landing and into her bedroom. Her eyes flew round the neat and tidy room and came to rest on a small velvet box on the dressing-table. Crossing to it, she quickly flipped the lid open. Inside was the diamond locket Mr Dickinson and Bradley had bought for Claire when she left the office. Nikki knew that her mum treasured it, but she had no time for sentiment at the moment. She needed something with which to pay Eddie for her next score, and this looked like it was worth a lot of money. She was aware that he had contacts who took stolen jewellery off him and sold it, so no doubt he would jump at the chance of getting his hands on this. Without a moment's hesitation she took the locket from the box and slipped it into her pocket, then returning the box to where she had found it, she left the room as quiet as a mouse.

'Oh hello, that was good timing. The dinner is just about ready,' Claire told Robbie when he came in a short while later.

'That's good, 'cos I could eat a scabby horse an' its rider along with it,' he told her with a wink. 'I'll just pop up and get changed first though, if you don't mind?'

'Of course I don't. I'll pour us both a drink,' Claire replied.

She listened to him whistling as he took the stairs two at a time and found herself smiling. The more time they spent together, the easier they seemed to get in each other's company, which Claire found strange when she thought back to how resentful she had felt about him such a short time ago. Things were looking up with Tracey too, it seemed, for she had phoned Claire only the day before to tell her that she would be bringing the twins over for a visit on Sunday. Claire suspected that Tracey was coming to see her father rather than her, but even so, if it meant them spending some time together she could live with that. Claire could hardly wait as she was totally besotted with her tiny nieces and couldn't see enough of them. She had already decided to do a picnic in the garden if the weather was nice, and was hoping that Nikki would come down off her high horse long enough to stay in and enjoy it with them.

By the time Robbie reappeared she had poured them both a nice cold glass of wine and they carried it out onto the patio.

'I was thinking, seeing as Bradley is coming to help me tomorrow, you could have the day off and spend some time with Nikki,' he told her thoughtfully, as he sank onto a chair and stretched his legs out contentedly.

Claire peered at him. 'It would be nice if you're sure you could manage,' she admitted. 'I've rather neglected the house with being so busy at the shop and I have to go and start buying stock next week if we're to open a week on Monday.'

He nodded. 'I wouldn't have said it if I didn't think I could manage, but do you have to spend the day working? Why don't you take Nikki to the pictures or something instead. You know, spend a bit of quality time together.'

'Huh! Chance would be a fine thing,' Claire muttered. 'Nikki doesn't seem to want to do anything with me any more. She lives, eats and breathes for Poppy, this new friend of hers.'

'Fairly normal for teenage girls, I should say,' Robbie replied. 'It's a well-known fact that half the time they'd rather be with their mates than their family. I shouldn't worry about it too much though, I'm sure she'll grow out of it, given time.'

Claire felt a flush rise to her cheeks. Since Robbie had moved in she had done her best to cover up the rows and arguments that she and Nikki were constantly having, but it seemed that he was a lot more astute than she had given him credit for.

Pulling herself out of the chair, she headed towards the open patio doors. 'Right, I'll give Nikki a shout and then we'll have dinner, shall we?' she said, and he smiled in agreement. Claire was having a rough time of it and there seemed to be nothing he could do to help her. There had been times lately when he had felt like shouting at Nikki himself; the girl seemed to rule the roost. But he knew that his interference would not be appreciated, so he had managed to remain quiet, although it was getting harder with every day that passed. It was obvious that this here Poppy was proving to be a bad influence on the girl, but what could he do about it?

Claire suddenly stepped out of the door again and he saw that her eyes were full of tears.

'Why, what's wrong, lass?' he asked.

'Oh, it's Nikki,' she said chokily. 'She's cleared off again without so much as a word, the little madam, and being a Friday God knows what time she'll roll in.'

'Well, happen she'll turn back up when she's ready,' he told her soothingly. 'Now come on, let's go and eat, eh? There's no sense in letting good food go to waste when you've gone to all the trouble of preparing it.'

Taking her elbow he steered her back into the kitchen, feeling her distress and a measure of resentment towards the person who had caused it.

Chapter Twenty-Two

When Nikki arrived at Poppy's she wondered what she was walking into. Roxy and Eddie were in the middle of a horrendous row and the air was almost blue.

They stopped abruptly when she walked in, and cocking her head towards the kitchen, Roxy told her, 'Go into our Poppy, love. She's through there.'

With her cheeks burning, Nikki scuttled past them, and once through the kitchen door she was shocked to see Poppy sitting at the kitchen table painting her nails without a care in the world.

'What's wrong with those two?' she asked, nodding towards the lounge.

Poppy sniffed. 'Oh, Dad's gone an' got himself into bleedin' debt wi' his boss again. I dare say they're rowin' 'cos he'll expect Mam to go back out on the streets again.'

Nikki felt sad for Roxy. Molly would definitely have classed her as 'common as muck', yet for all that, Nikki couldn't help but like her.

At that moment, Katie pottered into the kitchen and made straight for Nikki to give her a silent hug. Nikki hugged her back as sounds of the row started up again.

'I am *not* goin' back out there, Eddie, an' that's a bleedin' end to it! I'm too old to be doin' a turn now, do yer hear me? Yer got yourself into this mess so now yer can bloody well get yourself out of it. An' yer can knock me from pillar to post but I won't change me fuckin' mind this time so you'd better get used to it!'

A moment later, there was a crash and the sound of a cry, then Eddie stormed into the hallway and snatched up his coat.

'Huh! I thought husband an' wife were supposed to stick together,' he growled. 'All you're good for is sittin' on yer fat idle arse.'

'Well, piss off then, an' find somebody better,' Roxy hissed back.

'I might just do that!'

There was another crash as he slammed the front door and suddenly the silence was deafening. Nikki clung to Katie and seconds later, Roxy stumbled into the kitchen with blood streaming from her nose. Picking up a grubby tea-towel she held it to her face.

'I'm sorry about that, love,' she mumbled at Nikki apologetically. 'Best to take no notice of us, eh? He'll have forgot all about it by the time he comes home.'

Poppy sighed. 'One o' these days you'll learn,' she said, as if she was talking to a child. 'He'll do for yer yet, you just mark my words.'

'Not if I do fer him first!' Roxy lit a cigarette and inhaled deeply. Deep down she was beginning to wonder if Poppy wasn't right. But what could she do about it? Over the years she had stayed in numerous women's refuges but Eddie had always managed to find her and persuade her to go home. Now she just didn't have the energy to go all through it again. She was feeling her age and just wanted a quiet life, not that she was ever likely to get it, married to Eddie. And yet, for all that, she still loved him. He was her man, for better or worse.

Her eyes settled on Katie. Sometimes, God forgive her, she was almost glad that Katie was autistic. At least she was locked in her own little world where nothing seemed to trouble her.

'I ought to go,' Nikki said, gently disentangling herself from Katie's arms.

'No, there's no need fer that,' Roxy assured her. 'I'm goin' to go up an' have a bit of a lie-down. Yer weren't plannin' on goin' out, were you, love?'

When Poppy shook her head, the woman sighed with relief. 'Good, I'll settle Katie in front o' the telly then. You'll keep yer eye on her for me, won't yer?' She took the child's hand and led her back into the lounge, and finally the two girls were alone.

Crossing to the fridge, Poppy took out two cans of lager and, passing one to Nikki, she asked, 'So, how's things at your place then?'

'About the same,' Nikki informed her. 'I tell you, since my mum's dad has moved in I'm scared to breathe.'

'What's wrong wi' him then?'

'It's not so much him as my mum.' Nikki paused to take a swallow from her can. 'She's gone all goody-goody in front of him. You know, cooking a proper dinner every night and cleaning up all the time. She goes spare if I so much as leave my trainers in the hallway.'

Poppy chuckled and leaning towards each other, the two girls settled down to gossip.

Eddie had gone no more than ten paces along the road when his mobile phone rang. His heart began to race as he recognised the voice on the other end. He listened intently for a moment before babbling, 'I'm doin' me best, boss, really I am. I reckon she's just about ready now. It shouldn't be long now, honest.'

He listened for another minute then slowly replaced the phone in his pocket. It was time to put the plan that had been forming in his mind into practice. The boss was growing impatient and Eddie didn't fancy ending up in a concrete overcoat at the bottom of the river at all.

Nikki left Poppy's at almost half past ten after spending what had turned out to be a quiet evening with her friend. She felt nervy and on edge, but then she always seemed to feel like that just lately – apart from when Eddie had slipped her some coke – and that didn't look very likely tonight. Poppy hadn't even had a spliff to give her, so she could look forward to a sleepless night.

However, she had taken no more than a few steps when Eddie bobbed up from behind a hedge and hissed, 'Here, Nikki, over here.'

Glancing across her shoulder, she quickly joined him in the shadows and as he pressed something into her hand she sighed with relief.

'Have you got the money?' he asked.

'Well, not exactly.'

'What do you mean, "not exactly"? You either have or you ain't!'

'I daren't take any more out of my savings, but I've got this – look. It's worth much more than fifty pounds.'

As she held the locket out to him he peered at it in the glow from the street lamp. He could see at a glance that it was expensive, but he wouldn't tell her that, of course.

'Mmm, I ain't so sure about that,' he said instead. 'It's gettin' harder to pass jewellery on wi' all the police raids that are goin' on round the estate.'

Nikki felt the first stirrings of panic. If Eddie didn't accept the locket as payment it meant she would have to do without her coke.

He stroked his chin thoughtfully, enjoying her discomfort before saying, 'There is another way you could pay me though. A way that would mean yer could have as much o' this stuff as yer wanted whenever yer wanted.' He watched her eager face and felt a tiny stirring of guilt. She was little more than a baby, but what choice did he have?

'So, what is it then?'

'Well, I have this friend who's keen to meet yer.'

Nikki scowled now as she asked, '*What* friend?'

'Oh, just a bloke I know. He thinks you're the prettiest thing he's ever seen, an' if yer were to meet up wi' him an' be nice to him, he'd give you a real good time. He's a photographer see, an' he likes his models to be young an' pretty. He only wants to take a few photos.'

Nikki frowned into the darkness. She didn't like the sound of this at all, but even so, if it meant being able to have what she wanted, perhaps it would be worth considering. And besides, Eddie would never ask her to do anything wrong.

She was just about to answer when a voice snapped, 'Nikki, is that you?'

Pressing the locket into Eddie's hand she peeped from behind the hedge that had partly hidden her and was shocked to see Claire with Gemma on her lead staring at her.

'*Mum!*' For a moment she was speechless, but then pulling herself together she stepped towards her.

'What are *you* doing here? And how did you know where I'd be?' She was glad to see that Eddie had shrunk back further into the shadows.

'As it happens, I made it my business to find out where this friend of yours lives some weeks ago. I saw you get on the bus for the Chelmsey Park Estate with Poppy one evening and so I came here in the car and made a few enquiries. I figured that there couldn't be too many Poppys living hereabouts,' Claire said grimly. 'So from now on, if you decide to come in late I shall be after you. Now, I think it's time we were going home, don't you? We have rather a long walk ahead of us.'

Nikki resentfully fell into step beside her as Eddie slipped out from behind the hedge and went in the opposite direction with his head bent.

It was the following morning as they were having breakfast that Claire remembered the blocked toilet in Nikki's bathroom and asked, 'Dad, what are you like at plumbing?'

'Not too bad. I can turn me hand to most things if push comes to shove. Why do you ask?' He knew she had been out late searching for Nikki the night before and thought she looked worn out, but he was too tactful to mention it.

'It's just that Nikki mentioned her toilet seemed to be blocked and I wondered if you'd mind having a look at it?'

'Of course I wouldn't,' he assured her, 'but it will have to be this evening. I promised to meet Bradley at the shop at nine and Nikki isn't up yet, is she? I wouldn't like to go barging into her room while she's still in bed. I'd probably frighten her half to death.'

'No, she isn't up yet,' Claire admitted. 'And tonight would be fine. Thank you. I'm beginning to wonder how I'm going to manage when you've gone.' The instant the words were out she regretted them, but Robbie just kept his head down so that she would not see the flush of pleasure that was burning in his cheeks.

Hurrying on, she enquired, 'Are you quite sure you don't need me at the shop today?'

'Not at all. You have a day off, lass, you deserve it. You could perhaps try to find time to have a good talk to Nikki.'

'Why would I want to do that?' she flared up, and seeing that she was on the defensive again, he sighed. He felt as if he was walking on eggshells with Claire and could have bitten his tongue out. It seemed to be always one step forward and two steps back.

'Well, I couldn't help but notice that she was in late again last night and I thought perhaps spending some time together, you might be able to get to the bottom of what's troubling her. Something obviously is, lass. You can't shut your eyes to it. She looks like death warmed up, to the point that even I am getting worried about her now. I'm sorry to have to say this to you, but I am still your dad at the end of the day, whether you like it or not. Perhaps it's time you called that social worker you mentioned back in?'

He expected Claire to tell him to mind his own business, or flounce away from the table, but to his deep distress she suddenly buried her face in her hands and began to sob as if her heart would break.

'Oh Dad, I'm at my wits' end with her and don't know what to do for the best,' she admitted.

'Eeh, lass. It breaks me heart to see you so upset.' He was round the table in an instant and when he put his arms about her, Claire clung to him for the first time since she had been a little girl, and Robbie held his daughter close to his heart. Gently taking her elbow,

229

he steered her into the lounge and pressed her down onto the settee before taking a seat at the side of her, then taking her hand he asked, 'Would it help if you were to talk about it, lass?'

A million emotions flitted across her face but eventually she nodded. 'I think it would. You see, it goes so much deeper than you think. It's not all Nikki's fault. If I'd had the guts to be honest with her from the start, I might have avoided some of this.'

'Well, I'm a good listener.'

She looked down at their joined hands and then making a decision, she said quietly, 'I will tell you everything – but not now. As you said, Bradley will be waiting for you and it wouldn't be fair to keep him hanging around. Go on, I'll be fine and we'll talk tonight, eh?'

'If that's what you want.' Leaning across he planted a tender kiss on her cheek then stood up and walked towards the door where he paused to ask, 'Are you sure you'll be all right on your own, lass?'

'Positive. Go on, you get off.'

Raising his hand in farewell, he left – and once the front door closed behind him, Claire took a deep breath. It was time to come clean – to admit to being the person she really was. And who better to confide in first than her own father? Tonight she would tell him everything right from the start, and then maybe she would have taken a step towards being able to go to Christian with a clear conscience and an easy heart.

Mid-afternoon, Claire went into town to do some shopping and called in at Nikki's Boutique to see how her father and Bradley were getting on. The fitting room was already in place and they were busily painting it. She was delighted; the end of all their hard work was in sight.

'I thought I told you, you were to have a day off,' Robbie chided.

'Well, I've only popped in for a few minutes,' Claire assured him as she placed the bags on the floor. Bradley looked completely different. At the office he had always dressed in smart suits and shirts and ties, but today he was wearing jeans and a sweatshirt that were already splattered with paint.

'Oh dear, it looks like I'm going to owe you a new outfit,' she told him with a smile.

He looked down at his jeans and shrugged. 'Oh, I think I might let you off. But I'll tell you what: your dad has been telling me what a good cook you are. How about you invite me to dinner after we've finished here, and we'll call it quits?'

'Bradley King, you've got the cheek of the devil,' she scolded him, but then relenting she added, 'As it happens I've just bought enough lamb chops to feed an army so you're more than welcome if you want to follow Dad back. But don't get working too late. It is Saturday after all and I've no doubt you'll have plans for tonight.'

'No – I'm as free as a bird so I'll be more than happy to accept Madam's invitation.'

Claire shook her head as she saw the twinkle in his eye. She'd fallen for that one hook line and sinker, but then she supposed cooking him a meal was small payment for all the hard work he had obviously put in.

'Right, if you pair have quite finished nattering we have work to be getting on with,' Robbie told them, and with a smile, Claire lifted her bags and hurried away to leave them to it.

Nikki had just emerged from her bedroom when Claire got home and she looked absolutely dreadful. She was sitting at the kitchen table with a glass of milk in front of her and Gemma on her lap, and as Claire piled the bags onto the table she asked, 'Have you eaten?'

'Er . . . yes. I made myself some cereal.'

As there was no bowl in the sink, Claire thought that was highly unlikely, but she had no wish for yet another row so instead she told her, 'I've got us some nice lamb chops for tea tonight. Dad is bringing Bradley back here for a meal when they've finished at the shop and I've got all the food for the picnic tomorrow. I thought we could make a trifle for the twins. What do you think, perhaps a jelly too?'

'I shall be going out shortly.' As Nikki rose from the table, Claire's eyes were drawn to the stick-like legs poking out from beneath her dressing-gown. She looked like a bag of bones that had had skin stretched across them – and yet she had seemed to be eating better just lately. Claire had been taking loaded trays up to her room and they had all come down empty, so how could the girl be losing yet more weight?

Still hoping to avoid another argument, Claire asked gently, 'Couldn't you stay in tonight – just for me? I was hoping to make it a bit special. We hardly seem to have had any time together lately and I miss you.'

But Nikki was already disappearing through the door and her only answer was a shake of the head. Leaning heavily on the edge of the table, Claire's chin drooped to her chest with despair.

Half an hour later, Nikki came back into the room. She was dressed now and heavily made-up. Glancing towards Claire, who was peeling potatoes at the sink, she said gruffly, 'I'm off then. See you later.'

She saw at a glance that Claire had been crying and just for a moment she fought the urge to throw herself into her arms. But what good would that do? Nikki couldn't stop these feelings she had, the terrible feelings of guilt and worthlessness. Or the nightmares. She shuddered as she thought of them and her chin set as she turned about and walked away. And all Claire could do was watch her go, feeling totally helpless.

When Robbie and Bradley arrived home at six o'clock both men appreciatively eyed the table that Claire had set with her finest china.

'Crikey, that looks grand, lass,' Robbie commented. 'An' if havin' visitors gets us this sort o' treatment we'll have to start having them more often. Now what did you say we were havin'? Lamb chops, weren't it? Lord, I'm that hungry I could eat a nun through a hedge backwards.'

Claire laughed as she ushered them to the table. 'Well, sit down then and let me feed you. It's all ready to serve up.'

She carried the steaming dishes to the table and they had all just settled into their seats when the front door bell rang.

'Damn!' Claire wiped her mouth on a napkin before telling the men, 'Do carry on, I'll go and see who it is.' Seconds later she reappeared, closely followed by two police officers. Robbie saw that she was shaking like a leaf.

'Why, lass, whatever's the matter? What's happened?'

'It . . . it's Nikki,' she stammered. 'She's down at the police station. These officers caught her shoplifting. I have to go down there now.'

Bradley rose from the table, instantly taking control of the situation. 'I'll come with you,' he told her, and turning to the officers he informed them, 'I am a solicitor. You do know that Nikki is a minor, don't you?'

'Well, actually sir, she told us that she was sixteen,' the older of the two policemen replied. He looked slightly embarrassed and felt sorry for Claire, who was obviously deeply in shock.

'Has your daughter ever done anything like this before?' he asked.

'No, of course she hasn't! Why would she?' Claire cried out. 'Nikki knows that she only has to ask for anything she wants, within reason. She's still only a child! Are you quite sure it's my Nikki you have at the station?'

'I'm afraid so, madam. But now if you'll kindly come with us, we'll try to sort this out.'

Bradley steered Claire towards the door. 'We'll follow you to the station in my car,' he told the policemen. 'You do know that the worst you can do is give her a caution, don't you?'

The policeman nodded and led the way as Claire glanced imploringly over her shoulder at Robbie. She felt as if she were caught in the grip of a nightmare and had no idea at all how to handle this latest development.

'Shall I come too, lass?' Robbie asked as he wrung his hands together.

She shook her head. 'No, you stay here and have your meal. There's no sense in us all going. But thanks for offering.'

Once outside she climbed into Bradley's car, her mind in turmoil. Suddenly she could see herself as a child again, stealing from the village shop to give Tracey a treat or to get food for Tinker, the little dog she had once rescued from drowning. Then she had visions of herself stealing expensive outfits from designer shops in London flash in front of her eyes. How could she rant and rave at Nikki for doing the same thing? She would be a hypocrite, but then how could she not?

As she rubbed her forehead the thoughts spun around in her head and deep inside she was crying, *Oh Christian, where are you? I need you.* But it was Bradley's hand that snaked across to squeeze hers as she felt the beginnings of a headache start up behind her eyes.

They found Nikki sitting at a table in a small room with a stern-faced WPC keeping watch over her. When Claire and Bradley entered the room she raised her eyes to them and Claire saw that they were red-rimmed and swollen from crying.

'Oh Nikki!' Hurrying across to her, Claire sat beside her and squeezed her hand.

She had no chance to say any more before the policewoman informed them, 'We're waiting for the duty solicitor to arrive. He shouldn't be long now. Are you Nikki's parents?'

Under other circumstances, Claire would have found the question embarrassing, but right at that moment she was feeling so worried and so wretched that she merely shook her head. 'I'm Nikki's mum. This is a friend of mine.'

'A solicitor friend,' Bradley solemnly told the WPC. 'So who is on duty tonight?'

The policewoman looked him up and down. He certainly didn't look like a solicitor in his casual paint-spattered clothes, but even so she answered civilly, 'I'm not sure, sir. But I can go and find out for you.'

'Do that,' he told her with a note of authority. 'And ask the desk sergeant to tell him not to bother coming. I am Bradley King from Dickinson's Solicitors in the High Street and I will deal with this.'

'Well, if you're sure,' she said as she moved towards the door. It all sounded highly irregular to her, but she'd check it out with the desk sergeant as the man had requested.

An hour later, Nikki, Claire and Bradley left the station and Claire was sure that it was one of the longest hours she had ever been forced to endure in her whole life. Nikki had burst into tears at regular intervals throughout the interview and Claire had been glad of Bradley's presence. He had taken control of the whole thing.

The journey home in Bradley's car was made in silence and when he finally drew to a halt on the drive, Claire sighed with relief. Without a word he climbed out and opened first Claire's door then Nikki's before following them to the house. The second they entered, Nikki shot upstairs like a scalded cat as Robbie hurried out of the kitchen to meet them.

'How did it go, love?' His voice was heavy with concern.

Claire ran her hand distractedly through her hair. 'I think I can truthfully say I've had better times,' she admitted, on the verge of tears. 'I really don't know what I would have done without Bradley. He was absolutely wonderful.'

'Good, now come on in and have a hot drink. Everything's ready for you; I dare say you could both do with one.'

Claire managed a weak smile as she followed him along the hallway, and when she entered the kitchen she blinked with surprise. The whole room was as neat as a new pin with not a thing out of place. The only sound to be heard was the dishwasher buzzing in the background.

'I thought I'd have a tidy up while you were gone,' he explained as he saw her glancing around. 'The uneaten chops are on a plate wrapped in foil in the fridge if you want them heated up.'

'Thanks, Dad, but I've lost my appetite.' Sinking down onto the nearest chair she rummaged in her bag while Robbie switched the kettle on. She took out a packet of cigarettes and after lighting one she drew on it deeply as Robbie and Bradley exchanged a glance.

Minutes later, Robbie placed a mug of tea in front of her and after fetching Bradley's he told them, 'I shan't be a mo. I'm just going to take this up to Nikki. No doubt she'll be wanting one too. Have you had much chance to talk to her?'

'Not really, apart from while we were in the police station,' Claire admitted. 'I thought it might be best to wait until in the morning when we've all had time to sleep on it.'

'Happen that's wise, lass,' he agreed and hurried away upstairs as Claire looked across at Bradley.

'I really don't know how to thank you,' she told him sincerely. 'I'm not sure how I would have managed that on my own.'

'Then let's just be thankful that you didn't have to,' he told her. 'And you don't have to thank me. That's what friends are for.'

As she looked across at him she thought yet again what a lovely sincere man he was.

Robbie, meanwhile, was wrestling with his conscience. Claire was obviously at the end of her tether, so perhaps now wouldn't be the right time to tell her that while she had been gone he had also unblocked Nikki's toilet. That in itself was no big deal. It was what he had found *down* the toilet that was worrying. It had been absolutely clogged with uneaten food. That must be why Nikki was suddenly so keen to take her meals in her room nowadays. It was so that she could flush them all away. From where he was standing it appeared that Nikki had major problems but, he decided, it could wait till the next day. They had already had more than enough to cope with for one night.

Chapter Twenty-Three

'You gormless little bugger, you!' Roxy ranted as she strode along with Poppy at her side. 'What the bleedin' hell were yer thinkin' of? Yer dad will go mad when he finds out I've had to bail you out o' the cop shop.'

'Huh!' Poppy retorted indignantly. 'He's hardly Snow White, is he? So what can he say?'

'It ain't what he'll say I'm worried about, it's what he'll do,' Roxy snapped back. 'I've been on the receivin' end of his fists more times than I care to remember, so happen yer won't feel so cocky when he lays into you. Trouble is, I can't say as I'd blame him this time, so prepare yourself.'

Poppy went white as she thought on her mam's words. Her dad had always been a great one for telling them all, '*You do as I say, not as I do*' so she had no doubt at all that she'd be in for a rare old pasting when he decided to put in an appearance – if her mam told him what she'd been up to, that was.

Changing her tone now, she moved closer to Roxy and asked, 'Does he have to find out, Mam? If yer didn't tell him he'd probably never get to hear about it. An' I promise I won't do it again.'

Roxy frowned. Poppy's promises were a little like pie crusts – made to be broken. But then, did she really want the hassle of Eddie going off into one of his towering rages?

'Did anyone see yer getting taken to the police station?' she asked, and Poppy hesitated for just a fraction of a second before telling her, 'Well, no – no one except Nikki.'

'Nikki!' Roxy stopped in her tracks and grabbing Poppy's arm she swung her around to face her, heedless of the glances she was attracting. 'You're tellin' me that *Nikki* was with you?'

'Yes, she got taken to the station too,' Poppy admitted tremulously. 'She . . . er . . . had a top away, so she got caught an' all.'

'But why would *she* want to steal a bloody top?' Roxy asked in exasperation. 'Her mam is about to open her own dress shop so she could have any top she . . .' A thought suddenly occurred to her, and leaning menacingly towards her daughter again she hissed, 'She were stealin' it fer you, weren't she?'

Poppy tossed her head defensively as she hissed back, 'What if she was? You or Dad ain't bought me nothin' decent to wear fer ages so what am I supposed to do – walk around in rags?'

'I'll give you bloody rags, me girl!' Roxy was almost beside herself with rage, and turning abruptly she stormed away as Poppy ran to keep up with her.

'Please, Mam, don't tell me dad,' she beseeched her breathlessly, but for now, Roxy was too angry to answer her so they moved on in silence.

They had just turned the corner into Grove Road when Roxy swore under her breath. 'Looks like somebody's beat me to it,' she muttered as she saw the police car parked outside their house. All along the road the net curtains were twitching non-stop as neighbours peeped from behind them. Puffing her chest out, Roxy took a deep breath and hurried along.

Her son Luke was standing at the door talking to the police officers as she swung through the broken gate, and she saw relief flash across his face when he saw her. 'Mam, me dad's had an accident,' he gabbled and Roxy's mouth fell open with shock.

'He's *what*?' She had assumed that they were there because of Poppy's little escapade, but Luke's words took the wind right out of her sails. 'What's happened?' she demanded of the fresh-faced young policeman.

'I'm afraid your husband has been taken into Solihull Hospital,' he informed her solemnly. He cleared his throat and glanced at his colleague before going on, 'We had a report that a man had been found lying unconscious behind the Punchbowl in Wheeley Moor Road and when we got there we found your husband. He's taken a pretty bad battering by the looks of things, though they did say at the hospital that his injuries didn't look to be life-threatening. Can you think of anyone who might do this to him? Anyone that he might have upset recently?'

Roxy snorted; she could have drawn up a list. Eddie always seemed to be upsetting someone. However, she merely shook her head.

'Would you like us to give you a lift to the hospital?' the young man asked politely.

Roxy didn't really want to be seen in the back of a police car, but then she supposed it would be better than having to stand about waiting for buses and the neighbours had all seen the police there by now anyway.

She nodded ungraciously as she followed the two young bobbies back up the path, shouting across her shoulder, 'Poppy, you just keep yer eyes on our Katie while I'm gone.'

Keen to get back in her mam's good books, Poppy shouted, 'OK, Mam!' and hurried inside, slamming the door shut behind her. There was no concern for her dad; in her opinion, he deserved all he got. In fact, she was only surprised that someone hadn't given him a good hiding before now. And what perfect timing! Her mam would prob-ably forget all about her little misdemeanour now. Helping herself to a cigarette from the packet flung on the kitchen table, she inhaled deeply with a big grin on her face.

As they drove along Lode's Lane and the hospital came into sight, the first fluttering of fear sprang to life in Roxy's stomach. What state would she find Eddie in? And who could have done it? It would certainly be no one from the estate. Eddie was the king pin there and greatly feared. His boss? She pursed her lips; that was certainly the best possibility. He had been threatening Eddie about what would happen to him for some time now, if Eddie didn't get his finger out and repay him the money he owed him. But as usual her husband had gone along in his own carefree way, frittering away every penny he got his hands on, on the horses and booze, thinking that nothing and no one could touch him. Well, perhaps this would teach him a valuable lesson.

The car drew to a halt outside the Accident & Emergency Department, and nodding at the two policemen, Roxy clambered out of the car and with her heart hammering painfully in her chest, she strode towards the entrance.

'So how are you feeling this morning, lass?' Robbie asked as he strolled into the kitchen the next morning. Claire looked as pale as a ghost and one glance at the dark circles under her eyes told of the sleepless night she had just had.

'I'm fine,' she muttered, though he knew that she was lying through her teeth. 'I've just put some bacon on, would you like some?'

'No thanks, lass. I reckon I'll just have a bit o' toast this mornin' if it's all the same to you. Nikki still in bed, is she?'

'Yes, I couldn't see any point in disturbing her. I've got Tracey and Callum bringing the twins over this afternoon so I'm going to wait until they've gone before I talk to her.'

Robbie stared at his daughter's slim back. He could understand why she didn't want to start a row this morning, but even so he considered that what Nikki had done was serious enough to warrant a good telling-off at least. It seemed that the girl could walk all over Claire, which he found strange, for in every other direction Claire seemed to be a spirited young woman.

'Have you thought of how you're going to handle this?' he asked tentatively. 'You know, what punishment you're going to mete out?'

'Oh come on, Dad. Mete out? Anyone would think we were still in the Dark Ages. What do you want me to do? Put her in the stocks and throw rotten eggs at her?' When Claire turned on him he was shocked to see that her cheeks were flaming and tears were trembling on her eyelashes. She blinked them angrily away as she slammed some bread into the toaster.

He fiddled with the salt pot that was standing on the table. 'I'm sorry, lass, I don't mean to poke me nose in where it ain't wanted. But you know, if you let her get away with this, you'll be making a rod for your own back. She'll think that she can do as she pleases.'

'Do you really think I don't know that?' When she looked him in the eyes, the raw pain he saw there tore at his heart. 'I don't know how to handle it. There are reasons why I can't . . .' Her voice trailed away as she sank dejectedly onto the chair opposite him. 'Because of what happened with Nikki last night we didn't get to have the talk I promised you,' she muttered, 'but perhaps when we do, you'll understand why I'm in such a dilemma. You see, I haven't been an angel myself . . . but that's enough for now. When the time is right I'll tell you everything, I promise. Now I need to get started on the food for this afternoon, as I invited Bradley to come along too. It was the least I could do after he missed the meal I promised him last night and how kind he was to us. Nikki got let off with a caution, thank God, and I'm sure I owe that to Bradley.'

'All right then, lass. You do what you deem right. But remember I'm here an' I'm right behind you.'

She smiled and just for a moment he saw another glimpse of the brave little girl he had left behind all those long lonely years ago.

It was just after lunchtime when Roxy pushed through the doors to the ward. A large man was leaning over her husband's bed and Eddie looked none too happy about it. Drawing herself up to her full height, she advanced down the ward and when she stopped at the end of the bed the man straightened and flashed her a smile. Roxy stared coldly back at him.

'Right, Eddie, I'll be off now the missus has arrived,' the man said. 'You just remember what I told you, eh?'

'I'll do that,' Eddie told him in little more than a croak.

Roxy watched the man walk away. He was tall and she judged him to be in his late forties or early fifties. Immaculately dressed, she could only guess at what the smart suit he was wearing must have cost. It was certainly no cheap off-the-peg affair, of that much she was sure. Yet his clothes did nothing to enhance his appearance. His greying hair was receding and his belly was straining against the front of his jacket. But it was his eyes that were his most striking feature; they were a clear blue and as cold as marbles.

When the ward doors clattered to behind him Eddie let out a sigh of relief and dropped back against his pillows as Roxy scowled at him.

'So, *that's* the invisible boss I've heard so much about over the years, is it?' she asked sarcastically.

He flushed. There was no point in lying, Roxy had sussed it out. 'Yes, it is,' he muttered.

Putting her bag on the bedside cabinet she pulled a chair to the side of the bed, sat down and went on, 'An' I've no doubt at all that he had somethin' to do wi' you bein' in here.'

When her husband looked away, Roxy knew that she had guessed correctly. 'So,' she said, knowing that Eddie would say no more on the subject, 'what exactly is the damage?'

He gestured towards his wrist, which was heavily plastered and lying on the bedspread. 'Broken wrist, two cracked ribs. Three teeth missin' an' a few cuts an' bruises. I'll live. In fact, they're talkin' about lettin' me out tomorrow.'

Roxy frowned at the gaps where Eddie's front teeth had been. She had always considered him to be a handsome man, but right now he looked far from it. One eye had a great purple bruise spreading across it and was nearly shut, and his lip was split and swollen. His chest was heavily bandaged and when he coughed she saw him wince with pain.

'Let's just hope this teaches you a lesson then. Happen you'll keep away from the bookies an' pay your debts on time in future.'

He glared at her from his one good eye. 'You can be a callous fuckin' bitch at times, Roxy.'

'I've had to learn to be over the years, married to you,' she quipped. 'I was just thinkin' what a change it is to see yer lyin' in a hospital bed instead o' me. Happen you'll know what it feels like now, Eddie Miller.' With that she stood up, lifted her bag and walked away without another word as Eddie watched in amazement. Who would have thought it, eh? The worm had finally turned. But right at that moment, that was the least of his worries. If what the boss had told him was true, then this was just a taster of things to come if he didn't produce a new plaything or some cash for him soon. His mind raced back to the attack. It had been so unexpected he had had no time to defend himself, not that he could have done much against the two heavies the boss had set on him. They had been like bloody great grizzly bears, and he winced as he remembered the fists slamming into his mouth and the sound of his teeth cracking. It was just as well they were letting him out tomorrow; his time was running out.

When the knock came on the front door, Claire paused to tidy her hair in the hall mirror. She had made a huge effort to look nice though she couldn't think where she could have put the locket Bradley and Mr Dickinson had bought her. She had wanted to wear it today but for some reason it wasn't in its box on her dressing-table. Deciding that Nikki had probably borrowed it, she flung the door open.

'Tracey, Callum, come in.' They were each carrying a twin and the little girls stretched their arms out to Claire. Young as they were, they had soon recognised someone they could twist around their little fingers.

Claire laughed as she planted a kiss on their chubby cheeks. 'Come on, you two. I've got all sorts of goodies for you out in the garden. Grandad is out there waiting for you too. Shall we go and see him?'

The twins nodded eagerly and as they clung onto her hands she told Tracey over her shoulder, 'I'll just take the girls down to Dad and then I'll be back.'

Tracey watched Claire's unsteady progress across the lawn then listened to the girls' whoops of delight when they spotted their grandad. There was another much younger man in the garden too, though as yet Tracey had no idea who he was.

'Who is that?' she asked, when Claire rejoined them some minutes later.

'Oh, that's Bradley King. I used to work with him at the solicitors. He's Mr Dickinson's partner. I'll introduce you in a minute.'

Seeing the knowing grin that spread across Tracey's face, Claire hastily told her, 'It's nothing like that, I assure you. Bradley and I are just friends. He lives alone so I thought it might be nice for him to join us and meet you all.'

'I'll believe you, though thousands wouldn't,' Tracey replied. 'Mind you, he certainly looks a bit of all right.'

'Hey you,' Callum chided her teasingly. 'Just remember you're a married woman and the mother of twins.'

'As if I could ever forget it,' Tracey shot back, but the look she gave him was filled with love and Claire found herself thinking of Christian. They had barely spoken since the last disastrous visit to Seagull's Flight, which hurt her far more than she cared to admit.

'Where's Nikki anyway?' Tracey asked as she peered down the length of the garden.

'Oh, she's up in her room. She's . . . er . . . not feeling too well.' Claire avoided Tracey's eyes.

'Nothing too serious, I hope?'

'Oh no, it's just . . . er . . . you know, her monthlies.'

'Poor thing. It can be very draining,' Tracey sighed and then thankfully they all went out into the garden and the uncomfortable moment passed.

In no time at all, Callum and Bradley were chatting away like old friends. Claire and Tracey were sitting in the shade of the huge oak tree and Robbie was playing football with the twins, who were shrieking with glee.

An hour or so passed in the twinkling of an eye, and apart from Nikki's absence, Claire felt happier than she had done for a long, long time.

'Thanks for a lovely afternoon,' Tracey told her sister as she smiled indulgently at her twins' antics. 'It was a really nice tea, but I'm afraid we shall have to be going soon to get the twins ready for bed. It's perhaps as well, else Dad is likely to have a heart-attack, the way the girls are chasing him about.'

Claire followed her eyes and smiled. 'I think he's enjoying himself,' she remarked, and Tracey nodded in agreement.

'I can just about remember when he used to play with us like that in the garden back in Gatley Common when we were tiny.'

She was saved from saying any more when Bradley and Callum joined them.

'I hate to break the party up, but if we don't get these two home soon, I'm afraid we're going to have two wailing little gremlins on our hands,' Callum told his wife regretfully.

'I was just saying the same to Claire.' Tracey glanced at the dirty plates and food spread across the garden table and asked, 'Would you like us to give you a hand with tidying up before we go?'

'Oh, don't worry about that. I'll muck in.' Bradley had come to stand at Claire's side and Tracey found herself grinning in secret. Claire might consider him to be just a friend, but Bradley obviously didn't think of her that way. His whole face lit up every time he so much as looked at her, and Tracey thought what a nice couple they made. Still, there was no point in trying to play matchmaker. Claire had once told her that her affections lay elsewhere, with some vet or another from up North. She began to round the children up and herd them towards the house as the rest of the small party trailed behind them. Once they were all in the hall, Tracey kissed Robbie affectionately on the cheek but when she turned to Claire she merely extended her hand and Claire's heart sank into her shoes.

The barrier was still there between them despite all Claire's efforts to break it down. Even so she kept the smile firmly in place as she told her, 'It's been so lovely to see you. You will come again soon, won't you?'

'Of course. Thank you.'

Claire watched the couple strap the children into their little car seats and then waved until they were out of sight before closing the door. It was time to talk to Nikki now; she had put it off for quite long enough.

'Nikki, can I come in?' She knew that she should really wait until Bradley had gone but she felt the need to talk to the girl. She had seen nothing of her all day except a quick glimpse of her face at the bedroom window when she had gone out to get something from her car earlier that morning.

There was no reply, so taking a deep breath, Claire tried again, 'Nikki, it's no good shutting yourself away like this. You'll have to come out sooner or later. We have to talk, but don't worry – I'm not going to give you a roasting.'

'*Go away*,' came the surly response and Claire bit down on her lip. Nikki could be as stubborn as a mule just lately and Claire was wary of making things worse, if she wasn't careful.

'All right then, I'll go. But only until Bradley has left and then we need to talk, OK?'

Again there was only silence and Claire turned and walked away with a heavy heart.

'Well, thanks for having me. I can't remember when I last enjoyed myself so much,' Bradley told her when she walked out to his car with him some time later. 'I normally spend Sunday afternoons doing paperwork, so this has been a real treat. The twins are adorable. They've made me feel quite broody.' There was a twinkle in his eye and despite feeling wretched, Claire found herself smiling.

'Then perhaps it's time you found yourself a nice girl and settled down,' she told him.

'I already have. Trouble is, the girl's having none of it at the minute.'

'Oh, get off with you.' She pushed him gently in the chest. He shrugged his shoulders in mock defeat and after clambering into the car was gone within seconds. Claire went reluctantly back inside.

'Ah, there you are,' her father said. 'Come to the table, lass. I've made you a nice strong brew. There's nothin' like it when you're feelin' a bit off colour.'

'Thanks, Dad.' Claire joined him and sipped at the hot tea gratefully. She supposed that she should be bringing the remains of the picnic in from the garden, but the way she was feeling at the moment it could wait.

Staring at her thoughtfully over the rim of his mug, he commented, 'You look all in. I dare say you could have done without the family get-together today after what happened yesterday.'

'I suppose I could,' she admitted as she slipped her shoes off and wriggled her toes. 'But then again I didn't want to put Tracey off. She still hasn't fully forgiven me for leaving her and it took my mind off things for a while.'

'Well, it was certainly a good afternoon. Bradley and Callum got on like a house on fire. I think they've arranged to meet up to have a game of golf.'

He realised that she hadn't heard a word he'd said, so leaning across the table he squeezed her hand and asked softly, 'Why don't you talk to me, lass? They say a problem shared is a problem halved an' I'm a good listener. I'm no fool an' I know there's somethin' more than what happened yesterday on your mind.'

Indecision played across her face as she looked back at him. 'If I was to talk to you – *really* talk to you and tell you everything – it might completely change your opinion of me,' she said anxiously.

He shook his head in denial. 'Why don't you try me then?'

Christian's face floated in front of Claire's eyes. *Until you can be honest you'll never be free*, he'd told her, and perhaps now was the time to start.

'For you to understand, I suppose I'll have to go back to the time I was little after you left,' she began tremulously. 'Things were tight. Mam never seemed to have enough money for food or clothes and she started to drink, which just made things worse.'

Robbie bowed his head in shame as he thought of his daughters going hungry.

'After a time she started to have boyfriends. Some of them were nice, but some of them . . .' She shuddered as she remembered. 'Some of them started to come to my room at night and do bad things to me. I hated it, but as long as they left Tracey alone I could bear it. Anyway, eventually Mum met this particular man, Ian his name was, and one night after he'd abused me I caught him doing the same to Tracey. I didn't know what to do, but I did know that if we told anyone they'd take us away from Mam and I was scared we'd be split up, so I tried to look after her as best I could. But Tracey wasn't as strong as me and one day she told a teacher at her school what was going on. The next thing I knew, two social workers turned up and took us to Molly and Tom's. Tracey loved it there, but I . . . Well, looking back I suppose I'd put the barriers up. I couldn't let myself trust anyone, so I led them a right merry dance. Staying out late, stealing – you name it, I did it. I really don't know how Molly put up with me when I think back.' She gave a sorry sigh and took up the story again.

'Anyway, when I was fourteen I went and got myself pregnant. Molly told me that if I wanted to keep the baby she would help me all she could – but what sort of life could I have offered it? After what the men had done to me I felt dirty and I didn't want my baby to feel like that. So I . . . I gave the baby up for adoption shortly after it was born. It was a little girl and I called her Yasmin. She was so beautiful, Dad. It almost broke my heart and from then on I got harder still. Tracey didn't need me any more. Molly and her son Billy had taken my place. You see, up until we went to live with her, I had played Mum to Tracey and now even she didn't need me. I decided to run away. I was seeing a lorry driver at the time, a chap much older than me and I mistakenly thought that he loved me, so I went with him on a trip to London, thinking that he'd let me move in with him and we'd live happy ever after. Huh! That dream didn't last long. When he knew that I was running away he dumped me at a service station and I haven't seen him from that day to this.' Claire looked at her father, but he remained silent, listening.

'That left me with two options. I could either go back to Molly with my tail between my legs or I could go on. As you know, I've always had a stubborn streak so I chose to keep going, but once again I was disappointed because London was nothing at all like I'd expected it to be. I spent the first night sleeping in a cardboard box on the Embankment after being befriended by an old bag lady. I tried and tried to get a job, any job, but it was useless. Then not long after that, I got mugged and raped. They took every single penny I had. I was desperate and didn't know which way to turn. I fell into the hands of a pimp but managed to get away from him, and then I met a street girl called Cindy, who took pity on me and gave me a home. She had a tiny flat and she turned out to be the first real friend I ever had. I was still trying to get a job but eventually I gave up and . . .' She glanced at Robbie fearfully before saying in a whisper, 'I joined her on the streets.'

She watched her father visibly pale but it was too late to stop now. She had to tell it all.

'Right from the start I was determined that I wasn't going to end up like some of the other girls I worked with – hooked on drugs and old before their time – so I took elocution lessons and went to night school to improve myself. I didn't want to be Claire McMullen any more, you see. I wanted to be someone people would respect. Eventually I worked my way up to being a high-class call girl and that's how I earned the money to buy my hotel in Blackpool. I told everyone I was the orphan of wealthy parents and changed my name to Claire Hamilton, and for the first time in my life people respected me. Shortly after I'd moved in I took a little stray dog in who had been involved in a road traffic accident outside the hotel, and it was through him that I met Christian Murray. He was the vet who saved Cassidy's life,' she explained. 'I had promised myself I would never let my guard down or rely on anyone ever again, but somehow I fell in love with him. But that was the problem: how could I go to him? I was living an image but deep down I was still Claire McMullen, a common former prostitute. Christian deserved someone so much better than me . . .' Her voice broke, and she swallowed hard before resuming the story.

'And so I married my accountant, Greg Nightingale. He was wealthy, handsome and rich and I thought he would give me the stability and respectability I'd always craved. Once again, I soon found out how wrong I'd been. Our marriage was a sham. But then I got pregnant and thought that things would perhaps work out after all. I would have my very own baby, someone to love who would love me back for the person I really was.' She raised a hand to wipe a tear away.

'But then one night I went out and came home early. That's when I found Greg sexually molesting Nikki and I couldn't bear it. I threatened to shout what he was from the rooftops, and that night he took his own life rather than face the shame of it. The shock of what had happened made me have my baby prematurely. He was a lovely little boy and I called him William, but he died shortly after his birth.' She paused as the memories rushed back and then taking a deep, heaving breath she went on.

'Christian was there for me, but I knew I still couldn't go to him, even after he knew the truth about who I really was and still wanted me. I had Nikki to think about then and she still needs me so much, so we agreed that I would come back to my roots and face my demons as well as helping her to face hers. The trouble is, I haven't been able to do either up to now. Nikki has shut me out and apart from you, everyone still thinks that I earned my money by hard graft. But what would Tracey think of me if she knew how I'd *really* earned a living? Or Nikki, for that matter? So now you see why it's so hard for me to be strict with her. I've done everything she's done and a million times worse. I'm not quite what you thought I was, am I, Dad?'

'Oh, my poor lass!' Robbie was so choked that he was momentarily robbed of speech as he tried to take in what she had told him. But then suddenly he was round the table and rocking his daughter in his arms.

'I've caused all this, an' should I live to be a hundred I'll never forgive meself,' he sobbed.

She reached up to wipe the tears from his cheeks. 'No, Dad. You mustn't blame yourself any more. I used to, but recently I've come to realise that a lot of it was of my own making. If only I had trusted Molly and Tom and I hadn't run away, things would have been so different . . . Do you hate me?'

'Hate you!' Shock registered on his face as he held her at arm's length. 'Why, lass, I could *never* hate you. It's a crying shame what you've had to go through. But now you're able to talk about it, things will get better – you'll see. You've just taken the first step to facing up to your past. You shouldn't be ashamed of anything you've done. You've come through it and I'm proud of you.'

'*I* might have done,' Claire admitted in a hushed voice, 'but do I tell Nikki about my past? Will she be able to live with the fact that her mum used to be a common prostitute?'

Robbie stared reflectively through the open back door. He really had no idea how to answer her. There was so much to take in and he needed time to think about it.

'Let's sleep on it and decide what to do in the morning,' he said eventually.

Claire nodded wearily. She had hoped that, after confiding in Robbie, she would feel as if a great weight had been lifted from her shoulders, but it was still there, and deep inside she was afraid that it always would be, until she had plucked up the courage to confide in her other loved ones too. She had taken the first difficult step, but this was only the beginning.

Chapter Twenty-Four

'Mam, there's a taxi just pulled up outside,' Poppy shouted from the lounge as she flicked the grimy net curtain aside.

Roxy appeared in the lounge doorway with a cigarette dangling from the corner of her mouth.

'Is there? Are yer sure it's comin' here?'

She was halfway across the room when Poppy told her, 'It's Dad. He just got out.'

Roxy frowned. He had said the hospital was going to discharge him today but she hadn't expected him till later. She and Poppy watched him limp painfully down the path and then the front door opened and he was in the lounge staring at them as he hugged his chest.

'Well, ain't yer goin' to bleedin' say somethin' then? "Welcome home" would be nice. An' a good strong cup o' tea wouldn't go amiss either.'

'Anybody would think you'd come home from the wars,' Roxy quipped sarcastically, 'instead o' from the hospital after a beatin' that you were bloody askin' for.'

Eddie felt the rage welling up inside him, but for once he could do nothing about it. His cracked ribs were so painful it even hurt him to breathe let alone get into a full-scale barney. As he gingerly lowered himself onto the settee, Katie, who was playing on the floor, briefly glanced up before returning her attention to what she was doing. He sighed. Knowing Katie, she probably hadn't even noticed that he had been gone. Everything seemed to slip past her and he found himself almost envying her.

'I'll put the kettle on then.'

Roxy's voice brought his thoughts back to the present and he nodded. The second she had left the room he smiled at Poppy and she glared at him suspiciously. He looked so different without his front teeth and with his face all black and blue.

'So how are yer then, love?'

Her mouth gaped in surprise. She could count on one hand the times her father had shown any concern about her in the whole of her life. The one good thing to come from all this was the fact that, were he to find out about her shoplifting expedition, he was in no state to do anything about it at the minute.

'I'm fine, why wouldn't I be?'

'Good, good. An' Nikki, that little mate o' yours: is she all right an' all?'

She raised her eyebrows. Now she *knew* he was up to something. 'I'm fine, an' as far as I know, she's fine. Why the sudden interest?'

'Now that ain't very nice, is it?' he shot back. 'Can't a dad show an interest in his own kids any more?'

'I don't see why, if he's never bothered before.'

The conversation was stopped from going any further when Roxy reappeared to ask, 'Have you had any breakfast?'

Poppy took that opportunity to leave the room and Eddie cursed under his breath. He'd been about to ask her when Nikki would next be coming round, but now he'd have to wait till he got her on his own again. For some reason, Roxy had taken to the damn kid and clucked around her like a mother hen.

'No, I ain't,' he informed her. 'But wi' no front teeth I'm hardly goin' to tackle bacon an' eggs, am I?'

'Then I'll do you a bit o' porridge,' Roxy told him without a hint of sympathy, and with that she turned and went back to the kitchen.

Alone again, save for Katie, who was rocking to and fro locked in her own little world, he allowed his thoughts to run ahead and his insides felt as if they had turned to water. He had until the end of the week, the boss had told him, and if he hadn't delivered the goods by then, the beating he had just taken would be nothing compared to what he had in store.

'Claire, I forgot to tell you. I've got to go out for an hour or two this afternoon. Is that all right?'

Claire, who was busily sewing the voile for the shop window, glanced up in surprise. She and her dad had been working side-by-side in the shop all morning and this was the first she had heard of him going out.

'Why, of course it is,' she answered, taking a pin from the corner of her mouth. 'You don't have to ask permission. You're not on the clock, you know. Is it for anything important?'

'Not really. I've got to go to the hospital for the results of some tests I had a few weeks back.'

Seeing the look of concern on her face, he chuckled. 'Don't look so worried. It's nothin' serious, lass. In fact, it's quite embarrassin'. I've been havin' hot flushes. I thought women on the change got them, but perhaps I'm changin' sex.'

Claire smiled at him. The atmosphere had been a little strained between them this morning, made more so by Nikki who had got up and cleared off to school without glancing at either of them. She knew that she should have tried to address what had happened on Saturday, but somehow the time still didn't feel right and she wondered if it ever would.

'Well, in that case, I hope it turns out to be nothing serious. And have you thought on what I asked you last night – about whether or not I should tell Nikki about my past yet, I mean.'

Robbie stopped what he was doing and came to perch beside her.

'To tell you the truth, lass, I've spent the whole night tossin' an' turnin' an' thinkin' of nothin' else. And I'm no nearer to advisin' you. One part of me thinks it might help if Nikki knew you'd had it rough. But the other half wonders if it mightn't give her licence to do as she pleases. At the end of the day I think the decision has to be down to you, though I do think you should tell Molly an' Tom, an' especially our Tracey.'

Claire paled at the thought, but now he had started, Robbie went on, 'The thing is, I have a sneaky suspicion that Tracey is a teeny bit jealous of you.'

When Claire stared at him incredulously he held up his hand and hurried on. 'Think about it. You left her when she was just a little girl an' then you turn up years later with enough money to buy a lovely house, all sophisticated and well spoken. She thinks you've had it cushy. Happen she'd think differently if she knew how hard it had been for you.'

'But what if it went the other way and she despised me for what I'd done?' Claire asked fearfully.

Robbie shrugged. 'I don't somehow think that would be the case. But that ain't the main reason why I think you should tell her the truth. You see, from what I can make of it, this here Christian had about got it right. Until you've come out into the open and been big enough to be honest with other people, you can't be honest with yourself. Think on what I've said, eh?'

She nodded as he stood up and went back to what he had been doing. He was right, she knew he was, just as Christian had been right – but was she brave enough to go through with it yet? Dropping the voile she took a cigarette from her bag and lit it.

Robbie walked out of the George Eliot Hospital in a daze, hardly able to take in what the doctor had told him, yet he knew it was true: he had seen all the test results for himself. The disease was progressing far more rapidly than he had expected it would. But it wasn't just himself he was thinking of, it was Tracey and Claire. Particularly Claire. Tracey had a loving husband to look out for her, but Claire had no one but Nikki, and that wasn't exactly a match made in heaven. He shook his head in frustration. He had hoped to stay with her for the foreseeable future at least. They had been getting on so well for the past few days and he had wanted to make up to her for all the lost time. But that would be out of the question now.

Robbie walked to his car and sat inside, staring out across the busy car park. It was visiting time and people were streaming into the hospital with arms full of fruit, flowers and magazines. The last time he had come here was on the day Karen had died, and he had prayed that he would never have to set foot in the place again. Thoughts of his late wife brought tears stinging to his eyes and yet again he wished that he could go back in time. He would have done things so differently if he could have his life over again. He thumped the steering wheel. Life could be a cruel bugger at times, there was no doubt about it.

When he walked into Claire's lovely house almost an hour later he thought he had walked into a war zone, for Nikki and Claire were going at each other hammer and tongs.

'I am *not* staying in and that's an end to it! You can't make me!' he heard Nikki shout.

'Right, I've just about had enough of this,' Claire shouted back. 'I've tried to be reasonable but you've pushed me too far this time, young lady. I'm going to ring your social worker. I don't have any choice, you're beyond my control.'

'Oh yes, and just what do you think *she's* going to do?' Nikki retaliated furiously. 'Is she going to lock me in my room and throw away the key? Or are you saying that you're going to have me put into care? Is that it? You want shot of me?'

Claire's eyes stretched wide with shock as Robbie appeared in the doorway. 'Of course I'm not going to put you into care,' she gasped in horror. 'I would never do that. I love you, you know I do.'

'Then get off my back and stop treating me like I'm a baby.'

Nikki snatched up her denim jacket and with her blond ponytail swishing from side to side she elbowed past Robbie, who was watching the proceedings in dismay. He had always tried very hard not to interfere but now he saw that Claire was in need of a little help, so clutching at Nikki's arm and pulling her to a halt he told her, 'Hey, don't talk to your mam like that, lass. She's only trying to do what she thinks is best for you.'

'GET OFF ME, YOU!' Nikki knocked his hand away with a look of bitter contempt on her face. 'She's NOT my mum. And you're not my grandad, so stop trying to pretend that you are!' With that she ran down the hallway and out of the door before Robbie or Claire could stop her. They gazed at each other in shock.

'Oh Dad, I've lost her, I don't know what to do.' Claire's face crumpled and tears began to rain down her pale cheeks as Robbie hurried across to pat her arm consolingly.

'Don't take what she said too much to heart, lass.' His voice was gentle. 'She's young and she's just feeling her feet. She'll come through it, you'll see.'

At that moment they heard a screech of brakes and the sound of a car skidding to a halt in the road outside and now Claire's hand flew to her mouth. 'Oh my God, Nikki!'

As one they ran towards the front door, which they saw Nikki had left swinging open, and then they were running down the drive, each dreading what they might see.

A car was slewed across the road and a man with a stunned expression on his face was clambering out of it.

'I d-didn't have a chance,' he stammered. 'It just ran out in front of me from nowhere. I tried to miss it, really I did.'

'*It?*' Relief washed over Claire's face. He wasn't talking about Nikki then. Running round to the front of the car she looked down and began to sob. Gemma was lying motionless in the road with blood trickling from the side of her mouth.

'Oh no, she must have tried to follow Nikki,' she cried.

Robbie bent down and began to feel the dog's little chest. 'She's still alive,' he said. 'We have to get her to a vet.'

Claire felt as if she were paralysed. Her legs refused to do as she told them and she could only stare back at him.

'I'll take you to a vet,' the driver of the car offered. 'It's the least I can do. I'm so *very* sorry.'

'It wasn't your fault, lad,' Robbie assured him. 'Claire, run in and fetch a blanket or something that I can wrap her in, would you?'

By now there was a backlog of traffic building up and the sound of car horns piercing the air.

When Claire remained motionless he barked, '*Now!*' And as if she had been fired from a gun, she shot off back up the drive.

Seconds later, she was back with the warm woollen blanket from Gemma's basket. Robbie wrapped the little dog in it and lifted her gently into the back of the car.

'You go an' see if you can find Nikki,' he told her. 'She might be goin' a bit off the rails but I know she adores this little dog. We'll be at the vet's in Trent Road. Do you think you can do that?'

When Claire nodded numbly he slammed the car door shut and as the car pulled away, Claire stood in utter despair watching it disappear up the road.

Seconds later she pulled herself together with an enormous effort and raced back indoors for her car keys. She had no doubt where Nikki would be, and that meant that she wouldn't have to drive around looking for her, which was one good thing at least.

As she drove through the council estate past the great tower blocks of flats towards where Poppy lived, she felt as if she was slipping back in time. The fences that surrounded the gardens were broken or covered with graffiti and the snotty-nosed children who were playing in the streets eyed her car curiously or made obscene gestures to her. Gangs of youths with cans in their hands stood on street corners but Claire was oblivious to them. All she could think about was getting Nikki to Gemma, hopefully before it was too late. She was so distressed that she forgot exactly where Poppy lived and ended up once again knocking on doors until at last someone directed her to the right house. By then almost an hour had passed since the accident and Claire was in a panic.

Eventually she skidded to a halt outside the overgrown garden fronting Poppy's house and slamming the door shut, she raced up the path, stumbling over the rubbish strewn in her way. The sound of a Queen record was blasting from within but when she hammered on the door with her fists she heard a voice shout, 'All right, all right, I'm comin'! Keep yer bleedin' hair on.'

When a slovenly-looking woman with a cigarette dangling from the corner of her mouth opened the door, Claire swallowed her shock and said, 'Is Nikki here? I'm her mum, there's been an accident and I need her to come with me right now!' Having been one herself, Claire could spot a pro from a mile off and she had no doubt at all that Roxy was on the game.

Roxy gulped. So this was Nikki's mum then. She was really quite pretty and very well spoken. But then she would be, wouldn't she? She'd no doubt been born with a silver spoon in her mouth. Even so, she felt sorry for her at that moment. Claire looked almost wild with grief as Roxy held the door wide for her.

'Come on in fer a second,' she invited and Claire stepped past her into the gloomy hallway. And all the while she was silently chanting to herself, *Come on, come on, come on or it might be too late.*

'Nikki just got here,' Roxy informed her. 'She's upstairs with our Poppy. I'll give her a shout for yer, shall I?'

As Claire glanced into a room leading off from the hall she saw a man avidly watching her. He was sitting on a settee with his feet propped up on a stool and looked as if he had been in the wars. His face was covered in bruises and his chest was heavily bandaged. Normally she would have acknowledged him but for now all she could think about was getting Nikki to Gemma, so totally forgetting her manners she looked impatiently up the stairs again for a sign of her daughter.

She heard the woman who had answered the door shout something and the music stopped abruptly. Seconds later there was the sound of footsteps on the worn stair-carpet and Nikki peered over the banister at her.

'What are *you* doing here?' Her manner was rude and abrupt but Claire was willing to ignore that for now.

'I'm afraid there's been an accident,' she answered quietly. 'Gemma has been run over. She's at the vet's. I've come to take you to her.'

Nikki looked dumbfounded as the colour drained from her face like water from a dam. 'What do you mean, she's been in an accident? How did she get out?'

'You left the front door open when you stormed out,' Claire told her flatly and now tears sprang to Nikki's eyes as she stumbled down the rest of the stairs.

'How serious is it?' she asked, and Claire could detect the terror in her voice.

'I don't know yet, love,' she answered truthfully. 'Let's get along to the vet's and find out, eh?'

Nikki walked blindly towards the front door and Claire was about to follow her when Roxy gently caught her arm.

'Good luck, love,' she muttered, and as Claire nodded her thanks and looked into the woman's eyes she felt a certain affinity with her. After all, in other circumstances she might have ended up just like her.

She followed Nikki outside and once she got to the car, which now had a herd of children playing around it, she paused to look back at Roxy before ushering Nikki into the passenger seat and driving away.

They found Robbie sitting alone in the waiting room at the vet's. When he saw Claire and Nikki he sighed with relief.

'How is she?' Claire asked immediately.

He spread his hands. 'We don't know yet, lass, but she seems to be holding her own. The vet is X-raying her now to see what damage has been done. He'll be able to tell us more then.'

Nikki sank onto a chair with tears pouring down her face and despite the differences there had been between them recently, Claire's heart ached for her.

'She'll be all right, love, you'll see,' she whispered. To her surprise, Nikki suddenly launched herself into her arms, sobbing uncontrollably, and Claire stroked her hair. It felt so good to be able to hold her again and feel close to her. As Robbie watched them, a lump swelled in his throat. He had grown so used to seeing them constantly arguing that it was nice to see them close for a change, though he could have wished it to have been under better circumstances.

They sat together and waited and some time later the door to the surgery opened and the vet appeared. He was a middle-aged man and Claire found herself thinking that he had a kind face.

'I'm afraid Gemma has suffered some internal damage,' he told them solemnly. 'There seems to be some internal bleeding, though surprisingly there doesn't appear to be anything broken. I shall be doing a scan on her shortly. Meanwhile I've hooked her up to a drip to get some fluids inside her and I'd like to keep her here overnight for observation. She's had a very bad shock and that can sometimes be more damaging than physical injuries to small dogs.'

'Will she die?' Nikki asked falteringly as she clung to Claire's hand.

'It's too early to say yet,' the vet answered truthfully. 'But what I can tell you is that I'll do everything I can, although it won't be cheap.'

'That doesn't matter,' Claire assured him hastily. 'Just do whatever you have to, to get her through this, please. I don't care how much it costs so long as you get her well again.'

Nikki was heartbroken at the thought of having to leave the little dog there and asked, 'May I see her before we go?'

Mr Barrett considered her request. He had been a vet for many years and knew that if Gemma was to stand any chance of surviving she must be kept quiet at all costs. But then this young girl looked so upset that it was very difficult to refuse her.

'I'll tell you what I'll do,' he said kindly. 'I'll let you see her just for a minute. But only one minute, mind. It's paramount that she doesn't get excited so you must promise me you'll stay calm. Can you do that?'

'I'll try,' Nikki promised.

He turned about and they followed him into the surgery where Gemma was lying on a table hooked up to a drip. Her coat was matted with blood and her chest was heaving.

'Oh Gemma, I'm so sorry. This is all my fault.' Nikki bent to stroke the little dog's head. 'Now you just hurry up and get better, do you hear me? I've neglected you lately with keep going out all the while, but soon as you're better I'll take you for a walk every single day. How's that then?'

Gemma was conscious and her tongue flicked out to lick her hand, but when she tried to raise her head, Mr Barrett took Nikki's elbow and propelled her towards the door.

'That's enough for now. Peace and quiet is what she needs. And don't worry, you can ring to see how she's doing any time you like. She's in good hands, I promise you.'

Once in the waiting room again, Robbie held out his hand and the vet shook it as Robbie said, 'Thank you, sir. Goodbye.' He then steered Nikki and Claire out to the car and made them both sit in the back seat. Claire looked in no fit state to drive and he was happy to take control of the situation. When he glanced in the mirror on the way home and saw that mother and daughter had their arms tightly wrapped around each other it did his heart good. *Long may it last*, he silently prayed as he drove them home.

Chapter Twenty-Five

'Hello.'

Claire's heart sank as she heard the voice at the other end of the line, but she forced herself to say, 'Hello, Mandy, it's Claire. Is Christian or Mrs M there, please?'

'Oh hello, Claire,' Mandy replied brightly. 'I'm really sorry, but Mrs M is in bed and Christian's out in the surgery. We had a little dog brought in tonight that was in a really bad way – he's been in a road traffic accident. Christian's operating on him right now and I'd just popped in to make us a cuppa. Shall I get him to ring you back when he's done?'

'Er, yes, that would be lovely. Thanks.' Claire placed the phone down as a picture of Mandy's face swam in front of her eyes. She so wanted to dislike her, but there was really nothing about Mandy *to* dislike, as Mrs M had once pointed out to her. She wondered what Mandy would be doing at Seagull's Flight so late in the evening, but supposed she had stayed on to give Christian a hand with the poorly dog. No doubt he would tell her all about it when he rang her back.

She had just placed the phone down when her father walked past her, heading for the front door.

'Dad, where are you off to so late at night?'

Robbie paused to look blankly back at her. 'What? Eh? I'm going to the shop to finish the window platform off.'

Claire frowned. 'But, Dad, it's late at night.'

'Is it? Oh yes . . . yes, of course it is! What am I playing at, eh? I must be losin' me marbles. It's worrying about Gemma, I suppose. I'll get off to bed then, love. An' if the vet should ring, be sure an' wake me, eh? I can have you an' Nikki down there in two shakes of a lamb's tail if need be.'

She nodded, but as he slowly climbed the stairs a frown settled across her face. Was it her imagination or was he getting more and more forgetful? Only yesterday morning he had spent half an hour scouring the house for his car keys only to discover that they had been in his jacket pocket all along. And the day before that, he had fallen asleep on the bench under the tree in the garden. But then, he had been working hard, she was forced to admit, and decided that she was going to make him slow down a little. He had been under a lot of pressure lately with her mother dying and working so hard on the shop. She followed him upstairs, pausing on the landing outside Nikki's bedroom door. The girl had rushed upstairs the minute they had all set foot back in the house, but now Claire felt the need to check on her.

She tapped and called softly, 'Nikki, may I come in, love?' Without waiting for an answer she pushed the door open and Nikki, who was standing at the open window, quickly flicked something out of it before blushing furiously. That strange smell was in the room again, but seeing Nikki's bloodshot eyes, Claire chose to ignore it as she asked, 'How are you feeling?'

'Oh, come to gloat, have you?' Nikki flung herself onto the bed. 'Come to tell me what a wicked girl I am for leaving the front door open? If it wasn't for me, Gemma would be all right – that's what you're thinking, isn't it?'

'No, of course it isn't!' Claire looked horrified. 'Accidents happen and that's what this was – an accident. It wasn't anyone's fault. You didn't leave the door open on purpose, so stop blaming yourself. Gemma is a sturdy little thing and she'll pull round, you'll see. I've seen Christian save far worse than her so you mustn't give up hope.'

They surveyed each other uncertainly for a moment and then suddenly Nikki flung herself into Claire's arms and sobbed, 'Oh Mum, I'm so sorry for how I've been behaving. I don't mean to take it out on you, really I don't. It's just that I . . . well, I get so mixed up. I have all these horrible feelings inside me when I think of my dad and what he did to me, and I don't know how to handle them.'

Claire held her close to her chest just as she had when Nikki had been a little girl and rocked her to and fro. 'I know it's hard,' she crooned, 'but there are people out there who could help you, Nikki, if you'd only let them – counsellors and people who are trained to help girls who have been through what you have. That social worker who came to see us could put us in touch with them in no time, if that's what you want.'

'It's *not* what I want.' Nikki pushed Claire away and suddenly the gulf was between them again. 'Can you even begin to imagine what it would be like, trying to talk to a stranger about something like *that*?'

'Nikki . . .' Claire took a deep breath. There would never be a better time to tell her daughter about what she herself had been through. 'I perhaps ought to—' The harsh ringing of the phone stopped her from going any further, and cursing softly, she slithered off the bed. 'I shan't be a minute,' she apologised. 'I'd better just go and answer that, in case it's the vet.'

She pounded down the stairs and snatched the phone up, and instantly she heard Christian's voice. 'Hello there. Mandy said you wanted me to ring you. Is everything all right, Claire? Mandy thought you sounded a little upset.'

'Oh, Christian.' It was so wonderful to hear him and she wished with all her heart that he was there with her now. Haltingly she began to tell him of the accident, and by the time she was done she was sobbing uncontrollably.

'Aw, love, I'm so sorry. I know how much you and Nikki love that little mutt. I'll tell you what – I'm on my way. Expect me in two or three hours. Mandy can hold the fort here till I get back.'

'But I can't expec—' The phone went dead in her hand as a glow started in the pit of her stomach. Christian was coming, which could only mean that he still loved her. She hurriedly began to tidy the house as she waited for him to arrive.

It was three o'clock in the morning and still Claire was pacing up and down the lounge. She had told Christian, who looked ready to drop, of all that had gone on in the lead-up to Gemma's accident. He had listened patiently, but now she could see that he was struggling to keep his eyes open.

'Oh, I'm so sorry,' she said guiltily. 'I bet you've been up since really early, and here I am chewing your ear off. Come on – let me show you to your bedroom. We can talk some more in the morning when you've had a rest.'

He stifled a yawn and followed her up the stairs. She stopped outside the last door on the landing and as she pushed it open, she told him, 'I've made the bed up for you. Are you sure there isn't anything you want before you settle down? A hot drink or something?'

'No, nothing, thanks,' he replied with a smile. 'If I drink any more I've got a horrible feeling I'm going to be running to the loo all night. Now go on, get yourself off to bed too. You look completely done in. And try not to worry, Gemma will pull through.' He leaned forward to plant a gentle kiss on her lips then the door closed behind him and she made her way to her own room feeling strangely cheated.

She came downstairs the next morning to find Robbie already on the phone to the vet. She waited anxiously for him to finish his conversation as she tightened the belt on her dressing-gown. At last he put the phone down and slipping his arm across her slim shoulders, he told her, 'She's still holding her own, lass. The vet is going to ring you in an hour or so with the results of the scan and the X-rays he did.'

Claire nodded absently. She had hoped to hear that Gemma was much better today, but at least she was still alive, which was something to be grateful for.

'Christian, my vet friend, is upstairs,' she told her father, and Robbie was amused to see that she looked slightly embarrassed. 'He rang after you'd gone to bed last night and when he heard what had happened, he offered to come. He slept in the spare room,' she added hastily, as she saw Robbie grin.

'Makes no difference to me where he slept, lass,' he assured her. 'You're a grown woman an' more than capable of makin' your own decisions an' doin' as you please.' It hurt him to see her looking so pale and drawn. 'Why don't you sit yourself down an' let me wait on you for a change, eh?' To his amazement she did as she was told without a quibble as he filled the kettle at the sink and placed it on to boil.

He was just about to pour the tea when Christian strolled into the kitchen knuckling the sleep from his eyes. Robbie instantly saw why Claire was drawn to him. Tall and fair haired, the chap had somehow just missed being classed as handsome, and yet there was a kindness in his deep blue eyes that must make people and animals alike instantly warm to him.

'Ah, Christian.' Claire sprang up from her seat as colour flooded into her cheeks. 'This is Robbie, my father. Dad, this is Christian.'

'Nice to meet you at last, young man,' Robbie told him affably as he shook his hand.

'And you too, sir.'

'Good. Now you sit yourself down there next to Claire and I'll have you a brew in no time. Hot, strong an' sweet, is it?'

'It is actually,' Christian grinned. Robbie was nothing like he had imagined him to be, and the younger man took to him instantly. Claire was feeling very awkward but she needn't have done because the men seemed to be getting on famously.

'Will you be staying long?' Robbie asked and Christian shook his head.

'Unfortunately not. I shall have to be back for my afternoon surgery later on. Mandy, my assistant, will manage to hold the fort until then. By the way, Claire, did I tell you she had moved into Seagull's Flight?'

Some of Claire's tea slopped over the rim of her mug and splashed onto the table but she managed to stay composed as she told him, 'No, you didn't. Why is that?'

'Well, basically, the landlord who owns the flat she and her friend were staying in put the rent up again. That's three times this year he's done it and Mandy couldn't afford to stay there any more. She's at university, as you know, so Gran offered to let her stay with us for a while. She's there half the time working anyway, so it sort of made sense.'

Claire felt as if she had been thumped in the stomach as jealousy consumed her, but thankfully Robbie continued the conversation, giving her time to get a grip. She found herself watching Christian closely. Did he still love her? she wondered. Oh, admittedly he had driven through the night to be with her in a crisis, but had he come as a friend or a lover? He had never once tried to force himself on her since the day he had proposed and she had turned him down, and suddenly she found herself wishing that he wasn't so much of a gentleman. With Nikki behaving as she was they might go on like this for ever unless Christian put his foot down and gave her an ultimatum. But then if he did, would she be able to put her own feelings before those of her adopted daughter?

At that moment Nikki was answering her mobile upstairs and wondering who it might be that would be ringing her so early in the morning.

'Hello,' she muttered sleepily. She'd had less than two hours' sleep and felt awful.

'Mornin', sweetheart.'

Recognising Eddie Miller's voice, she leaned up on one elbow and asked, 'What is it? Why are you ringing me so early?'

'Well, to tell the truth it's about that little matter we discussed. You know, the photographer friend of mine? He wants to meet you this week. So how about we set a meeting up for two days' time, eh? Say Wednesday at seven.'

'I'm sorry, Eddie, but I can't. My dog has been run over, she's at the vet's and—'

Eddie's voice became menacing as he hissed, 'I don't give a flyin' fuck if yer *granny*'s bin run over, madam! You *owe* for all the stuff I've been supplyin' you with, an' now it's payback time. I'll expect you here at seven on Wednesday on the dot, or else.'

'Else what?' Nikki's voice was fearful.

'Let's just say you wouldn't want to know. It's this bloke who supplies me wi' the stuff you've been havin', an' you wouldn't want to cross him, believe me. Just be here or you'll live to regret it.'

The phone went dead in her hand as Nikki stared at it in amazement. What had Eddie meant – that she'd live to regret it? He had always been so nice to her before, so why the sudden change now? Swinging her legs out of the warm bed she padded towards the door and as thoughts of Gemma took over she forgot all about the phone call for now.

They were linked like a chain as they sat in the vet's waiting room, Claire, Robbie and Nikki, tightly holding hands. Christian had gone in to speak to Mr Barrett and now as they waited for the verdict, Claire felt sick to her stomach. Gemma was going to be all right, she told herself over and over again. She had to be – or how would Nikki cope? This morning, some of the old closeness that had once existed between them had returned as Nikki stuck to her side like glue, seeking reassurance that her pet would survive. But now all they could do was wait, and the waiting seemed endless.

At last the door to the surgery opened and Christian walked through it. One glance at his tight-lipped face told Claire that it was not good news.

'Come in,' Christian told them, acutely aware of the other animal owners who were staring at them curiously as they balanced pets of various shapes and sizes on their laps. Some of them had pitying looks on their faces as if they had somehow already heard what Nikki and Claire were about to be told.

Claire stood up, hauling Nikki up after her, and side-by-side they stumbled into the surgery. The first thing they saw was Gemma, lying on a table with a drip hooked into her leg. The veterinary nurse had made a valiant attempt at washing all the matted blood from her coat and this morning her soulful brown eyes were open and staring at her mistress.

Nikki whooped with delight, taking this as a good sign as she hurried over to her beloved pet and gently started to stroke her ears.

The vet and Christian exchanged a glance and then after taking a deep breath, Christian began, 'I'm really sorry to have to tell you this, but I'm afraid it's bad news. This gentleman here has done a sterling job. There is absolutely nothing more he could have done, but the tests revealed that Gemma has kidney damage. That's what is causing the internal bleeding.'

A deafening silence settled on the room for some moments until Nikki broke it when she demanded, 'So, what are you going to do about it?' She was addressing Mr Barrett now and he cleared his throat, looking decidedly uncomfortable. This was one of the aspects of his job that he hated.

'I'm afraid there is nothing more I *can* do,' he told her in a hushed voice. 'It's merely a matter of time now. The kindest thing you could do for Gemma is to let me put her out of her misery.'

'*What?* You mean put her to *sleep*?' Nikki's eyes were almost starting out of her head. She stared down at Gemma, who was looking up at her trustingly and then as Mr Barrett took a step towards her she hissed, 'STAY AWAY! Do you hear me? You're not going to put her to sleep . . . I won't *let* you.'

Christian took control of the situation as he politely moved the harassed-looking vet aside and placed his arms about Nikki's thin shoulders.

'If you don't allow Mr Barrett to end her suffering, she'll die in terrible pain.' He hated to see the girl so distraught, but he knew that it was up to him to hammer home the seriousness of the situation to her. Claire was certainly in no fit state to do so.

Nikki snarled as she shrugged his arm away and held Gemma protectively to her chest. It was a situation Christian had unfortunately seen many times before and he knew that he had to be cruel to be kind. 'Oh, so you want her to suffer then, do you? You surprise me, Nikki. I would have sworn that you loved her and would want the best for her.'

'I d-*do* want the best for her,' Nikki stammered. 'But I can't let you . . .' Her voice trailed away and suddenly tears were streaming down her cheeks and the wild look left her eyes.

Christian quickly moved close again. 'Now we're going to go out and give you two a few minutes alone together,' he told her gently. 'And then Mr Barrett will come in and put her out of her pain. We can take her home with us if you like and I'll bury her in the garden for you. At least that way you'll still have her close to you, won't you, love?'

He took Claire's elbow and they trooped back into the waiting room. Claire was deeply distressed and oblivious to the stares she was attracting. She found herself thinking of Tinker, the little mongrel she and Tracey had once saved from drowning when they were children living at home in Gatley Common with their mother. She then moved on to Cassidy, who had been the means of bringing her together with Christian. She had loved those two little dogs just as Nikki now loved Gemma and knew that it was going to break the girl's heart to lose her – but what option was there?

After a few minutes, Christian and the vet went back into the surgery, leaving Claire behind. Robbie grabbed her hand and squeezed it.

'I'm so sorry, lass.'

'So am I, Dad. So am I,' she whispered.

When the door to the surgery eventually reopened, Claire leaped from her seat. Nikki was standing there dry-eyed with a little bundle wrapped in a blanket they had brought from home clutched to her chest.

The girl walked past them all without so much as a glance, and after exchanging a concerned look with Robbie, Claire ran after her.

'Go on, I'll settle up the bill,' Christian urged her, and in that moment she could have kissed him for his thoughtfulness.

Claire caught up with her daughter in the car park. Nikki was standing next to the car staring blankly off into space. Chewing on her lip, Claire tried to think of something comforting to say but somehow the words just seemed to lodge in her throat. When Robbie and Christian joined them some moments later, they all climbed into the car and the journey home was made in silence except for the sound of Claire's quiet sobs.

The silence continued when they arrived back at the house. Claire hurried into the lounge to fetch the bottle of whisky from the sideboard.

'How about I put a bit of this in some tea for you, eh?' she asked Nikki. 'I'll only put enough in to warm you up. You're as white as a ghost.'

Christian was standing with his hands pushed down in his pockets as he stared out at the garden. Up to now he had not said a word but now he asked, 'Would you like me to bury her for you, Nikki, before I go? That looks a nice spot under the old apple tree.'

Nikki's head slowly wagged from side to side. 'No. I *do* want you to bury her for me, but not here. I want you to take her back to Seagull's Flight with you and bury her next to Cassidy in the pet cemetery. Would you do that for me?'

'Of course,' he said without hesitation, and to his amazement Nikki rose from her seat and placed her precious bundle into his arms before turning and walking from the room without so much as another word.

When Claire went to follow her, Christian caught her arm and stayed her. 'Let her have some time on her own, eh? She's in shock.'

Claire nodded and sank onto her chair again. The house wouldn't be the same without Gemma. Shortly after her father's suicide, Nikki had adopted the little animal from the sanctuary at Seagull's Flight, and ever since that day the two of them had been inseparable. It seemed fitting somehow that now Gemma would be returning there to lie at the side of her beloved Cassidy. Closing her eyes, she pictured it in her mind's eye. She could almost hear the sound of the wind in the grass that grew on the sand dunes, and the gentle roll of the waves as they broke on the beach. Yes, Nikki had made a wise decision. Gemma would rest easy there.

Chapter Twenty-Six

'For Christ's sake! What's up wi' you, Eddie? You've been like a bleedin' cat on hot bricks all bloody day.'

Stubbing his cigarette out in the overflowing ashtray, Eddie glared at Roxy, who was putting her make-up on in the nicotine-stained mirror above the fireplace.

'Just mind yer own bloody business an' piss off to Bingo, can't yer?' he shot back.

Roxy shrugged, and turning back to the mirror she gave her hair a final pat before snatching up her handbag. 'Suit yerself then, an' see if I care. I don't mind tellin' yer, I'll be glad when you can get out an' about again. I'm sick of havin' you under me feet all day. An' just mind as yer keep your eye on our Katie. Poppy should be back shortly if yer need any help with her.'

Katie was sitting cross-legged on the floor staring vacantly at the pages of a fairy-tale book spread out in front of her. Roxy swallowed hard when she saw that the book was upside down. It was probably just the pretty colours that were keeping the poor little mite interested. She paused to plant a kiss on the child's shining hair then moved on.

Eddie scowled as she passed him and listened to the sound of the door slamming behind her before struggling painfully from his chair and stumbling to the window. He looked swiftly up and down the road before glancing at the clock on the mantelpiece again. It was almost a quarter to seven, so where the hell could Nikki have got to? He'd told her how important it was that she be here tonight.

He hugged his chest. His ribs were still paining him to the point that it hurt to move, but somehow he would have to deliver Nikki tonight or else . . . He broke out in a sweat as he considered the alternative, and after lighting yet another cigarette he continued his vigil at the window.

When his mobile rang at seven on the dot his heart plummeted into his shoes.

'I trust you are on your way?' a voice muttered menacingly when he answered it.

'I . . . I'm just steppin' out o' the door even as we speak, boss.' Panic made his voice come out as a hoarse whisper. The phone went dead in his hand and Eddie frantically stared up and down the street again. The little bitch wasn't going to come, so what was he to do? With shaking fingers he punched Nikki's mobile number into the phone but only managed to reach her voicemail. Where the fuck was she anyway?

It was then that he heard the front door open and within seconds Poppy appeared and an idea was born. But no . . . what was he thinking of? Poppy was his daughter, for God's sake. His own flesh and blood. But then he asked himself, what alternative did he have? If he pushed enough treats her way, Poppy would never tell Roxy what had gone on, and if he was lucky he could have her back here before Roxy got home. His missus need never be any the wiser.

'Look, love. I've got a big favour to ask you,' he told Poppy. She narrowed her eyes. What was he after? He wasn't usually so nice to her. Seconds later when he had explained what he expected of her, her mouth dropped open.

'You're askin' me to come along to a party an' be handled by your pervy bleedin' mates?' she asked incredulously.

He raised his eyebrow. 'That's *just* what I'm askin'. An' don't look so shocked. I ain't thick, an' I happen to know you've already slept wi' half the lads on the estate fer nothin'. At least this way you'll get a good brucey bonus for yer trouble.'

Poppy's mind began to work overtime. If she were to go along with this, she'd have her dad right where she wanted him.

'All right then,' she told him eventually, and he breathed a sigh of relief. 'But what about our Katie? Who's goin' to look after her while we're gone?'

'Don't worry about her,' Eddie said quickly. 'We'll take her with us. She won't know where she's goin', an' when we get back I'll tell yer mam I took you both out for a treat to the pub. Now get a move on. We're late already an' my boss don't like to be kept waitin'.'

Poppy looked apprehensive for a moment as she stared at Katie, who was looking up at her trustingly, but then she thought of the new jeans she could buy tomorrow and within seconds she was following her dad out to the car like a lamb to the slaughter.

'Nikki, please open the door, I've brought you some supper.' Claire balanced the tray with one hand and tapped at the door with the other.

'I'm not hungry.'

'But you've got to eat, love.' There was a catch in Claire's voice. Nikki had scarcely ventured from her room since the day Gemma had died and now Claire was very concerned.

When she carried the untouched tray back into the kitchen some minutes later, Robbie, who was reading the *Daily Star* at the table, glanced up at her. 'No joy, lass?'

She shook her head wearily.

'Well, happen she'll pull herself together for the openin' o' the shop on Saturday, eh?' he suggested. 'I have to say it looks a fair treat an' the stock you've got in is incredible. I reckon you'll have the teenagers queuin' up to come in.'

Claire poured the drink she had carried upstairs untouched down the sink and came to join her father at the table. Under other circumstances she would really have been looking forward to the shop opening, but at present with the way things were with Nikki, she could summon up no enthusiasm for it.

Robbie reached across to pat her hand. 'She can't stay locked away for much longer,' he assured her. 'She's grievin' but she'll come round, you'll see.'

'I hope so,' Claire agreed, but at the moment she was feeling so down she could not allow herself to believe it.

Christian had been like a tower of strength to her, and now that he had returned home she was feeling his loss even more keenly than she had before. He had phoned to say that Gemma had been buried right next to Cassidy as Nikki had requested, but even that had not seemed to give the girl any comfort. She was blaming herself for the little dog's death and there was nothing Claire could say to make her believe otherwise.

The night before, Bradley had arrived with the most enormous bunch of flowers that Claire had ever seen and had been so genuinely sorry and attentive that she had felt herself warming to him.

'Mr Dickinson was saying at work today that he knows where there's a litter of shih-tzu puppies for sale,' he had told her earnestly. 'How about if I was to go and buy one for Nikki?'

'It's a lovely thought and very generous of you, but I don't think she's ready for another one just yet. Dogs are like people, Bradley. You can't just replace them.' She had felt instantly guilty as she saw him flush.

'No, of course you can't. I'm so sorry, Claire. I wasn't thinking.'

'No,' she sighed. 'It's me that should be sorry. I shouldn't have snapped at you like that. You were only trying to help and I do appreciate it, really I do. I'm just a bit edgy at the moment. Why don't you and Dad take a beer out into the garden? I'm afraid I'm not much company.'

Robbie had quietly taken two cans of lager out of the fridge and trudged out to join Bradley in the garden as Claire looked towards the ceiling. She was becoming more worried about Nikki with every day that passed. Since Gemma had died the girl had hardly eaten enough to keep a sparrow alive and Claire didn't have a clue what to do to change things. Perhaps it was time to get the social worker involved again? Or perhaps get the doctor to call in to take a look at her? She was unsure of what to do, but of one thing she was certain: she would have to do *something* – and soon – for things were just going from bad to worse.

Halfway between the villages of Bulkington and Bedworth, Eddie turned into a quiet lane. It was a beautiful evening, although he was so preoccupied with where he was going that he didn't even notice. Occasionally he glanced at Poppy and each time he did, guilt washed over him. He had delivered more young people to the bungalow he was heading for than he cared to remember, but never in his wildest dreams had he thought that one day he would take his own daughter there.

Poppy seemed oblivious to what she was letting herself in for, as she stared from the window. That's a blessing at least, he thought to himself, and it's not as if they're going to hurt her, is it? Soon there was nothing in sight but rolling fields and hedgerows, and Eddie slowed the car to a crawl. He wanted to turn the car around and take her home, but how could he? He pulled into the side of the lane and after fumbling awkwardly in his pocket, withdrew a crumpled packet of cigarettes and lit one. A glance at his watch and he put the car into gear and set off again. The way he saw it, he might as well go and get it over with.

Minutes later he turned off onto a rough track and about a mile down it, a sprawling bungalow came into sight. It was a magnificent place, far from prying eyes; his boss's home. The boss had had it built to his own specifications about ten years ago, and Eddie knew that if

Roxy ever saw it, she would drool. Set in ten acres of land, it had paddocks to one side of it and a large outdoor swimming pool to the other. But then the boss could afford it. He was heavily into property developing as well as other more shady businesses that never went through the books. To all intents and purposes the boss was a respectable man, but Eddie knew differently – not that he would ever dare tell anyone. That would be more than his life was worth.

He drew the car to a halt, flicked his fag end out of the window, then climbed from the car and waited for Poppy to join him.

'Phew, this is some place, ain't it?' She was staring around as if she could hardly believe her eyes. 'Your boss must be *loaded*, to own a place like this!'

Eddie found himself lost for words as he lifted Katie from the back of the car and nudged Poppy towards the front door. It opened and a middle-aged man appeared with a large glass of wine in his hand. The smile froze on his face as he looked first at Eddie and then at Poppy, and Eddie hastily told him, 'I hit a bit of a snag, Jackie. Nikki never turned up, the little bitch, but I've brought Poppy instead. An' yer needn't worry, she won't let yer down. She knows when to keep her mouth shut.'

The man's eyes swept over the girl as he swallowed his disappoint-ment before he said caustically, 'Trust *you* to get it wrong, Miller. I sometimes wonder why I keep you on. I'd told the blokes to expect a virgin an' you turn up with *her*!' Even as he said it there was a stir-ring in his loins. The girl was indisputably pretty and if what Eddie had said was true, then that was all to the good, a bonus. He glanced over his shoulder. He had customers waiting inside and if he didn't come up with something, he wasn't going to be in their good books.

'I dare say you'd best bring her in,' he barked. 'But this ain't the end of it, Miller. I want Nikki Nightingale here within the next week – is that *quite* clear?'

'Yes, boss.' Eddie felt as if his blood had turned to water as he followed the man into the luxuriously furnished bungalow. There were numerous doors leading off a long hallway and when the man threw one open he found himself staring back at half a dozen men who were sitting about drinking and smoking.

Ignoring them all, Jackie, as he was known, walked towards another door that was set against a huge mirror that took up almost the whole of one wall. He then turned back and told them, 'Right, gentlemen, the young lady we were hoping for hasn't arrived, as you can see, but I'm sure you'll all agree that this one will do us proud instead.' Looking towards Eddie he told him, 'You sit yourself down. I'll take it from here.'

Eddie fought the temptation to snatch Poppy back and run from this place as fast as his legs would take him, but one glance at the boss's face and he sank meekly down onto a chair with Katie pressed tightly to his side. The men all then crossed to peer into the enormous mirror as the door closed on Jackie and Poppy, who was looking slightly nervous now.

'So where the bleedin' hell is your dad an' our Katie then?' Roxy asked when she got in later that night.

'I've no idea,' Luke retorted. 'They were already gone when I got home about eightish.' As he turned his attention back to the motorbike magazine he was reading, Roxy chewed on her lip. It was really unlike Eddie to take Katie out. In fact, now that she came to think about it, she could count on one hand the number of times he had bothered to do so since the child had been born. But then, he had been like a bear with a sore head the last few days, trapped in the house, licking his wounds, so perhaps he'd decided to take her up the pub? That seemed the likeliest option so, feeling slightly easier now, Roxy went into the kitchen to see what was in the fridge.

Just then, the front door opened and Eddie walked in, clutching Katie's hand, with Poppy following closely behind. Katie looked slightly flushed but otherwise to Roxy's relief seemed to be perfectly all right, though the same couldn't be said for Poppy. She was as white as a sheet and shot off up the stairs before Roxy could say so much as a word to her.

'Just where the bleedin' hell have you been?' she spat. 'Fancy keepin' this poor little mite out till this time o' night. Couldn't you have waited for yer ration till Luke or our Poppy got in?'

Eddie could have cried with relief. Roxy obviously thought that he had taken Katie to the pub and he had no intention of telling her otherwise.

'Do you know, woman, I sometimes think there's no bleedin' pleasin' you,' he shot back. 'Yer forever tellin' me what a rotten dad I am an' how I don't spend enough bloody time wi' the kids, then when I do take 'em out yer have a go at me anyway! What do I have to do to fuckin' please yer, eh?'

Roxy sniffed, feeling slightly guilty. She supposed Eddie did have a point. Even so, she wasn't about to tell him so.

'Well, there's a time an' a place,' she scolded him. 'Perhaps next time you decide to play the dotin' dad you could do it at a more suitable hour an' not keep the poor little lamb up half the night. An' what's up wi' our Poppy? She looked as if she'd seen a ghost.'

'Oh, I reckon it's . . . yer know – women's problems. She's been quiet all night,' he mumbled.

Roxy eyed him suspiciously for a second but then she took Katie's hand and swept past him. Eddie listened to her talking to the child as she led her up the stairs and as his hand settled on the video in his pocket he broke out in a sweat. He would have to find a very safe place to hide this one, 'cos if Roxy ever happened across it, as sure as eggs were eggs, his life would never be worth living again.

'Nikki, please open the door. The doctor is here and he wants to talk to you.'

When there was no reply, Claire flushed and glanced back at the doctor, who was looking at his watch.

'I'm so sorry about this,' she told him. 'She's been locked away in there for days, which is why I wanted you to take a look at her.'

'I do understand your concern, Mrs Nightingale. But you know, if she has recently lost a beloved pet, she probably just needs time to grieve and I'm afraid I do have rather a lot of calls to make. Perhaps you could bring her down to the surgery when she feels ready?'

Claire's shoulders sagged in defeat. Apart from breaking the door down and forcing Nikki to see the doctor there was nothing more she could do.

'Very well, I'll do that,' she whispered flatly. 'Thank you for coming, Doctor. I'm sorry to have bothered you.'

'You haven't bothered me at all,' he assured her. 'But let's just let things take their course for a while, eh? I'm sure Nikki will come through this with flying colours once she's over the initial shock. Good day, and don't worry. I can see myself out.'

Once the doctor had gone, Claire sank down onto the carpet with her back against Nikki's bedroom door as tears spilled down her cheeks. Everything should be wonderful. The shop was due to open the following day, and she had pictured Nikki at her side when they opened the doors. With things as they were at the moment, she would be lucky to get so much as a glance at her, let alone enjoy her company. And then there was her dad. They had been getting on so well recently, yet now that the shop was finished he seemed a little nervy and on edge, and Claire wondered if he was about to leave her again. Drying her eyes on the sleeve of her cheesecloth top she sniffed loudly before trudging towards the bathroom to wash her face.

Nikki flicked through the messages on her mobile phone and was shocked to see that nearly all of them were from Eddie. But why would he be ringing her?

As she began to read through them her face grew even paler than it already was. He was angry with her because she hadn't turned up for his friends to take photos of her on Wednesday, but then she had been so sick with grief over losing Gemma that she had forgotten all about it.

She was still reading the messages when the mobile rang yet again and this time she answered it.

'You little bitch,' Eddie snarled. 'Just who the fuck do yer think you are, eh? You owe me, girl, an' yer let me down. Now it's time to find out what happens to people who upset the boss.' The phone went dead as Nikki stared at it in consternation. What did Eddie mean? He could hardly hurt her while she was shut away in her room, and she hadn't meant to let him down. What with the upset of losing Gemma she had forgotten all about the fact that they were supposed to meet. Shrugging, she tossed the phone onto the bedside chair and curled herself up into a miserable little ball again.

It was the early hours of the morning when a thundering on the front door brought Claire starting awake. Through the drawn curtains she could just distinguish faint blue flashing lights and she wondered what could have happened now. Dragging her dressing-gown on, she pushed her feet into her slippers and ran for the door just in time to see Robbie heading down the stairs. He had already opened the door by the time she joined him and she stared across his shoulder at two police officers.

'Mrs Nightingale?' The older of the two flashed his identity card at Claire and she nodded. 'Are you the owner of Nikki's Boutique in the High Street?'

'Yes . . . yes, I am,' she stuttered, completely bewildered.

'Then I'm sorry to have to tell you that a fire has been reported there. The fire service are dealing with it right now.'

'A *fire*?' Claire gasped incredulously. 'But how? We were due to officially open the shop tomorrow. Everything was fine when I left it earlier on.'

The officer shrugged. 'I'm afraid we have no idea how the fire started. But perhaps you'd like to come with us?'

'No, it's all right,' Robbie butted in. 'You go on, we'll just throw some clothes on and then I'll take us there in my car. We'll meet you at the shop.'

'Very well, sir.' The two officers turned away as Claire stared at Robbie open-mouthed.

'They must have got it wrong,' she whimpered. 'It can't be *my* shop. I had everything ready for the opening. It all looked so—'

'Now then, lass.' Robbie squeezed her hand soothingly. 'There's no point in goin' an' gettin' yourself all hot an' bothered. Let's just get dressed an' get down there, eh? How soon can you be ready?'

'Five minutes,' she promised. Minutes later, as Claire hastily buttoned the shirt of her blouse, she knocked at Nikki's door and called, 'Nikki, are you awake?' There was no reply, so she went on. 'There's a fire at the shop. Me and your grandad are going there now.' Still no reply but Claire was too harassed to stand there any longer so she hurried away and left Nikki to it.

'Oh my God!' As Robbie screeched to a halt just down the road from the shop in the High Street, Claire's hand flew to her mouth in horror. Flames were licking out of the shop window and firemen had hosepipes trained on it, though even from here it was apparent they were fighting a losing battle. The front window had shattered with the heat and broken glass twinkled like diamonds on the pavement in the light from the street lamps. Robbie had parked on double yellow lines but seeing as the road was deserted save for two police cars and two fire engines he didn't think that anyone would take much notice. The vehicles were parked over the road from the shop, their blue lights flashing like sleepy eyes in the darkened street.

Grim-faced, Claire and Robbie strode towards them but they had gone no more than a few yards when a fireman approached them and urged, 'Best not go any closer. We don't know if there's anything in there that might explode.'

'There . . . there's a small gas cooker in the back room,' Claire stuttered as she gazed in shock at the thick black smoke belching up into the sky.

'Oh, it's your shop is it, miss?'

'Yes. How bad is the fire?'

'Well, I don't think there's much chance of saving anything,' the fireman told her truthfully. 'It was already well alight by the time we got here. The best we can hope for now is that we can stop it spreading to the shops either side of it.'

Claire nodded numbly as she stared up at the smart red sign she'd had made for above the door. *Nikki's Boutique*, it had said, but now it was nothing more than a mess of melting paint that dripped to the floor like drops of blood.

'Oh Dad, all that hard work and now everything's ruined.'

Seeing her deep distress, Robbie patted her arm. 'Never mind, lass. It could have been worse. At least no one has been hurt, and when everything's sorted and you've got the insurance money, we'll start all over again and we'll make it even better, you'll see.'

When Claire didn't immediately answer him, he asked, 'You *did* insure it, didn't you?'

She gulped. 'The actual building is insured – I had to do that before I could rent it, but . . . well, I hadn't got round to insuring the stock or anything. I was going to, but we've been so busy and what with Gemma and one thing or another, I never actually did it.'

Robbie sighed deeply. 'You mean to tell me that you've lost the lot?'

She nodded miserably. It had cost thousands to stock the rails and the shelves, and now it was all gone before she had even had a chance to open the doors. But how could it have happened?

Turning back to the fireman she asked, 'How do you think the fire started? Could it have been an electrical fault or something?'

'I suppose it could have been.' The fireman removed his helmet and scratched his head. 'But I have to say I think it's highly unlikely. The door was open at the back so my guess is someone broke in and started it deliberately.'

Appalled, Claire stared at him. 'But who would do such a thing?'

'Your guess is as good as mine, love. We'll just have to wait and see what they find when they've managed to put the blaze out.' At that, he put his helmet back on and strode away.

'Right, miss,' said one of the policemen. 'You may as well go home. There'll be nothing you can do here tonight.'

She gazed back at the shop for one last time. The shop was to have been something she and Nikki could share together, and now this was ruined too. She saw the place in her mind's eye as it had been just a few short hours ago: the shiny red sign above the door, sparkling in the sunshine. The gossamer-fine voile draped across the trendy window display; the shelves bulging with shoes of every colour and size. Racks of dresses, skirts, jeans and tops, the counter crammed with jewellery and knick-knacks, all designed to appeal to teenage girls. And now everything was gone; nothing but charred remnants and blackened walls remained.

Seeing that she was close to breaking down, Robbie took her elbow and steered her back to the car. He wanted to scold her for not taking out insurance on the contents of the shop but he could see that she'd had more than enough for one night and wisely stayed silent.

'Come on, lass. Let's go an' get a good stiff drink inside you, eh? There's nowt to be gained by stayin' here.'

Trance-like, Claire allowed him to gently lead her away.

Chapter Twenty-Seven

'Well, there's one good thing that's come out of tonight,' Robbie remarked, nodding towards the table when they arrived back at the house. 'Looks like Nikki's decided to come out of her pit for somethin' to eat.'

Claire followed his eyes to the empty plate and glass. He was right. It looked as if the girl had come down for a snack, which Claire supposed was something to be grateful for at least, although right at that moment she was feeling so wretched it would have taken a lot more than that to cheer her up. Robbie meanwhile had fetched a bottle of vodka from the lounge and pouring her a stiff measure he ordered, 'Get that down you. You look like you need it.'

She gulped at it, coughing slightly as it burned its way down into her stomach.

Robbie joined her, and when he had refilled their glasses he asked tentatively, 'You can't think of anyone who might do this, can you, lass? Someone who might have a grudge against you?'

When she shook her head he frowned. 'Then it must have been either some sort of an electrical fault or vandals. Perhaps a group o' youths or sommat on their way home from the pub.'

'I doubt it.' Claire took a swallow from her glass. 'Why would they choose my shop from all the others?'

'I've no idea,' he admitted regretfully. 'But sittin' here frettin' about it ain't goin' to change nothin', is it? So come on, finish your drink an' let's get back to bed. We'll see what's to be done come mornin'.'

'I'll be up in a minute. You go on.' Claire poured herself yet another drink under his watchful eye. 'I don't have to worry about getting up early to open the shop now, do I, so there's no rush.'

Robbie opened his mouth to say something but then thinking better of it, he hastily snapped it shut and strode away without so much as another word. It was taking him all his time to come to terms with the latest catastrophe Claire was faced with, so he could only begin to imagine how she must be feeling. Poor lass. Trouble seemed to follow her about like a shadow, from what he could make of it, and it was a crying shame.

It was mid-morning the following day when a policeman arrived to tell Claire that the fire had been no accident. As the police had initially suspected, someone had forced the door in the small yard at the back of the shop and gone in and deliberately started the fire. He went on to ask her questions, much as Robbie had the night before. Did she know of anyone who might bear a grudge against her, someone who was capable of doing such a thing? She answered the questions dully before asking one of her own.

'What are the chances of catching whoever did it?'

'Well, of course we'll continue with our investigation,' the solemn-faced policeman told her. 'But I have to be honest and tell you that we have very little to go on. Any fingerprints et cetera were destroyed in the fire. I dare say you'll be fully covered with insurance though?'

Claire flushed to the roots of her hair. 'Actually, I hadn't got around to insuring it,' she admitted, feeling a complete idiot. 'The shop was due to open today. My father and I had just finished refurbishing and stocking it.'

The police officer's attitude softened then and Claire realised with a little start that he must have thought she might have had something to do with it. Perhaps he'd thought that she had done it for the insurance money?

With all his questions answered, the officer now stood and closed his notebook.

'Right, Mrs Nightingale. Please accept my condolences, and rest assured we'll keep you informed of any developments. We have finished at the shop now so you may go back in whenever you wish.'

'Thank you.' Claire saw him to the door and once it had closed behind him she leaned wearily against it. 'You may go back in,' he had said – but go back in to what? Who could have done this wicked act? Her heart began to pound as a frightening possibility occurred to her. Could it be someone from her past who had managed to track her down?

It was at that moment that Nikki appeared on the stairs. Under other circumstances, Claire would have been thrilled to see her up and about again, but this morning she could only manage a feeble smile.

Nikki followed her into the kitchen and sat down at the table. 'Was there much damage done in the fire?' she asked.

'Oh, you did hear me last night then?' Claire's voice was uncharacteristically sarcastic. 'Truthfully, until I've been in there I can't say for sure, but if what we saw from the outside last night is anything to go by, I'd be shocked if there's anything salvageable at all.'

Robbie, who looked almost as bad as Claire did, joined them now and suggested, 'Do you feel up to going and taking a look? There's no point in putting it off and you never know, it might turn out to be not as bad as we think.'

'Huh! And pigs might fly, but I suppose you're right – we may as well go and get it over with,' Claire agreed. 'I'll just go and tidy myself up a bit first. Are you coming with us, Nikki?'

Nikki nodded and minutes later they all left the house together and piled into Robbie's car.

They entered the shop, or what was left of it, through the rear, and as Claire stared round she felt angry tears stinging at the back of her eyes. The place where the front window had been had already been boarded up and there was no electricity on, but even in the gloom it was plain to see that the whole place and everything in it was ruined. Even the clothes rails were blackened and charred, and the fitting room that Robbie had worked so hard on was burned to the ground – nothing more than a pile of black ashes.

She kicked at some beads that had fallen from where the counter had been and they crumbled to dust.

'I think we can safely say there's nothing going to be saved in here, don't you?' she muttered, more to herself than anyone else.

It was then that Nikki took her hand and with tears in her eyes told her, 'Oh Mum, I'm so sorry. I know you did this for me, and . . .'

Suddenly they were in each other's arms and it did Robbie's heart good to see them so. At least there would be something positive to have come of this sorry mess if it brought them closer together again.

'Come on,' he said softly. 'Let's be gettin' you two home, eh? There's nothin' we can do here today.'

Nodding, they slowly turned about and followed him.

Tracey and Callum turned up late that afternoon after reading about the fire in the Nuneaton Tribune.

'I can't believe it!' Tracey declared and she sounded so genuinely upset that Claire felt a warm glow inside. 'All that work you and Dad put into the place and then for this to go and happen before you'd even had a chance to open it. Molly sends her love and said to tell you that if there's anything at all she can do, you just have to say the word and she'll be over. Perhaps we could all stick in and get it ship-shape again?'

'I don't think there's much chance of that,' Claire told her regretfully as she scooped one of the twins onto her lap. 'I'm not even sure that I'm going to bother. I paid for the lease on the shop for twelve months in advance, but I think it could take that long to get the place sorted out. Then I'm not so sure that I have the heart to do it again. What's the point, when some mindless vandal could spoil it all again? No, I reckon I might just count my losses and put it down to experience.'

Tracey sighed. She had always been slightly envious of Claire since she had returned home. After all, her elder sister seemed to have everything – money, looks, a beautiful house – and now for this to go and happen.

'Well, look, how about I stay and fix us all a nice meal, eh? I don't suppose you're feeling up to cooking after the shock you've had, on top of losing Gemma. Callum and I stopped off to get some steak and salad on the way here, but I don't want to intrude, of course. Just say if you'd rather we left.'

'Oh no,' Claire told her hastily. 'That would be lovely. It would take our mind off things.'

'Good, then you get yourself off for a nice hot bath or a lie-down, and I'll call you when it's ready,' Tracey urged her.

Claire meekly left the room enjoying the feeling of being looked after. Now that the initial shock of what had happened was wearing off a little, she did feel tired and decided that she'd not bother with the bath but just shut her eyes for a few minutes before going back down to help with the meal. Yawning, she strolled over to the windows to look out, and frowned when she saw a man standing across the road with his hands stuffed in his jacket pockets. There was something vaguely familiar about him, though she couldn't think why. And what was he doing just standing there with his hands in his pockets? Deciding that he was probably just waiting for someone, she slid under her duvet and settled down for a nap.

When a tap came on the bedroom door she jumped awake, amazed to find that she had fallen into a deep sleep. Tracey was peeping round the door at her and Claire told her, 'I'm so sorry. What must you think

291

of me? I only intended to close my eyes for a few minutes but I must have gone out like a light.'

'Well, you obviously needed it.' Tracey smiled at her. 'Now go and rinse your face and come and eat this meal I've cooked. Oh, and by the way, Bradley is downstairs. He stopped by to see if there was anything you needed doing, so I've invited him to stay for dinner too. I hope you don't mind?'

'Of course I don't mind,' Claire assured her. 'But how did Bradley find out about the fire?'

'The same way as we all did – local newspapers.' Tracey raised her eyebrows. 'You know what it's like, the least bit of trouble and the papers blow it up out of all proportion. Though I'm not saying that what happened at the shop wasn't awful, of course.'

Then, fearing she might put her foot in it even more than she already had, Tracey scooted away as Claire hastily pulled a brush through her tangled blond hair and tried to pinch some colour into her cheeks.

You've looked better, my girl, she told herself as she stared at her reflection in the mirror, then after straightening her creased blouse as best she could with the flat of her hands she smoothed her jeans and returned to the window. She was relieved to see that the man who had been standing there earlier on had gone. I'm getting paranoid, she scolded herself, then turning about she went down to dinner.

'Claire, this certainly hasn't been your week, love, has it?' Bradley greeted her.

She smiled at him ruefully. 'I think I can truthfully say you got that right!'

He held a chair out for her and she sat down, pleased to see that Nikki had joined them. The girl had swept her long fair hair high onto the top of her head in a ponytail, and without the heavy layers of make-up she had taken to wearing she looked incredibly young and pretty.

'Nikki's been a great help,' Tracey informed her as she placed a large bowl of Caesar salad in the centre of the table. 'She's been showing me where everything is.'

'You should have woken me,' Claire reproached her, but as Tracey strapped Jessica into one of the high chairs she and Callum had brought with them, she retorted, 'I certainly wouldn't have done that. You look dead on your feet. It won't hurt you to be waited on for once. And what's more, when we've eaten, Nikki and I are going to clear up while you put your feet up, aren't we, Nikki?'

Nikki nodded obligingly and Claire's heart soared.

Despite the disaster of the night before, the meal turned out to be a relaxed affair. Callum and Bradley chatted non-stop and Nikki was obviously enjoying herself as she helped the twins with their meals. Robbie was clearly in his element too, having his two girls together, and so the time passed pleasantly. By the time they had finished their dessert, which was a delicious apple pie that Tracey had managed to rustle up, Claire was beginning to feel a little better about things. After all, as had been pointed out to her, no one had been hurt in the fire, which was one blessing at least, and she supposed she could always ask Mr Dickinson for her old job back – if he hadn't already found someone to replace her permanently, that was. As yet, she hadn't had time to total up what the fire had cost her, although she knew that it would run into thousands of pounds. But then, she still had money in the bank, so she was hardly going to become bankrupt through it, which was another blessing.

Eventually, Tracey bossily ordered them all out into the garden with a bottle of wine while she tidied the kitchen up. Nikki took the twins up to her room for a nap and so Claire found herself with three men pandering to her under the tree in the garden.

'I think I could get quite used to having three men all at my beck and call,' she told them jokingly.

'Well, I for one would certainly volunteer for the job full-time,'

Bradley replied, which brought a stain to her cheeks and had Callum and Robbie laughing.

Up in her bedroom, Nikki had just got the twins off to sleep in her bed when her mobile rang. She snatched it up hastily, fearful that the noise would waken the little ones, and whispered, 'Yes?'

'How does it feel to have your own shop then?'

She instantly recognised Eddie's voice but something about it made her bite her lip and remain silent.

'Oops, sorry! I forgot – you ain't got your own shop any more, have you?'

Nikki's stomach did a somersault.

'Shame about the fire, weren't it? But I did warn you what the boss were like if he got let down, didn't I?'

The hairs on the back of Nikki's neck stood to attention as horror washed over her. 'It was *you* who burned the shop, wasn't it?' she choked.

A throaty chuckle was her answer. 'Don't talk such rubbish. Yer should know I'd never harm so much as a hair on yer head. Let's just say you don't mess about wi' the boss, eh? Not if you know what's good fer you. Now . . . shall we try again? Me friend is still very keen to meet yer. Be here at seven o'clock next Wednesday, or somethin' else bad might happen to sommat of you or yours again.'

The phone went dead in her hand and Nikki clutched at the bedside table for support. Eddie's boss had had the shop burned down! And just because she hadn't done as he had asked. Indignation took the place of shock. Well, she'd show him. She'd go downstairs right now and tell Claire who was responsible for the fire. The police would be round to Eddie's to question him about this boss of his in no time!

She was almost at the door when common sense took over and her footsteps slowed. If she told Claire who was responsible for the fire,

Eddie might retaliate and tell Claire that he had been supplying her with drugs! This invisible boss of Eddie's had her over a barrel and he obviously knew it. What a mess she had got herself into! If Claire ever found out that she'd been taking drugs she would never forgive her, so what was she to do?

Dropping onto the edge of the bed she began to cry noiselessly as the soft snores of the twins floated around the room.

'Eddie, get your arse over here right this minute!'

'What? Who is this?' Eddie rubbed the sleep from his eyes and glanced at Roxy, who was fast asleep at his side in a tangle of grubby bedclothes. The bedside clock showed that it was almost two o'clock in the morning. Slightly more awake now, he slid off the edge of the bed and, holding the mobile close to his ear, he tip-toed out onto the landing, where he hissed, 'Is that you, boss?'

'Of course it's me, you arsehole. We've had a bit of a disaster here an' I need you.'

'But it's the middle o' the night,' Eddie objected, and then a tremor of fear spread up his spine as the voice on the other end of the phone told him, 'If you ain't here in half an' hour you'll be sorry.'

Eddie had worked for Jackie, as his boss was known to everyone, for more years than he cared to remember. He had visited tenants who owed the boss rent. He had handled stolen goods and sold drugs for him. He had supplied the boss and his kinky friends with kids who were little more than babies, and he had also participated in their parties – but never before had he been summoned in the middle of the night. Something serious must be afoot.

The sound of Shania Twain, warbling 'That Don't Impress Me Much' was wafting from Poppy's room and he cursed softly. She'd obviously fallen asleep and left her music on again. It's no wonder the bleedin' electric bills are always through the roof, he thought to himself. I'll whack her one in the mornin', but for now I ought to get goin'. That was one thing about the boss: when he told yer somethin' he meant it, so there wasn't a moment to lose.

As he drew the car to a halt outside the sprawling bungalow some time later, he was shocked to see that almost every window in the building was lit up. A number of expensive cars were parked outside, and even as he made to climb out of his own, a smart-looking bloke in a suit that looked like it had come straight off a tailor's dummy hurried out and climbed into one of them, before roaring off as if the devil himself were after him.

Bewildered, Eddie limped to the door; hurrying had made the pain in his ribs worse again and he only hoped that whatever it was the boss had got him out of bed for was worth it.

'Eddie? Thank God – come in.'

The boss had clearly been waiting for him, but this was a man Eddie had never seen before. Jackie was normally as cool as a cucumber, but tonight he was bordering on the edge of panic.

'What's up then?'

Jackie grabbed Eddie's elbow and hauled him into the bungalow.

'I'm afraid there's been a little . . . accident.'

They were walking through the lounge towards the door where Jackie had taken Poppy and Katie only nights before, and Eddie was aware of a dozen pairs of eyes tight on him. Men were sitting about; some were pacing up and down while others stood with their hands in their pockets furiously puffing on spliffs or cigarettes.

Eddie followed the boss into the room and his eyes almost started from his head as he found himself staring down at a young girl who was sprawled out on the bed. She looked to be no more than thirteen or fourteen at most, and one glance at her was enough to tell Eddie that she was as dead as a dodo.

'*Christ almighty!*' He paled to the colour of lint. 'What the fuckin' hell has been goin' on here?'

'One of my friends got a little . . . er . . . carried away,' Jackie gulped.

'Yer can say that again.' Eddie stared at the livid red fingerprints on the girl's neck that stood out in stark contrast to her white skin. 'He's bleedin' *killed* her! Who was she, anyway?'

'That's of no consequence. Just some little scrubber he picked up in Brum earlier on.'

'Well, I want no part of it. It's murder, whichever way yer look at it.' Eddie was backing towards the door, but Jackie's voice stayed him.

'You just hold fire. You're here to get rid o' the body.'

Shock robbed Eddie of speech for a moment but then he stuttered, 'Y . . . you must be fuckin' *jokin'*! What am *I* supposed to do wi' her?'

'We've thought of that. If you were to take her and dump her in the Blue Lagoon there's every chance she won't be found for some time. There's loads o' courtin' couples use that place, so when she is found the cops will think it's some lad done it an' then dumped her in there. At this time o' the mornin' it'll be quiet so there ain't much chance o' you bein' seen.'

'Oh no yer don't!' Eddie held his hands up as panic gripped him. 'You ain't dumpin' this job on *me*, boyo! I've done some bad things for you over the years, but even I call a halt at gettin' rid o' dead bodies.'

'You ain't got no say in the matter – unless you want to get dumped with her,' Jackie spat. 'Now get a grip on yerself an' help me put her clothes back on so there's nothin' can be traced back here.'

Eddie shuddered as he lifted a crumpled denim skirt from the floor and advanced slowly on the lifeless corpse.

'I'll do what yer ask,' he said resignedly, knowing that he had little choice, 'but I'll have to have somebody come along to help get her into the water.'

'Why?' Jackie's narrowed eyes were heavy with suspicion.

''Cos o' these.' Eddie tapped his chest, which was still tightly bandaged. 'Cracked ribs, remember? It's a good walk to the water from where you have to park an' there's no way I can carry her on me own.'

Seeing the sense in what he said, Jackie continued to struggle with the cheap top he was trying to get over the girl's head while Eddie battled with the skirt. His eyes were drawn to a whip lying discarded on the floor and now that he was closer he could see angry red weals on the girl's stick-like legs and skinny thighs.

'Don't feel sorry for this piece o' trash,' Jackie told him harshly as he followed his eyes. 'She loved it rough. The rougher the better, in fact. She's been here a few times now, an' soon got to know that there's no gain without pain. As long as she went home with a fat pocket the punters could do what they liked to her. Well, she'll line my pocket now. The film we have o' tonight will fetch a bundle abroad, especially when it gets on the internet.'

Eddie felt sick as he thought of the video he had back at home with Poppy on it. He hadn't been able to bring himself to watch it – and it would be God help him if Roxy ever came across it, or any of the others he had tucked away, for that matter. But he couldn't let himself think about that for now. All he wanted was to get this over with and get himself home. The girl was dressed by now and Eddie was horrified to see urine trickling down her leg. Jackie clucked with annoyance when he saw the expression on Eddie's face and turning abruptly, he strode into the other room. Eddie caught snatches of a muttered conversation and then Jackie returned with a man in a smart pin-striped suit whose eyes were almost popping out of his head with fear.

When they went to lift the girl, Eddie told them, 'Hey, hang on a bit. Ain't yer goin' to wrap her in sommat? I don't want her . . . yer know . . . leakin' all over me car.'

Sighing heavily, Jackie tugged a sheet from the bed and roughly tucked it round her then addressing the other man he told him, 'You take her legs an' I'll take her arms.'

Once outside, they threw her unceremoniously onto the back seat of Eddie's car.

'I'll . . . er . . . follow you in mine,' the man who had been dele-
gated to help him told Eddie.

Eddie sneered. He might have guessed as much. That way, if he got
stopped by the Old Bill, the other crafty bugger could clear off and
leave him to face the music.

'Just make sure as yer do then,' he snarled.

'Eddie.' Jackie's voice stayed him just as he was about to get into
the car. 'Once it's done, be sure an' keep away from here till I tell you
otherwise. Just lay low an' try an' keep out o' trouble, eh?'

Eddie stared at him with contempt but as he drove along, his heart
was in his mouth. He could see the headlights of the car following
him in his mirror, but every other car he spotted made his heart leap
painfully. What if someone had tipped the cops off and they were on
to him?

It was not until he finally turned off Heath End Road in Nuneaton
onto Bermuda Road that his heart settled into a slightly steadier rhythm.
They were almost there now; surely nothing could go wrong now?

Halfway down the lane he turned the car onto a rough dirt track.
There were no street lamps here and the car headlights sliced through
the darkness as it bounced along on the uneven track. He was half-
tempted to turn them off in case they drew attention to him, but was
too afraid of going over the edge of the cliff into the deep reservoir
below. Soon the car was going downhill and he saw the glitter of the
dark water reflecting in the light from the moon. He drove on until
he came to a fence that prevented him from going any further then
stopped and switched the lights off as the car that had been following
him pulled up alongside.

The men both climbed from their cars and stood looking about
them. The Blue Lagoon was a popular place for courting couples, and
most nights it was commonplace to see vehicles with steamed-up
windows parked in regimental rows all along the fence. Thankfully, at
this time of the morning it was deserted, and Eddie breathed a sigh

of relief. The Blue Lagoon was also popular with youngsters, who loved to swim there during the summer months, despite the signs that were placed strategically warning them not to. It was treacherously deep and the waving weeds growing beneath the surface and the undercurrents had claimed more than one young life. By day it was a breathtakingly pretty place when the sun was glinting off the water, but tonight it was eerie and looked dark and forbidding.

'Right, let's get this over wi' then, shall we, eh?' Eddie wondered why he was whispering and his heart started to hammer again as he and his accomplice began to manhandle the lifeless body from the car. Eddie's ribs were paining him and each breath he took was an effort. The girl hit the ground with a dull thud and Eddie and the man then began to drag the sheet along the dewy grass until at last they came to the edge of the water. At that moment the moon sailed from behind the clouds, illuminating the scene with frightening clarity.

'I reckon we're goin' to have to wade in deep enough for the current to catch her,' Eddie told him. 'Otherwise she's just goin' to float around the edge.'

The stranger looked down in horror at his smart suit and Eddie felt his anger building. He knew the bloke from somewhere, he was sure he did, but up to now he hadn't been able to place him. He was no youngster and nothing much to look at, though he was impeccably turned out and obviously had money, as all of the ring Jackie ran did. Suddenly it hit him like a thump in the gut.

'Why, *you* were one o' the magistrates when I were last in court!' he said incredulously. 'Jenkins, ain't it? You've got the butcher's shop in Cross Street.'

The man looked as if he might faint clean away there and then. 'Who I am is fairly irrelevant at the moment, don't you think? Now . . . shall we just get this done?'

They each grabbed a corner of the sheet again, gasping as they dragged it into the water, which was surprisingly cold. A mist was floating across the surface and Eddie wasn't sure if he was shivering from cold or fear. If anyone should see them now, they would be locked up and the key would be thrown away. Once the body was afloat it was slightly easier, and they felt their way along the uneven bottom until their jackets were floating around them and they were chest deep. A sound from the woods made them both stop dead and now Eddie felt sweat break out on his forehead although he was freezing cold.

'It's all right,' he whispered after a few moments. 'It's just some creature in the wood. Probably a fox.'

They moved on until Eddie paused. 'I reckon this should do it.' Tugging the sheet from around the body he then pushed it as hard as his ribs would allow him to. The body floated still farther out, the girl's skinny arms and legs seeming luminous on the black water, and then a current snatched at it and they watched as it slowly began to sink and finally disappeared from sight.

As one, the two men turned and waded back towards the bank where Eddie chucked the sheet into some bushes, the wind sighing through the trees the only witness to the dastardly deed that had just been committed.

Jenkins was looking down at his soaking suit in dismay, no doubt wondering how he was going to explain it away to his wife, and Eddie felt the urge to hit him. 'It were you as killed the poor little sod, weren't it?' he ground out.

Ignoring his question, the man turned away and they climbed into their cars without another word.

The job was done, and as far as Eddie was concerned, after this night's work he and the boss should be quits now.

Chapter Twenty-Eight

'I was thinking – now that I've done what I came to do, you'll be wanting me to move out?'

Claire stared at Robbie. They were sitting together having breakfast. The schools had broken up for the long summer holidays and she assumed Nikki was still in bed fast asleep. She buttered some toast before saying cautiously, 'Actually, I was wondering if you'd mind staying on for a bit longer, Dad? The thing is, this place is long overdue for a facelift and a bit of redecorating, and I was wondering . . .'

'If I would do it?'

She nodded nervously, though if truth be told she didn't want him to stay on just for that reason. She had got used to having her father about the place and was glad of an excuse to postpone him leaving.

'I'd be happy to,' he assured her as a warm feeling started to grow in the pit of his stomach. 'You just choose the paint and wallpaper and tell me which rooms you want doing and I'll start as soon as you like.'

'Fantastic,' Claire beamed, but then becoming solemn she went on, 'the only thing is, I *insist* on paying you this time. You wouldn't take a penny for all that work you did in the shop and I feel as if I'm taking advantage of you.'

'Rubbish!' He laughed good-naturedly. 'You've given me free board and lodgings for weeks and I'm not short of a bob or two, I can assure you. I've lived very frugally over the years and I've got quite a little nest-egg tucked away. That will come to you and Tracey when anything happens to me. I've already instructed my solicitor.'

'Don't talk like that. That isn't going to happen for years and years yet,' Claire scolded him.

Unable to meet her eyes, Robbie looked away. There was so very much he wanted to confide in her, but how could he without breaking her heart again? She had been through so much already, without him giving her something else to worry about. He would tell her, of course, but not until the time was right – and that time wasn't now. There was still a lot of catching up to do yet.

'Well, lass, that remains to be seen,' he said softly. 'Look at your mam. Here one day and gone the next, just like that.' He snapped his fingers to emphasise his point. 'Life is a funny old thing and you never know what it has in store for you or when your card is marked.' His face was sad, and once again Claire realised that he still had deep feelings for his late wife even though they had been apart all those years.

A silence settled between them as they became lost in their own thoughts, broken by Nikki who walked into the kitchen still in her pyjamas and yawning widely.

'Morning, love. Come and join us and I'll pop you some toast in,' Claire told her cheerfully.

Nikki sank down, rubbing the sleep from her eyes. Mornings were always hard without Gemma there to greet her when she came downstairs.

'So what have you got planned for today then?' Robbie enquired.

Nikki shrugged. She should have been helping Claire out in the shop over the summer holidays, but that wouldn't happen now, and the way she saw it, it was all her fault, though she couldn't tell Claire that, of course. If only she had done what Eddie had requested, the shop would still be intact instead of a burned-out shell.

'I thought we might go and see Christian and Mrs M sometime

over the next couple of weeks,' Claire suggested. 'That is, if you don't mind being left here on your own, Dad?'

'Not at all. You just supply me with a load of paint and paper and tell me what rooms you want decorating and I shall be as happy as Larry,' he assured her.

Nikki bit on her lip. The idea of getting away for a while was appealing after all that had gone on, but what would happen if she didn't turn up for Eddie's boss again? She knew what he was capable of now and dreaded to think what he might do next.

'How about we go shopping for some wallpaper for the lounge after breakfast?' Claire asked, but Nikki shook her head.

'If it's all the same to you I'll pass on that one.'

'Suit yourself.' Claire was obviously not too happy with her decision but there had been so many rows and arguments just lately that she was eager to avoid another one. 'Got something planned, have you?'

'Not really.'

'Well, as it happens I was planning on popping over to Nuneaton after breakfast to see Tracey and the twins,' Robbie piped up. 'How about you come too and keep me company?'

Nikki again shook her head as Claire sighed and turned away. She knew by the look on Nikki's face that enough had been said.

It was eleven o'clock that morning when Nikki left the house. She could hear Robbie, who had decided to postpone his trip into Nuneaton, in the lounge dragging the furniture into the centre of the room in readiness for stripping the old wallpaper from the walls. Nikki knew that she ought to offer to help but her mind was on more pressing things. Claire had left over an hour ago, off on the hunt for some new wallpaper, and Nikki knew that she ought to take this chance to go and face Eddie.

The thought of it made her go weak at the knees, but the way she saw it, the longer she put it off the worse it would be; and besides, she had run out of spliffs days ago and was dying for one. She had just reached the end of the drive when she nearly collided with Erin, who was walking past.

'I . . . er . . . I was sorry to hear about your mum's shop,' Erin muttered.

'Thanks. I dare say we'll survive.'

'Have they caught who did it yet?'

Nikki shook her head and the two girls eyed each other awkwardly before falling into step and moving on. They hardly saw each other any more since Nikki had become close to Poppy, which was surprising seeing as it had been Erin who had introduced them to each other in the first place.

'Off out somewhere nice, are you?' Erin asked, and she had the satisfaction of seeing Nikki flush.

'Not really. I was just popping over to see Poppy. Why don't you come?'

'No, thanks. I get the feeling I'm not welcome any more.'

Nikki had the good grace to look embarrassed and they walked on in silence until they came to a bend in the road where Nikki told her, 'I'll be off then. See you.'

Erin nodded and went on her way with her chin touching her chest feeling very sorry for herself indeed.

Poppy's bedroom window was wide open, and as Nikki approached the house, she could hear her friend singing along to 'When You Say Nothing At All' with Ronan Keating. Poppy had a dreadful voice; her dad often told her that she was tone deaf, and some children who were playing in the street were giggling and pointing up at the window in glee.

Nikki tapped at the door and let herself in as she had been told to do. The first person she saw was Roxy, who was in the lounge trying to brush Katie's hair as the child struggled fretfully.

'Oh, hello, love. I don't know what's up wi' this little madam again, I'm sure. She's not been herself for days.'

Katie turned her head to see who her mother was addressing and before Roxy could stop her she launched herself across the room at Nikki and wrapped her arms around her waist.

'Oh Katie, whatever is the matter?' Nikki crooned as she stroked the child's hair. Indistinguishable sounds uttered from Katie's mouth as Roxy looked on in bewilderment.

'I just don't understand it,' she muttered in concern. 'Katie is usually so placid. She's not been sleeping right either, ever since she went out with her dad the other night. The silly bugger. He should know better than to go upsettin' her routine! She keeps waking up and crying, and when I go into her she won't let me near her. Something's upset her. If it keeps up, I'm having her off to the doctor's. Now come on, love, let's get you upstairs an' see if a little lie-down does the trick, eh?'

Roxy prised the little girl's arms from about Nikki's waist and led the child away as Nikki looked indecisively towards the kitchen. Eddie was probably in there, but did she have the nerve to go in and face him? As it turned out she didn't have to because he suddenly appeared in the kitchen doorway and beckoned her to come and join him.

She glanced at him nervously as he closed the door behind her.

'While we've got the chance to be on our own I thought I'd tell you you've had a reprieve. The boss don't want to see you this week after all now. Somethin's come up so he'll tell me when he's ready.'

Nikki felt almost sick with relief. Eddie was speaking so normally that it was hard to believe he could have been in any way responsible for her mum's shop being burned to the ground.

'Here.' He fumbled in his jacket and winked at her as he passed her a small wrap of white powder, which she hastily shoved down into the pocket of her jeans. 'Just remember – I look after me own. But I expect the same back in return. *Next* time when I tell you to come, you come . . . understand? An' keep yer bloody mouth tight shut if you know what's good fer you. The boss ain't one to cross, an' if you upset him he gets upset wi' me too.'

She nodded, relieved when she heard Poppy's footsteps on the stairs.

The next second, Poppy burst in only to skid to a halt as she looked from one to the other of them.

'Christ, what's up wi' you two?' she asked. 'You've got faces on yer like wet weekends. What's wrong wi' everyone?'

'Nowt,' Eddie informed her shortly, and elbowing past he moved back into the lounge with a last knowing glance at Nikki.

Suddenly she just wanted to be out of there. The house and everyone in it had lost its appeal. Thankfully, it looked like Poppy was ready to go out anyway, so Nikki asked politely, 'Off out somewhere nice, are you?'

'Well, I ain't so sure about that.' Shutting the door, Poppy leaned towards her and whispered, 'I've got a date.'

'So? Why so secretive about it? You've had loads of dates.'

'Yes, but not like this one. I'm meetin' the landlord from the Pig an' Whistle.'

'What for?' Nikki was all wide-eyed innocence and Poppy sighed.

'God, yer can be thick as mud at times, gel. I'm meetin' him to . . . *yer know*. He's gonna pay me.'

As realisation dawned on her, Nikki stared at Poppy in horror. 'But he's even older than your dad . . . and it's only the middle of the day!'

Poppy grinned. 'He might be old but he ain't tight-fisted. Let's face it – one bloke is much the same as another when they get their kit off. An' if they're prepared to pay for it then it's all to the good. I'm hopin' to get enough to treat meself to another tattoo. I want one on me shoulder this time.' She paused to stroke the rose on her arm before going on, 'The yobboes round here will use you forever an' a day, then when they get yer belly full they piss off an' leave yer to it. An' what does it matter what time it is? Sex ain't somethin' yer can only do after dark, yer know. His missus has gone out shoppin' fer the day so he wants to make hay while the sun shines, if yer get me meanin'.'

She winked as she added another layer of lipstick to her already shocking-pink lips. Ever since the night her dad had taken her to the bungalow she had had her tail up. 'Now come on, I'll walk wi' yer to the corner an' yer can tell me what's gone on about this fire. Bloody shame, that were. Yer mam had got some crackin' gear in that shop. What a waste, eh?'

Nikki glanced at Eddie as she walked through the hallway and he smiled back at her, making shivers run up her spine.

She was glad when they were outside and gulped in air. She wondered what Poppy would say if she were to tell her that it was her father's boss who had burned the shop down? Not that she ever could. Looking at her now from the corner of her eye she wondered how Poppy could appear so calm, knowing what she was about to do. Whenever Nikki thought of sex she immediately remembered the feel of her late father's hands crawling across her body and broke out in a cold sweat. It was a feeling that she had hoped would lessen with time, but if anything it was getting worse – and sometimes she wondered if she would ever be able to have a normal relationship with a boy. There were a few recently who she had felt attracted to, though she had done nothing about it.

Her thoughts were interrupted when they came to the corner and Poppy told her, 'Right then, I'm off. See yer soon.'

Nikki watched her walk away then despondently turned around and set off for home with the day stretching endlessly in front of her.

When Claire pulled onto the drive a couple of hours later she was pleased to see Molly and Tom's car parked there. They hadn't said that they were going to visit, but even so she would be glad to see them. She hauled the bags of wallpaper and the huge tin of paint she had bought into the house, dropped them onto the hall floor and walked into the kitchen. Robbie and Molly were deep in conversation but the second they saw her they sprang guiltily apart.

'Hello, what's going on here then?' Claire asked with a grin. 'Is it a private conversation or can anyone join in?'

'Oh, we were . . . er . . . just t-talking about the shop,' Robbie stammered.

'Yes, we were.' Molly's head wagged in hurried agreement. 'It was a terrible thing that happened, just terrible. I only hope they catch the lousy buggers who did it, and that they'll throw the book at them.'

'I think there'll be very little chance of that,' Claire said, as she filled the kettle at the sink. 'I'll just have to put it down to experience and get on with things.'

'But you'll restock and start again when the shop's been sorted out, won't you?' Molly enquired. 'Otherwise the ones who did it will have won.'

Claire shook her head. 'I doubt it. I don't know if I could face all that work again. I ran round like a lunatic for a whole week before it was due to open, stocking up the shelves and rails – and all for what?'

'Where's your old fighting spirit, girl?' Molly retorted. 'The Claire I know would have picked herself up and got on with it against all the odds.'

'Perhaps the Claire you know is fed up of trying to fight the world.' Claire's voice was tired. 'Sometimes it's just easier to concede defeat.'

'Over my dead body!' Robbie was indignant and colour had crept into his cheeks. 'I've got an idea I've been meaning to put to you, and I was going to wait until everything had settled down a bit. But seeing as Molly is here and the time feels right, I may as well put it to you now, love, and see what Molly thinks of it too.'

Claire cocked an inquisitive eyebrow, intrigued despite herself. 'So go on then.'

'Well, I think your original idea of starting a teenage boutique was sound but, to tell you the truth, I've been having a good look around the town and what I found was that almost all the dress shops here are chainstore branches. Now that's fine for everyday wear but there doesn't seem to be anywhere where women can buy special occasion outfits – you know, for weddings, balls et cetera. Now it's more than obvious that you have a flair for smart clothes after living in London. When you dress up, you look the bee's knees, so what I thought was, how about if you were to open a select ladies' shop – something very

309

upper class – and stock the sort of clothes that ladies around here would normally have to travel to London to buy. Classy expensive stuff – and I'm not just talking about the outfits. You could sell hats and shoes and bags to coordinate, even jewellery too. You could make it into a place where women could come in empty-handed and walk out again with their whole outfit complete, without having to visit a single other shop. I know the stuff wouldn't come cheap but I don't mind betting it'd sell once word of mouth spread. Eventually you could expand – get a shop in another town too . . . and then another. You could end up with a whole chain of them in time. And you could give it a classy name too – something like Fifth Avenue, perhaps?'

Claire frowned, but the more she thought on what he'd said the more excited she became about the idea. Again, it would be something that she and Nikki could do together, and after Nikki left school she might even be able to manage one of the shops. The possibilities were endless and could mean that Nikki would be set up for life if she showed an interest.

'Why, I think that's a wonderful idea,' Molly declared, deeply impressed at the thought Robbie had obviously put into it.

'It is,' Claire admitted a little more cautiously. 'But if I decided to go ahead with it, and I say *if* . . . it couldn't happen for months. I spoke to the people from the insurance company and they said it will take that long to get the shop habitable again.'

'I thought of that too,' Robbie told her smugly. 'So I've been havin' a bit of a ride round and I found another shop over in Coleshill. Like this one, it's in the High Street so it would be ideal for catching passing trade and it doesn't need that much doing to it.'

'You seem to have thought of everything, Dad.' He was relieved to see that there was an amused twinkle in her eye. 'The one thing you don't seem to have taken into consideration, though, is funds. Like an idiot I didn't have the stock at the shop insured, as you know, and for the type of clothes you're talking about it would mean another considerable outlay.'

'Oh, but that's where I may be able to help,' he informed her. 'As I was telling you earlier on, I just happen to have a little nest egg stashed away – and what better way to invest it than in a new business?'

'Oh no.' Claire's pride was to the front now. She had been fiercely independent for some time now and had no intentions of borrowing money, even from her own flesh and blood.

'Fine. We'll come up with some other way then,' he said.

Molly was beginning to see where Claire got her stubborn streak from now as she watched the two sparring.

'We'll sit down together when you have time and roughly work out how much you think the venture might cost, then we'll draw up a business plan if you find you haven't enough funds and we'll go to the bank.'

Claire tapped her lip thoughtfully and after a moment her face broke into a rare smile. She had had so little to smile about lately. 'I'll tell you what I'll do. I promise I'll give it some serious thought. Is that good enough?'

'For now.' He grinned and the conversation turned to other matters as Claire poured them all a cup of coffee.

Nikki came in shortly afterwards. Since Gemma had died, the fight seemed to have gone out of her; instead, she just looked miserable.

'Why don't you come back and stay with me for a couple of days?' Molly suggested as she looked at the girl's downcast face. 'We could go to Tracey's and see the twins tonight, if you liked?'

Nikki replied politely enough, 'Thanks, Molly, but I won't if it's all the same to you. I've got some revision I could be doing.'

'Lord, you have the whole o' the summer holidays ahead o' you to do that,' Molly pointed out, but Nikki merely shook her head and wandered away upstairs.

'How's she been?' Molly asked when they heard the slam of her bedroom door.

'Oh, you know – up and down. Gemma's dying has affected her really badly.'

'Then why don't you get her another dog, the next time you visit Seagull's Flight?'

'I'll willingly do that if there's one that takes her fancy,' Claire replied. 'But I have to say I seriously doubt there will be. Gemma helped Nikki through a very difficult period after her father died, and I think it will be some time before she feels she can replace her. I have an idea she might feel that she's being disloyal to Gemma if she had another one just yet.'

Molly nodded sadly, seeing the sense in what Claire said. Her eyes then moved to Robbie and she frowned. He wasn't looking too chipper today and she determined to try and snatch another quiet word with him before she left.

Chapter Twenty-Nine

'But it's only been two weeks, boss! Don't yer think it's a bit too soon?' Eddie was standing at the bottom of the overgrown garden with his mobile phone pressed tight to his ear. When it had rung and he saw the boss's number flash up, he had exited the kitchen like a greyhound. Roxy had ears like an elephant when it came to overhearing things that didn't concern her.

'There's been nothing in the papers about the body being found, has there? So I reckon we're home an' dry,' Jackie's voice came back. 'Even if they do find it, there's nothin' to trace her back to us – not if you did your job right. I'm tellin' you, Eddie, I'm *rakin'* it in since the film got abroad. The punters can't get enough of it. I've told the blokes to be here on Wednesday, so you just make sure you supply us with that little Nightingale bird.'

The phone went dead and Eddie stared at it in consternation. He had barely slept for two weeks now, and when he did his dreams were filled with the vision of the girl sinking down into the Blue Lagoon as if some great hand were pulling her beneath the water.

Still, the boss seemed pretty clear on what he wanted, and as he'd been keeping Nikki happy with drugs, Eddie didn't see how she could object. Especially after what had happened to her mam's shop.

He considered ringing her but then decided to wait. She usually called round to see Poppy most days so he'd have a word with her then, when he caught her on his own.

His chance came the following evening. The boys were both out and up to no good. Poppy had nipped upstairs to get changed and Roxy had taken Katie up to tuck her in, leaving him and Nikki alone in the kitchen.

Seizing the opportunity, he closed the kitchen door and whispered, 'Tomorrow night, seven o'clock. Be at the corner – an' I don't need to tell yer not to let him down this time, do I?'

'N . . . no,' she stuttered, taken completely off-guard. She had lulled herself into a false sense of security over the last couple of weeks, but now she felt as if she was being backed into a corner again.

'Good girl!' There was a smug expression on Eddie's face and Nikki hastily looked away from him. But then she supposed that she was worrying about nothing. After all, Eddie's friend only wanted to take some photos of her – and how hard could that be? And Eddie was her friend, he would never let anyone hurt her.

At that moment, Roxy walked back into the room with a wide grin on her face.

'Ah, Nikki, I almost forgot. I treated you while I were up the market the other day. Remember that top I got our Poppy that you liked? Well, I got you one too. Here, try it on, but don't worry if I've bought the wrong size. The chap on the stall promised he'd change it if it weren't right.'

Eddie scowled as he stamped out of the room, slamming the door behind him. He couldn't understand why Roxy had taken such a shine to Nikki but she obviously had, and big time.

Meantime, Nikki blushed prettily as she took a bright T-shirt from the cheap plastic bag that Roxy had passed her.

'Oh, thank you, it's lovely,' she declared.

Roxy smiled with pleasure. 'Well, try it on then.'

Nikki hated undressing in front of anyone, even Claire, so she self-consciously turned her back and slid her arms out of the top she was wearing.

As Roxy glanced at the girl's bare back as she pulled the new T-shirt over her head, the colour suddenly drained from her face. There was a little triangle of moles on her right shoulder blade. Nikki was wreathed in smiles as she turned back to her with the new top in place, but the smile vanished as soon as she saw Roxy's expression.

'Roxy, what's the matter?' The woman was trembling.

'Oh . . . nothin'. I . . . er . . . I just went a bit dizzy, that's all,' the woman stammered.

Nikki frowned with concern. 'Why don't you go up and have a bit of a rest, then. You do look a bit tired.'

'I reckon I might just do that.' Roxy stumbled away from the table as Nikki watched her in bewilderment.

'Thanks for the top,' she shouted as Roxy headed for the stairs, then she shook her head. God, it was hard to understand grown-ups sometimes. Roxy had been bright as a button one minute, then looking like death warmed up the next. And yet they reckoned it was teenagers who were the trouble . . .

Meanwhile, Roxy was battling the tears that were stinging at the back of her eyelids. It had suddenly hit her like a punch between the eyes why she had so taken to Nikki. And these three moles, the little triangle, albeit on the wrong side of her body, were uncannily like the birthmark on her own lost baby. The lost daughter whom she tried hard not to think about. The child she would probably never set eyes on again, though she thought of her every single day.

When Nikki came down the following morning she found Robbie and Bradley moving all the furniture back into place in the lounge.

Bradley grinned when he saw the surprised look on her face. 'I've got a few days off work,' he explained, 'so I thought I'd come round and give your grandad a hand before whipping him off for a game of golf. He's done a lovely job, hasn't he?'

Nikki looked around the room. The colour of the paper Claire had chosen was almost identical to what had been on before, so Nikki could see very little point in having it done in the first place.

'It's all right, I suppose,' she muttered gracelessly. She still struggled when anyone referred to Robbie as her grandad.

Bradley chuckled. 'Right, why don't you go into the kitchen to your mum? I think you'll find she has a nice surprise for you.'

Nikki looked curious and turning about, she did as she was told for once. Claire was standing at the sink rinsing some pots when she entered, and she smiled at her.

'Ah, there you are. I was just going to give you a shout. I've noticed that you've been a bit bored the last couple of days and moping about the place, so I rang Mrs M this morning and told her to expect us.'

If she had been hoping for Nikki to be happy with her idea she was sadly disappointed, for the girl looked thunderstruck.

'*What?* When?'

'Well, I thought we could get off as soon as you'd had some breakfast and packed a few clothes.'

'You mean TODAY?'

'Yes, I mean today. Why, did you have something else planned?'

Nikki struggled to think of something but her mind had gone a blank. If she didn't show up at Eddie's this evening, there was no telling what he might do.

'Not really, but why can't we go tomorrow?' she asked lamely.

'Why should we put it off until tomorrow if you haven't got anything special planned?' Claire asked, trying hard to be reasonable.

'Because I don't *want* to go today,' Nikki said petulantly. 'In fact, I'm not that keen on going at all. It's boring there. Why can't you go on your own? I could stay here with Robbie.'

'Oh no, you could not!' Claire was getting annoyed now. It seemed that everything she tried to do for Nikki backfired on her lately.

'Well, I'm not going and that's an end to it,' Nikki declared flatly.

Claire felt her temper rising. She had been so looking forward to seeing Christian and it appeared that Nikki was just being awkward for no good reason.

'Oh yes, you *are*, young lady. It's about time you remembered who the adult and who the child is in this house. I'm getting a little bit sick of you trying to rule the roost lately!'

'So put me into care then!'

The discussion had turned into a full-scale row now, but both of them were beyond caring at this point.

'For two pins I would,' Claire shot back.

'So do it then, and see if I care,' Nikki screamed. 'It would be better than having to put up with your nagging all the time!'

As Nikki made to step past her Claire's hand shot out and smacked her firmly around the face. For a long moment in time a stunned silence settled between them but then Claire's face crumpled and she put her hand out towards her.

'Oh Nikki, I'm so sorry. I didn't mean to do that and you know I would never put you into care. You're my whole life.'

Nikki was still on her high horse and she stared back at her mother with contempt as she stroked her stinging cheek.

Claire's shoulders sagged. Never once had she raised a hand to her daughter before and she could hardly believe she had hit her, but this time she was determined not to back down. 'I *am* sorry,' she repeated quietly, 'but I do still feel that a break would do us both good after what's happened at the shop and losing Gemma. And so I'd be grateful if you could be ready to leave in an hour.'

Nikki was red in the face as she stared back at Claire incredulously. She had grown accustomed to getting her own way and was feeling desperate. What would happen if she didn't turn up for Eddie's boss this time? It hardly bore thinking about.

'What you really mean is, it would do *you* good to see Christian,' she snapped spitefully. 'Why don't you admit it? You blame me for keeping you two apart, don't you?'

Claire wearily ran a hand through her hair. 'I'm afraid this isn't up for discussion, Nikki. I know you're trying to goad me into another row, but I'm not going to bite – so just go and get ready, can't you?'

Nikki stormed from the room, almost colliding with Bradley who was walking through the hallway.

'Can I take it your surprise idea of a break didn't go down too well then?' he asked as he joined Claire in the kitchen.

'That's a bit of an understatement,' Claire admitted. 'But for once I didn't give in to her and I've told her to go and get ready. I'm sure that when we get there, she'll calm down. She might even enjoy it, if she allows herself to.'

Bradley blinked. Teenagers were a complete mystery to him and he was glad that it was Claire having to deal with Nikki and not him.

'Anyway, if you'll excuse me I'm going to pop up and get ready myself now,' she told him, and quietly left the room. In truth, wanting to see Christian wasn't the only reason Claire was eager to get away for a time. Over the last few days she'd had the strangest feeling that someone was following her, and the silent phone calls had increased to the point that she was almost afraid to answer the phone. But then, she told herself, I have been under a lot of pressure one way and another, so it's probably just me imagining things.

An hour later the car was loaded and ready to go. It would be the first time Claire had visited Seagull's Flight since Gemma's death and the back seat looked ridiculously empty without her basket and her favourite toys, which Nikki had always insisted on taking with them.

'All ready for the off then, are you?' Robbie had come to join her

318

on the drive, looking fresh and smart after a quick shower and a change of clothes.

She glanced towards Nikki's bedroom window. 'Ready as I'll ever be. I'd better go and see if Nikki's ready now and in a slightly better mood.'

'I wouldn't count on that,' he muttered as Claire strode back into the house. He and Bradley were all ready to go off and enjoy a game of golf but he would wait and see Claire off first. She was back within minutes with a face as black as thunder.

'She's not in her room,' she told him, unable to keep the anger from her voice. 'She hasn't come past you, has she?'

'No, she hasn't,' Robbie told her truthfully. 'She must have sneaked out the back way earlier when we were getting ready. What are you going to do now? You could always leave her here with me. I'd look after her, and you look like a break would do you the world of good.'

'Thanks, Dad, I appreciate the offer but I can't do that.' Claire looked so disappointed he could have cried for her. 'You get off and have your game of golf and I'll wait here for her to come back. If she's not too late we might still make it today.'

'If you're quite sure, lass,' he said uncertainly, feeling totally useless.

Robbie and Bradley had been gone an hour when temper finally got the better of Claire and she snatched up her car keys. She had no doubt at all where Nikki would be. She would have gone to see that Poppy again on the Chelmsey Park Estate. Up until now she had refrained from going there and dragging her home because she didn't want to embarrass the girl, but enough was enough. It was time she taught Nikki a lesson that she wouldn't forget – and if her daughter hated her for it, then so be it.

The car looked strangely out of place when she parked it next to Eddie's outside the Millers' house. Climbing out, Claire looked up and down the street. Children were playing football in the middle of the road with no thought to their safety and the whole area looked unkempt and neglected. Even the council estate she had been brought up in looked posh compared to this. Squaring her shoulders, she strode down the weed-strewn path and rapped sharply at the door.

Roxy opened it and when she recognised Claire, her mouth dropped open.

'Is Nikki here?' Claire asked, completely forgetting her manners.

'No, love. As far as I know, we ain't seen her yet today. But hold on an' I'll just go an' see if our Poppy knows where she is.' Roxy moved away from the door, feeling very frumpy in comparison to Claire who was dressed in a smart two-piece suit and high heels. She came back minutes later to tell her, 'Sorry, love. Poppy has no idea where she might be – she ain't seen her.'

When Claire raised an eyebrow, Roxy became indignant. 'I'm tellin' you the truth. Why would I lie?'

'Well, if she should show up, can you tell her I'm waiting at home for her? We were supposed to be going away for a few days this morning but she's chosen to do a disappearing act.'

''Course I will.'

Unsmilingly, Claire turned about and hurried back to the car as Roxy watched her go. No wonder Nikki's so well spoken, livin' wi' *her*, Roxy thought to herself, and closing the door she returned to Katie, who was once again demanding her attention.

Nikki showed up at Poppy's two hours later after a long wait in the churchyard. She had had an idea that Claire might come looking for her, so had decided to keep a low profile for a while. The moment that Roxy told her that her mum had been there, she flushed guiltily.

'Why don't yer get yourself back home an' go off an' enjoy yourself?' Roxy said persuasively.

'Enjoy myself? Huh! Would *you* enjoy being stuck in the back of beyond with a vet, an old lady and pack of stray dogs for company?'

'As a matter o' fact I think I would, if the back o' beyond happened to be at the seaside.' Roxy sighed. 'I can't remember the last time I had a holiday, an' come to think of it, I don't think our

Katie has ever even seen the sea. Yer don't know how lucky you are.'

'Lucky!' Nikki repeated scornfully. 'Oh yes, I'm *really* lucky, I am. My first mum gave me away, my second mum died tryin' to protect me from my dad who was abusing me, and my third mum thinks she can rule me. She hit me today – what do you think of that? I don't even know who I really am or where I came from. Yes, that's what you'd call lucky, isn't it?'

'Oh, Nikki.' Roxy's heart went out to her and it was all she could do to stop herself from pulling the girl into her arms there and then. She looked so sad and vulnerable, as if she was carrying the weight of the world on her shoulders.

'I'm not ever going back there,' Nikki stated. 'And I was wondering if perhaps you'd let me stay here for a while?'

Roxy swallowed hard and steeling herself she replied, 'I don't think I dare let yer do that, love. You know Eddie ain't no innocent an' I can't risk havin' the coppers sniffin' round the place – which I undoubtedly would if I let yer stay. Your mum would have 'em down on us like a ton o' bricks. For what my opinion's worth, I get the feeling that your mum loves yer very much. She wouldn't worry and fret about you as she does if she didn't, would she? She probably slapped yer out o' frustration. Now why don't yer just get yourself off home and go and forget about everything for a few days?'

Suddenly, Nikki would have loved to do just that. But she couldn't, not with Eddie's threats ringing in her ears. Look at what had happened the last time she had let him down. As she gazed into Roxy's tired eyes she longed to pour out all her worries. She wanted to feel normal, but how could she ever be normal after what her father had done to her? She was dirty, tainted and sure that no decent boy would ever want to touch her with a bargepole once they knew what had happened to her.

'Let's not talk about it any more. I'm not going back and that's an end to it,' she muttered stubbornly. Roxy sighed and went to make Katie a drink.

When Robbie and Bradley arrived home after their game of golf they were surprised to see Claire's car still parked on the drive, and more surprised still when they entered the house to find her in a towering rage storming up and down the lounge in a haze of cigarette smoke.

'Nikki's done a disappearing act again,' she seethed. 'I've just about had enough now. In fact, I've just phoned the social worker and asked her to come and speak to her. Perhaps she'll be able to talk some sense into her and get to the bottom of what's troubling her.' Deep down she knew what was troubling her, but felt powerless to help. It might be that someone from outside might have more success at getting through to her daughter.

'But I thought you wanted to keep social services out of it.' Robbie placed his golf clubs down in the hall and scratched his head in bewilderment.

'I did,' Claire admitted. 'But I've got to do *something*, haven't I? She's going completely off the rails and I don't know how to stop it.'

'She'll probably be round at that Poppy's,' Robbie remarked.

'She isn't. I've already tried there.'

Seeing her frustration, Robbie took her elbow and steered her into the kitchen.

'Look, getting yourself all worked up isn't going to do any good, is it?' he pointed out sensibly. 'Have you let Christian and Mrs M know that you're going to be late? They'll be worrying about you.'

'I rang them about ten minutes ago and told them I wasn't going to be able to make it,' she said miserably.

'Well, let's have a nice cup of tea and see if we can't think of something,' he suggested.

Claire sighed. Like Molly, Robbie seemed to think that a cup of tea was the answer to everything. If only it could be that simple.

* * *

322

Nikki left Poppy's mid-afternoon and spent the next few hours killing time once again in the deserted little churchyard, but at seven o'clock sharp she was waiting on the corner of Grove Road for Eddie.

Her stomach was churning, but when he pulled up beside her in his car she climbed in without a word.

He smiled at her approvingly. 'Good girl . . . and don't look so scared. He's not going to hurt you. He's only going to take a few photos.'

She stared out of the window, suddenly wishing with all her heart that she was back at home with her mum, but after all the silly things she had done over the last few months she had no choice but to go through with this now. If Claire ever found out that she had been taking drugs, there would be hell to pay. But after tonight she was determined that things would be different. She would stop going round to Poppy's and would avoid Eddie like the plague. Perhaps then she and her mum would get close again as they had used to be.

The journey to the bungalow was made in silence, and when it came into sight at the end of the long sweeping drive, Nikki's eyes almost popped out of her head. It was beautiful, almost like a mini-mansion, and made the house she lived in with Claire look positively small. She sat tight in her seat as Eddie climbed out of the car and went to speak to a man who had appeared in the doorway. The man was smiling at Eddie and kept looking towards the car and nodding. He was old, or he appeared so to Nikki. He was balding and his stomach hung over his trousers but he looked friendly enough as he walked towards the car.

'Nikki, how lovely to meet you at last,' he said, as he opened her car door for her. 'I'm so glad you agreed to come. Has anyone ever told you that you could be a model?'

'A model?' Nikki looked back at him incredulously. No one had ever said that to her before and she felt herself blush with pleasure. Everyone else but Eddie treated her like a kid, but this man was also talking to her as if she was a grown-up.

'Oh yes,' he assured her with a friendly grin. 'You're very beautiful and I just know you're going to be very photogenic. With me behind you, you could end up on a catwalk. Your face could become known all over the world.'

Nikki climbed out of the car, feeling as if she was stepping into a dream. Perhaps this wasn't going to be as bad as she had thought. Suddenly she was glad she had come.

'Will you be wantin' me to pick her up?' Eddie asked, and Nikki noticed that he looked nervy and ill at ease.

'No thanks, Eddie,' the man said. 'I shall personally take Nikki home after we've finished. Now, shall we go and make a start?'

Nikki nodded, no longer even minding the fact that Eddie was going to leave her there.

'I'm Jackie, by the way,' the man introduced himself as he held out his hand. She shook it shyly, aware of Eddie's car starting up and moving slowly past her. She didn't even look at him but followed Jackie into the bungalow like a lamb being led to the slaughter.

Eddie had gone some way up the drive when he glanced in his mirror just in time to see Jackie leading Nikki into the bungalow. A cold shiver ran up his spine. Over the years he had lost count of the number of youngsters he had delivered to this bungalow to be left to the mercy of the perverts who frequented it. If he were to be honest with himself, he would have had to hold his hands up and admit that he had done it without a second thought. Jackie paid him well to keep his mouth shut and the way Eddie saw it, once he'd taken them there, what he didn't see couldn't hurt him. But tonight something didn't feel quite right, although he couldn't put his finger on what it was. Perhaps it was the fact that Jackie had been so insistent on him taking Nikki there? He had never cared who Eddie delivered before – boy or girl either sex – it didn't matter so long as they were young and willing. But this time he had gone out of his way to make sure that it was Nikki.

His thoughts moved to Roxy and he shuddered. God help him if she discovered that he had brought Nikki here. And if she ever found out that he'd been here with Poppy – with young Katie in tow – she'd do for him. For some reason she seemed to have taken to Nikki big time, to the point that she had even changed some of her slovenly ways. Roxy had never professed to be Housewife of the Year, yet since Nikki had come on the scene she had suddenly started to make a concerted effort to keep the house a little tidier. Why, only yesterday she had suggested out of the blue that it was time the whole house was redecorated. Huh! As a picture of the nicotine-stained walls flashed in front of his eyes, he grunted aloud. If she thought *he* was going to tackle it then she had another think coming.

Eddie glanced in the mirror again. Nikki and Jackie had disappeared into the bungalow, and then he turned a bend in the drive and it was no longer in sight. He shrugged. Out of sight and out of mind. Nikki was well and truly on her own now.

Chapter Thirty

'Do you think we ought to call the police, love?' Robbie was looking anxiously at the clock. 'It's nearly eight o'clock now and we haven't seen hide nor hair of her all day.'

'No!' Claire took a deep drag of her cigarette as she continued to pace up and down the kitchen. Bradley had left almost an hour ago at her insistence, and she almost wished that Robbie would leave her to her own devices too. She was certainly no company at the minute.

'If we involve the police as well as the social services, how is it going to look?' she snapped. 'They'll think she's beyond parental control and they might—'

'Take her into care? Is that what you were going to say?'

Claire stopped pacing and nodded miserably before saying forlornly, 'Oh Dad, what am I going to do?'

He stood up and put his arms about her heaving shoulders. 'I don't know, lass,' he admitted quietly, and there they stood, each trying to draw comfort from the other.

Nikki's eyes were on stalks as Jackie led her into one of the most beautiful lounges she had ever seen. It was absolutely enormous, with huge floor-to-ceiling windows all along one wall that gave magnificent views over open countryside. Huge settees were dotted here and there, and an enormous flat screen television took up nearly all of one wall. On another wall hung the largest mirror she had ever seen, and her feet were sinking into a thick pastel carpet.

'This way.' Jackie led her to a door set into the wall next to the mirror. She glanced uncertainly at a number of men who were sitting about the room, but seeing her concern, Jackie told her, 'Don't worry about them. They're just some photographer friends of mine who've popped over for a drink. But it will be me doing the photographing tonight, never fear.'

She followed him into yet another enormous room containing a large bed set against one wall and a number of cameras on tripods. Behind the door was a large mirror, almost identical to the one she had seen in the lounge, and in a far corner was a large roll-top bathtub with ornate gold taps.

'It's an American idea,' Jackie informed her, seeing her glance at it curiously. 'They often have their bathtubs in their bedrooms over there.'

Nikki wasn't sure if she liked this open-plan idea. She had always considered that bathing was a private affair, something to be done behind closed doors where no one could see you, but afraid of upsetting him, she kept her opinion to herself.

'Now then, how about we have a little drink before we start, just to relax you, eh?'

From a mahogany cabinet set close to the bed, he took out two crystal glasses and a bottle of vodka. 'You *are* sixteen, aren't you?' he asked with twinkle in his eye.

Nikki gulped then nodded, and he smiled with satisfaction as he poured two generous measures. 'Good. Here you are then. Bottoms up!' Jackie then took a couple of roll-ups from his pocket and after lighting one, he handed it to her.

'Thanks.' She took the spliff eagerly, feeling very grown up.

After a time he told her, 'Right, let me tell you what I want you to do. I want you to have a bath and put on the clothes that are laid out on the bed for me.'

327

For the first time she noticed the outfit that he was referring to. It looked suspiciously like a school uniform, and a very short one at that. He saw the fear in her eyes and laughed. 'It's all right, you needn't look so worried,' he said kindly. 'I'm going to leave you in peace. You didn't think I was going to stay in here with you, did you?'

He saw the relief on her face as he walked towards the door, where he paused to tell her, 'You can lock it from this side if you like and give me a shout when you're ready. I can see you're not too keen on the outfit, but trust me, I know what the magazines want – and if I can sell any of your pictures to them you'll be made. You're on your way to being a top model, believe me. Take as long as you like. Oh, and do help yourself to another drink if you want one. When you're done I'll come in, we'll take a few snaps and then I'll drive you home. How does that sound?'

Nikki stared at him starry-eyed. This was every girl's dream come true; a man who treated her like an adult and offered her the stars. When he left the room, she moved quickly to lock the door behind him. Turning to gaze at the room again she then crossed to the bath, turned the taps on and slowly began to peel her clothes off.

In the next room, Jackie's friends were clambering to watch her through the two-way mirror. From the bedroom, the mirror on her side appeared to be just that, but in the lounge, one flick of a switch made the mirror in there into a window through which the men could watch Nikki's every move unobserved.

'Set the video rolling,' Jackie commanded as he watched Nikki's jeans sliding down her legs.

It was half past ten when Jackie's luxurious Mercedes cruised into Lovelace Lane.

'So, how did you enjoy your first photographic session then?' he asked pleasantly as he pulled the car into the kerb some distance from Nikki's home.

'Oh, it was *wonderful*,' she gushed, her eyes shining in the light from the street lamps. There was fifty pounds tucked into her pocket, she was slightly tiddly and on top of that Jackie had given her enough drugs to last for a week and it wasn't just spliffs but coke, too. He had been true to his word, not entering the bedroom again until she was ready, and then he had taken some photos and left the room, telling her to put her own clothes back on without so much as laying a finger on her.

'Would you consider coming again then?' he asked, and she nodded eagerly.

'Oh yes, whenever you like. But do you *really* think you might be able to sell the photos?'

'I've no doubt about it,' he told her convincingly. She was so gullible that this was turning out to be even easier than he had anticipated. 'The only thing is,' he looked at her regretfully, 'you and I both know that we've done nothing wrong, but mums . . . Well, you know what they're like. It might be better if you weren't to tell yours anything about this. It could be our little secret. When I've actually sold some photos of course, then we could consider telling her, but until that happens . . .'

'Oh, I won't breathe a word, I promise,' Nikki sighed happily.

He smiled with satisfaction. 'Good, then how about I get Eddie to bring you over again on Saturday night?'

Swallowing her disappointment, Nikki nodded. She had been hoping that Jackie would say he would pick her up himself. His car was so much nicer than Eddie's. But at least he wanted her to come again, and soon she might be a famous model with her name in all the magazines. As she wondered what Poppy would think about that, a little glow started in the pit of her stomach.

'I'd love to,' she told him shyly.

'Excellent. It's a date then. Goodnight, Nikki.'

Hugging herself with excitement she watched him drive away, then pulling herself up to her full height she slightly unsteadily headed for home. It was time to face the music.

Roxy was still up when Eddie got home in the early hours of the morning, and judging by the look on her face he guessed that she was ready to do battle.

'Been proppin' the bar up again, have yer?' she demanded, the second he set foot through the door.

'Wharr if I have?' His voice was slurred and her lip curled in contempt.

'Yer can drink yerself into an early grave fer all I care, Eddie Miller,' she flung at him, 'but what were Nikki doin', gettin' into your car earlier on? An' don't bother to deny it 'cos she were seen fair an' square.'

Eddie looked guilty. He hadn't expected this. 'She just asked me fer a lift to a mate's house,' he floundered.

'Oh yes, an' just where did this *mate* live then?'

'How the fuckin' hell am I supposed to know, woman? I ain't her bleedin' keeper, am I? I dropped her off near Touchwood an' where she went from there I couldn't say.'

His wife's anger started to build as she stared at him suspiciously. That was the trouble with Roxy, she never knew when to back off.

'Look, if you've quite finished yer interrogation I'm ready fer me bed,' he told her. 'I'll be havin' to ask yer permission to use the bathroom next.'

'If I find that you're lyin' to me—'

His fist suddenly shot out and connected firmly with her chin, and the next minute all hell broke loose as she swung back at him.

'Why, you lowdown bastard . . .'

Roxy fought back valiantly, but even though Eddie's ribs were still sore she was no match for him. Within seconds he had slammed her to the floor where she lay in a whimpering heap with blood pouring from her nose, which he had just broken for the third time.

Looking down at her, he asked, 'Why the fuck do yer make me do it, Roxy? Why can't yer just keep that great gob o' yourn shut an' keep yer nose out o' what don't concern you.'

"Cos,' she gasped, "cos . . . Nikki is an innocent. She's the same age as the daughter we lost, an' I don't want no harm to come to her.'

The look on Eddie's face was a picture as the room swam around him, and now he helped her to her feet, pressing her into a chair as he mumbled, 'What did you 'ave to go an' bring that up for? It's all in the past now.'

'So it is,' she shot back. 'But it don't stop me missin' her, wonderin' how's she's doin'. When they first took Rebecca off us an' put her into care, I thought we'd get her back. But we didn't, did we? She were just a baby when they took her, an' eventually some posh family adopted her from up North, an' all 'cos they didn't think we were fit parents, or have yer forgotten?'

'O' course I haven't forgotten,' he shouted. 'But what's that to do wi' Nikki?'

Roxy was crying now. 'I don't know. There's just somethin' about the girl that reminds me of our baby. I can only pray that wherever Rebecca is, her new mum an' dad are keepin' her safe, an' I want Nikki to be safe too.' Roxy's eyes were already beginning to swell and a dark shadow was spreading across her cheek as the bruises started to appear as if by magic. 'I bought her a little top up the market today, an' when I got her to try it on, it hit me – she's the same age, everythin'. I think that's why I've so taken to her. Somewhere out there is a girl who's our flesh an' blood. Don't you hope that she's all right too, if you ever think of her?'

The floor spun up to meet him as Eddie sank into a chair, and bile rose in his throat. Suddenly the painful memories that he had tried to lock away were flooding back. What had he done? He had delivered yet another innocent into Jackie's evil clutches, and should Roxy ever find out, he would be dead meat.

As he wiped the sweat from his forehead he muttered, 'I'm sure Nikki will turn out all right, love. An' yes, I do hope that wherever our Rebecca is, she's all right too.' He saw the despair in Roxy's eyes and a silence settled between them.

Claire lay staring up at the ceiling as tears trickled down her cheeks. The house was silent. Nikki had stormed off to bed some time ago after yet another raging row. Robbie had discreetly left them to it the second Nikki had come through the door, but Claire wondered what he must think of her. She was turning into a poor apology for a mother and yet when she had first adopted Nikki, the future had looked bright. She had been so sure that she could help Nikki come to terms with what had happened to her. After all, hadn't she been through the same thing herself at the hands of her mother's boyfriends? But it seemed that Nikki was slipping away from her, possibly for ever.

Nikki had told her in no uncertain terms that the social worker could '*go and get stuffed*' when Claire revealed that she had rung her; she had no doubt at all that Nikki would refuse to see her – so what was she to do?

Her thoughts moved on to Christian and the tears flowed even faster. When she had rung him earlier in the day to explain that she wouldn't be able to make it, she had expected him to sound upset and disappointed. Instead, he had told her very politely that he was sorry to hear it and that he hoped she would be able to make it another time. She had felt as if she was talking to a polite stranger instead of the man she loved, and it had almost broken her heart.

And then there was Bradley. She had sent him packing, thinking that he would go home to the pile of paperwork she knew he had waiting for him, but instead he had spent the whole evening cruising the streets looking for Nikki. Her heart ached for him. He obviously had deep feelings for her, but she knew that she would never be able to return them – not while she was still so in love with Christian.

Everything was such a mess, the only bright spot on the horizon being Robbie's idea about the new shop. She had given it some serious thought and he had been delighted when she had agreed to go and look at the shop in Coleshill with him. As she thought of her father, sleeping in his room along the landing, she felt a little better. She had resented him turning up out of the blue after all their years apart, but now she was beginning to realise that it was the best thing that had happened to her for some long time.

Turning on her side she looked at the moon through the window and offered up a silent prayer: *Please let things get better soon.* She then snuggled down beneath the duvet and as the first cold fingers of dawn licked at the sky, she finally slipped into an exhausted sleep.

It was Nikki's third visit to the bungalow, and on the journey there, she felt not a trace of nerves. She had come to know what Jackie expected of her and had no fear of him. But for some reason tonight, from the second she walked through the door, things felt different. He always had some male friends visiting, but tonight she found one of them in the room she considered to be hers.

'Ah, Nikki. How are you?' he greeted her.

She eyed him suspiciously as Jackie came to stand at her side. 'This is Don,' he told her. 'He's a good friend of mine and the thing is, well . . . I'm not quite sure how to tell you this. Don is the editor of a magazine. I've shown him your photos and he says that if you were prepared to be *nice* to him, he might think about publishing some of them.'

Nikki shuffled uncomfortably from foot to foot. Don was of a similar age to Jackie – old, like her grandad – and there were suddenly butterflies in her stomach.

'Wh . . . what do you mean by "nice"?' she asked in a small voice.

Jackie poured them all a drink in the long-stemmed cut-glass goblets that Nikki loved so much. She always felt very grown up, drinking from them. Unseen by her he slipped a small tablet into the one he handed to her and it dissolved almost instantly.

'Let's have a drink while we talk about it,' he soothed. 'And don't look so worried. You trust me, don't you?'

Nikki nodded as she sipped at her drink and within seconds she started to feel more relaxed.

'That's better,' Jackie said encouragingly. 'Now why don't you have a lie on the bed and I'll give you a nice massage to relax you, eh?'

It suddenly seemed like a very good idea and she slid onto the bed as Jackie took a seat at the side of her. She felt all warm and happy and smiled at him as he bent over her.

'That's a good girl. Now . . . let's get these clothes off you. I can't give you a massage with all these on, can I?'

Nikki felt uneasy again but powerless to stop him as he slowly undressed her with Don's help. And then for the next hour she was subjected to acts so horrendous that she thought she would die – and once again she was back in her bedroom at Bispham and it was her father's hands she could feel moving all over her before he entered her – and she thought she would die of shame.

Don and Jackie were getting dressed with huge grins on their faces.

'Now tell the truth – that wasn't so bad was it?' Jackie asked her as he zipped up his flies.

'Do you reckon we got it all?' The man called Don was moving towards a camera that was trained on the bed and to Nikki's horror he now turned it towards the wall, which acted as a screen as the last hour played out in front of her. It was like a nightmare and she wished that she could die right there and then. Jackie and his friend however seemed thoroughly pleased with themselves.

'We'll get a fortune for this from our friends abroad,' Don muttered approvingly.

Jackie nodded in agreement. 'Didn't I tell you I would make you into a star, Nikki?' he chortled as he turned to look back at her.

'I . . . I'll *tell*,' she gabbled desperately, but Jackie shook his head.

'Oh, I don't somehow think you will.' His voice was menacing now and nothing like the voice of the man she had come to trust. 'Just think what your mum would say if she were to see this. I mean, it hardly looked like you were putting up a fight, did it? In fact, from where I was standing it looked to me like you were enjoying it. Wouldn't you say so, Don?'

'Absolutely.' As Don ran his tongue round his thick lips, Nikki felt sick. They had her over a barrel, and she knew it. From now on she would have to do whatever they said, otherwise her mum might find out what she had done and disown her.

'Get yourself dressed,' Jackie told her abruptly, all pretence of friend-ship gone. 'And make sure that you're back here for six o'clock tomorrow. I have another friend who wants to spend some time with you. And here . . .' He tossed a bag of white powder onto the bed. 'Now hurry up and put your clothes on. Don will give you a lift home.'

As the men strode from the room, Nikki curled up into a ball and sobbed with humiliation as she realised how foolish she had been. She couldn't go home and face her mum now, she just couldn't – but there was someone who she felt would help her . . . Swiping the tears from her cheeks with the back of her hand, she gathered her clothes together.

The dark street was deserted as Nikki staggered up the path leading to Poppy's front door. Unable to face Claire, she had decided to seek refuge with Poppy, but now she was concerned to see that the house was in darkness. It looked like they were all in bed and she was afraid of waking them.

Knowing that she had no other choice, she tapped tentatively on the door and after a moment the upstairs window creaked open and Roxy peered out. 'Who is it?'

'It's me . . . Nikki. May I come in?'

The window closed and seconds later, the hall light clicked on.

'Why, lovie. Whatever's the matter?' Roxy gasped as she opened the door and looked at Nikki's pale face.

'I was wondering if you'd let me stay the night?' the girl mumbled in a small voice. 'I . . . I didn't mean to wake you. I'm sorry.'

Roxy took her arm and hauled her over the step. 'What's happened?' she demanded, but Nikki merely bowed her head.

'Please don't ask me to tell you, Roxy,' she implored. 'Just say if you don't want me to stay and I'll go.'

'You'll do no such thing!' Roxy whispered indignantly. 'Do you really think I'd let a young girl like you go wanderin' the streets at this time o' night? Come on, get yourself up them stairs. You can go an' get in wi' Poppy, an' perhaps in the mornin' you'll feel ready to tell me what's happened.' After ushering Nikki up the stairs ahead of her she paused outside Poppy's bedroom door and kissed the girl gently on the cheek, as Nikki eyed her swollen face.

'Go on, go an' get some shut-eye,' Roxy murmured tenderly. 'Happen everythin' will look different after a good night's kip.'

Nikki smiled sadly. She doubted that anything would ever look right again but she kept her thoughts to herself as she slipped silently into Poppy's bedroom. She had somehow known that Roxy wouldn't turn her back on her and she had been right.

Chapter Thirty-One

Claire's eyes blinked open and she glanced blearily at the alarm clock. It was only 6 a.m. but she could have sworn she had heard something. She hadn't really slept properly all night, but lain on top of the bed fully clothed hoping that Nikki would come home.

Going to the window, she peered down onto the drive and swallowed her disappointment. She had hoped that it would be Nikki, but instead she saw a woman tapping softly at the door. Who on earth could it be, at this time of the morning?

When she opened the door she recognised Poppy's mother and immediately beckoned her inside. Roxy Miller looked as if she had been in a boxing ring. Her nose was swollen out of all proportion and her eyes were black and blue with bruises.

'Do you know where Nikki is?' Claire said immediately.

'She's at my house,' Roxy answered without hesitation. 'She turned up late last night an' asked to stop. I couldn't turn her away, could I? But I thought you'd be worryin' so I just came round to let yer know that's she's safe.'

As she watched Claire's shoulders sag a wave of sympathy passed through Roxy. The woman obviously loved young Nikki and was worried sick about her.

'Thank you, I appreciate you letting me know,' Claire sighed, then said: 'But . . . are you all right?'

Roxy's hand self-consciously flew to her face. 'Oh, this. It's nothin'. Just a bit of a barney wi' the old man last night. I've had far worse, believe me.'

The two women surveyed each other until Claire broke the silence when she asked, 'Would you like a cup of tea?'

Roxy screwed her hands together uncertainly. 'Well, I really ought to be gettin' back in case I'm missed . . . but go on then. I'll have a quick one. There was somethin' I was wantin' to say to you anyway.'

'Oh?' Claire was curious as she put the kettle on and prepared two mugs. 'Do sit down.'

Roxy did as she was told as her eyes flicked round the spacious room. How could Nikki possibly prefer to spend time round at her shit-hole when she had a place like this to come home to? And Claire seemed a decent enough sort an' all. A bit la-di-da, granted, but she did appear to care about Nikki.

When Claire placed a mug in front of her some minutes later, Roxy noisily sipped at it, wincing as the hot liquid came into contact with her split lips.

'What I wanted to say to yer was . . .' Roxy hesitated, uncertain of how to go on. 'I think it might be a good idea if yer were to keep Nikki away from around our parts in future. I can see she's been brought up decent an' I think our Poppy might be havin' a bad influence on her. I know that's a wicked thing to say about me own daughter, but I ain't got shit in me eye. I know what goes on, on the estate. It's full o' villains an' thieves, an' I'm ashamed to say I have to include me own brood in that. I'm shocked as one o' me lads ain't ended up in nick afore now.' Shrugging her shoulders despondently she warmed her hands on the mug and Claire saw that there were tears in her eyes. 'Even so, I think you'll want better than that for Nikki, so as I say, if I were you I'd try to keep a tighter rein on her.'

'Don't you think I've been trying to?' Claire snapped despairingly, and then instantly felt guilty. This woman was only trying to help her, after all, and she hadn't had to drag herself out of bed at this time of the morning to tell her that Nikki was safe.

'I'm sorry,' she muttered as she ran her hand distractedly through her hair. 'I know you mean well and I appreciate it. It's just . . . well, Nikki is pushing me to the limits at the minute and I don't know how to handle her any more. Sometimes I think she hates me.'

'Naw, love. Don't go thinkin' that.' Roxy was round the table like a shot, and when she placed a sympathetic arm around Claire's shoulders it was just too much and the younger woman began to sob.

'I . . . I think I've lost her,' she sniffled. 'She won't talk to me; she won't do as I tell her; she won't even go to school half the time any more.'

'It's all part o' growing up, love,' Roxy told her sagely. 'I've gone through it wi' each an' every one o' mine in turn but they ain't had the privileged upbringin' that Nikki has. If yer stand by her you'll get her back on track, you'll see. Meantime we have to be a bit crafty. I won't tell her as I've been round here an' don't you mention it neither. Next time she comes to my house I'll tell her Poppy ain't in an' send her packin'. She'll soon get the message if I do that a few times, an' then happen she'll start to calm down a bit again.'

Claire stared up at her gratefully. The woman might be what Molly would term 'as common as muck' but she obviously had a big heart and Claire felt herself warming to her.

'So where was she last night before she turned up at your house?'

Roxy pursed her lips and looked quickly away from Claire's prying eyes. She had a pretty good idea but hoped to God that she was wrong. Her Eddie thought she was as thick as mud, too daft to see past the end of her own nose, but she knew a lot more about what he got up to than she let on. She was aware that he often went off with youngsters in his car and always came back without them, and it was usually following a call from his so-called boss. Well, you didn't have to be the Brain of Britain to figure it out really, did you? This boss was clearly some kinky pervert who was into youngsters. Her biggest fear at the moment was that Nikki was the latest to have caught his eye. If this was so, then Roxy was prepared to move heaven and earth to keep the girl out of his evil clutches, although she couldn't tell Claire that. Instead she stroked Claire's hair for a minute before turning wearily towards the door.

'I'd best be off before the old man realises I'm missin' – not that he usually surfaces much before dinnertime. I'll send Nikki back an' you try an' keep her in, eh? There's some on the estate that yer wouldn't want her mixin' with. Bye, love.'

'Roxy . . .'

The woman paused when Claire's hand settled on her arm.

'Why are you doing this for me?'

Roxy seemed to be struggling with herself before she finally mumbled, 'Let's just say I have a daughter out there somewhere who's about the same age as Nikki. I'd like to think someone is watchin' out for her too.'

Claire's heart flooded with sympathy. So this woman had lost a child too, just as she had. That was another thing they had in common. She took her hand from Roxy's arm and let her move on towards the door

'Goodbye. And Roxy . . . thank you.'

Roxy lowered her head and let herself out without another word as Claire sat down at the table, her own head reeling. Somehow she felt that in Roxy she had found an ally, and the feeling brought her comfort.

Robbie and Bradley had finished stripping the old wallpaper from the dining-room walls. Now they were in there painting the skirting boards. Nikki had come in shortly after nine o'clock that morning, gone straight to bed without offering any explanation as to where she had been and had stayed there ever since. Claire was feeling thoroughly miserable as she prepared the vegetables for the evening meal. She had almost finished when there was a knock on the front door, so wiping her hands on a cloth she walked through the hallway to answer it.

When she saw Christian as large as life standing there on the doorstep her whole face lit up and her hand flew self-consciously to her hair. She must look dreadful. She'd had very little sleep and was dressed in old jeans and an out-of-shape T-shirt that was spattered with paint.

For a moment she was so thrilled to see him that she was speechless, but then she stuttered, 'Why didn't you let me know you were coming? This is such a lovely surprise, but I look such a state. I'm so sorry, we're decorating, you see. Well, Dad and Bradley are; I tend to get more paint on me than where it's supposed to go when I try to help. Come in, are you on your own?' After glancing over his shoulder she took his hand and gently pulled him into the hall.

'Yes, I am, and don't worry, you look just fine.'

She wanted to fling herself into his arms and tell him how much she had missed him, but something about the way he was standing away from her stopped her. He was probably aware that Robbie and Bradley were there, she supposed, as she led him into the kitchen.

'Sit down, I'll make you a drink,' she prattled as her heart did somersaults in her chest. He looked so handsome and she was so thrilled that he had driven all this way to see her that suddenly she felt herself climbing out from the depths of depression she had allowed herself to sink into.

'How is Mrs M?' she asked, as she tried to straighten her hair with her fingers.

'She's fine and she sends her love.'

'Good, good.' All the time Claire was dashing about, fetching biscuits from the cupboard, preparing mugs and laying a tray for Robbie and Bradley.

'And how is Nikki?'

The cloud that crossed Claire's face was Christian's answer.

'Still pushing the boundaries,' she admitted sadly. 'But she'll come through it, you'll see.'

He nodded, and although she had tried to pretend that she was imagining things, she saw that he looked very ill at ease and unhappy.

'Christian, is there anything wrong?' she asked finally.

'Not wrong exactly, but I do need to talk to you,' he answered.

'Oh well, fire away then.'

'Is there anywhere we could talk in private?'

Claire stared back at his solemn face. 'I dare say we could go for a walk down the garden. Would that be private enough for you?'

'Yes, yes of course.'

She led the way, very aware of him just two steps behind her. When they came to the bench under the old apple tree, she sat down and patted the seat at the side of her.

'Come on then, out with it. It must be something important, for you to have come all this way.'

When he hung his head, a cold feeling settled around her heart.

'The thing is, Claire, I know that there's always been an unspoken agreement between us since you came to live here. The agreement being that once you had Nikki settled and you'd sorted yourself out, we'd all get together and live happily ever after. But . . . well, there's no easy way to say this, so I'm just going to come out with it. Things change and I'm afraid that I've . . . I've fallen in love with Mandy and we've decided to get married. I never meant it to happen, neither did she; it just sort of crept up on us. I'm so sorry, Claire. I hope you'll forgive me. But it would never have worked for us, I can see that now. You've been back here for a couple of years now, and I dare say that you still haven't told anyone about your past, have you?'

'Oh, but I *have*. I've told my dad,' she babbled breathlessly.

'And what about Nikki, and Molly and Tom, and your sister Tracey?'

When she lowered her head he sighed. 'I thought as much. And you would always have felt that you had to put Nikki first because of what she had been through too. But the thing is . . . I want a family too, while I'm still young enough to enjoy it. Time is moving on, yet we are still as far apart as we ever were. I'm telling the truth, aren't I?'

342

Shock rendered Claire temporarily speechless as the dream she had treasured for so long slowly fell apart around her. She wanted to rant and rave at him, to tell him that he was wrong, that they could make it work. But deep down she knew that he *was* telling the truth. The dream was finally over.

Seeing her stricken face, he took her hands in his and gently shook them up and down. 'Please don't look like that, Claire. I never set out to hurt you, I swear I didn't. In another time and another place I think you and I would have been perfect together, but the gods have been against us all along the way, haven't they?'

She nodded, but strangely there were no tears. The pain she was feeling went way beyond tears at that moment in time. For years his face had been the first thing she saw in the morning and the last thing she saw at night in her mind's eye, and now he was telling her it was finished. She couldn't blame him really. As he had said, he was still young enough to start a new life with someone else, someone who would love him as he deserved to be loved. Someone clean and fresh like Mandy, not soiled as she was.

'I hope you'll both be very happy.' She felt like a robot, going through the motions, saying the right things, but inside she felt as if she was dying.

'Thank you. I couldn't bring myself to tell you on the phone. I thought you deserved to be told face to face and I hope that we'll be able to remain friends, Claire. I will always care about you.'

'Of course.'

'Right, I'd better be setting off back then.' He seemed keen to be gone now that he had said what he had come to say, and when he rose and started away back up the garden she followed him automatically.

As they were walking through the hall, Robbie suddenly appeared in his overalls and his face broke into a grin. 'Why, I thought I heard someone. It's Christian, isn't it?'

'Yes, sir.' The two men shook hands as Claire looked numbly on.

She felt as if she was seeing everything through a thick fog and was detached from reality.

'Staying for long, are you?' Robbie was confused; Christian could only just have arrived, and yet he looked as if he was about to leave. Suddenly noticing Claire's pale face, the smile slid from his face. Feeling in the way, he said hastily, 'Right, I'd better get back to work then, before the boss here starts to crack the whip. Goodbye, son.' And disappearing back into the dining room, he closed the door behind him.

They were on their own again, for the very last time, and Claire wasn't sure how she would bear it. She was staring at Christian's face, drinking in every feature so that she could lock them away in her memory, and then he was holding his hand out and she was shaking it as if he was a complete stranger.

'Goodbye then, Claire. I hope everything works out for Nikki. Have a good life and take care of yourself.' He was walking away and she was fighting the urge to run after him. He couldn't leave her, not like this; he was the centre of her world and she had no idea how she would cope without him.

She watched him as he drove away and then after closing the door, her legs buckled beneath her and she slowly slithered to the floor.

After a while the door to the dining room opened and Robbie peeped out. Seeing her sitting there as if she had been cast in stone, he dropped the paintbrush he was holding and bounded over to her.

'Eeh, lass. Whatever is it?' he cried as he gathered her into his arms, and then at last they came; hot gushing tears that seemed to pour out of her like a waterfall. She felt as if she were drowning and though she opened and shut her mouth, no sound issued from it save for huge, gulping sobs.

'He . . . he's left me, Dad,' she managed to choke eventually.

'But why, lass?'

'He's fallen in love with Mandy – a girl who's been working at Seagull's Flight for him. They . . . they're going to be married.'

Robbie's heart broke afresh as he witnessed her despair. Claire had had so very much to contend with in her life, and now for this to go and happen . . . He wanted to offer words of comfort but what could he possibly say to soften the pain she was experiencing?

And so they sat there with their arms entwined until another knock at the door behind them made them both start.

'Come on, lass. Get yourself away into the kitchen an' I'll see who it is, eh?' Robbie helped her to her feet, waited until the kitchen door had closed behind her and only then did he open the front door to find Tracey, Callum, Molly, Tom and the twins all standing on the doorstep.

'It was such a lovely evening we thought we'd come and surprise you and treat you to a barbecue,' Tracey told him brightly as she held up two bulging carrier bags. 'You haven't already eaten, have you?'

'Er . . . no, lass, we haven't.' Robbie glanced worriedly towards the kitchen door. Under other circumstances he would have been delighted to see them all, but as it was he wondered how Claire would cope with visitors. They all piled into the hallway just as Bradley, who was completely oblivious to all that had gone on, appeared in the doorway of the dining room.

'Hello.' As he scooped to lift a twin into each arm, the little girls giggled. 'I've finished painting the skirting boards and I don't know about you but I reckon I'm about ready to call it a day now,' he said to Robbie.

'Oh good. In that case you can relax now and stay for something to eat,' Tracey told him.

Bradley didn't need to be asked twice. 'Well, whatever you have in mind, I'm sure it will be better than the microwave meal I was going to have back at the flat. Thank you.'

Tracey breezed past him, but Robbie caught her arm. 'Tracey, I think I ought to warn you. Claire is in there and you'll find she's upset. She's just had a bit o' bad news.'

She stopped abruptly. 'Nothing's happened to Nikki, has it?'

'Oh no, no, nothing like that,' he hastened to assure her. 'I'm sure she'll tell you herself if she has a mind to, but in the meantime go steady on her, eh?'

She nodded and with her lips set in a straight line she set off for the kitchen while the rest of the visitors trooped into the lounge.

Claire was sitting at the table and when Tracey entered she raised a tear-drenched face to her. Her younger sister took a seat at the side of her and gently took her hand. Claire had always appeared so sophisticated and composed to her before, but suddenly she saw her differently.

'Is it anything you care to talk about?' she asked softly.

For a moment there was silence but then between sobs, Claire told her brokenly, 'Christian came to see me today, to tell me that he's going to be married. It's over between us.'

'I see.' Tracey sought for the right words to say. 'I'm so sorry, Claire. I know you thought you had a future together.'

'Huh! Since when have any of *my* dreams come true?'

Tracey looked confused. What could Claire mean? As far as she knew, since Claire had left them all those years ago, she had led a charmed life.

As if she could read her thoughts, Claire's lip curled. 'I know what you're thinking,' she said. 'You're thinking it serves me right, aren't you?'

'No, I was not!' Tracey retorted indignantly.

'Good! Because if you did but know it, this is just another disaster to add to the list that my life has amounted to.'

Tracey was still staring at her in bewilderment and suddenly Claire was sick of pretending to be someone she was not. It was time to tell the truth about what her life had really been like.

'Go and fetch Molly in, would you?' Her voice was so weary that her sister was afraid. 'I have something to say that I'd like you both to hear.'

Without a word, Tracey rose and hurried away. Robbie was hovering in the hall and catching her arm he asked her, 'Is she all right?'

'Well, she's certainly very upset,' Tracey replied. 'But there's something she wants to tell me and Molly, so I'm just going to fetch her. Do you have any idea what it might be?'

'As a matter of fact I think I just might.' Robbie looked suddenly very old and weary, but he hoped that Claire was about to be honest about her past with them as she had been with him. If she was, he felt that it would go a long way towards giving her some peace of mind. The only person she would need to be honest with then was Nikki, but he suspected Claire wasn't ready for that. Still, the way he looked at it, she was about to take another major step forward, which couldn't be a bad thing whichever way you looked at it. And he was convinced now that she *would* tell Nikki – when she felt the time was right.

'So what's all this about then?' Molly huffed into the room and after taking a seat she crossed her arms beneath her chest.

Tracey was watching her expectantly and Claire gazed from one to the other of them. They were both so very precious to her and she hoped that they would still love her when she had told them the truth.

'I think it's time I was honest with you both,' she began falteringly. 'About how I earned my living in London before I moved on to Blackpool . . . When I first arrived in London I spent days trying to get a job. Then I got mugged and raped and taken in by a pimp. I managed to escape from him and finally I was taken in by . . . a prostitute.' And so she went on, leaving out nothing as the two women listened in open-mouthed amazement.

By the time the sorry tale was told, Molly was openly sobbing but Tracey had said not so much as a word.

'Oh Claire, I can't even begin to imagine how awful it must have been for you.' Molly was round the table now, raining kisses onto the top of Claire's head, but the latter's eyes were fixed on Tracey and she was holding her breath as she waited for her sister's reaction.

When it finally came it was not what she had hoped for. Tracey stood up, her back as straight as a broomstick and her mouth set in a grim line as she declared, 'We are leaving now.'

'Eeh, but we've only just come! Don't go yet,' Molly pleaded. 'Your sister needs a bit o' support tonight.'

'I hardly think so. I believe *prostitutes* are quite notorious for looking after themselves.'

Molly was horrified to hear the contempt in Tracey's voice. 'Don't you dare talk like that,' she scolded. 'Surely you can see the poor love didn't have a choice?'

'From where I'm standing, she did.' Tracey's voice was as cold as ice. 'All she had to do was pick up the phone and you would have gone and fetched her home like a shot – and don't deny it! Claire could always wrap you around her little finger. But no, *we* weren't good enough for Claire. She wanted better than we could give her, even if it meant going on her back to get it! What am I going to tell Callum, eh? How is he going to feel when he knows that my sister is no more than a common ex-pro? And to think that I thought she was some-body to be proud of, when all the time—'

'TRACEY! That is quite enough!'

Tracey glared at Molly before flicking her hair over her shoulder and striding from the room. Seconds later they heard muttered voices coming from the direction of the lounge and then the sound of the front door slamming.

Robbie and Bradley appeared looking totally bewildered, and Claire told her father, 'I can't take any more tonight, Dad. I'm going to my room.'

'You do that, lass.'

She slipped past them. Her head was throbbing and she just wanted the privacy of her room.

'What's going on?' she heard Bradley ask, but then the voices faded away as she climbed the stairs. She didn't care any more what anyone thought of her. Without Christian her life was meaningless and she prayed as she slipped into an uneasy sleep that she might never wake up again. She had finally faced her demons – but it was too late.

Chapter Thirty-Two

Well into November, Claire stood back to admire the cake she had iced for Nikki's fifteenth birthday.

The last few months had been painful, but as time slipped by she was adjusting to the fact that Christian had gone from her life. Bradley had been marvellous. She knew that she would only have to say the word and he would marry her tomorrow, but as much as it flattered her she wondered if she would be doing right by him when her heart still belonged to someone else. Robbie had been marvellous too, and she was now the proud owner of Fifth Avenue, the shop in Coleshill which had opened the month before and was doing remarkably well. She had been lucky enough to find a very efficient woman called Sandra who now had the shop running like clockwork, and this gave Claire time to devote to Nikki – when she was home, that was.

Nikki had changed. She no longer visited Poppy or stayed out all night, but she would disappear two or three nights a week with no explanation of where she was going and return home when she felt like it. Claire had given up trying to find out what she was up to and could only pray that Nikki was doing something harmless like visiting a friend. The sparkle seemed to have gone out of the girl and she was sullen and lethargic, but then Claire had to admit that she herself had hardly been a barrel of laughs, so she didn't comment on it and was just grateful for the fact that Nikki came home at all.

She hadn't seen Tracey since the night she had confided in her and this was another hurt to add to all the others. Molly on the other hand had been wonderful, supportive and caring and always there when she needed her.

'Why, lass, that cake looks great. Whose birthday is it?'

She had been so deep in thought that she hadn't been aware of Robbie, who had come to stand beside her.

'Dad, there you go again – you'd forget your head if it wasn't screwed on just lately. It's Nikki's. Let's just hope she comes straight home from school tonight to eat it,' she muttered.

'Sorry, lass.' Claire was right, Robbie thought; he was becoming more and more forgetful as the weeks passed. It would be time to leave soon. His poor daughter had enough on her plate without having to worry about him. He determined to talk to Molly about it the very next time he saw her, but trying to be cheerful for now he dipped his finger into the bowl that had contained the icing and sucked it off his finger.

'Mmm, that's grand. I reckon you should have opened a cake shop instead of a dress shop,' he teased her.

'Fifth Avenue is doing very well, thank you very much,' Claire told him as she waved the spoon at him. 'And Sandra is an absolute gem. I don't know what I'd do without her – or you, for that matter. I would never have taken the plunge if you hadn't talked me into it but your idea has proved to be spot on. The customers love having somewhere classy to go where they can buy their outfits all in one go, and they don't mind paying for the quality and the privilege either.'

'Well, there you go then. It just goes to prove I have me uses, doesn't it?'

Claire smiled at him with genuine affection. She was glad her dad had come back into her life now.

As if he were able to read her thoughts he suddenly said, 'You know, Claire, these last few months have been the best of my whole life. I wouldn't have missed a minute of them, and no matter what happens in the future I want you to know that I'm very proud of you and I love you.'

'Oh Dad.' Claire was deeply touched but as she leaned over to peck him on the cheek, she noticed how pale he was. 'Are you feeling OK?' she asked with concern. 'You look a bit peaky.'

'It's just me age,' he joked. 'It has a habit o' catchin' up on you when you least expect it.'

They turned as one at that moment when they heard the front door open and the next minute Nikki strolled into the room.

'Happy Birthday!' they chorused in unison and as Nikki's eyes dropped to the cake she flushed and smiled tentatively.

'Let me just go an' get your present.' Robbie hurried from the room with a bright smile on his face, and once they were alone, Claire lifted an envelope and handed it to her.

'Here. I know this may seem like an odd sort of present, but I hope you'll like it,' she told her daughter.

Nikki split the envelope and after taking a photo from it, she frowned. It was a picture of a little shih-tzu who looked very like Gemma. A litter of fluffy puppies was playing around her.

'What's this?'

Claire laughed. 'Well this, or should I say, *that* one there,' she pointed at one of the puppies, 'is your birthday present. A lady who lives by Molly owns the mum and I thought it was time we thought about getting you another dog. It's a little girl and we can collect her on Saturday . . . Do you like her?'

A thousand emotions seemed to play across Nikki's face and her lips began to tremble but she suddenly flung the photo onto the table and said harshly, 'No, I *don't* like her! Do you really think we could ever replace Gemma?'

'No, I don't,' Claire replied truthfully. 'And Gemma never replaced Cassidy. But we grew to love her for herself. Dogs are like people –

they each have their own personalities. We can't bring Cassidy or Gemma back, unfortunately, but we could offer that little one a good home, so what do you say?'

Robbie chose that moment to come back into the room. He handed Nikki a brightly coloured gift bag. 'Now the lady in the shop said you can go back and change them if you don't like them,' he told her. 'And your mum told me the size so I hope they'll do.'

Nikki opened the bag and withdrew a pair of Levi jeans. 'Oh, they're wonderful,' she declared with genuine pleasure. 'I've had my eye on these for a while.'

'So your mum told me,' he grinned. 'Now here's your other present. It's something I'd like you to keep.'

Nikki took a tiny velvet box from him and when she opened it, a small diamond on a thin gold band winked up at her.

'It was your grandma's engagement ring,' he told her solemnly. 'I gave her wedding ring to your mum, but I thought you might like this.'

'Oh . . . Grandad!'

Robbie's chest swelled. That was the first time Nikki had ever addressed him as such, and he felt as if he had taken a great step forward.

'It's really lovely,' she told him. 'Thank you, I'll keep it for always. And Mum . . . I'll think about the puppy.' Turning abruptly, she hurried from the room as Claire and Robbie exchanged a smile. All in all, that had gone down rather well.

Up in her room, Nikki slipped the ring onto her finger as tears welled in her eyes. Her mum had seemed so sad since Christian had ended their relationship, and yet she had still gone to the trouble of trying to make her birthday special for her. She looked into the mirror. She was now fifteen years old and yet she felt like an old, old woman. She wished that things could go back to how they had been before she met Poppy, but it was too late for wishing now. Jackie had her well and truly in his clutches and she knew that he would never let her go until he and his friends had grown tired of her. She shuddered as she thought of the despicable things they made her do to them, but then as her eyes fell on the drawer where she kept the drugs he supplied her with, she knew that she was not entirely blameless. She was totally dependent on them now, and if she didn't have them at regular intervals she would start to get the shakes, a fact that Jackie was aware of and took full advantage of.

Slithering out of her clothes she surveyed her body with contempt, then slowly she pulled on the jeans that Robbie had bought her and a long sleeved T-shirt.

'Well, would you ever believe it, eh? And practically on our own doorstep!' Molly waggled the evening newspaper at Tom. 'It says here that they've pulled the body of a young girl out of the Blue Lagoon. It had been in there for months, according to this. They're trying to identify the poor little lass at the minute. It makes your blood run cold, doesn't it? Our Billy and Tracey used to swim in there when they were nippers and all! Oh, I always warned them not to but I know they did.'

Shaking her head, she went back to reading the report as Tom turned the television on.

At almost that precise moment, Eddie walked into Jackie's bungalow and threw an identical newspaper onto the coffee-table. 'They've found her,' he told his boss shortly.

'Found *who*?'

'The girl you asked me to dispose of, o' course! Who do yer fuckin' think!' Eddie was clearly in a panic so, lifting the paper, Jackie hastily read the report.

'Look, calm down,' he snapped. 'She's been in there for months.

There'll be nothin' left to identify, an' certainly nothin' to link her to us.'

'*US!* Oh no, yer on yer own wi' this one, Jackie. I might have got rid o' the body but I never killed her. You ain't bringin' *me* into this.'

Jackie leaned menacingly towards him. 'Pull yerself together, man,' he barked. 'I've told you, we're home an' dry on this one.'

'What do yer mean, on *this* one?'

Realising his mistake, Jackie tried to cover his tracks. 'It was just a figure of speech, that's all. I just meant we're as safe as houses. And as for bringing you into it, well, from where I'm standing you're already in it, mate, right up to your fuckin' neck, an' don't you forget it. If I go down for this I'll make sure as you come with me . . . do you understand?'

Eddie choked as Jackie caught him by the throat. 'All we have to do is stay schtum. No talkin' out o' school . . . *right?*'

'Yes, boss.'

'Good. Right – you've told me what you came to tell me, so fuck off an' forget you ever came here. When I need yer, I'll send fer you.'

Eddie moved towards the door but there he paused to ask, 'Is Nikki still comin' here?'

'Why do you want to know?'

'Oh, just curious really.'

'Fuck off, Eddie, you're beginnin' to seriously annoy me now.'

As Eddie left the bungalow, the day seemed to darken, and he had the strangest feeling that somewhere down the line he would be made to pay for his sins.

'So, how are you feeling then, love?'

Robbie stared into the heart of the living-flame gas fire Molly had just had installed and shrugged. He had to admit it looked very realistic and Molly was over the moon with it.

'Oh, you know, not too bad, but . . . Well, I reckon I'll get Christmas over with and then I'll make me way back to Scotland. I have a place all lined up; it's very nice, if the brochures are anythin' to go by.'

Molly hung her head as tears pricked at the back of her eyes before she asked, 'Are you going to tell her?'

Robbie pondered for a moment before replying. 'No. Happen it would be best if I just slipped away. She'll think I've abandoned her again, an' then she can go back to hatin' me.'

'For what my opinion's worth I think you're wrong,' Molly told him soberly. 'It's been lovely to watch the two off you grow close, and after all Claire's been through and all the trouble she's having with Nikki, I think she'd appreciate you being honest with her.'

'I can't do that!' he gasped as panic gripped him. 'If I told her the truth she'd feel obliged to ask me to stay an' I don't want to add to her worries and turn into a burden.'

Molly sighed. 'Well, at least you'll be staying put till after Christmas so I suppose that's something. But do think about what I've said. I reckon honesty would be the best policy.'

Robbie snorted in disgust. 'Oh yes, an' how do yer figure that out, Molly? Claire was honest with Tracey and look where that got her. They haven't spoken for months, an' if Claire rings her, Tracey puts the phone down. She hasn't said much, but between you an' me I think it's breaking Claire's heart.'

'Tracey always was a stubborn little madam,' Molly conceded. 'But give her time and she'll come round. I'm more concerned about Claire and Nikki at present. They both look dreadful.'

'Claire's not been herself since that vet bloke finished with her,' Robbie admitted. 'She's runnin' herself ragged – tryin' to keep her mind off things, I think. She's been out buying stock for the shop all day. She looks so worn out, an' the way Nikki is behaving ain't helping matters.'

'Still staying out all night, is she?'

Robbie shook his head. 'Strangely enough, no she isn't. She stays out late and refuses to say where she's been, but she always comes home. It's as if a spark has gone out in her since she lost Gemma. Claire offered to get her a puppy for her birthday as you know, but Nikki decided against it in the end.'

'And how is the shop doing?'

'Splendidly.' Robbie smiled now. 'At least that's something that's going right. There was very little to do in it and Claire had it open in no time. According to her books she's showing profit already, even after the rent, wages and stock she's laid out for.'

'Good.'

They fell silent for a while until Molly asked, 'What do you think Nikki is up to, Robbie?'

He hesitated, then replied tentatively, 'I reckon she might be into drugs.'

'*No!*' Molly looked horrified. 'But she's only a little slip of a thing.'

'All the signs are there,' he told her regretfully. 'I have a feeling Claire is thinking along the same lines but doesn't know what to do about it. She's begged Nikki to go to the doctor's with her. She even got him to come to the house once but Nikki refused to see him. I'm tellin' you, Molly, that child ain't no further through than a line prop. She's got bags under her eyes that you could do your shopping in, an' if you so much as ask her where she's off to she almost snaps your head off. It makes you wonder where it will all end.'

'They reckon as the Good Lord never sends you more than you can deal with,' Molly muttered stoically and Robbie frowned.

'From where I'm standin' it looks as if Claire has already had her quota of unhappiness,' he mumbled. 'There's Bradley who worships the very ground she walks on yet she looks straight through him as if he isn't there. If only she'd open her eyes an' see what's in front of her, she'd see that her future could be bright if she took to him. I'd lay odds she'd never want for nothing, least of all love if she'd only let go of this feeling she had for Christian. Though I have to admit, he would have been me first choice for her.'

'Ah, but love is a funny thing,' Molly pointed out. 'Seems to me this young vet was the first chap to ever show Claire any kindness, so it stands to reason that she was going to put him on a pedestal. That said, time is a great healer and she will get over him – and then, who knows? What will be will be, and there isn't a thing that will change it.'

They slipped into a compatible silence and stared into the dancing flames of the fire.

'So I was thinking we might go into Birmingham for the day on Saturday and get some of the Christmas shopping done out of the way. What do you think, Nikki? We haven't had a whole day to ourselves for ages, what with the shop opening and one thing and another.' Claire glanced across at Nikki who was pushing her meal around the plate as if it was poison.

'*Nikki!* Have you heard a single word I've been saying?' Claire's voice came out more sharply than she had intended it to.

'What?' As Nikki glanced up, a guilty flush sprang to her cheeks. 'Oh sorry . . . what were you saying? I was miles away.'

Claire took a seat at the side of her. 'I said, how about we spend the day together on Saturday?' she repeated patiently.

'I can't, Mum. I've got something planned.'

Swallowing her disappointment, Claire kept her voice even as she said, 'Aw well, it was just a thought. Perhaps next week, eh?'

'Perhaps.' Nikki pushed her plate away and rose from the table.

Despair washed over Claire. The wall between them was getting higher by the day despite all her efforts, and she thought back to her own adolescence. She had been just fourteen when she had given birth to her baby Yasmin – even younger than Nikki was now, which was why she was so careful to try and treat Nikki like a young adult, rather than a child.

As she watched the girl walk from the room, her shoulders stooped, Claire sighed. It looked like this was set to be another miserable, depressing Christmas – and there wasn't a damn thing she could do about it.

That evening, Claire set off to visit Molly. Nikki declined to go with her as she had a thumping headache and Robbie, who was feeling unwell, had retired to bed for a very early night. Claire had been gone for no more than an hour when the headache became unbearable and Nikki loped along the landing to Claire's room. There were no Paracetamol in the bathroom cabinet but she knew that her mum usually kept some in her bedroom. She decided that she would take a couple, if she could find them, and then she would get an early night too. There was nothing on TV she wanted to see, and she couldn't be bothered to do any revision for her mock GCSEs in January.

Once inside Claire's room, Nikki clicked on the light and looked around. The bedside drawers seemed to be the obvious place where Claire would keep the tablets, but a quick glance in each one proved her wrong. She then moved on to the chest of drawers that stood next to the wardrobe. It contained nothing but underwear. It suddenly occurred to the girl that Claire might have some aspirin in one of her handbags in the bottom of the wardrobe, and this time she was successful. She had just taken two tablets from the packet and was about to return the bag to the warbrobe when two large books beneath a tidy pile of Claire's shoes caught her eye. They were leather-bound and looked quite old. Intrigued, Nikki removed some of the shoes and withdrew the first one – and when she opened it to the first page she was shocked to see that it was a diary. Her *mum's* diary.

Nikki's heart began to race. She knew that it was wrong to intrude into something so personal, but her curiosity was aroused now. Hastily snatching up the second diary, she positioned the shoes back in the bottom of the wardrobe and crept from the room. Once back in her own room she lay on the bed and turned to the first page. As she was

358

slowly drawn into Claire's childhood tears streamed down her thin cheeks. Nikki read long into the night, and by the time she finally fell asleep with the first diary resting on her chest, she had read of Claire's heartbreak when she had given her baby away. *Did my birth mother feel like that when she gave me away?* Nikki wondered, as sleep came to claim her, and her dreams were troubled. She was awake and eager to start reading again at the crack of dawn, and by the time Claire called her down to breakfast, she had almost finished the first diary.

'Had a good night, have you, love?' Claire asked as she placed some toast in front of her.

Nikki didn't answer but suddenly stood up from the table and flung her arms about her. 'I really love you, Mum,' she whispered.

'Oh sweetheart, I *really* love you too.' Claire was deeply touched as she returned the hug, though she had no idea what had brought it about. Whatever it was, she hoped it would continue. It had been a long time since Nikki had managed more than a cursory glance at her, and this made a welcome change. When she left for the shop that morning after seeing her daughter off to school, there was a spring in her step that hadn't been there for some time. Little did she know that Nikki was hiding across the road just waiting for her to leave so that she could creep back into the house to continue her reading, which is just what she did.

As the story of Claire's life slowly unfolded, Nikki's tears were replaced by shock, and any sympathy she had felt for her fled as she read disbelievingly of Claire's time as a prostitute in London. Her mum had been a *pro*! Nothing more than a dirty little hooker who would drop her knickers for anyone who would pay for her. Disgust and revulsion made Nikki gag. She could forgive Claire for the abuse she had suffered at the hands of her mother's boyfriends. She could even forgive her for giving her baby away. But she had believed that Claire had earned her living in London as a secretary, not a common prostitute. It just didn't bear thinking about. For months she had lived in shame because of what she was doing at Jackie's bungalow. She had been terrified of Claire finding out, while all the time Claire had presented a façade of respectability to the world. But she *wasn't* respectable. Her fancy clothes had been earned by lying on her back. She was scum – the lowest of the low – and Nikki wasn't sure that she would ever be able to respect her again. Throwing the second diary across the room, she turned onto her stomach and sobbed into her pillows as the world she knew crumbled around her.

'I'm telling you they're on to us!' As Alan Jenkins paced up and down the luxurious lounge in Jackie's home, he ran his hand distractedly through his thinning grey hair.

'For fuck's sake, stand still and tell me what you're prattlin' on about,' Jackie growled at him.

Alan stubbed his cigarette out in a cut-glass ashtray before taking a packet from his suit pocket and lighting another.

'The Old Bill. They've been sniffing around,' he muttered. 'They called into the shop the other day an' asked if they could have a word in private out the back.' His hand began to shake and Jackie scowled as he dropped fag ash all over his carpet.

'A word about what?'

'The girl they fished out of the Blue Lagoon, o' course,' Alan Jenkins spluttered. 'They'll be questionin' everyone who's got a history of child abuse. I've no doubt they'll come here before much longer. I reckon the best thing you could do is clear the place of all the computers and films an' stuff, an' get off abroad for a while till things cool down.'

Jackie stiffened. What Alan was saying made sense. If the coppers were to raid this place, they'd throw the book at him. He shuddered as he thought back to his stretch in prison, when he had had to be placed in a separate wing for his own safety. The men inside were happy to rub shoulders with cold-blooded murderers and villains, but when it came to sex offences against kids . . .

A feeling of panic fluttered to life in his stomach. 'You could be right,' he was forced to admit. 'Ring round the rest o' the blokes an' tell 'em to get their arses over here.'

'Where are you going to put everything?' Alan asked.

Jackie thought, then an idea occurred to him. 'I've just bought a warehouse in Nuneaton. I haven't rented it out yet so we could store everything in there. No one knows it's mine so they wouldn't think of looking there.'

Alan shuffled uncomfortably from foot to foot. 'An' what about the drugs?'

'They can go in there an' all,' Jackie decided. 'Meanwhile, I'll lay low in one o' me rented houses till everything cools off a bit. There's one or two empty at the minute so it shouldn't be too hard. I'll take Nikki wi' me.'

Jenkins stared at him as if he had completely lost his senses. 'You can't do that! The kid is just fifteen, for God's sake – the coppers would be lookin' for her as well then. What is it with you an' that kid anyway? You've usually lost interest in them after a couple o' weeks but you seem to be obsessed with this one.'

Jackie grinned, a smile of such pure evil that it turned the other man's blood to water.

'It ain't really the kid I'm interested in,' he admitted for the first time. 'It's more *who* she belongs to. Let's just say this is my way o' getting revenge on someone who once caused me a load o' grief an' were inadvertently the cause o' sendin' me down.'

'Revenge is all well an' good,' Alan pointed out. 'But there's a time an' a place for it. Do you *really* want to risk it at the minute?'

'I ain't got no choice.' Jackie glared. 'Yer know what they say, Alan – revenge is sweet – an' they weren't wrong. Oh no, they weren't wrong. As far as I'm concerned, this ain't over till it's over.'

He walked into the next room and began to unplug the computers that he used to transmit his child images to people all over the world, and as Alan watched him go, a cold finger played up and down his spine.

Chapter Thirty-Three

As Nikki walked along the road with her hands tucked deep in her coat pockets she shuddered. It was a miserable afternoon and although it was only just gone four o'clock the frost was already sparkling on the pavements, turning them into a skating rink. The high-heeled boots she was wearing didn't help, and more than once she thought she was going to slip and had to reach out to steady herself. Added to this, there was a thick fog forming that made her feel strangely alone; almost as if she was the only person left on earth. Here and there, brightly coloured lights festooned Christmas trees standing in people's front windows and winked into the gloom. Nikki ignored them, hurrying on as best she could. She was in no mood for festive activities or anything associated with them.

Jackie had informed her that Eddie would be picking her up tonight and she knew that she should go and get ready. She had bunked off school all day, but hopefully, her mum wouldn't get to know about it. Claire had been in the shop all day. Tossing her long fair hair across her shoulder, Nikki contemplated the evening ahead. Her nights at Jackie's had fallen into a pattern now. When she arrived she would be left alone to bathe and change into the school uniform that would be laid out on the bed. She would then twist her hair into two long plaits and scrub every bit of make-up from her face, and then . . . She shuddered as she stopped her thoughts from moving on any further. Not that it mattered any more. After all, she was doing no worse than her mum had done in her early days. Strangely enough, Jackie always treated her like an adult yet insisted she should dress as a child. It was all very weird. Not that she was not well rewarded. Even so . . . there was always the temptation to run away – just go somewhere where no one knew her and where she could start again. But then, her mum had tried that once, and look where it had got her. Also, where would she get her drugs from?

Nikki felt depressed. It had been really hard since reading the diaries to even look at her mum. She wanted to scream at her and tell her what she thought of her, but up to now she had managed to stop herself. The time would come though, and then she would let Claire know what she thought of her in no uncertain terms. Her thoughts shifted back to Jackie and the evening ahead. She knew what Jackie was capable of, if she should let him down now. Strangely, she didn't feel so bad about what she was doing any more, and if push came to shove she would rather spend time with Jackie now than Claire. At least he wasn't a hypocrite.

Claire put her bag down on the hall chair and walked wearily into the kitchen where Robbie was waiting to greet her.

'Hello, pet.' Crossing to the fridge, he produced a bottle of chilled white wine as Claire sank into a chair and kicked her shoes off. 'Everything all right at the shop, is it?' he asked, pouring her a small glass.

'Fine.' Taking the slide from her hair, she shook it loose. 'Sandra has everything under control as usual, and the new line in evening dresses is selling like hot cakes. The handbags and jewellery I bought in are selling well too.'

'Aye, well, it's the right time o' year for party frocks an' a bit o' glitter,' Robbie commented with a twinkle in his eye.

Claire glanced around before asking, 'Is Nikki in?'

'Aye, she is, though the last I saw of her she looked as if she was getting ready to go out.' The words had barely left his lips when Nikki sauntered into the kitchen, pointedly ignoring the two of them.

'Off out, are you?' Claire asked.

Nikki looked at her resentfully. 'What if I am?'

'I was only asking. I do have a right to, as your mum.'

'Yes, of course you do. You're so concerned about what I might be up to, *aren't you*?'

The words were said so cuttingly that Claire was momentarily speechless, but then she spluttered, 'What's got into you, Nikki? Is there really any need to talk to me like that?'

'How am I supposed to talk to you?' Nikki shot back. 'With respect? Huh, from where I'm standing you don't deserve it! You're a hypocrite, that's what you are. Nothing but a bloody hypocrite.'

It had been some days since Nikki had returned Claire's diaries to her room, and during those days the revulsion she had felt for her mother had bubbled away inside her, and now it exploded from her lips as she shouted, 'I know all about you! Oh yes, I just happened to come across your diaries. You, who always acts so righteous when you were nothing more than a common *prostitute*! Well, I'll tell you now, your days of ordering me about are well and truly over. In fact, I wouldn't care if I never set eyes on you again! Why didn't you tell me how you'd earned your living in London instead of acting so prim and proper? Wasn't I important enough?'

'Oh Nikki, of course you are, and I always m-meant to tell you,' Claire stammered. 'I did, I promise you. I . . . I was just trying to choose the right moment. I was afraid of how you'd take it – of what you'd think of me.'

'Well, I'll tell you what I think of you. I think you're *scum*!'

'Now, Nikki, there's no call to be talkin' to your mum like—'

'And *you* can shut up as well.' Nikki's eyes flashed fire at Robbie as he spoke in Claire's defence. 'I never wanted you here in the first place, poking your nose in and interfering. Perhaps if you'd been a proper dad to my mum, none of this would have ever happened!'

With that she swung about and crashed from the room as Claire gazed after her with her mouth hanging slackly open and tears pouring down her cheeks. After the initial shock of Nikki's attack she made to go after her but Robbie caught her arm and pulled her back into her seat. 'Let her go,' he advised. 'There'll be no talkin' any sense into her till she's had time to calm down. An' you know, at the end o' the day she were bound to find out sooner or later.'

'Oh Dad, I should have told her, but I've been such a coward! For her to have to find out like that . . . I doubt she'll ever forgive me.'

In actual fact, Robbie was glad of the chance to talk to his daughter alone, and Nikki's outburst had just shown him that he had made the right decision. It was how to begin that was the problem. He waited until he was seated opposite Claire and they had both taken a sip of wine before beginning. 'Actually, there was something I needed to talk to you about an' all, lass.'

As she stared at him dully, he felt his colour rising. She was still reeling from Nikki's attack, but if he put off what he had to say now, he might never find the courage to say it in the days ahead. 'The thing is . . . I've decided to go back to Scotland after Christmas. I feel in the way here now, an' what Nikki just said proved it. I've done all the odd jobs about the place an' I reckon it's time I left you an' her in peace.'

There was a stunned silence that seemed to stretch into infinity, but then Claire gulped and blurted out, 'But . . . I thought you were happy here.'

'I have been, lass,' he hastily assured her. 'More than happy, if truth be told. I wouldn't have missed the time we've had together for all the tea in China, but I think it's time to move on again now.'

Claire placed her glass on the table and stared at him. She wanted to cry at the thought of him leaving her again, especially now, but she had no intention of showing him how hurt she was at his decision.

'Very well.' Her words cut into him like a knife. 'You must do as you see fit. Nikki and I will be fine. We managed before you came, so I'm quite sure we'll manage again after you have gone.'

'Aw, lass.' He was lost for words as he heard the coldness in her voice.

She rose from the table and he watched her put her shoes back on and make for the door.

'You're not thinkin' of goin' out again, are you?'

'Yes. I just remembered I told Molly I'd call over tonight. I'll see you later.'

'But, Claire, the weather's atrocious. The roads are like glass. Couldn't it wait until tomorrow?'

'No, it couldn't.' Claire was in the hallway now, keeping her back turned so that he wouldn't see the tears that were shining in her eyes.

Two minutes later, the door closed quietly behind her and Robbie bowed his head. Well, that had gone down like a lead weight and no mistake. But, he asked himself, what choice did I have? The answer came back loud and clear. *You should have waited till she got over the shock of Nikki having a go at her like that.* He slammed his fist onto the table in his frustration, making the wine glasses dance. One of these days he just might get it right.

Outside in her car, Claire leaned heavily on the steering wheel. So, Nikki finally knew of her sordid past. She had only herself to blame, since she should have told her the whole story long ago – but it was too late to worry about that now. And now on top of that, her dad was about to leave her again. She supposed she shouldn't have been so surprised and hurt. After all, he had turned his back on her once when she was a child, so why shouldn't he do it again now? Pain throbbed through her. Over the last few months she had gradually let down the barriers she had built against him and allowed him back into her heart – and for what? So that he could abandon her all over again, it appeared. He hadn't changed, not really. He was still the same man who could walk away without a second glance. She ached as she thought of all the things he had told her. Of how he had missed her and Tracey and thought of them every single day. Huh! And she had fallen for it hook, line and sinker. Well, let him go and see if she cared.

One thing was for certain: she had no intentions of going down on bended knee and begging him to stay. From now on, Nikki would be the only one she would worry about. Nikki was all she had left and somehow she had to try and put things right between them.

Starting the car, Claire drove out onto the road, not even sure of where she was going. And then it came to her: she would go and see Bradley. There had never been any arrangements to visit Molly but Bradley would listen. He always did.

The journey to Jackie's home was made in silence and when they arrived, Nikki was surprised to see a number of Jackie's friends loading monitors and computer towers into the back of a large van.

'What's going on here?' she asked curiously.

Averting his eyes, Eddie shrugged. 'Ain't got a clue,' he lied as she opened the car door.

She found Jackie in the hallway loading video tapes into a large cardboard box.

'You look busy,' she commented, and he nodded before thumbing towards the lounge.

'I am, and we'll be going out shortly, so don't bother going through.' Usually he seemed pleased to see her, but tonight for some reason he was preoccupied and edgy.

'And where will we be going?' she asked.

'That's for me to know and you to find out. Wait there.' As he turned away to speak to one of the men, Nikki felt herself flushing.

Inching towards the lounge door she glanced inside. She recognised some of the blokes there from earlier visits. They were all standing by the huge mirror that took up almost half of one wall with their backs to her. They had glasses of spirits in their hands and appeared to be looking into the mirror, which she found strange, to say the very least.

'What the hell do you think you're doin', bringin' *her* here tonight?' Jackie ground out as Eddie drew abreast of him.

'You told me to bring her!' Eddie exclaimed indignantly.

'Not tonight I didn't,' Jackie said irritably. 'I said tomorrow, you idiot! Can't you get anything right?'

Eddie frowned. He could have sworn the boss had said tonight but knew better than to argue with him.

'Well, seeing as you're here you can give me a hand with this.' Jackie nodded down at the box, which he had finished packing. 'Come on, I want it in the back o' the van with the rest o' the stuff.'

Between them they lifted the box, and once they had disappeared outside with it, Nikki seized her chance and slipped silently into the lounge. The men were so intent on gazing into the mirror that they didn't even notice her as she crept up behind them.

She positioned herself so that she could peep between two of them and the sight she saw made her gasp and had the men turning towards her.

'What the fuck do you think you're doing?' one of them shouted, and at the same time the man nearest to her caught her arm in a vice-like grip.

'*Get off me, you dirty old pervert!*' Nikki screamed as Eddie and Jackie erupted into the room.

Jackie slewed to a halt as he saw Nikki struggling before spitting out, 'What the bloody hell is goin' on here?'

Nikki meanwhile had looked back towards what she realised now was a two-way mirror with a look of horror on her face. There was a young girl in the room beyond and she had just climbed from the bathtub, whilst one of the men on this side of the window was filming her. An elderly man with thick grey hair who looked vaguely familiar was drying her with a towel and touching her intimately. As she suddenly realised what was going on, shame washed over her. All the time she had spent in that room with Jackie or one or another of them, she had been being filmed. But who was the man? She knew him from somewhere, she was sure of it.

Jackie looked absolutely livid. 'Lock her in the kitchen,' he instructed the man who had hold of her. 'We'll deal with her later.'

Nikki began to kick and scream but it was no use. The man holding her was built like an all-in wrestler and dragged her along as if she weighed no more than a feather. Within seconds he had flung her into the kitchen and shut and locked the door behind her and as Nikki sagged against it, tears started to roll down her cheeks.

'Come on, it's not the end of the world,' Bradley comforted Claire as he pressed a glass of brandy into her hand. They were in the little sitting room in his flat and Bradley could see that she was as taut as a wire. 'I'm sure your dad has his reasons for leaving, and I've no doubt he'll keep in touch.'

'He needn't bother,' Claire declared with a toss of her head. 'I should never have got taken in by him in the first place when he decided to come back. He hasn't changed at all.' She deliberately didn't tell him about what had happened with Nikki. That would mean yet more ex-planations and Claire felt as if she had taken all she could for one night.

Bradley wondered what to say. Claire was obviously hurting, though she was trying desperately hard not to show it. That was something he had discovered about Claire: she was fiercely independent and found it difficult to share her feelings with anyone – except Nikki. He some-times felt jealous of the girl. It was plain that Claire worshipped the very ground she walked on, not that Nikki seemed particularly deserving of her devotion lately. It was as if she was on a self-destruct mission and it pained him to see Claire trying to cope with her tantrums and moods, though she rarely complained.

She took a long swig of her drink and held the glass out for a refill.

'Here, steady on,' Bradley joked. 'If you have much more of this you won't be fit to drive home tonight.'

'So what?' Claire shrugged. 'Would that be such a bad thing?'

His heart began to hammer. This was a one-bedroom flat as Claire knew full well, so what was she suggesting? He wanted her so much that sometimes his need for her was like a physical pain, but when and if she came to him, he had hoped it would be because she was returning the feelings he had for her, not because she was stinging about her father leaving her.

'How about I make us both a nice cup of coffee?' he suggested as he placed the brandy bottle out of her reach.

She grinned at him coyly. 'Why, Bradley, if I didn't know you better I could almost believe that you were afraid of me,' she told him teasingly.

Bradley almost tripped in his haste to get to the kitchen, and laughing now, Claire held her bare feet out to the warmth of the gas fire.

Robbie stared down into the dark garden below his bedroom window with a look of great sadness on his face. He knew that Claire had taken the news of him leaving very badly, but what choice did he have? If he stayed he would only cause even more heartache than if he left. He would have liked nothing better than to remain here for the rest of his days, keeping a watchful eye on the daughter that he had missed and yearned for over the years. But as Robbie had discovered early in life, happy endings were not meant for the likes of him. In his mind's eye he saw them working together in the first shop before it had burned down, happy and content in each other's company as the weeks had passed by. And tomorrow he would have to tell Tracey that he was leaving too; yet more unhappiness to face.

Sighing, he crossed to the bed and lay on it fully dressed. Somehow he must stay strong and follow through with his plans for both their sakes. Tracey would be all right, he was sure of it. She had a loving husband and two beautiful children to keep her occupied, but Claire . . . She had changed in the months since Christian had ended their relationship, but still, there was always Bradley waiting in the wings. The young man had made no secret of the fact that he adored her and would have married her tomorrow if Claire would just say the word. Still,

Robbie consoled himself, all was not lost. Claire seemed to have warmed to him lately, so who knew what the future might bring? His thoughts then moved on to Nikki. Now there was a lost, mixed-up little soul if ever he had seen one. She walked about as if she had the weight of the world on her shoulders, but was it really any wonder after all she had been through? And then to have to discover about Claire's past by reading her diaries. Even so, he was sure she would come through it with Claire's support. His daughter loved young Nikki unreservedly and would never give up on her, no matter what Nikki threw at her. Feeling his eyelids begin to droop, the man soon slipped into an uneasy doze.

'Right, that's about it then.' Jackie ran his sweating hands down the sides of his trousers. 'I'll fetch the car round while you go an' get Nikki from the kitchen.'

Eddie nodded, feeling more uncomfortable by the minute. He had no idea why Jackie seemed so intent on taking Nikki with him. What he *did* know was that Roxy would have his guts for garters if she ever found out he had had a hand in it. Most of the men had left by now with firm instructions to keep a very low profile until Jackie got in touch, which could be some time away. The plan to move into one of his rented houses had been brought forward when he had learned that the police were dredging the Blue Lagoon where his last unfortunate victim had finished up. Eddie was ignorant of the fact that they might find at least two more bodies and Jackie had no intention of enlightening him. As far as he was concerned, ignorance was bliss and he just wanted to lay low until everything had blown over again. It was every man for himself now, and if any of the others in the ring were to get their collars felt it was up to them to talk themselves out of it. Unfortunately, the recorded sexual offenders were always the first to be dragged in for questioning when a youngster went missing. As long as it wasn't him and they didn't mention his name, he couldn't have cared less.

He looked regretfully round at his luxurious home. The house he would be living in for the immediate future was nowhere near as comfortable as this, but then he had lived in worse and it was only a temporary arrangement after all.

Eddie went to do as he was told and arrived back with Nikki walking at the side of him. Her chin was held high and there was a defiant look in her eye.

'Now just get in an' don't argue,' Jackie told her, but to his surprise Nikki retorted, 'I have no intention of arguing. Where are we going?'

Bemused, he glanced at Eddie before replying, 'To one of me rented houses for a while.'

'Good. The longer we're gone the better, as far as I'm concerned.' During her time in the kitchen, Nikki had decided that anything was better than having to go home. After all, nothing she had done was any worse than what Claire had done before her and it would do her mum good to sweat about her for a while. She climbed into the front seat and slammed the door as Eddie scratched his head.

A thrill rippled through Jackie. He was so close to getting his revenge now, but just taking Nikki away wasn't enough. Oh no, it wasn't nearly enough for what he had suffered. He stood for some minutes as he thought of what else he could do and then Eddie's blood ran cold as he turned to him and told him, 'Get to her mum's house an' torch it!'

'WHAT?' Eddie was horrified. Burning the shop down had been one thing, but burning a house down . . . What if Claire and her father were in it?

'Aw, come on, boss. What we get up to here is one thing, but *murder*—'

'Do it, yer bastard, otherwise it might be *you* feelin' me fuckin' wrath,' Jackie spat.

Eddie paled to the colour of putty. He knew that the boss was more than capable of carrying out his threat.

'I'll be layin' low at me house in Nuneaton,' Jackie now told him. 'Keep yer distance till yer hear from me. I don't want nothin' linkin' the coppers to what's been goin' on here, do you understand?'

372

'Yes, boss.' Eddie was clearly terrified now and Jackie nodded with satisfaction as he strode towards his car. All he had to do now was wait for his revenge to be complete.

Almost opposite Claire's house a new property was in the process of being built and it was to this that Eddie now made his way. From here he had a clear view of Claire's home. The roof was on although it had no windows in at present. He saw that it was going to be a beautiful house when it was finished. Not that he was in the mood for appreciating much tonight. He entered through what would be the back door and picked his way across the tools that were strewn across the floor, which was no mean feat, for it was as black as pitch in there and freezing cold. His fingers were blue and he swiped the back of his hand across his dripping nose, cursing softly to himself. Once at the opening that would eventually be the window in what he presumed would be the lounge, he peeped across at Claire's house. It was in total darkness and he felt a wave of relief rush through him as he noted that Claire's car was not on the drive. Well, that was one good thing at least. As far as he was concerned, there was a world of difference between arson and murder.

Shifting the petrol can from one hand to the other, he glanced up and down the road. There was not a soul in sight so he hurriedly crossed the road and slipped onto the drive leading to Claire's front door. The tarmac was white with frost and he picked his way around to the back of the house, glad of the darkness that had wrapped itself around him like a cloak. It took only a couple of minutes to pick the lock of the back door. Eddie prided himself that there wasn't a lock yet that had been invented that he couldn't get into.

The warmth of the kitchen made his cheeks glow as he stood, his ears straining into the darkness. When he was sure that he was alone he stole into the hallway and entered the lounge. This too was in darkness, but from the faint light of the street lamp outside he could see that it was a lovely room. The sort his Roxy would have killed for. It was a shame

really that he had to ruin it. But still, if that was what the boss wanted . . .
Unscrewing the top off the petrol can he began to sprinkle it about. First
on the fancy curtains and the heavy Chinese rug that lay in front of the
fireplace; then over the furniture. Next he moved back into the hallway
and proceeded to do the same there. He had almost reached the kitchen
again when a light suddenly snapped on and he blinked in surprise.

'Claire, Nikki, is that you?' a man's voice from the staircase asked.

Panic gripped him as he turned, dropping the can, which immediately spilled petrol all over his shoes and the hall floor. And then a middle-
aged man appeared and gaped in surprise as he saw Eddie standing there.

'What the—?'

Eddie snatched up the first thing that came to hand – a heavy brass
candlestick that stood on a small hall table to the side of him. As the
man lunged towards him, Eddie raised it and brought it crashing down
on his head, and the man dropped like a stone at his feet, blood trickling from the gaping wound on his temple.

Trembling uncontrollably, Eddie wiped the spittle from his mouth and
looked down at the man in horror. If and when the bloke regained
consciousness he would be able to identify him and if he did, they would
lock him up and throw the key away. Putting the murder weapon down,
Eddie fumbled in his pocket for the matches that he had ready there. His
first three attempts to light one were in vain; his hands were shaking so
badly that all he managed to do was burn himself. But on the fourth
attempt the match flamed into life and after waiting a few seconds to
make sure that it was really going, Eddie flung it down onto the floor.
Almost immediately it licked greedily at the petrol spilled there and ran
like a flaming river towards the figure lying on the floor. To his horror,
the figure twitched and began to crawl towards him. Whimpering in terror,
Eddie snatched up the candlestick, then ran through the kitchen and back
out into the freezing night, slamming the door resoundingly behind him.
Once outside, he hurled the bloody weapon far into the bushes of the
house next door and ran as if Old Nick himself was snapping at his ankles.

Chapter Thirty-Four

'Come on, madam. I think it's bedtime for you,' Bradley told Claire indulgently as he slid his arm around her and helped her to her feet. 'I'll put you in my bed and I'll sleep on the settee. Would you like me to ring your dad and tell him you'll be staying over?'

'No, don't do that, he'll be ashleep,' she slurred, stifling a giggle.

'But what about Nikki?'

'She'll be all right. We had a row but when she gets home, Dad will watch her till I get back in the morning.'

Bradley sighed as he glanced at the almost empty bottle of brandy. All his attempts to sober her up with coffee had failed dismally and he had realised hours ago that she was in no fit state to drive home. Normally he would have offered to take her, but seeing as he had had one too many himself, he hardly thought that was a good idea. Not that he was anywhere near as tipsy as Claire, of course. She had been alternately going from floods of tears to hysterical laughter for the last hour now, which only went to show him how deeply upset she was at the thought of her father leaving. Bradley's eyes drew together in a deep frown. If only he could have told Claire why Robbie was *really* going – but if he did he would have broken the promise he had made to the man some weeks ago. 'Why don't you come into bed with me?' Claire giggled as he led her across the room, keeping his arm tightly around her waist.

There was nothing that Bradley would rather have done but he had a horrible feeling that if he did, Claire might well regret it in the cold light of day and he didn't want that. She was perfect to him and deserved to be treated with respect.

'There is nothing in this world I'd like more,' he told her truthfully. 'But I don't want you to come to me like this, Claire, when you're blotto. I want you to come to me because you have genuine feelings for me, as I have for you.'

Dragging him to a halt she peered up into his face. 'Do you? I mean, do you *really* have feelings for me?'

He smiled sadly. 'You must know I do. I fell in love with you the very first day I set eyes on you, and one day I hope you will do me the very great honour of becoming my wife.'

'Ish that a proposal?' Her eyes were twinkling and he found himself smiling again.

'Yes, it is, though I doubt you'll remember it in the morning.'

'Then in that case,' she tried to straighten up, 'the ansher is yesh. I will marry you, Bradley. I'm tired of being on my own.'

Planting a gentle kiss on her forehead he moved her on again. 'Well, I'm very pleased to hear it. But as I said, let's see if you remember any of this tomorrow before we book the church, eh?'

Once in his room he pulled back the duvet and swung her legs into the bed before tucking her in and kissing her again. Then crossing to the window he closed the curtains against the bitterly cold night. 'Now, is there anything you need?' he asked, turning back to her. He smiled indulgently; she was already fast asleep and as he looked down on her, all the love he felt for her shone in his eyes. Moving quietly, he crept from the room and softly closed the door between them before settling himself on the sofa.

It was during the early hours of the morning when he became aware of someone standing beside him, and opening his eyes he blinked up to see Claire staring down at him. She was dressed in her underwear and smiling.

Bewildered, he pulled himself up onto his elbow and as he did so, Claire bent to kiss him on the lips.

'Come to bed,' she murmured, and unresisting, Bradley took her hand and led her back to the bedroom where he tenderly made love to her. And all the time she was crying inside, for no matter how hard she tried, it was Christian she saw behind her closed eyes and Christian she longed for. On the one occasion when she and Christian had made love, their coming together had been urgent and passionate, yet tender. Bradley had waited so long for her that he wanted it to be perfect, but within minutes of lying with him she knew that she had made a grave mistake even though she clung to him as if he was a lifeline.

Nikki was so tired that she could barely keep her eyes open. It had been raining heavily when she arrived at the house with Jackie, only for him to discover that he had left the key behind at his bungalow. She had no idea what time it was, although she guessed that it must now be the early hours of the morning. Her jeans were soaking wet from the time she had spent cowering in the back yard of the little terraced house waiting for him to return with the key, and they clung to her legs, making her shiver uncontrollably. She wondered what Claire would do when she didn't arrive home. Shuddering at the thought, she wished Jackie would hurry up or she was sure she would freeze to death soon.

'Come on, sleepyhead. I've got work to go to even if you haven't.'

Claire blinked as Bradley threw the curtains back, allowing an eerie grey light to filter into the room. Just before dawn the rain had turned to snow and now as he glanced from the window he saw that everywhere looked clean and bright in its crisp white overcoat.

He placed a cup of tea down on the bedside table as Claire groaned and pulled herself up onto the pillows.

'Ooh, what time is it?' she asked as she stroked her forehead. She had a thumping headache but then as she thought back to how much she had drunk the evening before, she supposed it served herself right. Suddenly realising that she was in Bradley's bed she flushed and pulled the covers up under her chin.

'Oh Bradley, I'm so sorry about what happened,' she said, as embarrassment flooded through her.

'I'm not,' he told her truthfully.

Unable to look at him, she lowered her eyes. 'Look, I . . . I was feeling a bit lonely and . . . Well, it was a mistake. Can we try and forget it ever happened?'

Bradley felt as if someone was twisting a knife in his heart but he hid his hurt as he told her, 'We can, if that's what you want.'

'It is,' she told him miserably. 'I'm so sorry.' She stared guiltily up into his face. He was such a kind man.

Avoiding her eyes, Bradley made towards the door, telling her, 'Use the bathroom when you're ready. I'll go and rustle us up some breakfast.'

He closed the door between them and only then did the smile slip from his face. Just as he had thought, Claire obviously had no recollections of him asking her to marry him. And he was far too much of a gentleman to remind her – but then he thought, I'm not beaten yet. At least it was me she turned to when she needed someone. Slightly heartened, he hurried into the kitchen to see what he could find in the fridge.

Half an hour later, Claire lifted her car keys but Bradley instantly took them off her.

'Oh no, you don't,' he chided. 'After what you put away last night you're still in no fit state to drive. I'll run you home on my way to work and then I'll bring the car around this evening for you.'

'Are you quite sure?' she asked, knowing that he must think she was an awful nuisance.

Nodding, he lifted his briefcase and headed for the door and Claire meekly followed him. The journey to her home was made in silence. She was feeling very uncomfortable and could hardly bring herself to look at him. What must he think of her, dragging him off to bed like that?

They were nearing the house when she exclaimed, 'There's a police car outside! What do you think has happened?'

As she leaned forward in her seat with a look of deep concern on her face, Bradley momentarily took his hand from the steering wheel to squeeze hers reassuringly.

'I've no idea but we'll soon find out.'

The second he drew the car to a halt at the end of the drive, she spilled out onto the pavement, her eyes wide with horror as she looked at the burned-out shell that only hours before had been her home.

'Oh, my dear God.' She was crying as she ran towards a policeman who was standing outside the front door. 'My daughter, my father – are they all right?' she demanded.

Ignoring her question for now, he asked, 'Are you the owner of the house? Mrs Claire Nightingale?'

'Yes, yes I am . . . but *where* are my family?'

He beckoned to another officer who was just stepping out of the charred front door. Walking briskly, the man came to join them and again Claire babbled out her question, but she was in such a panic that the words were almost incoherent. Bradley had come to stand beside her and she clung on to his hand. Thankfully he took control of the situation and with a voice of authority he asked the policeman, 'Are Mrs Nightingale's family safe?'

'There was a gentleman brought out, sir. I believe he has been taken to Solihull Hospital, but I don't think there was anyone else in there.'

'Is my father all right?' Claire now choked out but the policeman shook his head.

'I couldn't tell you. Perhaps it would be better if you got to the hospital and asked there. A neighbour gave us your name but sadly they didn't have a contact number for you.'

Claire cursed inwardly. Why oh why, had she stayed out all night? If only she had been at home where she belonged, this might never have happened and her father and Nikki would be safe. But the policeman had said that only a man had been in the house, so where was Nikki, and was her father injured?

As she glanced towards her home her spirits sank even further. It had been such a beautiful house, but now . . . Through the shattered glass of the front window she could see what remained of the curtains flapping gently in the falling snow and beyond that, the blackened remains of what had been her elegant cream leather three-piece suite.

'Come on, Claire. I think we ought to get to the hospital now, don't you?' Bradley suggested. Seeing that she was in deep shock he went on, 'And then we'll have to find out where Nikki is. This is the only time I think I can say I'm genuinely pleased she didn't come home last night. She's probably still fast asleep tucked up at a mate's somewhere, so that's something to be grateful for at least, isn't it?'

'What?' Claire dragged her thoughts back to him with an enormous effort and slowly nodded. 'Yes, I suppose it is.'

She stood silently whilst Bradley had a muttered word with the police sergeant and then he and Claire got back into his car and drove to the hospital.

When they arrived, Bradley once again took control of the situation. He sat her in a chair in the reception area and strode off to the desk. When he returned, his face was solemn and Claire's heart began to pound so loudly that she was sure he would hear it.

'I'm afraid it doesn't look good,' he told her. 'Your father is in the Intensive Care Unit. He was very badly burned, by all accounts, but they're sending someone down to take you to him now.'

Claire gulped, and started to pray that soon she would wake up and the events of the last couple of hours would all prove to be a bad dream. Within minutes they saw a nurse in a crisp white uniform walking towards them.

'Mrs Nightingale?' she enquired, stopping in front of Claire.

Claire nodded, her eyes wide with fear.

'Would you follow me, please?'

'I'll wait here, shall I?' Bradley asked, but Claire grasped his hand and said, 'No, *please* come with me, Bradley. I don't think I can do this on my own.'

Without a word he fell into step beside her as the nurse led them through a labyrinth of corridors. After what seemed like hours she stopped in front of some double doors and smiled at Claire sympathetically.

'Your father is in here,' she told her, 'but I think you should prepare yourself. He's got third-degree burns over the majority of his body and on top of that he suffered a lot of smoke inhalation. He's quite heavily sedated at the moment, so I can only let you have a few minutes with him. Are you ready?'

Instead of concentrating on what the nurse had just told her, Claire found herself thinking how pretty the woman was and then mentally scolded herself. What was she doing? The woman had just told her that her father was seriously ill and here she was, trying to block it from her mind. All the way to the hospital she had stopped herself from thinking of what she might find there, but now she could put it off no longer.

'Is he going to die?' she forced herself to ask, and when the nurse lowered her eyes her heart broke. 'Very well. I'm ready.' She could hear the words yet had no idea that it was she who had uttered them.

The nurse opened the doors and ushered Claire and Bradley through them, and then she led them down yet another corridor towards the ICU.

'He's in here,' she told Claire. 'I'll help you get gowned up, then I'll leave you alone for a while, but if you need me just ring the bell at the side of the bed.'

'Look, Claire, I'm going to go and make a few phone calls,' Bradley told her diplomatically. 'I'll let Molly and Tracey know what's happened,

381

eh? You could do with your family around you at a time like this.' He inclined his head at the nurse and walked away.

The first sight Claire had of her father lying on the snow-white sheets brought her fist to her mouth and tears stinging to her eyes, for the poor soul lying on the bed looked nothing like Robert McMullen.

His head and most of his face was swathed in bandages, but the parts that were exposed looked raw and angry, as if someone had peeled the skin from him. There seemed to be drips and tubes running into him from every angle and he was lying so still that she suddenly became fearful that he was already dead.

'Oh Dad,' she breathed as she approached the bed, and now his eyes fluttered open and he lifted his hand feebly from the covers. And then suddenly she had covered the distance between them and she was touching his bandaged hand, afraid of disturbing the drip that was attached to it as she sank down beside him. He was hooked up to a heart monitor that slowly beeped in time with his heartbeats, and for a few moments that was the only sound in the room now as they looked deep into each other's eyes.

'What happened, Dad?' she asked eventually, but he shook his head, the effort making him gasp with pain.

'N . . . never mind that for now, pet. I . . . I have things that I need to say.' He took a great gulp of air and then went on, 'I'm sorry for dropping it on you like that – about me leavin', that is. Molly told me I should be honest with you.'

She stared at him quizzically and after a time he said, 'I don't want you getting upset about this. Me days were numbered anyway, you see. That's why I was goin', but now I feel it's only right to be upfront with you. The thing is, lass, I have Alzheimer's disease. It was diagnosed some time before I came back. I was goin' back to Scotland so I could book meself into a hospice an' not be a burden to you when I got worse.'

Claire could hardly believe what she had just heard and stared at him in horror. How could she ever have thought that he would just up and

382

leave again for no good reason? But she had to admit to herself that she had, and now guilt was added to her grief.

'Oh Dad . . .' There was so much that she wanted to say but the words were lodging in her throat and threatening to choke her. Eventually she placed a tender kiss on his burned hand as tears slid down her cheeks. 'Why didn't you tell me? I would *never* have let you go. You're my dad and if you are ill then *I'll* take care of you. You shouldn't die surrounded by strangers.'

'That's why I didn't tell you, lass,' he gasped painfully. 'I knew you would say that and I think you've gone through enough. But you know, things will work out for you in the end, an' I'm so grateful that we had this time together. That's why I'm not afraid to die. Just promise me one thing though, will you?'

Blinded by tears, she nodded. 'Anything.'

'When I'm gone, I want you to have me cremated an' then take me ashes an' scatter 'em in the same place as we scattered your mam's. Will you do that for me, pet?'

'Yes, of course I will, but not for a long, long time yet,' she told him. 'You and I still have lots of catching up to do. You're going to get better, you'll see.'

There was a wealth of sorrow shining in his eyes. 'No, lass. Now I've seen you I don't want to fight any more. You're a good girl, Claire, an' you know I love you. I . . . I always have.'

His eyelids were fluttering now and she could see that he was tired. 'I love you too, Dad,' she whispered. 'I never stopped loving you, even though at times I thought I hated you for leaving me.'

The heart monitor suddenly began to beep erratically and then suddenly the doors flew open and a doctor and nurse rushed into the room and pushed her out of the way as she screamed, 'What's the matter? What's happening?'

Another nurse appeared and manhandled her into the corridor.

'Please wait there,' she told her shortly before flying back into the

383

room. Claire could only stare helplessly at the doors that were flapping behind the nurse. She was still standing there when Bradley reappeared and grasped her hand.

'I . . . I think something is really wrong,' was all she could manage to say and then he had her head cradled against his chest as they waited for what seemed like an eternity.

Eventually the doctor opened the door and told them bleakly, 'I'm sorry. We did everything we could but I'm afraid he's gone. To be honest, I don't know how he hung on as long as he did with the injuries he sustained. I think he must have been waiting for you.'

Claire stared sightlessly past him as another little part of her heart died.

Chapter Thirty-Five

Nikki stretched painfully on the narrow single bed. She felt hot and cold all at the same time and knew that she had a fever, no doubt from the soaking she had got the night before. Turning on her side she looked around the tiny bedroom. It was sparsely furnished and none too clean either, not that she cared any more. As the events of the night flashed before her, tears squeezed from the corner of her eyes. Already she was beginning to wonder if she had done the right thing by agreeing to come here with Jackie. No doubt her mum would be beside herself with worry by now, but then the girl's face hardened. It would serve her right. Why couldn't she have been honest with her about her past?

Downstairs she could faintly hear voices, so rising from the bed she padded towards the door. She felt shivery and ill, but no doubt she'd feel better after a hot cup of tea and something to eat.

When she entered the small living room she found Eddie and Jackie in deep conversation, but as soon as she entered they stopped talking and Eddie looked furtive.

'You've got something to tell her, ain't you?' Jackie urged and Eddie cleared his throat before saying falteringly, 'Yes. Nikki, I've just been to see your mum. I were thinking, see, that she'd worry about where you were.'

As Nikki glared at him suspiciously, Eddie hurried on, 'The thing is, she weren't worried at all. In fact, she said she were sick of yer and never wanted to see you again.'

'No!' The girl shook her head in disbelief. Even though they had parted on a row she could never imagine Claire saying that.

'I'm afraid she has, an' when yer see what Jackie has to show yer, you'll see why.' Eddie shook his head sadly. 'You see, she happened across something that concerns you, and when she'd seen it she said she had washed her hands of you. From now on there's only me an' Jackie to watch out for you, take my word fer it.'

'So why did Jackie lock me in the kitchen before I agreed to come here then?' she sputtered indignantly.

''Cos he were tryin' to look out for you, yer silly little mare. Now sit still and shut up an' you'll soon see why.'

And so Nikki sat back in her seat and waited while Eddie inserted a video into the video recorder and for the next five minutes she watched in shock as she saw herself being used by the men at Jackie's bungalow.

'Oh my God!' she gasped, feeling nauseous, and when Eddie nodded she started to cry. What must her mum have thought, watching this? It was too awful to contemplate. No wonder she had disowned her. Tears slid down her cheeks and she wished that she could just go back in time and start all over again. But it was too late for that now and suddenly all the fight went out of her.

From now on she would have to do just what Jackie told her. But how had her mum got hold of the film? Then Nikki decided she didn't really care any more. Ever since the day her father had first laid his hands on her she had known deep down that there would be no happy ever after ending for her. She was soiled goods: who would ever want her when they found out? There were compensations, however, to living with Jackie. For a start-off she could have drugs whenever she felt like it and she wouldn't have to go to school ever again. Without a word she rose from her seat and made her way back up to her room.

386

Once alone she wondered what Eddie and Jackie would be doing now. No doubt they would still be watching videos – films like the one she had just seen. The one that had made her stomach churn and finally made her mum turn against her. She had no idea why Jackie had suddenly decided to stay here in one of his rented houses instead of the bungalow, but no doubt he had his reasons. He had told her it was only for a short time, so at least she wouldn't be stuck here for good. Compared to the houses Nikki had been brought up in, this place was a dump. Cheap carpets, cheap curtains, tacky furniture. It was a marvel that anyone had ever paid rent for it, but then she supposed that there were those who weren't as financially well off as Jackie and her mum had always been.

She licked her dry lips. Part of her wanted to lie down and go back to sleep, but she had a raging thirst on her. It was no surprise; drugs always had that effect on her. Dragging herself from the bed she made for the door. Her Levi jeans had dried on her and now they clung to her thin legs like a damp second skin. Shivering, she descended the stairs again, trying hard not to admit to the fact that she was missing her mum and her grandad already.

'Oh love, I can hardly take it in!' Molly exclaimed as she wrapped her arms protectively about Claire. 'Do the police have any idea at all how the fire started?'

When Claire continued to stare off into space as if she had not even heard her, Bradley told Molly, 'I don't think so, not yet. No doubt they'll be looking into it today.'

Molly and Tracey had come straight to the hospital following Bradley's phone calls and now Molly declared, 'Well, let's get her back to my place, eh? The poor love is obviously in shock and she can't go home, can she? Then when we've got her settled we'll set about finding out where Nikki is.'

'If you don't mind, Molly, I'd rather she came home with me.' Tracey spoke up, causing them all to glance towards her in surprise. Tracey hadn't spoken to Claire for months yet here she was, offering her a temporary home. The young woman had the good grace to flush. 'Well, she *is* my sister,' she said defensively, 'and I have got two empty bedrooms so it makes sense for her to come to me until we know what's going to happen at least. We've both lost our dad so we might be able to prop each other up.'

Seeing the sense in what she said, Molly nodded. What a mess everything was. Nikki had gone awol, Claire's house had burned down, and poor Robbie had passed away all in the space of a few short hours. It just went to show, she thought, that you never knew what life had up its sleeve waiting for you. Both Tracey's and Claire's eyes were already red-rimmed from crying, so now Molly told them bossily, 'Come on, let's get you both home. There's nothing to be gained by hanging around here any longer. We can make the funeral arrangements from there.' Glancing towards the room where Robbie's body lay, she made the sign of the cross on her chest.

Back at her car, she turned to Bradley and asked, 'Shouldn't you be at work?'

He flashed her a weak grin. 'Yes, I should as it happens – hours ago, but I could hardly leave Claire to it, could I? I've spoken to my boss and he's fine about it and told me to take the rest of the day off to look after Claire. He grew very fond of her during the time she worked for us.'

'Then in that case, perhaps you could go back to Claire's and give the police the address of where she'll be staying? I've no doubt they'll need to talk to her at some stage today. And then you could have a snoop round and see if you can find Nikki.' Taking a scrap of paper from her bag she hastily scribbled down Tracey's address and passed it to him.

'Consider it done,' he told her, and as he walked away, Molly found herself thinking, Eeh, if only Claire could see what a catch he would be. Sighing, she then clambered into her car and drove the two young women back to Tracey's house.

It was almost lunchtime when Bradley rapped on the door of Poppy's home on the Chelmsey Park Estate. A woman in a faded dressing-gown opened the door and peered suspiciously at his smart suit.

'I'm sorry to trouble you,' Bradley began, giving her a charming smile, 'but I'm a friend of Claire Nightingale – Nikki's mum. I believe Nikki and your daughter Poppy are friends, and I was wondering if Nikki might have stayed here last night?'

Roxy smothered a sigh of relief. She had thought he was a plain-clothes copper. 'I can truthfully say we ain't seen hide nor hair o' Nikki for weeks,' she told him, and then seeing the look of concern on his face she asked, 'She ain't in any bother, is she?'

'I don't know,' he said truthfully, 'but if she goes home she's in for a shock because her house burned down last night. Her grandfather was inside it at the time and sadly he died in hospital early this morning.'

'Oh, my dear God!' Roxy's hand flew to her mouth as her heart sank into her down-at-heel slippers. Suddenly she remembered the smell of petrol that had entered the bedroom with Eddie in the early hours of the morning and a gut feeling told her that he had had some-thing to do with it. Keeping her emotions under control with a great effort she asked, 'Are you quite sure that Nikki weren't in the house as well?'

'Quite sure,' he told her. 'But look, if she should turn up here, could you tell her that her mum is staying at her sister's in Nuneaton? I'll write her address and my phone number down for you.' He handed her one of his cards after hastily scribbling Tracey's address on the back of it.

She watched him stride away before closing the door and staring down at the card in her hand. After a moment or two she slipped it into her pocket before looking thoughtfully up the stairs where Eddie was still sleeping in their bed. If he had been the cause of the fire, then he had also been responsible for a murder, that was how the law would look at it. At that moment Poppy appeared at the head of the stairs.

'Who was that?' she yawned.

'Oh, just somebody lookin' fer Nikki,' Roxy flapped her hand dismissively. 'She didn't go home last night. You haven't seen her, have yer?'

Poppy shook her head as she passed her mother on the way to the kitchen and slowly Roxy climbed the stairs and made her way into the bedroom. Eddie was spark out, his mouth gaping open like a goldfish. Crossing to the clothes that he had discarded in a heap on the bedroom floor she lifted his jeans. Her eyes smarted as the smell of petrol assailed her nostrils. Hastily she went through his pockets. There was a small amount of change and a piece of paper with a Nuneaton address written on it. She pocketed them before bundling his clothes up and heading back down the stairs where she rammed them into the washing machine. She then went back upstairs and snatched up his shoes. They stunk of petrol too so she would soak them in a bucket of hot soapy water. It would be tough luck if it ruined them. Better that than have his collar felt. Poppy was staring at her as if she had taken leave of her senses.

'They're me dad's Ben Sherman shoes,' she told her in exasperation. 'He'll slaughter yer if you ruin 'em.'

'Well, he'll have to slaughter me then, won't he?' Roxy told her with a nonchalant shrug. 'You know what yer dad's feet smell like. I couldn't sleep fer the stink last night an' I can hardly put 'em in the washer, can I?'

'Rather you than me,' Poppy giggled but she soon stopped when Roxy asked her, 'An' why ain't you at school again, miss? I'm sick o' the truant officer knockin' on me door. Did yer know that I could get sent to nick if yer keep bunkin' off?'

Poppy stared back at her sullenly, 'I shall be left soon so what's the point?' she sniffed. 'I hate the fuckin' place.'

'You watch yer language, miss,' Roxy scolded her as she slopped some tepid tea from the pot into a grimy mug. 'An' when you've had yer breakfast yer can get your arse up them stairs an' tidy that shit tip of a room up. If you're stayin' off school I may as well give you a few jobs to do.'

'Huh! I'd 'ave gone to school if I'd known yer were goin' to give me so much grief,' Poppy declared sulkily and with that she flounced out of the room leaving Roxy alone with her disturbing thoughts. There would be no chance to talk to Eddie while Poppy was in. Roxy knew that the girl had ears like an elephant and she didn't want what she had to say to Eddie to be overheard. The lads were probably still in bed too, and if they were following their usual pattern they likely wouldn't surface till lunchtime. Lately they were becoming as big a pair of wasters as their dad. The only one who seemed to live by any rules in this house was Katie, and Roxy had seen her off to school in the minibus looking bright as a button hours ago. She sighed heavily. She'd had such high hopes when she had married Eddie all those years ago. They were going to live in a cottage with roses round the door and live happily ever after. Instead of that, what had she got?

Her thoughts moved on to Nikki and now tears started to her eyes. Why would Eddie have burned her house down, and was the child all right? She had missed her in the weeks since she had stopped coming to see them, more than she would admit. If Eddie had done one single thing to harm a hair on her head, she would . . . She stopped her thoughts from taking that road, it was too dangerous – and in that moment she realised with a shock that the love that she had once felt for him had finally died. The only reason she was still here now were the three young people upstairs, for lazy as they were, they were still her children and she loved them. But one day in the not too distant future they would fly the nest and then she would take Katie and clear off, make something of their lives. First though, she would find out what hand Eddie had had in the fire at Nikki's house and it would be God help him if he couldn't come up with a good explanation.

Nikki paused outside the door. It was slightly ajar and she could hear Jackie in the room beyond having a conversation with someone on his mobile.

'So, they found the other body then?' she heard him say and her stomach turned over.

'Right,' he went on. 'Just make sure as everyone stays schtum if they get a visit from the Old Bill. An' don't let none of 'em know where I am, have yer got that?'

There were more muttered words but then silence. Slowly she pushed the door open and walked into the small kitchen.

As he eyed her up and down she flushed with embarrassment. She knew she must look a sight but she didn't even have so much as a hairbrush to tidy herself up. Added to that her stomach was churning and she felt sick.

'There's a loaf in the bread bin,' he informed her shortly. 'Make yerself a bit o' toast an' then get yerself a bath. You have a visitor comin' tonight.'

Nikki gulped. No doubt the visitor would be a male and she knew exactly what Jackie would expect her to do with him. He tossed her a spliff and she lit it eagerly. A few more of these through the day and she wouldn't much care by tonight. She thought of her mum but pushed the thought away. Her mum was in the past now; Claire didn't want her any more and because Nikki knew that she was bad through and through, she didn't really blame her. So why then, she wondered, was she missing her so much?

'So what you are saying then, is that the fire was lit deliberately?'

The policeman nodded at Bradley. They were standing in the hallway of Claire's home and the officer told him, 'No doubt about it, sir.

Forensics have been in here for most of the day and they're quite sure. Someone forced the back door then tipped petrol about before setting light to the place. Going by the wound on Mr McMullen's head, I would think he disturbed whoever it was and they clobbered him and left him there to die before setting fire to the place.'

'Good God!' Bradley was horrified. To think that the fire had been started by an accident was bad enough, but to know that it was arson was another thing altogether. How would Claire take this second attack on her life and property? And who could be behind it?

'What will happen now?' he asked sombrely.

'Well, there will have to be a post-mortem on the man who died, and it will be treated as arson.'

'I see.' Bradley stared around at the ruined home. Robbie had worked so hard on redecorating it; he would have been heartbroken if he could see it now. Pulling the collar of his overcoat up he inclined his head at the policeman. 'Thank you, officer. I'm going to get over to Nuneaton now but you have my number if I can assist in any way. Good evening.'

'Evening, sir.'

Bradley walked down the drive and climbed wearily into his car before running his hand across his eyes. He felt as if he could have slept for a month, so he could only imagine how Claire must be feeling. He would get over to Tracey's, have one last look at her, and then get himself home to bed.

The snow was still falling in soft white flakes that sparkled like diamonds in the light of the street lamps when he pulled up outside Tracey's home. The instant he walked through the door, the twins, who were fresh out of the bath and looking totally adorable in their little pyjamas, launched themselves at him with cries of glee.

Callum was sitting in the lounge reading a newspaper and he nodded towards the kitchen. 'Tracey's in there,' he informed him. 'She's rustling us all up something to eat, though I don't think any of us much feel like it. You're more than welcome to join us.'

Bradley hadn't eaten all day and his stomach growled with hunger at the appetising smells that were issuing from the kitchen.

'I might just take you up on that offer,' he told Callum as he lifted the twins one onto each hip and hurried towards the kitchen.

Tracey was standing at the stove stirring a huge panful of bolognese sauce and he instantly saw the stress on her face as she smiled at him weakly.

'That was good timing,' she said. 'This will be ready to serve up in a minute. You will stay and join us, won't you?'

'I'd love to,' he told her as he placed the twins back on the floor. They instantly scampered away to join their father in the lounge and now that they were alone, Bradley asked, 'Where's Claire?'

Tracey thumbed towards the ceiling as she strained the spaghetti into a colander at the sink.

'I sent her upstairs for a lie-down about an hour ago. She looked as if she was about to drop. But has there been any news? And is there any sign of Nikki yet?'

'In answer to your first question, yes, there has been some news and it's not good, I'm afraid. I just came from Claire's house and an officer there informed me that they have now established that the fire was started deliberately. It looks like someone broke in and your poor father disturbed them. They must have hit him with something and knocked him out and then set light to the place and left him there to die, the lousy bastards.'

'Oh no.' Tracey began to sob as she tried to picture it in her mind's eye.

'As for Nikki, there's still no sign of her though I shouldn't get overly concerned about that just yet. I happen to know that she's been going off on walkabouts for months, so no doubt she'll turn up when she's good and ready. She's been leading Claire a merry old dance.'

'But why didn't she tell me then?' Tracey bit down on her lip as she realised how ridiculous the question must sound. She hadn't even acknowledged Claire for weeks, so how could she expect her to confide in her? Guilt washed over her. Looking back, she had been very harsh on her sister. It must have taken Claire a lot of courage to confide in her about her past as she had, and what had she done? Instead of trying to understand what had led Claire to a life on the streets, she had turned her back on her just when she had needed her most.

Bradley came to stand beside her and put his hand on her shoulder. 'Don't whip yourself, Tracey,' he urged. 'We all do things that we live to regret. Your sister left you when you were very young so she won't hold it against you that you didn't welcome her back with open arms. But you've both lost your father and you can help each other through this now. I think that's what Robbie would have wanted. He loved you both very much, you know.'

Tracey realised in that moment that Bradley had no idea of Claire's past and she had no intention of enlightening him. That would be up to Claire, when she felt ready. Her chin drooped to her chest and now her tears spilled freely. 'Claire and Nikki will have a home here for as long as they need it,' she told him. 'When Nikki decides to put in an appearance, that is. But how will she know where Claire is when she arrives home?'

'Don't worry. The police are going to be in there for a couple of days,' he assured her. 'And I've given them this address. She's pulled this stunt before so no doubt she'll turn up sooner or later and they said they'll run her over here as soon as she does. But now, would you like me to go and get Claire for her meal?'

'Yes, that would be lovely, thank you, Bradley. I really don't know what we would have done without you today. She's in the second bedroom on the right along the landing.'

Bradley had half-expected Claire to be fast asleep, worn out with the day's events, but he found her lying on the bed in the dark staring dry-eyed up at the ceiling.

It had been a long hard day for her; not only had she had to face seeing her father die, she had then spent the rest of the day being interviewed by the police.

She looked towards him when he entered the room as if it was the most natural thing in the world to see him there, and before he had a chance to say anything she asked, 'Has Nikki shown up yet?'

'No, I'm afraid she hasn't, but try not to worry. She'll breeze in when she's good and ready.'

She nodded as he cleared his throat and went on, 'I'm afraid I have some news for you, Claire, concerning the fire. I just came from your house and the investigating officer told me that they are treating it as arson.'

Pulling herself up onto her elbow she gaped at him incredulously. '*What?* You mean the fire was started deliberately – like the one at the shop?'

'Yes, there's no doubt about it, apparently. Someone broke in through the back door and poured petrol about and then . . .' His voice trailed away as he saw the stricken look on her face. If what he was saying was true, it meant that her father had been murdered. But who would do such a thing? Since coming to live back in the Midlands, Claire had taken a pride in keeping herself very much to herself. Now as she thought back to the fire at the shop she and her father had refurbished, it suddenly occurred to her that the two incidents might be linked. She shuddered. Someone, somewhere obviously wished her harm . . . but who could it be? Was her past coming back to haunt her yet again?

Chapter Thirty-Six

'Is there anywhere else at all where you think she might be?' the police-woman asked Claire as she scribbled frantically in her notebook. It was now four days since the fire and still there was no sign of Nikki, so Claire had had no choice but to report her daughter missing. By now, she was almost beside herself with fear and worry. If anything should happen to the girl now, Claire felt as if she might give up; she would have nothing left to live for. It seemed that for the whole of her life, just as she had thought things were beginning to go right for her, something had happened to snatch her happiness away and now she was growing tired of trying.

'I've tried every single person I can think of who she knows,' Claire told her resignedly, 'but no one seems to have seen her since the night of the fire.' As a frightening possibility occurred to her she blanched. 'You don't think that whoever started the fire might have taken her, do you?'

The policewoman glanced uncomfortably at her colleague. 'We can't rule that out as a possibility,' she admitted, 'but try not to worry too much just yet. By your own admission, Nikki had taken to staying out, so it could be that she's just lying low at a friend's somewhere. I'll get her description on air right now though and you can rest assured that we'll have every car keeping an eye out for her.' She looked at Claire. 'I know this is hard for you, but I have to ask, had you and Nikki had a row before she left home that evening?'

Claire blinked back tears of shame. 'I'm afraid we had. To be honest, Nikki had been acting strangely for some time. I put it down to teenage moods at first but then . . . Well, I had my suspicions that she might be on drugs. I never found anything to substantiate that feeling but, she just wasn't herself, if you know what I mean. The row wasn't about that, though. It was . . . personal.'

'I see.' The policewoman again scribbled furiously in her book for a moment before snapping it shut. Whatever the row had been about, it was obvious that Mrs Nightingale wasn't going to elaborate about it.

'Thank you, Mrs Nightingale,' she said. 'You have been most helpful and I promise we will keep you closely informed of anything we hear that might lead us to Nikki. Now if you will excuse us, we ought to go and get her description out over the radio.'

The police officers rose and headed for the door. Tracey let them out then turning to Claire she asked, 'How about a cuppa? I could certainly do with one.'

Callum was upstairs reading the twins a bedtime story and now that the police had gone the room was unnaturally quiet.

Tracey drifted away to put the kettle on as Claire rose and walked towards the large picture window that overlooked the front garden. The lawn was now beneath several inches of snow and she shuddered. What if Nikki had met with an accident and was lying out there somewhere? She would not survive for long in this weather.

Tracey interrupted her thoughts when she re-entered the room bearing a tray of tea and biscuits. Claire smiled at her tremulously. Over the last few days the closeness that had once existed between the sisters had returned. That was the only good thing to have come from this whole sorry mess, the fact that she and her sister were finally back on good terms again. Tracey had gone out of her way to make Claire feel welcome. She had lent her some clothes and held her while she had wept. She had listened to her worries over Nikki and they had cried together over the loss of their father. Only today someone from the insurance company had come to see Claire about the house. Thankfully it had been well insured but he had told her that the fire damage was extensive and had explained that it could be months before the place was habitable again. The downstairs was the worst. Nearly all of the furniture was ruined as well as all of the kitchen, and the whole place would need re-plastering and redecorating. Claire had listened half-heartedly, wondering if she would ever be able to live there again after what had happened. The house was tainted now as far as she was concerned, as she had told Tracey when the insurance man had left.

'Then why don't you sell it when they've put it to rights and come back to live in Nuneaton?' Tracey had suggested.

Claire could see the sense in what her sister said but at the moment she was too worried about Nikki to think that far ahead. She could not sleep or eat for fretting, and Tracey was concerned to see that Claire appeared to have aged years in days. The weight was dropping from her and her eyes looked deep and sunken like those of an old, old woman. Now she wondered how she could have ever felt jealous of the woman standing beside her, and much as it hurt to admit it to herself, she *had* been jealous of Claire. Her older sister had always appeared so poised and sophisticated – nothing like the wreck she saw before her now. Thinking back, Tracey realised that Claire's decline had started after Christian had finished their relationship. She had lost her sparkle and gone slowly downhill.

Bradley had been wonderful and Tracey wished with all her heart that Claire could just open her eyes and see how much he cared for her. He had come every evening straight from work and nothing was too much trouble for him. Yet Claire scarcely seemed to know that he was there and seemed to be retreating into her own little world where none of them could reach her as she waited for news of Nikki.

Sighing, Tracey placed the tray down and slid her arm about her sister's frail shoulders and there they stood staring out into the dark snowy night.

'How about some tea then, eh?' Tracey asked after a while.

Claire shook her head. 'No, thanks, but I wouldn't say no to something stronger.' She lit yet another cigarette and inhaled on it deeply. Tracey pursed her lips before crossing to the drinks cabinet and taking out a bottle of brandy. Maybe this was the only way Claire could dull what was happening to her. It certainly appeared that way from the amount of spirits she was consuming. Only last night she'd had to send Callum down to the off-licence to restock the cabinet. Still, Tracey told herself, just so long as it gets her through it, and she poured out what she knew would the first of many generous measures that evening and handed it to her sister.

'Tidy yourself up. You have a visitor comin' in an hour.'

Nikki stared up into Jackie's cold eyes. Her own eyes were dull and lacklustre, and she had never felt so ill in her life. Ever since the night he had brought her here she had alternated between being soaked with sweat and shivering with cold. She knew that Jackie had noticed but chose to ignore the fact, and she had given up telling him how ill she felt. Apart from giving her the odd meal, which she was unable to eat, he had totally ignored her. He had spent the most part of every day sitting in front of the television watching videos that he had filmed back in his bungalow. Pictures of young girls and boys being sexually violated by the men who Nikki had thought were his friends. She was amongst the children on the films and now she understood why her mum had turned her back on her. Now she looked at him and dared to say, 'I don't think I'm well enough to have a visitor tonight.' She began to cough so violently that her small frame shook.

His lips curled back from his teeth. 'Stop bein' such a baby,' he snapped. 'All you've got is a little cold. Pull yerself together. You're neither use nor ornament to me in this state.'

Nikki clutched at her chest. It hurt her to breathe and every breath she took seemed to make the sweat stand out on her brow. For the first time, Jackie looked uncertain as he stared down at her. She did look ill, he was forced to admit, but what could he do about it? There was no way he could get a doctor in to look at her, that would only land him in bother.

'I'll tell you what. I'll let you off tonight but I want you better by tomorrow, do you hear me?'

She nodded miserably and watched as he turned and walked from the room, slamming the door behind him. Nikki stared up at the cracked ceiling as tears squeezed from the corner of her eyes and she wanted her mum so much that it hurt. It suddenly didn't matter any more about finding her birth mother. She realised now that Claire had been her real mother ever since the day they had met, in everything but name. And what had she done? She had thrown all the kindnesses Claire had ever shown her back in her face. But it was too late to do anything about it now. Eddie had told her that Claire never wanted to see her again and after the way she had behaved over the last few months, Nikki couldn't blame her.

The sweat had dried on her brow and she was shivering uncontrollably as the pain in her chest increased. Her lips were cracked and dry and she wanted a drink but felt too weak to get out of bed to fetch one, so instead she curled herself up into a ball and prayed that she would soon fall asleep so that she wouldn't be aware of the pain any more, or better still that she could die so she would never have to feel any more pain again. As sleep claimed her she saw herself in her mind's eye with Claire walking along a sandy beach. Cassidy was frolicking ahead of them on his three legs and they were laughing. Her last conscious thought was how much she would like to turn back the clock so that they could be happy again, but even in her feverish state she knew that it was too late for a happy ending for her or Claire. Both of their pasts had seen to that.

Poppy was bored. Roxy had gone into town some time ago, her dad was down at the Pig and Whistle and the boys were out. Katie was off school with a slight cold and Poppy had promised to look after her until her mum got back. Katie was sitting on the hearthrug playing with her dolls and so Poppy wandered upstairs. She had seen her dad pushing some videos under his bed the other day and wondered if there would be anything worth watching amongst them. Kneeling down, she peered under the bed, wrinkling her nose as the smell of unwashed socks and underwear hit her. There was enough fluff under there to stuff a pillow, along with bits of old food that was growing mould on it. But then her eyes lit on a black bin bag. Reaching over, she pulled it towards her. Sure enough she found about half a dozen videos inside it. They were all in cases and looked for all the world like blank videos. There was nothing written on them to tell her what they were, but knowing her dad, they would probably be blueys. She had caught him watching them more than once and had always wondered where he hid them.

Grinning, she carried a few downstairs and slotted one into the video recorder. Katie didn't even look up, so Poppy settled herself into a chair and hit the play button. The next second her eyes almost started from her head and her mouth gaped in horror. It was then that she heard a key in the front door and her mother's voice floated to her. 'I'm back, love.'

Roxy appeared in the doorway of the front room with a heavy carrier bag loaded with food in each hand, looking very pleased with herself. 'Yer dad had a bit of a win on the horses yesterday,' she told Poppy with a grin, 'so I thought I'd treat us to a bit o' steak for dinner today. I nicked some notes out of his pocket while he were asleep last night. What he don't know won't hurt him, will it? The tight git, he wouldn't have . . .' Her voice trailed away as she saw the look on Poppy's face and dropping her bags she hurried across to her to ask with concern, 'What's up, love? You look like you've seen a ghost.'

Poppy gulped as she dragged her eyes away from the screen to stare up at her mother then without so much as a word she fumbled to turn the video off with shaking fingers.

'Oh no you don't, miss. What's on there that you don't want me to see?' As Roxy looked towards the screen the colour drained from her face and her hand flew to her mouth in denial.

'It . . . it weren't my fault, Mam, honest it weren't. Dad made me go an'—'

'Oh dear God, no. He wouldn't sink that low, he *wouldn't*.' Roxy reeled back. She had never been under any illusions that Poppy was a saint, but even so she was still little more than a child at the end of the day, and for her own father to put her to this was unthinkable. What sort of a monster was he?

Suddenly Poppy was afraid. Her mother looked almost demented, horrified at what she was seeing yet unable to drag her eyes away from it. It was Poppy on the screen with a man who was touching and fondling her bare body as the girl shrank away from him. Snatching the remote control from Poppy's hand, Roxy snapped it off before barking, 'Get yourself an' Katie away next door to Vera's. An' *don't* come back till I come to fetch yer. Tell Vera I've got some trouble on – she'll understand.'

Normally, Poppy would have argued but something about the set of Roxy's face made her scramble to her feet and grasp Katie's hand. She had never seen her mother like this before and prayed that she would never see her like it again, for she looked like a woman possessed.

Without a word she led Katie towards the door, where she paused when Roxy told her, 'Not a word about what you've just seen, do you understand? I'm goin' to deal with it.'

Poppy nodded and then dragged Katie out into the snow with a sinking feeling deep in the pit of her stomach. It would be God help her dad when he decided to come home, if she was any judge.

Once alone, Roxy turned the video on again and within minutes she had leaned over and vomited all across the carpet. When she could bear to watch no more she ejected it and inserted another. This time she saw another young girl who looked to be about fifteen with two men who were soaping her in a large bathtub. Again she ejected the video and snapped another one in. As a picture of Nikki appeared on the screen, Roxy sank onto the nearest chair and now tears of despair washed down her cheeks as she watched the naked girl struggling into a school uniform that was laid out neatly on a bed for her. She saw a man enter the room from a door behind her and the look of resignation on Nikki's face as she stared towards him. Unable to bear to watch any more, Roxy hit the stop button and buried her face in her hands and now the upset was replaced by white-hot rage that seemed to consume every inch of her. How could Eddie have done it? she asked herself. She had always known he was no Snow White, but this . . . He was part of a paedophile ring, there could be no other explanation for it, and he had even sacrificed his own daughter to it.

His own daughter!

A strange sort of calm came over her as she walked into the kitchen to wait for him. It was almost an hour later when he came in from the pub with a drunken grin on his face and a sway on.

'Hello, me little kitten,' he greeted her. 'Why don't yer come an' give yer old man a nice likkle kiss, eh?'

'Come with me,' she told him, and as the smile slid from his face he followed her unsteadily along the hallway into the front room, wrinkling his nose as he looked at the pile of vomit on the floor.

'What's been goin' on 'ere?' he demanded, but Roxy ignored him as she hit the play button on the remote control. The moment he saw what was on the television screen he was instantly sober.

'Roxy, I can explain. It ain't what yer think,' he spluttered as he held his hands out towards her.

'No? An' I suppose the one wi' our Poppy on ain't what I think neither, is it?' Her eyes were flashing fire and in that moment she felt a hate so intense and all-consuming that it frightened her.

Eddie gulped. 'Look, let me explain,' he pleaded as she faced him across the room.

'I don't think you need to. I reckon that just about says it all,' she ground out. 'I always knew you were capable o' bad things, Eddie, but

I never thought you'd sink to sacrificin' yer own flesh an' blood to somethin' as sick as that. The thievin' an' the stolen goods, even the drugs, I could turn a blind eye to 'cos I ain't never been a saint or whiter than white meself. But there's a line yer don't cross an' *you* just crossed it. Even an animal will defend its own. Now where is Nikki? I know it were you as burned her house down an' the girl is still missin' – an' I have a feelin' you know where she is.'

She was coming towards him now and suddenly he was afraid. He had never seen Roxy like this in all the years they had been together.

'Look, I had no choice, the boss made me do it,' he choked out. 'He's got Nikki at one of his rented houses in Nuneaton. I owed him money an' if I hadn't—' He stopped abruptly when she raised her arm and he saw the glint of a knife. And then it was flashing down towards him and he felt a coldness in his chest. Roxy yanked it out of him and as his hand flew to the wound he felt hot blood trickling through his fingers though strangely there was no pain.

She was lunging at him again and now his knees started to buckle beneath him and a curious warmth was bubbling from the sides of his mouth. Again and again the knife flashed up and down until at last he lay still at her feet. Only then did she stand and stare breathlessly down at the remains of her husband. She felt nothing – no remorse, no sorrow; he might have been no more than a slab of meat on a butcher's block. She had done what had to be done and now she needed to find Nikki. To make sure that she was safe. What was it Eddie had said? *The boss has her at one of his rented houses in Nuneaton.* But where could it be? She suddenly remembered the scrap of paper she had taken from his jeans pocket on the night he had come home reeking of petrol. That had a Nuneaton address on it, she was sure of it. Calmly she made her way to their bedroom where she took the paper from her dressing-gown pocket. It was worth a try, she supposed, or should she phone the young man who had called the other day looking for Nikki and tell him where she was? Deciding on the latter she went back downstairs. She had two phone calls to make, the first to Bradley and then one to the police. Still remarkably calm, she took up the card Bradley had given her and dialled his number.

Bradley was in the office when the call came through and he listened to Roxy intently.

'You'd better come round to my place,' she told him. 'There's somethin' I need to show you. I think I know where Nikki is, but I reckon you'll need to involve the police.'

The phone then went dead in his hand and after staring at it for a moment he snatched up his jacket and headed towards the door.

'Bradley, where are you going!' Mr Dickinson exclaimed. 'You're due in court in an hour.'

'Sorry, you'll have to ring and ask for an adjournment,' Bradley flung across his shoulder and then he was clattering away down the stairs as the elderly solicitor gawped after him open-mouthed.

When he screeched to a halt in front of Roxy's house a short while later the car slewed around on the snow, but heedless of how badly it was parked, Bradley ran down the path and through the front door that she had left swinging open for him.

When he looked into the lounge, he had to grasp the doorframe for support as shock coursed through him. He was no doctor, but from where he was standing it looked like Eddie Miller was as dead as a dodo.

'I killed him,' Roxy told him matter-of-factly, then clicking on the video she pointed towards it and told him, 'Because o' this . . . look.'

His eyes followed hers and he felt vomit rise to his throat as a vision of Nikki, stark naked, appeared on the screen.

'The bastard let 'em have my Poppy an' all,' she told him, 'but I reckon I know where they've got Nikki. I found this address in Eddie's pocket. It were him that burned down Nikki's home an' I would bet he had a hand in gettin' her to where she is now. If I were you I'd take the police with you. God only knows what state you'll find the poor little mare in, though.'

And as he stared back at her, unmoving, she snapped, 'Well, don't just stand there gawpin'! Call the police. They'll need to come here an' all. But will yer just do one thing for me?'

Bradley nodded numbly.

'Will yer wait with me till they get here? I . . . I don't want to be alone here wi' . . .' As her voice trailed away and the tears finally sprang to her eyes, he reached out and gently stroked her arm.

'Of course I will,' he promised, then reaching over, he dialled 999 with shaking fingers.

Chapter Thirty-Seven

As Eddie's body was carried out to the ambulance and Roxy was led to a waiting police car in handcuffs, the sergeant standing in the hallway turned to Bradley.

'Right then, have you called Nikki's mother?'

'Not yet.'

'In that case it might be best if we went to this address first and checked it out.'

The Millers' grubby terraced house was swarming with policemen who appeared to be tearing it apart. The video that Roxy had shown to Bradley was already in one of numerous plastic bags that would be taken away and used as evidence.

Sergeant Jones turned to a young constable and told him, 'Get round to the local magistrate and ask for a warrant to search this house. And radio through for at least two more cars to join us. And step on it, lad.'

'Yes, Sarge!' The young officer almost ran down the slippery path in his haste to do as he was told, and Sergeant Jones turned to Bradley.

'I've dealt with some cases in my time,' he said sadly, 'but this one takes the biscuit. Fancy being called out to a murder *and* a paedophile ring all in one day!' He had met Bradley numerous times in court and so knew that it was safe to talk off the record to him. 'There are some sick bastards about, aren't there?' he went on. 'Between you and me, I feel sorry for that woman that we've just arrested. If I were to discover that someone had just done that to one of my kids, I reckon I would have committed murder an' all. But now what's that address?'

Bradley silently passed it to him.

'Thirty-eight Queen Victoria Street. Um – I reckon that's off Edward Street,' the sergeant remarked. At that moment the young constable flew back into the hallway, almost going his length as he skidded on the snow that was still falling thickly.

'The cars are on their way, sir,' he informed him and as one, the men walked out to wait for them.

The journey to Nuneaton took an hour, for the icy conditions hindered their progress, but at last the three cars turned into Queen Victoria Street and parked at the end of it, as they had been instructed.

Sergeant Jones climbed from the car and looked up and down. The road consisted of rows of terraced houses that all fronted directly onto the pavement with nothing much to distinguish one from another apart from the different curtains that hung at the windows.

Walking to the car behind him, he leaned into the driver's window and told the four policemen inside, 'Get yourselves round to the back entrance and go in that way. Break the door down if you have to.'

'Right, gov.'

The car immediately started back up, did a three-point turn and went back the way it had come. The sergeant waited a few moments then moved to each of the other cars and instructed his team to get out and follow him on foot.

They set off as quickly as they could, aware that by now, net curtains were twitching up and down the length of the street.

Once outside number 38, the sergeant nodded at the tallest of the policemen. 'Give it a good loud knock and if it hasn't been answered within one minute, break it down.'

The officer nodded, glad to note that the door in question was an old wooden affair that looked as if a strong gust of wind would blow it in. It would have been a different matter altogether if it had been double-glazed, as most of the doors were now.

There was no door knocker so he rapped on it loudly with his fist. From within they could hear the sound of a television set, but no one came to answer the door. The sergeant waited impatiently, then grunted, 'Do your worst.'

The young policeman stood well back, took a deep breath and then lunged at the door. As his shoulder connected with it, the sound of wood cracking echoed down the deserted street and the door flew in, bouncing on its hinges.

The officers surged forward, just in time to see a man running towards the back of the house. He was halfway through the kitchen when the back door burst open and more officers poured through that opening too. One of them grasped the man by the shoulders and quickly handcuffed him.

The sergeant immediately began to read him his rights then snapped, 'We have reason to believe that you are keeping Nikki Nightingale here – and that's just for starters. Now where is she?'

'I . . . I don't know what you're on about,' Jackie stuttered. 'What yer playin' at, burstin' into a law-abidin' citizen's house like this?'

The sergeant turned to the assembled officers and said tersely, 'Rip this place apart if you have to. I want that girl found.'

The men began to scatter as Bradley took his mobile from his pocket and hastily dialled Claire's number. He had a feeling that she would want to be here.

Claire was sitting in a chair staring off into space when the call came. She lifted her phone and stared at the number. Seeing that it was Bradley she briefly thought of ignoring it, but then felt guilty and snapped it open.

As his voice floated down the line her face paled and Tracey, who was just giving the twins a snack, looked at her in alarm.

'What is it?'

Claire held her hand up to silence her sister then listened intently. 'I'll be there in ten minutes,' she said, and a bewildered Tracey watched her spring towards the hall where her shoes and her coat were.

'Please tell me what's going on,' she implored as she followed Claire.

'It's Nikki. Bradley thinks they might have found her. He's at a house in Nuneaton with the police and—'

'Claire, now *calm down!*' Tracey grasped her sister by the shoulders and shook her. She had been babbling incoherently and Tracey had not understood a word she had said.

Claire repeated what she had said a little more slowly and Tracey called urgently, 'Callum! Come quickly.' Removing the car keys from Claire's trembling hand she told her, 'You're in no fit state to drive anywhere. Callum will take you.'

Her husband had joined them in the hallway now and after she had quickly told him of the call he snatched up his coat and grasped Claire's elbow. In no time at all he had her seated in the car and was pulling away as Tracey watched from the doorway with a look of deep concern etched on her face. What Claire had failed to tell her was if they had found Nikki safe. She dreaded to think how her sister would react if anything had happened to the girl. During the days that Claire had been staying with her, Tracey had come to realise just how much Nikki meant to her. Claire loved her as her own and Tracey began to pray that they would find Nikki safe and sound as she closed the door on the fast-falling snow and hurried back to her twins.

Callum shot across the Leicester Road bridge on two wheels, heedless of the slippery roads. Claire had said not a word but he could feel the fear and the tension coming off her in waves.

Minutes later, he drew the car to a halt outside the house in Queen Victoria Street. People had begun to gather outside, huddled up in overcoats, shivering with cold but too curious to go back inside. Claire saw the shattered front door hanging off its hinges and an icy hand closed around her heart. Two more police cars had arrived, and uniformed officers seemed to be everywhere. The sound of sirens pierced the air and she glanced down the street to see an ambulance hurtling towards them, its flashing lights standing out in stark clarity against the snow. Her heart sank even further. Could the ambulance be coming for Nikki? And if it was, what had happened to her?

She remained seated in the car, paralysed, until Callum yanked the door open and helped her out.

As they approached the front door, the policeman who was standing there held his hand out to stop them from going any further.

'I'm sorry, you can't come in here,' he told them. 'Would you please stand back?'

'I . . . I'm Nikki's mum,' Claire heard herself say and instantly he retreated into the room behind him to return seconds later with a stern-faced inspector from the Nuneaton branch who had come to join the sergeant.

'Is she all right?' Claire asked, without giving him time to speak. He took her elbow and drew her into the room.

'No, I'm afraid she isn't,' he told her quietly.

'Then where is she? I want to go to her.'

He nodded towards the ceiling. 'She's up there. We're waiting for an ambulance.' Even as he spoke, a look of relief flashed across his face. 'Ah, here it is now, Mrs Nightingale. Perhaps it would be better if you waited here and let them do their job.'

Claire was just about to object when her eyes were drawn to the television set. A pornographic video was playing on it and as she recognised Nikki her hand flew to her mouth in horror.

'Oh my God!' Her face was ashen. 'Th . . . that's my daughter,' she gasped. 'And Mr Dickinson, the solicitor I used to work for. He has an office in Coleshill.'

The inspector nodded at a colleague who was standing behind him. 'Make a note of that,' he instructed him. 'Get his address and send someone out to arrest him.'

'Yes, sir.'

As shock coursed through her, Claire leaned heavily on Callum who was looking as white as she was, as he noted what was happening on the video.

'Is it him that has kept her here?' Claire demanded as shock was replaced by a huge surge of rage.

'No, it wasn't. The man who was keeping her here is under arrest in there,' the inspector replied. Before he could stop her, Claire had broken away from Callum and was striding into the back room where she confronted a man who was seated at a table in handcuffs. There was something about him that was vaguely familiar, but until he opened his mouth to speak she could not think what it was.

'Hello, Claire. Long time no see, eh?' His lips curled back in a sneer and suddenly the years fell away and Claire was a child again, lying in her little bed in Gatley Common waiting for this brute to come and abuse her and her sister.

'*Ian!*'

He laughed, a low laugh that made the hairs on the back of her neck stand up. 'Yes. It's me, Ian Jackson, or Jackie as I'm now known to me friends. I've waited a long time for this, Claire. *A very long time.*'

'B . . . but why?'

'*Why?* Because *you* were the cause o' me doin' a stretch in the nick – that's *why*, you bitch,' he ground out.

Her head wagged from side-to-side in denial. 'But you didn't go to prison for what you did to me and Tracey! None of the men involved did!' she shot back.

'Not for what we did to *you*, no, we didn't. They couldn't prove anythin' that time. Trouble was, me cards were marked after that an' the next little family I befriended they caught me bang to rights wi' me trousers round me ankles so to speak. Four fuckin' years I were locked up for that an' all because o' you! When I finally got out I swore I'd get me own back on you. I'm a wealthy man now, yer know?

I went into property developin', as well as me other little sideline, an' then I bided me time – an' sure enough, one day you came back an' almost handed the kid to me on a plate.'

Claire clapped her hands over her ears as the bad memories flooded back. She didn't want to hear any more. She didn't know if she could bear it. This animal had violated Nikki just as he had violated herself and Tracey all those years ago – and all so he could have his revenge. It was almost too much to bear.

An officer was yanking Jackson none too gently to his feet and propelling him towards the door. 'Come on you,' he said with contempt. 'Let's get you locked back up in a cell where you belong, an' let's pray you'll rot in there this time, you filthy pervert.'

'It'll be worth goin' back inside this time,' Ian taunted. 'Ooh, she were a lovely lay, that little Nikki were.'

Callum went to take a swing at him as he passed, but another officer stopped him. 'Don't waste your time on him,' he warned Callum sympathetically. Claire also laid a restraining hand on her brother-in-law's arm as Ian was propelled from the room and then watched as two paramedics sped past her on their way up the stairs.

She couldn't think of Ian now. Nikki needed her. She took the stairs two at a time and stopped outside the room that the men had disappeared into. Nikki was in there, but what state was she going to find her in? Half of her wanted to turn and run as far away from this godforsaken place as she could get, but taking a deep breath and forcing herself to move forward, she stood in the doorway. One of the paramedics was leaning over the slight figure on the bed while the other talked urgently into a radio. But that couldn't be Nikki; Claire was sure of it. Nikki was young with her whole life ahead of her, whilst this poor girl looked a wreck.

They were bundling her onto a stretcher now and asking Claire to stand aside as they carried the girl from the room. She was lying so still that Claire was convinced she was already dead, and then suddenly Bradley was standing at her side.

414

'Come on,' he urged. 'You should go with her in the ambulance.'

It never occurred to Claire to ask him where he had popped up from. The whole day had taken on an air of unreality and everything seemed to be happening in slow motion now.

Within minutes she was in the back of the ambulance with Nikki and they were speeding towards the George Eliot Hospital. Two doctors and two nurses were waiting for them with a trolley when the ambulance screeched to a halt minutes later, and Claire was shouldered aside as they loaded Nikki onto it and rushed her away.

'Come on, I'll get you a nice cup of tea while they have a look at her, shall I?' a nurse offered kindly as she put her arm round Claire's shaking shoulders.

Claire found herself in a small waiting room. There was nothing in there but four hard-backed chairs and a small coffee-table strewn with magazines. Minutes later the nurse returned with a steaming mug of tea. 'Try and drink this,' she urged.

'Is she going to be all right?' Claire was so terrified that she could taste the fear.

'The doctors are with her now,' the nurse assured her. 'As soon as they have any news for you, someone will be in to see you. Try not to worry.'

Claire sank into a chair to wait, and when Bradley appeared some minutes later she could have wept with relief.

'How is she?' he asked.

Claire could only shrug. 'They don't know yet. The doctors are with her. They haven't told me anything.'

'Well, at least she's in the best place now.'

A silence settled between them until Claire eventually told him of the video she had briefly caught sight of, and said, 'It was Mr Dickinson in that awful room with her.'

Bradley stared at her incredulously. 'Are you *quite* sure? What – our Mr Dickinson?' It barely seemed credible.

'Of *course* I'm sure,' she sobbed. 'I have worked for him long enough to recognise him. They've sent a police car and some men to arrest him. I *loved* the man and all the time he was nothing more than a stinking paedophile!' Wiping her eyes, with her voice breaking now and then, Claire went on to tell him all about Ian Jackson and how he had once been her mother's boyfriend and of how he had been the cause of her and Tracey going into care.

Bradley could hardly take it in. He too had had a great respect for the elderly solicitor for whom he worked, and he felt physically sick now as he realised that he was part of a paedophile ring – and yet he looked as if butter wouldn't melt in his mouth. A kindly old grandfather figure whom you could pass in the street without looking at him twice.

'There's something else you ought to know,' he told Claire gravely, wondering how much more she could take. The way he saw it, what he had to say would be better coming from him than from some police officer she didn't know.

'It was Roxy who discovered what was going on. Poppy found one of the videos at home, and when Roxy saw Nikki and her daughter on them she just flipped. They've arrested her, Claire. She stabbed Eddie to death then rang me to tell me where Nikki was. If it wasn't for her, we might never have known.'

Claire was reeling from this latest shock, but she had no time to comment, for just then a nurse pushed the door open and asked, 'Mrs Nightingale? Would you like to come with me. The doctor is ready to see you now.' Claire and Bradley followed her along the corridor to a room at the other end where a tired-looking young doctor was waiting for her. Claire clung to Bradley's hand, afraid of what she was going to hear but needing to hear it all the same.

'Ah, do come in.' The doctor motioned towards a chair but Claire shook her head.

'I'm afraid it is not good news,' he went straight on. 'Nikki has pneumonia and one of her lungs has collapsed.'

'But she'll be all right, won't she?' Claire said hoarsely.

He bowed his head, unable to look at the hope shining in her eye.

'I'm afraid I can't say at this stage, Mrs Nightingale. She's suffering from malnutrition, which doesn't help, and she's in a very bad way, although we are of course doing all we can. The next forty-eight hours will be the testing time. If she can get through them and come out of the fever, then she has a chance. I have had her put into intensive care. Would you like to see her now?'

Unable to speak for the fear that was constricting her throat, Claire nodded and the doctor crossed to the door and summoned a nurse who was hovering outside like a little bird.

'Would you take Mrs Nightingale to the ITU please, Nurse?'

'Of course, Doctor.'

Bradley had to practically hold Claire up as they followed the girl down yet more corridors that all smelled of disinfectant and death.

'Your daughter is in there,' the nurse told her, pointing at a door that had glass in the top half of it. 'Don't be afraid of all the tubes and drips. They are all there for a purpose.'

'Look, I'll wait out here,' Bradley told her, suddenly feeling like an intruder, as he had when Robbie McMullen was dying. 'I'll see you later, eh? Take your time.' He too needed a few minutes on his own to absorb the shock of the revelation about his employer.

After following the nurse's instructions to gown up, Claire entered the ICU and, for the second time in days, found herself staring down onto a hospital bed at someone she loved. The nurses had washed Nikki and brushed her hair, and now she was dressed in a plain white cotton robe that reminded Claire of a shroud. She looked so little and vulnerable that it was all Claire could do to stop herself from snatching her into her arms. And the most terrible thing about it was the fact that this was all her fault. Ian had hurt Nikki to get back at *her*. It seemed as though she had been cursed – and this curse was destroying everyone she loved.

Chapter Thirty-Eight

It was now almost two days since Nikki had been taken into hospital and Claire had not once left her side except to visit the toilet and splash cold water on to her face to try and keep herself awake. Every bit of energy she had left was directed at the silent figure lying on the bed as she willed her to come back to her. The way she saw it, Nikki was all she had left in the world now. Christian had deserted her, her mother and father were dead, and Molly and Tracey had their own families to love. She had no one but Nikki.

Bradley was supporting her; only leaving to go home to wash and change and snatch a bite to eat. He sat outside in the corridor, refusing to impose but wanting to be there should she need him. She would have liked to thank him, to tell him how much his presence meant to her, but the words stayed trapped inside. The only words she could spare were for Nikki, who she talked to constantly as she told her how much she loved her and begged her to get well. Claire had no idea if the girl could hear her but she kept up the chatter just in case. Doctors and nurses slipped in and out, silently taking her pulse and checking her vital signs, but each time Claire looked at them for encouraging words they bowed their heads and bustled from the room.

During the second night, Claire could no longer keep her eyes open and fell into a fitful doze in the chair at the side of the bed. The dawn light brought her awake and after she had yawned and stretched, she looked towards the bed. Nikki was awake and watching her from feverishly bright eyes.

'Nikki!' Springing towards her, Claire wiped the damp hair from her daughter's forehead and smiled down at her with tears in her eyes. 'My goodness, you gave me a scare,' she told her as she kissed her hot lips. 'I ought to ring the bell, sweetheart, and let the nurse know you are back with us.'

'No, not yet,' Nikki whispered, and gripped her hand. 'I want to talk to you first.' She went on in a weak thread of a voice: 'I never meant to hurt you, Mum. I just felt so dirty after what my dad did to me, so I thought . . . Well, it doesn't really matter what I thought. But I *do* love you, Mum. I love you so much.'

'I know you do, darling,' Claire told her. 'And I love you too – more than anybody else in the whole world.'

'So . . . are we friends again?'

'We were never *not* friends,' Claire assured her. 'But now I really ought to run and fetch the nurse. The doctors are going to be so thrilled that you're awake.'

'I'm sorry about the way I reacted to what I read in your diaries,' Nikki whispered. 'I had a lot of time to think while I was at the house with Jackie, and I realise now that you just did what you had to do to survive.'

'And so did you,' Claire told her gently. 'In a funny sort of way we were both victims of our past but there are no secrets between us any more and soon we'll be able to put all this behind us.'

Niiki smiled weakly as with a final kiss, Claire dashed out into the corridor, disturbing Bradley who had been fast asleep in the chair.

'What's happened?' he mumbled groggily.

'It's Nikki, she's awake,' Claire told him across her shoulder as she hurried towards the nurse's station at the end of the corridor.

Seconds later she was coming back with a young doctor in a starched white coat and a nurse following close behind. The doctor paused at

Nikki's door to tell her, 'Wait here, please, Mrs Nightingale. We'll go in and check her over then you can come back in.'

Claire nodded as Bradley caught her hands in his. 'There, didn't I tell you she'd come through it?' He looked almost as excited as Claire, and for the first time since the night they had slept together in his flat she really smiled at him.

'Yes, you did, but I didn't dare believe it. But she's going to have to go through all sorts of interrogations now. They'll be wanting to take statements from her and—'

'Ssh, none of that matters. All that matters is that she's conscious now and hopefully on the mend. Everything else is unimportant.' As he glanced towards the window leading into Nikki's room he offered up a silent prayer that Claire was right. The alternative was just too terrible to think about. He almost dragged her down onto the seat that had served as his bed for the last two nights. 'Let's just wait here now and see what they have to say about her, eh?'

Claire sat silently clinging to his hand. What if she was wrong? How would she cope if she were to lose Nikki now? The minutes stretched on like hours until eventually the doctor appeared in the doorway.

'Mrs Nightingale, I don't want to raise your hopes too high, but it's a good sign that Nikki's come round. She isn't out of the woods yet, not by a long shot, but I'm feeling much more optimistic. I suggest you go home now and get some sleep. We've given Nikki a sedative and you'll be more use to her tomorrow when she wakes up if you've had a rest.'

Claire allowed Bradley to help her out to his car. Tears were streaming down his face but her eyes were dry. Once more in her life, the pain she was feeling went beyond tears.

Tonight, when Nikki had looked at her with love shining from her eyes, Claire had once again caught a glimpse of the little girl Nikki had been, and happy memories had flooded back. They were in Greg's beautiful house, and Mrs Pope the housekeeper was holding a birthday cake for Nikki to blow the candles out. Now Claire was at the school, proudly watching Nikki in her school play as her heart thumped with pride. They were shopping for things for the new baby's nursery and Nikki was holding up a teddy bear for Claire's approval. But she had never met the little brother she had so looked forward to, for he was born prematurely and died following the trauma of Greg's unmasking. And now she had come so dangerously close to losing Nikki too . . . the one person who made her life worth living.

As Bradley drove smoothly along the deserted roads, a comforting darkness crept towards her and she opened her arms and sank gratefully into it.

Inspector Ford stamped his feet on Tracey's doormat as he asked, 'How is she today, Mrs Brady?'

'Oh, still fussing round Nikki like a mother hen,' Tracey told him as she took his coat and hung it over the bottom of the banister. 'Won't you come through and have a cup of tea with us, Inspector? It's Callum's day off and he's just made one.'

'That would be most welcome,' the inspector told her as he followed her through the lounge. The twins were playing with their toys on the floor and he smiled at them as he passed them on his way to the kitchen.

'Ah, Inspector – any more news?' Callum asked as he lifted down another mug and started to pour the tea.

'As a matter of fact there is,' the inspector answered, then glancing around the room he asked, 'Where's Mrs Nightingale?'

'Upstairs with Nikki.' Tracey sighed heavily. 'She's hardly been out of her room since we got her home from the hospital. It's as if she's afraid to leave her side in case someone snatches her away again. But what's the news?'

The officer cleared his throat. 'Well, the results of the post-mortem showed that your late father, Mr Robert McMullen, was clubbed on the head on the night of the fire.' Tracey reached for her husband's hand as the inspector went on: 'Mrs Miller informed us in her statement that she had reason to believe that her husband had started the fire at your sister's house, and going on that, the search of a neighbouring property revealed a heavy brass candlestick containing Eddie Miller's fingerprints and traces of the deceased's blood. Had he been alive, Eddie Miller would be facing a murder charge now, but as it is, his wife got to him before us.'

'But why would she kill her husband because of starting a fire?' Callum was baffled.

'It went much deeper than that.' The inspector paused to sip at his drink. 'It was their daughter, Poppy, who stumbled across some of the videos. While she was watching them, her mother walked in and saw them too. When Roxy learned that Eddie had involved their daughter and Nikki in a paedophile ring she snapped and stabbed him to death.'

'I can understand her wanting to protect Poppy,' Tracey chipped in, 'but why would she be so angry about Nikki?'

'Because . . .' The inspector paused. 'She has a daughter somewhere who was once taken into care and eventually adopted. She would be the same age that Nikki is now, which is probably why she grew so fond of Nikki and felt so maternal towards her.' Tracey's hand flew to her mouth as she stared at him in stunned silence. It was so sad and just too much to take in all at once, but the inspector wasn't finished yet.

'The whole thing seems to have been set up by Ian Jackson, who was the leader of the paedophile ring. It was he who was the cause of you and Claire going into care when you were little girls. He was your mother's boyfriend – do you remember him?'

Tracey shuddered and nodded. She would never forget him.

'Quite by chance, Mr Dickinson, who Claire used to work for, was part of the ring. When Jackson called at the office one day, he happened to spot Claire leaving and realised instantly who she was. It seems that he has always blamed you and Claire for him being sent to prison, for although no one could prove that he had abused you both, after that the police kept a close eye on him and the rest of the men who were questioned. When Jackson then attached himself to another family, they caught him red-handed abusing a little girl and he got sent down. He saw Nikki as his means of getting at Claire. Personally, I hope the jury will be lenient with Roxy Miller when her case gets to court. Eddie Miller was the biggest rogue on two legs; he ran that estate and Dickinson was always getting him off the hook when he got arrested for one thing or another. If she did but know it, Roxy has done him a favour because the other prisoners would have given him a hard time of it in nick if word got out that he was part of a paedophile ring.'

Tracey shook her head in stunned disbelief. 'It's all very well to think that the men who have been arrested will finally get their come-uppance, but I don't mind betting none of them will suffer as much as Claire,' she muttered brokenly.

The inspector nodded in agreement. It seemed the ring they had just cracked had had a worldwide reach, with the men involved sending images of the children they had abused to every corner of the globe in return for extortionate amounts of money. The police had found yet more videos in a deserted warehouse, and these and Alan Jenkins the butcher's statement had led them to link the deaths of the two girls who had been dragged from the Blue Lagoon to the gang too.

'How long do you think those scum will get?' Callum now asked.

Inspector Ford shrugged. 'Let's just say I reckon by the time they come out − *if* they come out − they'll be too old to be a threat to anyone. But anyway, another reason I called round, Mrs Brady, is to tell you that we are willing to release your father's body for burial, now that the post-mortem is done.'

Fresh tears sprang to Tracey's eyes as the inspector smiled at her sympathetically. It would be hard for the young woman to have to bury her father, but harder still for Claire, because she was blaming herself for his death.

'Can I leave you to fill Mrs Nightingale in on all that's happened then?' he asked.

Callum nodded. 'Yes, Inspector, you can – and thank you for all you've done.'

'Huh! I just wish I could have done more,' Inspector Ford said sadly. 'All this heartache and for what, eh? Life can be a bitch at times, can't it?' And with that he turned and followed Callum to the front door as Tracey stared out across the snowy garden. It was far from over as yet. Now they had a funeral to plan.

'Do you think Claire will come through this?' Callum asked, on his return.

Tracey nodded without hesitation. 'She'll come through it,' she told him with certainty. 'One thing I've discovered is that my sister has guts and more spirit than anyone else I know. Most women would have gone under long ago, but Claire is a fighter. As long as she has Nikki she'll pull through.'

Callum nodded slowly. 'I think you might just be right,' he agreed. 'Let's hope that once this is all over, things will get better for her.'

'I have a funny feeling they will,' Tracey told him and then she slid into his arms, realising just how very lucky she was.

Epilogue

It was now early March, and as befit the season a cold wind was blowing as Tracey and Claire once more stood on the hillside overlooking their old home in Gatley Common.

The last few weeks had been difficult, full of ups and downs as Nikki battled to recover from her illness. Slowly, she was regaining her strength. The antibiotics and her mother's and her aunt's devoted nursing, as well as the love of her little cousins, was bringing the girl back to life. Months of near-starvation and drug abuse had hampered her recovery, but small frequent meals were building her up gradually, and she was rediscovering the joy of being alive. Far below them she was sitting in the car, out of the biting wind, with her new pet cuddled on her lap. They had come across the little dog quite by chance, or perhaps she had come across them, when they found her on the doorstep one morning, pathetically thin and freezing cold. Tracey had immediately brought her into the kitchen and fed her before wrapping her in a warm towel, while Nikki looked on with tears in her eyes. Callum had reported her as a stray but agreed to keep her at Nikki's request while the police tried to trace her owners. Three weeks later the police had rung to inform them that her owners had not come forward to claim her and that they could keep her if they so wished, and so she had duly been christened Lilibet, and was now Nikki's shadow.

Claire felt that the little honey-coloured mongrel had gone a long way towards helping Nikki on her slow road to recovery. Nikki had insisted that the little dog should sleep in her room with her as Gemma had once done, and since then Nikki's bedroom had become a happy place where the twins would spend hours giggling and laughing with Nikki at Lilibet's antics, or listening to Nikki's music while she read stories to them.

If Claire had been forced to admit it, she would have had to say that Lilibet would never win a prize at Crufts. The little dog had long floppy ears that were far out of proportion to the size of her body and her legs looked barely long enough to carry her. Her tail would have looked more at home on a fox, but her saving grace were her wonderful soulful deep brown eyes that reminded Claire of Cassidy's.

Callum had teasingly asked Nikki where she had come up with the dog's name from, and Nikki had solemnly informed him that it was the nickname the Queen Mother had used for Princess Elizabeth when she was a child. 'So,' she had told them with her chin in the air, 'if it was good enough for the Queen then it's good enough for her!' Which had them all smiling and nodding in happy agreement.

Claire and Nikki had also spent a lot of time talking about their pasts, and it had been therapeutic for both of them. Claire had assured Nikki that as soon as she was eighteen they would start to search for her birth mother in earnest but, strangely, it didn't seem so important to Nikki any more. She was enjoying being at the heart of a loving family. A home tutor was now calling at Tracey's home three afternoons a week to help Nikki prepare for her exams and she had also finally agreed to counselling with a child psychologist, who was slowly helping her to come to terms with the abuse she had suffered at the hands of her father.

Another thing that had lately brought a twinkle to Nikki's eye was a certain young man by the name of Ashley Vince. He was sixteen years old and painfully shy; tall and dark with a gentle nature, he was the son of one of Callum's friends. He had called round with his father one day to see Callum, and Claire had been amused to notice the blush on both young people's cheeks when they saw each other for the first time. Since then, Ash, as he preferred to be called, had been a frequent visitor to the house and Claire had a strong suspicion that he might soon turn out to be Nikki's first real boyfriend. She was quite happy with the idea; she was happy with anything that made Nikki smile.

Now she dragged her eyes from the car below to gaze at the panoramic view spread out before her. Since the day that her father had been cremated, Claire had asked if she could keep the urn containing his ashes in her bedroom at Tracey and Callum's house. She had not felt ready to let him go. But then one day, quite out of the blue, Claire had informed Tracey that it was time to set his spirit free. So now here they were, about to keep the last promise that Claire had made to her father.

Down below they could see Callum and Bradley waiting for them, close by the car but not wishing to intrude on the final goodbye.

As her eyes rested on Bradley, Claire smiled fondly. What a tower of strength he had been for them all over the last few months. He had stood by her, and despite her inability to love him back, his friendship had never wavered, for which she would be eternally grateful. She would miss him when he moved away in April. Having resigned from his partnership with the disgraced Mr Dickinson, Bradley was about to take up a new post in a large, busy legal practice in the heart of Manchester. He had family there, and would be well looked after. It was time for him to move on, find a woman who was free to love him, one who was not burdened by her past.

Claire sighed, then turned her attention back to the matter in hand. 'Do you want to say anything?' she asked Tracey.

Tracey nodded. She was crying, her blue eyes red-rimmed as she removed the lid from the urn containing their father's ashes.

'May you rest in peace, Dad,' Tracey whispered, and together, the sisters tossed the contents of the urn into the air.

The ashes were instantly snatched away by the wind as Claire spoke the haunting words from the Bible: '*The wind/spirit blows where it wills, but you do not know where it comes from or where it goes.* Goodbye, Dad. May your spirit be free now and may you find peace with Mum.'

As the two sisters clung together, Claire was crying not only for her father but for all the lost dreams.

'Come on.' Tracey took her hand. 'Let's get home, eh?'

And silently the two women picked their way down the hillside to the people waiting below.

By the time they arrived back at Tracey's comfortable home, and she had settled Nikki back into bed with a nourishing, hot snack and her CD-player for company, Claire's tears had dried and she was strangely calm. Molly had been babysitting the twins and had fussed around them all, knowing it had been a difficult day.

'You had a call from your insurance company while you were out, love,' she informed Claire. 'Apparently your house should be ready to move into again by the end of the month. They've replaced the kitchen, and the decorators are almost finished now. You'll have to buy all new furniture, of course. They didn't manage to salvage much, from what he was saying.'

Claire nodded. Apart from visiting her shop, Fifth Avenue, in Coleshill, which her manageress Sandra still had running like a dream, she had barely been out of Tracey's house in weeks, and had certainly been nowhere near Lovelace Lane. All her attention had been centred on Nikki and the bond between them was renewed, as strong as ever now.

'I shan't need any new furniture,' she told Molly solemnly, 'since I'm going to put the house on the market. Nikki and I need a new start somewhere else.'

'Well, I can't really say that I can blame you. There could only be unhappy memories for you there now after what's happened,' the woman agreed. 'But I hope you weren't planning on moving too far away?'

Claire smiled at her warmly. 'Don't worry, Molly. Now that I've found you all again I have no intention of ever disappearing out of your lives for good.'

428

Molly saw the pain that briefly flared in Bradley's eyes. She had guessed long ago that he adored Claire but sadly, it seemed that her heart was still at Seagull's Flight with the young vet who had jilted her. Molly wondered why life could be so cruel. Claire had lost her parents, her business and her home within months of each other. And then on top of all that, she had very nearly lost Nikki. It made Molly's blood run cold just to think of it.

She wished that she could wave a magic wand and take all the young woman's hurt away, but was wise enough to know that no one could do that. Claire would bear the scars of everything that had happened for the rest of her life.

She waited until Tracey had drifted away into the lounge to check on the twins before asking casually, 'Ever hear from Christian nowadays?'

Claire stiffened at the sound of his name, which still had the power to disturb her. 'No, I haven't. Why?'

'I just thought it was a bit strange, that's all. That he hasn't been to see you,' Molly said innocently. 'After all, you were very close, weren't you? I'd have expected him to show his face and offer his condolences at least.'

'I haven't been in touch,' Claire told her sadly. 'There didn't seem any point.'

'Well, I think you should have let him know, all the same.'

Claire shrugged. 'Christian has his own life to lead. And he made his choice long ago, Molly.' And with that, she rose from her stool, kissed Molly and went off to run a bath leaving the older woman staring thoughtfully after her. She was more worried about Claire than she cared to admit. Oh, she knew that Claire adored Nikki, but one day, no matter how close they undoubtedly were, the girl would fly the nest and Claire would be left alone. She needed someone to love her and take care of her. But what could Molly do to help? As she strummed her fingers on the worktop an idea began to form in her mind.

★

Molly and Tom were in their lounge that evening and he noticed that she seemed to be strangely on edge. Normally she would be engrossed in whatever was on the television, but tonight she seemed to be alternating between chewing her nails down to the quick and staring into the fire.

'What's up, love? Been a bit of a hard day, has it? Nikki's all right, isn't she?'

'Oh, Nikki's coming along nicely,' she assured him. 'It'll be a long job till she's really properly well again, but Claire is wonderful with her. And no, it hasn't been the easiest of days.' Then pulling herself out of the chair she told him, 'I reckon I'm going to get me an early night. Would you mind?'

'Of course I wouldn't,' he said. 'You go and get your head down, love. These last months, it's been one thing after another, and everything's probably caught up with you.'

Planting an affectionate kiss on his forehead, Molly hurried into the hallway, closing the door between them. Then, fumbling in her pocket, she took out the scrap of paper with an address that Tracey had written down for her. Molly had always prided herself on never interfering in anyone else's business, but on this particular occasion she felt that a little interference was called for – and she hoped that she would be forgiven. With nervous fingers she dialled the number and waited for her call to be answered.

It was the following Saturday. Tracey was in the kitchen and had just finished giving the children their lunch when the door bell rang. 'Get that for me would you please, Claire?' she called.

Claire called back, 'Will do.'

She opened the door to find Bradley standing on the step with the most enormous bunch of red roses she had ever seen clutched in his hand and her heart sank. Could this mean that he was going to try and woo her again, she wondered.

'Come on in,' she invited him, and as he stepped past her he pressed the flowers into her arms.

'I've been thinking,' he said before she had a chance to say so much as a single word. 'Nikki is well on the mend now and I reckon it's time we had a talk.'

'What about?' she asked nervously.

'Well, I'm leaving soon, and I know I can't go without saying what's been on my mind.'

This was what Claire had been dreading.

'Look, why don't we go in here.' She opened the door to the dining room and after laying the roses on the hall table she followed him inside.

Once she had closed the door behind them he instantly caught her hands in his own and told her, 'I love you, Claire. I've *always* loved you. I know the last few months have been difficult, so I've kept silent, but now I think it's time to speak out. I don't want to leave you behind. I want you and Nikki to come to Manchester with me and be a family. Make a fresh start. What I'm really saying is: I want you to marry me.'

Claire bit down on her lip. Bradley had been kind to her, so why was she reminded of Greg now as she looked up at him?

'I think you'd better sit down,' she told him quietly and when he did as he was told she took a seat opposite him and joined her hands as she began, 'I really appreciate your offer, Bradley, and I don't know what I'd have done without you over the last few months. But I don't love you. And the thing is, I'm not who you think I am.'

When he raised a bemused eyebrow she took a deep breath. It was time to place the final demon to rest. Bradley deserved to know the truth, and so slowly, for the last time, she began to tell him of her life. Of running away from Molly and how she had earned a living in London. And as the tale was being told she saw his face alter, saw the look of revulsion that flared in his eyes and watched him withdraw from her.

'And so now you know who I really am,' she ended. 'I earned my living as a call girl. Do you still want to marry me, Bradley?'

'Well, I . . . er . . .' He was floundering for words, but Claire remained silent as he struggled with his feelings.

He was rising from his seat and she now understood why he had reminded her of Greg. Greg had fallen in love with an image too, the image she had created around herself.

Bradley's face suddenly flushed and now he looked angry as he glared down at her and asked, 'Why didn't you tell me this before?'

She shrugged. 'It's not easy to admit to your mistakes, and I'm sorry, but I can't turn back the clock. What's done is done. Do I take it that you don't want to marry me any more?'

She could see the confusion and the hurt shining in his eyes and she was sorry for hurting him, yet overriding all her other feelings was a huge sense of relief. He walked from the room without another word and as she watched his car pull away she knew that she had seen the last of Bradley King.

It was early evening. Nikki had already gone to bed as she still tended to tire easily, and Claire had sent Tracey and Callum out for a meal while she babysat for the twins, who were also tucked up in bed fast asleep. She was engrossed in the newspaper when a knock came on the door. When she opened it and saw who was standing there, larger than life, the colour drained from her face. It was Christian, clutching a large bunch of beautiful spring flowers. His face was heavily tanned a golden-brown.

'Hello, Claire,' he said quietly. 'I've been away and only just got to hear about what's happened to Nikki and your father, so I thought I ought to come and check on how you are. I'm so very sorry.' He stopped and looked at her, indecisively, as if he wanted to say something, but then changed his mind and told her: 'Gran sends all her love. She would have liked to come and see you too, but the journey would have been a bit too much for her now. She said to tell you she's thinking of you though.'

Claire stared back at him as if she had been struck dumb as he shuffled uncomfortably from foot to foot.

'Well, aren't you going to ask me in?' he joked after a time. 'It's a bit wet and windy out here and I could kill for a cup of tea.'

'Oh yes, of course, I'm so sorry. Do come in.' She motioned towards the lounge. 'Go through.'

Once inside they fidgeted and darted glances at each other like two strangers until, suddenly remembering her manners, Claire told him, 'I'll go and put the kettle on then, shall I? Do make yourself comfortable.'

'Um, you might want to take these with you,' he said, holding out the flowers to her. With a nervous smile she took them from him and hurried away to the kitchen.

In the lounge, Christian hung his head. He was shocked at the change in Claire; she seemed to have aged years since he had last seen her. There were lines on her face that had not been there before, and she had lost an enormous amount of weight. But then he supposed it was hardly surprising after all she'd been through, going by what Molly had told him.

'So, how are you?' Christian asked some minutes later when they were finally sitting face to face with mugs of tea in their hands.

'I'm fine, but I have to admit to being surprised to see *you*.' 'Surprised' was not the right word, she thought. There was no one word to cover her mix of emotions.

He said in a low voice, 'Yes, I suppose I should have phoned to let you know I was coming, but when I heard what had happened I just didn't stop to think.'

'And just how *did* you hear?'

Christian paused before replying. 'It was Molly who let me know, actually. But I was surprised that you didn't contact me, Claire. You must know I would have been here like a shot!'

433

Claire shrugged. 'There didn't seem much point in letting you know. You have Seagull's Flight and Mandy to worry about now, so I wouldn't expect you to concern yourself with what's happening to me any more.'

'Oh Claire, please don't say that. You were the whole world to me once. In fact, you . . .'

When he stopped abruptly, she frowned as she tried to make sense of his words. What was he trying to tell her? 'Does Mandy know that you're here?' she asked eventually, and when he raised his hand to swipe the lock of fair hair from his forehead, the gesture that she remembered so well, her heart lurched and she knew in that moment that she still loved him with all her heart. During the last awful months she had tried to convince herself that he was no great loss, but now after seeing him again, she realised that she had been fooling herself. He was still the only man she had ever loved or ever would.

'Mandy dumped me some months ago,' he told her with a rueful grin. 'We were halfway through planning the wedding at the time.'

Claire stared at him in disbelief. 'B . . . but why would she do that?' she stuttered.

'Because she said that she didn't want to be married to a man who was in love with someone else. I can't say that I blame her, really. She was a nice girl and deserved better.'

Claire looked so confused that he laughed softly as he caught her hands in his and gently shook them up and down. 'You silly goose! Don't you see? She was talking about *you*! Mandy could read me like a book, and I think in the end she knew that if I couldn't have you I'd never truly settle with anyone else. It wouldn't have worked and she was wise enough to see it.' He paused. 'I feel such a fool, Claire. Who was I trying to kid? I lost you through my own selfishness because I was tired of waiting. Mandy was there and she was kind, and a good friend to me and Gran, and now I've hurt her. After she finished with me I ran away like the coward I am, thinking that I could put you out of my mind once and for all. I got a couple of friends of mine,

434

who are both retired vets, to come in and run the practice and keep an eye on Gran for me while I cleared off to South Africa for three months. I worked on a large farm there and was so busy I barely had time to think. But I soon discovered it was no good. You were in my mind every second. And I realised then that I'd made a huge mistake. I should have been more patient and given you chance to do things in your own time.'

'*Oh!*' It was all she could think of to say. She was terrified that at any moment now she would wake up to find that she had been dreaming.

Christian could see that she needed a few moments to get her thoughts into some sort of order and so, changing the subject, he said, 'Would you like to tell me everything that's gone on? You see, I only got a very sketchy picture from Molly. But don't if it's too upsetting.' Tenderly, he squeezed her hands again as she blinked to hold back her tears.

And so, Claire falteringly began to bring him up to date with everything that had happened. It was a litany of violence and tragedy that had Christian turn white beneath his tan.

'I can't take it in,' he gasped when she was finally done. 'You mean to tell me that this Jackie, or Ian Jackson, was selling porn images of the children he had abused to paedophile rings all over the world? Why, it's like something you read about in the newspapers. I hope the bastard rots in hell.'

'Oh, I think there's a very good chance of that, *and* the rest of the ring they exposed,' she told him, her face wreathed in sorrow.

They lapsed into silence, each lost in their own thoughts for some moments until Claire finally plucked up the courage to ask, 'Why didn't you tell me that you and Mandy had finished?'

Christian sighed heavily. 'I didn't think you'd be interested. The last time I saw you, I got the impression that something was going on between you and that Bradley chap.'

Claire shook her head in hasty denial. 'No – at least, not on my part. I do admit that I tried to become fond of him after you told me that you were going to marry Mandy, but I couldn't think of him as anything other than a friend. The thing is, Christian, I felt that I'd let you down, by not doing what I'd come back here to do. Telling my family about my past was the hardest thing I've ever had to face. But it's done now and I finally feel that I can move on.'

'Good.' There was the old familiar twinkle in his eyes that could still set her heart racing. Had he really meant what he'd said? Could he really still love her? There was only one way to find out. Once, what seemed a lifetime ago, he had proposed to her and she had turned him down. Now, it was her turn.

Sitting straight in her chair she looked him in the eyes and said, 'You once asked me to marry you, but there were too many ghosts that needed to be laid to rest, that would otherwise have come between us. I've finally faced those ghosts, so now I'm asking *you*: are you ready to put me out of my misery and marry me?'

There was a lump in Claire's throat and she felt as if she was going to choke as she waited for his answer.

And then his arms were around her and he whispered, 'Yes, I would *love* to marry you, Claire, and I promise I will do my level best to make sure that no one ever hurts you again, even if I have to wrap you in cottonwool and put you in a plastic bubble.'

'Then that's settled,' she told him. 'You can go ahead and organise the wedding as soon as you like.'

Christian Murray looked like a man whose birthdays and Christmases had come all at once as he gently brought his lips down on hers, and Claire felt a warm safe glow spread through her.

'So,' he said tenderly when they eventually broke apart, 'how soon exactly do you mean when you say soon? This month? Next month?'

'The sooner the better,' she replied, as her heart swelled with love. She was ashamed as she thought of all the pain she must have caused this man. But she would have a whole lifetime to make it up to him now. And she would, every single minute of every single day.

Her life had never been easy and she knew that she would carry the scars of her past to the grave. But there need be no more looking over her shoulder any more. No more living up to an image. She could be herself and with Christian at her side she could face each new day and take it as it came.

He kissed her again with such tenderness that it brought tears springing to her eyes and for the first time in her life she saw a bright light at the end of a very long dark tunnel. And it came to her then in a blinding flash! This wonderful feeling that was spreading through her . . . *this* was the peace she had always craved . . .

Rosie Goodwin has worked in social services for many years. She has children, and lives in Nuneaton with her husband, Trevor, and their four dogs.

Praise for Rosie Goodwin:

'A gifted writer . . . Not only is Goodwin's characterisation and dialogue compelling, but her descriptive writing is a joy' *Nottingham Evening Post*

'A heart-throbber of a story from Goodwin that puts many other so-called emotional blockbusters in the shade' *Northern Echo*

'Goodwin is a fabulous writer . . . she reels the reader in surprisingly quickly and her style involves lots of twists and turns that are in no way predictable' *Worcester Evening News*

'Goodwin is a born author' *Lancashire Evening Telegraph*

'Rosie is the real thing – a writer who has something to say and knows how to say it' Gilda O'Neill

'Rosie is a born storyteller – she'll make you cry, she'll make you laugh, but most of all you'll care for her characters and lose yourself in her story' Jeannie Johnson

'Her stories are now eagerly awaited by readers the length and breadth of the country' *Heartland Evening News*

Also by Rosie Goodwin and available from Headline

The Bad Apple

No One's Girl

Dancing Till Midnight

Moonlight and Ashes

Forsaken

Our Little Secret

Crying Shame

Tilly Trotter's Legacy

The Mallen Secret

The Sand Dancer